Clouds
of
Love
and War

Also by Rachel Billington

Clouds
of
Love
and War

A NOVEL BY

Rachel Billington

UNIVERSE

This edition first published by Universe in 2020
an imprint of Unicorn Publishing Group

Unicorn Publishing Group
5 Newburgh Street
London W1F 7RG

www.unicornpublishing.org

A catalogue record for this book is available
from the British Library

5 4 3 2 1

ISBN 978-1-913491-13-0

Cover design illustration by Dawn Monks
Typeset by Vivian@Bookscribe

Printed by Fine Tone Ltd

'I'm finished with the earth.
From now on our place is in the sky.'

Dr. Jacques Charles, 1783
(After ascending 2 miles in a hydrogen balloon)

For Nat
1970–2015

PROLOGUE
October 1940

The clouds swirling around a pale sky opened and closed like a camera shutter. For one second Eddie could see the plane, a Messerschmitt Me 109, its belly the same blue as the sky, the next it had vanished. He assumed it was the same for the enemy as he saw the Spitfire fly in and out of the clouds. You'd expect the clouds to be neutral. Although as they were fighting over the English Channel, they should have supported the Allies, if anybody. Indeed, sometimes it felt as they were players in this dance performed by men – the dance of death.

It had been a surprise to spot a single fighter over the sea.

Should be easy prey this one, unless it was a trap. It didn't feel like a trap. It felt more like some idiot out for an adventure. Well, he'd found one, all right.

For a full three seconds Eddie did not see the Me 109. This cloud was bigger, that was it. The dance would end if the Hun found enough cloud to cloak his escape to France. Now was the time to head home himself.

But there was the 109 again. The clouds, a curtain now, had parted to reveal him centre stage. One on one. Almost too good to be true. How could he resist after a week of daily blanks or planes so high you'd need to be a spaceman to reach them. Eddie felt his knees knocking as they sometimes did in the excitement of an approaching fight. He had the advantage of height, about twenty thousand feet to the other's nineteen thousand, but enough, and the sun was behind him. If only the clouds would hang in the air just as they were, he would have a clear view of his prey.

He was diving now, closing in for the kill, like an eagle, with talons outstretched, beak thrusting. One more second and he'd squeeze his forefinger and let loose the streaming lance of lead. He could already picture the spurt of flame, the gorgeous burst of fire, the twist, the turn, the screaming corkscrew descent. He'd seen it all before. A kill. One more kill. How bloodthirsty he felt today!

The Spitfire shuddered. It shook. It slithered. Clouds whirled above and below. They had become malignant. Eddie blinked, then stared. The sweat, in droplets on his forehead, turned to ice. He thought, I'm so tired. Even though I've been flying much less, I'm still so tired. And he saw the tracer lines and the bullets from a second Me 109 which had crept up on his tail. They fired into the flesh of his Spitfire, into the heart of his stupid pride. The plane sped passed him and disappeared into the cloud ahead. The two of them could do what they pleased now.

Two of them. The oldest trick. One engages, the other sneaks onto your tail. How could I fall for it? 'Because I'm tired and I'm on my own.' Eddie spoke out loud and a terrible loneliness took hold of him. *I chased him because the others turned for home and I saw the 109 and I thought I'd be clever but now I'm hit and soon I'll be on fire.* Liquid splashed across the windscreen, thick tears of glycol. The engine had been hit.

The Spitfire gave a wobble and seemed to sigh as if in sympathy with its pilot's pain. Shame and pain. You never allow the enemy to surprise you from behind. Number One Rule.

Eddie pushed up his goggles, rubbed his eyes, put them back down again and pulled himself together. He was not alone. He spoke into the radio telephone. 'Red 2, Red 2. I've been hit. Two bandits. I've been hit.' But nothing came from the headset and the plane seemed to sag in his hands.

Only bullets, he told himself, a spray of bullets. He realised he was still heading towards France. Desperate to see the English coast, he pushed up his goggles again and tried to swivel his head.

But it would only move so far. Had he been injured too? How far had he chased that German?

Turn, he needed to turn and that's what he'd been trying to do automatically since he was first hit, turn for home. But his head wouldn't turn, nor would the Spitfire. Nothing was happening. The Spit continued on. All you need are wings and an engine or if that fails and you can reach land, wings on their own will do. *As long as you are going in the right direction.*

Eddie pictured the green fields around the airfield where he and his Spitfire lived. Any strip would do or even one of those green fields. He'd done that before now. Where exactly had those bullets hit, he wondered. But none of this mattered if he couldn't turn.

He glanced round and realised with a shock that all the clouds had gone, leaving him in an expanse of empty blue sky. So they had been *Boche* clouds guarding their friends as if some Wagnerian opera had taken to the air.

His eyes returned to the front but not before they'd caught a bright flicker. The sun glinting on his wing? He knew better than that. The flicker grew into a flame which he could see without moving his head. It hurt to move his head and anyway at last he could see the coast ahead. The end to another perfect summer's day. Both shoreline and water were burnished by the lowering sun. They merged into a mysterious, vibrating, probably unobtainable line.

No! No! It was the wrong coast. 'Get out, Eddie!'

If he was a bird, he'd land on the water, fold his wings and rock gently on the waves.

'Jump out, now!' Who was shouting at him?

Eva's pale oval face stared at him with dark luminous eyes.

CHAPTER ONE
March 1939

'They're training you to be a killer.'

'It's about flying, not killing. We're not even at war.' Eddie took an angry step towards his father. Eddie was six inches taller and his fists were clenched, but Fred grabbed his arm. He used his left hand because his right was missing.

'You have no idea.' Fred tightened his grip but Eddie shook him off.

'Of course you know everything! You don't talk about it but your beastly stump talks for you. Your war turned you into a cripple but it was a different war. Your war, not my war. And there isn't a war! I'm flying. I'm a pilot. It's the only time I'm happy. You don't believe in happiness. You believe in 'the Workers' and 'Communism' and 'Pacifism'. But you're bitter and old. You can never understand. I can't understand about your war and you can't understand about my flying.'

'You've drunk too much to make any sense.' Fred drew away and looked up at the sky. It was a darkening blue above the university quadrangle in which they stood.

'You don't make any sense to me!' Eddie's voice rose even louder.

'I shouldn't have come. At least not to the lunch.' Now Fred seemed weary of the argument. 'I never liked your godfather, the Professor. Except for a short period in the war.'

'The war again! You came to see *me*, or so you told me.'

Fred turned his back on his son and looked up again.

'Why do you keep staring up at the sky? I've told you. You're old. You can't understand what I feel about it.'

'Wouldn't you like me to try?' Fred turned round.

Both men paused as a group of undergraduates passed by. The black gowns floating from their shoulders gave them an Elizabethan swagger. The leader called to Eddie, 'Afternoon, Chaffey!'

Eddie frowned without answering and the men disappeared into a stairway, leaving behind the word 'pater', spoken in disparagement.

Their appearance and disappearance seemed to change Eddie's mood. He pushed his hand through his thick yellow hair and glanced at his father. They both had the same electric blue eyes. 'The Professor's claret was good at least. He's a dour old thing.' His voice was conciliatory.

Fred seemed unphased by the change in tone. 'Your mother assures me he's a prized tutor. Then he's always impressed her. Once upon a time they were engaged. I bet you never knew that.'

'Engaged to that old queen!' Eddie's face expressed such a mixture of disbelief and horror that Fred suddenly laughed. 'He's only a few years older than me.'

'Was he ever young?'

'Let's say he's more interested in *mens sana* than in *corpore sano*.' Once more Fred took his son's arm. 'How about visiting your rooms since that's why I'm here?'

'I've only been in them for a year.' Eddie's sarcasm was good-natured and the two men continued across the quad, as if the row had never been. They entered a stairway, two doors down from the swaggering students.

⚞

Fred sat watching his son make the tea, laid out by his scout. He'd always felt it necessary to bring Eddie down. He was too beautiful, too much a product of his mother's privileged background. Fred's occasional lover, Sonia, once enquired why he couldn't make his son a project like the other isms in his life. Sonia had her own ism which included 'Free Love'.

Fred looked at his son, assessingly. Where was his blood, the blood of Dorset labourers in this gilded youth? Perhaps Sylvia had enjoyed a secret fling with Professor Lamb. Fred smiled at such a ridiculous idea.

'Milk?' Eddie held up a white jug. Fred's occasional visits to the family home in Dorset where Eddie spent his childhood with his mother and grandmother had inspired excitement and fear. Sometimes he used his stump like a pink baton to conduct his oratory. Sylvia would challenge him but that made things worse as if he enjoyed disgusting her. As a boy, Eddie had taken it for granted that his father lived mainly in a London flat and his mother in a large country house. Now he knew it was unusual, like most things about Fred.

'Milk?' repeated Eddie, as Fred continued to stare without answering.

'Why not? Give the farmers a living.' Fred paused. 'Are you serious about the flying?'

'Oh, yes.' Eddie's voice was negligent. He handed Fred his tea and sat down. 'I even thought you might approve. It's run on far more democratic lines than the army or navy.'

'The Oxford University Air Squadron?' Fred's scorn was moderate.

Eddie wondered what he could say which would avoid the usual lecture. 'I plan to join the RAF,' he announced simply.

'You just said that there wasn't going to be a war.'

'As you pointed out, I was talking nonsense.'

'Are you telling me that when the little gnome in the bow of your boat commands you to scupper your oar or feather your spoon, he's interrupting a spirited debate over the choice between a rampant Churchill and a cringing Chamberlain?'

'I didn't know you followed my rowing career.' It struck Eddie that his father sounded childish. 'Even we can see Hitler's creating a vast war machine and that no other country is preparing for war. Not the sort of war Germany is planning. France is ruled by old men still resting on the laurels won in your so-called Great War and England's not much better. Hitler's like a wolf baring his teeth while we're the silly sheep too busy nibbling grass to see the danger.'

Fred put down his cup. 'Simple, isn't it?'

'Who said it's simple? I'm talking about massive armies, guns, bombs, tanks, millions blown to pieces in ways we can't imagine.'

'You talk as if no lessons have been learnt. As if there wasn't a whole new way of looking at the world. To many people the misery of their everyday life is just as important as the prospect of bombs.'

So I didn't avoid the lecture about the wondrous good of Russia and Communism, thought Eddie.

But Fred held back. 'And you'll be thousands of feet up in the sky, looking down on us poor things.'

'That's the general idea,' agreed Eddie cheerfully.

Fred thought of the last article he'd written for the *Daily Worker*. It contradicted everything expressed so comfortably by these deep-panelled walls, the presence of a servant not far away and this healthy, lounging boy. Images of illiterate men going to their pointless deaths in 1915 had accompanied the writing. It was harder to be a Pacifist when Fascism was sweeping through Europe. 'I suspect I'm a natural cynic and disbeliever.'

He saw Eddie look at him in astonishment. Certainly he had believed in the Workers' Education Association. 'Do you expect me to believe in the League of Nations?'

'You always seem loaded with beliefs,' said Eddie.

As he spoke the outer door to the set was pushed open, followed by a whistle of air as the inner door sprang open. It revealed a woman, sleek in a silvery dress. Pale hair, fluffed around a velvet cap, caught what light remained in the room.

'Why are you two sitting in the dark?'

'We're having tea, mother dear, can't you see?' Mother and son smiled at each other as if they hadn't been together an hour earlier.

'Your son's impressing on me the need for war.' Fred, who had not stood when his wife came in, looked up at her provocatively.

'Oh, don't spoil the day, Fred.' Sylvia extended a placatory smile to her husband. She put down the small handbag and white gloves she was carrying and turned on a couple of lamps before pausing at one of the three stone mullioned windows. 'It's more like autumn than spring. Why don't you light the fire, Eddie.'

'You don't eat enough, mother dearest.' Eddie opened a drawer and picked out a box of matches.

'Arthur's lunches are too disgusting to eat.'

'He must like them or he wouldn't be so fat.' Eddie laughed and crouched by the gas, watching the blue flames spurt at the bottom of the cones, then turn red and orange and yellow as they spread upwards. It reminded him of a sunset he'd seen coming in after a flight. The colours had burst into his head, making the whole sky glow. He stood up and walked back to his chair.

Sylvia sat down on the nearest chair and watched her son. 'You look pleased with yourself.' As she spoke, she glanced at Fred.

'It's nice playing at host with you both,' Eddie stared contentedly at the fire.

Sylvia put out a hand to Fred. 'Arthur appreciated that you came. Did you think the other guests were very dull?'

'I liked his goddaughter.'

'The young girl. What was she called?'

'Eva,' said Fred.

'Oh, you *did* like her.'

'I liked her conversation. She told me that, although her father was a professor at some college …'

'Magdalen,' supplied Sylvia. 'He talked intensely about things I didn't understand.'

' … she had never been to school,' continued Fred, 'and scarcely had any education. Her mother who was highly educated, taught her when she had time, but was away a lot.'

'The daughter came instead of the mother,' said Sylvia, adding vaguely, 'I think she might be abroad.'

'I asked her,' remarked Fred, 'how this lack would affect her future. She answered calmly that both her parents had left behind their parents when they were eighteen, her mother moving country, and she planned to do the same and make her own life.'

'I thought her quite shy and ordinary.' Sylvia said, turning to Eddie. 'Did you notice your fellow godchild, darling?'

'She was dark, wasn't she? Long, dark hair down her back and a pale face like a Leonardo.' Eddie paused. 'We didn't exchange a word.' But he remembered her now, the dark red stuff of her dress and her smooth white hands. He didn't usually remember girls he met at dreary lunch parties.

'I think her mother might be German,' said Sylvia.

'You mean Jewish,' said Fred.

'Oh, do I?' Sylvia looked away. 'Anyway, it's time I went.' She stood up immediately, smoothing her skirt and pushing up her hair round its little hat. Are you coming to London, Fred? I have the car and a driver.'

Eddie watched as his parents negotiated their departure. It was always like this, neither of them willing to admit that they wanted the other's company. It used to make Eddie anxious but now he was able to see it as a rather absurd dance, about pride and other pointless sentiments.

'I'll walk you both out,' he said and handed Sylvia her bag and gloves.

Together, they pushed through the two heavy doors and down the dark stairway. Fred's steps, in boots, echoed noisily.

Once they reached the quad, Eddie glanced up at the darkening sky with the greedy, secretive eyes of an addict.

CHAPTER TWO
April 1939

Eva was walking slowly, slowly reading a letter. When she reached the Turl where her bicycle was chained, she stopped, clasping the letter to her breast, then, self-consciously, looked around. The letter was from Eddie. His third letter. It was all very surprising. She had received the first almost immediately after their meeting at Professor Lamb's lunch party. He had informed her that she was his 'muse', that nothing would be hidden from her because she was 'the inspiration for everything.' They had scarcely spoken a word to each other so Eva assumed that muses were most inspiring when remote and virtually unknown.

The letter in Eva's hand was, it must be said, more like a diary. Over Easter Eddie had gone on a walking tour with Oz and Henry. Eva darted a look at the letter, 'Oz is a hearty rower like me and planning to be a doctor but because he was named after Ozymandias, made famous by Shelley describing his fallen broken statue as 'King of Kings: Look on my works you Mighty and despair...' he also has a romantic side. You might call him a hearty with a heart. Henry, on the other hand, is a Yank.'

Eva smiled and put the letter away again. It was the randomness of Eddie's thoughts and the headings 'April 20th Kendal... April 30th Windermere'. She would look up all the places he mentioned and Shelley's poem. He couldn't know how alone she was. Cabined, cribbed, confined.

Of course she was not literally alone and at this moment her father would be waiting for her return. It was such a beautiful spring day and the windows in his study were curtained with heavy blue brocade. Her father, Professor Speke, was trying to make up for the many absences of her mother and, at the same time, continue her education which meant he spent an hour talking about books and she listened. Books were his thing. His voice droned on but now and again he rattled the cup on the saucer and his pale eyes under their shaggy eyebrows fixed wonderingly on her.

He's an old man, thought Eva scornfully as she pedalled along, although the scorn disguised affection. She was important to him, even if he could not get much beyond her dust cover. She laughed and the wind brushed the sound behind her to join the dark hair lifting off her shoulders. I will never grow old, she thought happily. Eddie would never grow old either. He was too golden, *gemütlich* as her mother might say, although she'd given up using German words recently. Her accent was embarrassing enough, *muzzer* for mother, *anozzer* for another. You'd think after twenty years she could do better.

When she'd been at school – she'd lied to Eddie's father about that – some of the girls had imitated her mother's accent and their parents whispered behind their hands, 'What must it feel like to have a German as a mother...Although of course there're plenty of good Germans...' Once she'd cried out, 'Don't you know? My mother's a spy!' That had been fun, although nobody had laughed, not even her so-called friend, Betty.

She'd left school last summer. A step towards independence, she'd hoped. She'd asked Betty, stolid hard-working Betty who had five younger siblings, to leave with her but she'd pretended it was a joke. She would never be a muse. She'd be a head girl.

Eva speeded up as she turned into the driveway of one of the smaller houses and skidded to a halt. Usually at this point, she bent to smell the secret perfume from little white flowers hidden in a dull shrub but the day before she'd confided this discovery to her father who'd found its name, *Osmanthus burkwoodii*, and smothered her delight. At least Eddie was still a secret. Eva rang the doorbell which was immediately opened by the German maid.

'*Guten Tag, Fräulein* Eva.'

'Good afternoon, Valtraud,' responded Eva sympathetic-ally. The girl who had arrived two weeks ago was not much older than herself. She was supposed to speak English but seldom managed it. She cried in her bed at night. Even in the dark hallway her eyes were surrounded by white puffy skin. She'd probably opened the door so promptly in the hope it was Mrs. Speke returning.

'Is my father in his study?' asked Eva as the girl still waited. It was hard not to be impatient with someone so stupefied, even if grief was the stupefying agent.

'The Herr Professor has telephoned with the message that he will be home in one hour.' She spoke in German.

Eva wandered through the house into the garden. Here nature was in the ascendancy. Seated on a stone bench, she was tickled by grasses, stared at by tall daisies. She thought it was hard to be young in a house where the only other young person longed impossibly for her far-away home. A couple of years ago there had been talk of Eva continuing her studies in Germany with some cousins. But the political situation had put an end to that.

At the lunch party where she'd met Eddie, guests had talked names of politicians, crossing European leaders with effortless knowledge which she seemed too young to acquire but too old to ignore. She must, as her father told her often, read more history books or, if she preferred, books about politics or economics. Or indeed anything which could fill her head with more information rather than her habitual state of vague dreaming. He didn't understand that her dreams were filled with pictures, images, outlines, forms, colours, shapes…

Suddenly filled with energy, Eva returned to the house, dashed up the stairs and into her bedroom. Going to her wooden chest of drawers, she brought out a book of cartridge paper, crayons and a pencil. Clasping book and colours, she ran back downstairs and into the garden.

Only an hour! Her parents were complete intellectuals and could quote Kant, Shakespeare and Goethe in the same paragraph and music, particularly piano, meant more to Gisela Speke than almost anything else in the world, but they had minimal interest in the visual arts. When Eva had raised the subject of her attending The Ruskin College of Art, they had looked at her blankly. The only pictures in the house were etchings by Durer and prints by gloomy Dutch masters, inherited from Speke's father. Duncan Bell, Eric Gill, David Bomberg, Paul Nash, even Kandinsky, her current favourites, meant nothing.

While these thoughts, too habitual to be distracting, passed through Eva's mind, she completed a delicate study of grasses, flowers and bench. But its delicacy annoyed her. Turning the page, she tried again, this time using only crayons.

Professor Speke put down his briefcase in his study and took off his coat. Tall and thin with grey, wild hair, he seemed like an ageing student. He sat down at his desk before getting up immediately and going to the window.

There he saw Eva drawing and looked at her with more approval than she would have expected. 'Eva! I'm here now.'

He returned to his desk without noticing her petulant frown.

'I apologise for postponing our session.'

Eva saw at once that her father was trying to hide anxiety. It was a sign of her second-rate nature, she suspected, that she noticed other peoples' moods. Any first-rate mind was preoccupied with some great idea and did not waste time on moods. This afternoon, because she was pleased with her crayon drawing – the colours well-chosen, the lines bold – she did not feel as second-rate as usual.

'I've finished *Crime and Punishment*,' she said brightly. 'It's very bleak,' she added, still brightly.

'Bleak? Bleak. Yes, indeed. Bleak.' The Professor looked at her as if surprised.

Valtraud came in with the tea tray. Eva helped her to put it on a low table and pour. Meanwhile the Professor sat with his head down and did not even acknowledge the arrival of the tea cup.

'I expect you are missing your mother,' he announced suddenly.

Valtraud, already at the door, stopped with a startled expression and let go of the door which, caught by a draught, banged shut.

The Professor looked up, nudging his cup which spilled tea into the saucer. Valtraud rushed forward and Eva, sitting composedly, thought, what a storm in a tea cup, and smiled at her own joke. Of course she was missing her mother.

'Ah, Valtraud,' said Professor Speke in German, 'You will be glad to hear that Frau Speke has seen your father. Your family are well and in the country.'

'Well,' repeated the girl in English. She stared at him as if not understanding.

'Yes,' agreed the Professor. 'My wife will be back in a week when we will know more.'

'Where is she?' asked Eva in what she hoped was an adult conversational tone.

'Indeed,' said the Professor. 'We will know all when she returns.'

Eva saw she was not going to get an answer and wanted to cry out, 'I am not a child!' But that would have sounded childish so she said nothing. If her mother had seen Valtraud's family she must be in Germany. Could her father believe that she had not heard of *Kristallnacht*?

Eva said nothing and Valtraud, sniffing a little, left the room.

'Yes,' said Professor Speke. He picked up a book on the desk and put it down again. Vaguely, as if he didn't know what he was doing, he turned the pages.

Eva watched him for a few seconds and then began to think of the daisies, the grasses and the stone bench, three varying forms which needed to be considered in relation to each other. She would try it in pencil again – charcoal would be better but she had none. She could get an effect in colour but it had no substance. She must look at more paintings by Matisse. Her father began to speak again.

'I judge you perfectly intelligent enough to learn Greek,' he said. 'As I impressed on your mother when she was my student, it's impossible to play a role in the world without first reading the Greek philosophers in their own language.'

CHAPTER THREE
June 1939

'The rain's never going to bloody well stop.'

'You're such a pessimist, Charlie.' Eddie glanced at his companion, dressed like him, in flying gear, leather helmet, dungarees, boots, with goggles and gauntlet in his hand and parachute over his shoulder.

Eddie kept his eyes on the sky, even when Charlie shouted goodbye and walked off. He didn't mind getting wet and wanted to learn everything about the all-important world above his head: the permanent blue underneath, shrouded now by massing layers of grey, nimbostratus, fronted by puffy white clouds with dark underlining, cumulus of some sort. This was another dimension, which became his own when he flew through it.

Soon the rain turned to drips and the darker bands thinned and parted, while the rounded clouds softened and became whiter. A brisker wind blew them from West to East and at last slivers of blue appeared like bright eyes.

'You the last man left standing?'

Eddie turned and saw the instructor peering at his watch. 'Half an hour left. Aren't you the lucky one.'

'It was only a shower,' said Eddie, as they walked briskly towards a Tiger Moth.

'You'll be out in storms soon enough, don't worry.'

It wasn't just luck, thought Eddie. I was willing those clouds to part. I'd stood staring at them for half an hour and I'd have stood for as long as it took.

'Right-ho! Let's see if you can get everything in the right order this time. Routine, that's what you lads lack. Routine doubles your speed. Don't have to bloody think. Don't have to bloody panic. Go on then. Do the lot. I'm not saying a word.'

The man sat behind him not saying a word. As if Eddie was flying solo. His heart beat a little faster. Buckled in, goggles, gloves, feet on the rudder boy, hand on the joystick and the men on the ground to turn the propeller. Taxi into the wind, open the throttle, push the stick forward, keep a straight line and off the ground. Smoothly up, smoothly into the sky.

'Not too bad,' said the instructor, breaking his promise.

But then the Moth took to the air, as light as its namesake, and the instructor did keep quiet.

Eddie took a deep breath. The aeroplane belonged to him, the sky was his, the remaining clouds floating away. Into the blue. One circuit. One perfect circuit. A perfect world. His world.

≫

Eva took her bicycle and rode into the centre of town. She propped it against the wall of the Cadena Café and wandered inside, failing to spot Eddie who sat at a table by the window. He was waiting for her, their first meeting since lunch at the Professor's.

'I'm here!' he called to catch her attention.

Eva came back to him and settled, like a seabird on water in her white blouse.

'You're beautiful!' admired Eddie, truly meaning it. Once he was down from the sky, he seldom noticed how things looked, but Eva had impressed him from the start. Today she looked different, her face flushed above the white.

Pleased at this reception, Eva assumed a 'muse' expression. 'I've been painting in the garden.' She watched for a response. Eddie's appearance which bordered on the dishevelled with an open-necked shirt and baggy trousers tucked into boots, surprised her.

'I've been flying. Came straight from the airfield.'

"Do you think there's going to be a war?' Since Eddie didn't answer, she added, 'My father was a Pacifist in the last war.'

'But not now?'

'Oh no. The Jews...' Eva didn't complete her sentence.

'I'm not an anti-Semite,' he said self-consciously because some response seemed to be needed.

'Of course not.' Eva stared, surprised, then recovered herself. 'Hitler is though.'

'We call him the mustachioed midget.'

'We've got two refugees staying. First there was Valtraud then Hildegard...' Eva could tell Eddie wasn't listening and stopped.

'Frankly, I'll be relieved when the war comes. This on-off business is making everyone jumpy. I mean what's the point of being at university this term when if the war comes I'll join the RAF *tout de suite*? And people argue so much.'

Eva thought about this. In her house, nobody argued but, having met Eddie's father, she could see he might argue even though he'd been so nice to her.

'I suppose it's different if you've been through a war already.'

Don't let's talk about it anymore!' Eddie flung himself back on his chair which creaked alarmingly.

Eva noticed two women at the next table staring at him. She wondered if she might tell him about her mother going to Germany but she knew so little and anyway he clearly wanted to change the subject.

'Let's go and see a friend of mine.'

Eva stared up at Eddie who had suddenly stood. He looked down on her inquiringly.

'Who...?' She began.

Eddie was already out of the café. He was vaguely aware that his impulsive surges of energy were a kind of flight but he didn't see any reason to control them. He dashed along the High and Eva followed.

'My bicycle!' she called but he didn't seem to hear.

'It's not far!'

Eva caught up with him as he turned left down the Turl. He felt pleased she'd come with him. 'Henry's a member of the Toxophily Society. He says when he lifts his bow he feels the blood of King Arthur's knights coursing through his veins. Not joking.'

They crossed a bridge and turned right into the courtyard of a small college. Eddie led them confidently through it and out into a large garden bounded with tall trees.

'Am I allowed in here?' asked Eva.

'I'll say you're my sister. Look, there's Henry.' He pointed.

Eva saw a row of figures holding stretched bows. One after the other they loosed arrows in the direction of a target propped far away on an easel.

Eva thought, so toxophily is archery. Then she thought, I'm a nothing and nobody, in a self-pitying way.

Eddie turned round at this moment and caught sight of her stricken expression. 'I'm such a bully,' he said penitently. 'You were looking forward to jolly tea cakes in the Cadena, not cavorting round Oxford. But you'll like Henry.'

'I want to meet him,' Eva felt challenged. 'He appeared in your letters.'

Eddie stared at her for a second – a second longer than he'd give any other girl. The archers were clustered around the target as they approached them. They were tall with broad shoulders and wore leather shields on their left arms. The oldest who had greying hair cut very short, seemed to be the instructor.

'You're still pulling to the left, Mr. Walker.'

Henry nodded. 'A one-legged kid would have shot better.' He turned and saw Eddie and Eva. 'We're just finishing'.

Eva blushed and fixed her gaze on the target which was stuffed with straw and painted in bright and beautiful blues and reds.

'Who's this tree sprite?' asked Henry.

Eddie, seeing his friend as Eva might perceive him, realised he sounded like a brash American. 'My sister,' he said vaguely. 'We were passing.'

'I'm happy to meet you.' Henry shook Eva's hand while the other men drifted off. Eva noticed his arms were rather long and his face broad with a short nose and wide mouth.

Eddie stood by Eva frowning. 'We're off to tea with our parents,' he said.

Henry seemed to be concentrating on Eddie's boots. 'Your brother's always trying to make me learn to fly with him. As if rowing together wasn't enough.'

'I just wanted to show her this place,' said Eddie. 'We're off now.' He started away quickly with Eva following, her pleated skirt swinging over the green grass. She looked back once but Henry was fiddling with his bow.

'Wasn't that rude?' she asked when they were outside the college.

'Yanks are very informal. Anyway, he's a good friend. He's twenty-four.'

'How old!' exclaimed Eva.

'I was afraid he'd want to have tea with us.'

Eva had nothing to say about this so they carried on side by side at a more sociable pace. After a bit Eddie began to quote Wordsworth, '*It was an April morning: fresh and clear/The rivulet, delighting in its strength/Ran with a young man's speed...*' He broke off. 'Such tosh!'

When they were nearly back at the café, Eddie asked, 'Do you think age is important?'

'Oh yes,' replied Eva, thinking of her father. 'The old can be very rigid.' Then she thought of Betty. 'But so can the young.'

'Age isn't important at all QED,' said Eddie, seeming pleased. 'Tea at last', he said as they went up the steps to the café. 'Shall I take you on the river?' He pictured how beautiful she would look lying back in the punt, her dark hair spread about her.

'Not in one of your rowing boats, I trust.' Eva pursed her lips together. They were red and full.

Eddie watched her. 'Our table's still free. I'll get a waitress.' He lifted his hand.

'I mustn't stay long.' Eva felt shy under his gaze. He was so close across the table.

'One day I'll take you up in a plane. Would you like that?'

'Do you feel like a bird?'

'When the prop is swung and the engine roars...' Eddie swung his arms. He looked too big for his chair.

'Yes, sir?' An old, skeletal waitress inquired with an aura of suffering. She softened as she looked at Eddie. 'Tea and cake?' she crooned.

'Spot on,' agreed Eddie, noticing his conquest. 'My sister and I are going up in a plane later. Shall you come too?'

'Oh gawd!' The waitress backed away hastily.

Eva laughed and Eddie gave a smug smile.

'I mustn't stay long,' repeated Eva. She wondered whether Eddie in the flesh, rather than in a letter, was too much for her. She didn't know any young men.

'I'm going up to London,' announced Eddie carelessly.

'Will you drive?'

'If my motor's out of the garage.' He began to eat hungrily.

'It must be strange doing exactly what you want.' Eva sipped her tea. 'I sit on my own at home.'

'I've always done what I wanted. That's why I kept being thrown out of my schools.' He noted the awe in Eva's face and added kindly, 'What would you do if you could do anything you like?'

'Paint!' The single word flashed back and Eva's face went bright pink. She tore apart a cake.

Eddie was taken aback by her vehemence, then rallied. 'Girls often like messing with paints.'

'That's not what I mean.' Her flush deepening, Eva stared at her demolished cake.

'What else can you mean?'

'I'm going to go to The Ruskin. I'm going to be a painter. I'm working at home at the moment.'

'I see. Good for you.' He imagined her in a smock standing in front of an easel. Perhaps she would paint his portrait. 'You've made a right mess of that cake.'

They stared at each other, Eva defiantly, Eddie with a mix of emotions. So far Eva's only reality was in his imagination. He tried to see a painter was just what she should be.

'I'm glad you have an aim in life,' he said, 'most girls only want to get married.'

'I don't see the point of marriage,' said Eva.

'You will,' Eddie smiled knowingly.

Eva stared at his grinning face with sudden horror. 'I've got to go home.' Her eyes filled with tears which she rubbed away angrily. 'You don't know what it's like being a girl, being told what to do all the time!' She stood up and remembered her role as a muse. 'I thought you realized I was different.'

'Eva,' pleaded Eddie but without much conviction.

'You're just like everyone else.' It was too late to turn back so she fled.

Eddie didn't follow her. He poured some more tea and promised himself he would send her a letter. People in a state were best left alone. He drank his tea and ate the crumbled remains of Eva's cake. Perhaps it was true that females had less self-restraint than males. They were called 'the weaker sex' after all, although some were tough, like Amy Johnson, the American flyer. He began to think about flying and wonder whether he'd ever get aboard this new aeroplane everyone raved about, the Spitfire. It was being rushed through for the war that much was clear. But he'd never seen it at a university squadron, let alone had the chance to fly it. Besides, it was a monoplane and he hadn't gone solo yet.

'Your sister went along, did she?' The skeletal waitress stood over him with the bill.

'She's not my sister, she's my lover.' Eddie smiled charmingly.

CHAPTER FOUR
June 1939

Gisela Speke was pouring tea but her hand shook. She had arrived at the house an hour earlier.

'Go and play the piano, Mama.' Eva took the teapot and her mother went obediently to sit on the long bench in front of the piano. But she didn't play. She folded her hands in her lap and turned to face Eva.

'You are happy, my darling? No more school. What shall we do with you?' She smiled, making friendly creases in her grey face.

'I'm learning Greek with Father.' Eva carefully poured three cups of tea and added milk for two of them. 'When are you going away again?'

'It is not a good time.' Gisela played three notes on the piano. 'It is sad you do not make music.'

'Even you wince when I play and you're my mother.' Eva noticed that there were more silver strands in her mother's hair but at least her hands were now still. 'Do you have to go?' She took over the cup without milk and watched her mother place it on the top of the piano.

'Sit with me a moment.'

Eva felt her mother's warmth as they sat together but she was not as soft as she used to be.

'Will you ask Papa if I can go the Ruskin School of Art?'

Gisela hugged her and kissed first one cheek, then the other. She still smelled the same, like no-one else. Her hair which had been cut short, pricked Eva's cheek. 'I will do whatever you want.'

Except stay, thought Eva and eased herself apart.

'So you've come to help deliver leaflets,' Sonia looked up from the table stacked high with slips of paper printed with 'NO WAR'. 'That makes a change.' She smiled at him affectionately with her wide mouth and her speckled eyes crinkled at the edges.

Eddie who had come for something totally different, much more fun, and knew she knew that, smiled back at her. 'I'll do two streets,' he said, 'as long as you like.'

'Agreed.' Sonia shoved a large bundle towards him and a canvas shoulder bag with 'Royal Mail' on it.

'I'll be back.'

'I have no doubt.' Sonia watched him go. His lack of resemblance to his father, apart from those blue eyes, amused her. She supposed having sex with a father and his son was unusual, although she knew plenty of men who chased after a mother and daughter. Always different rules for men, of course. Come to think of it, Fred had introduced her to Eddie. The small room was stuffy. Sweat crawled down from under her hair. She looked forward to his return.

Eddie enjoyed walking down the busy East End street. He delivered to shops and houses impartially, even though he was sometimes chased out of the shops by furious small men who flung the leaflets after him. When he reached blocks of brick-built flats, he ran up the exterior staircases and along the walkways, noting sometimes the smell of poverty that came through the letterboxes. He didn't mind being used in this way by Sonia. If he'd gone with a tart, he'd have had to give money and this was a more interesting form of payment. Besides, the delay and the energy needed made the thought of Sonia's naked body, her small pointed breasts and her musky smell more exciting. Early on, he'd wondered whether his father knew of their liaison but decided it didn't matter one way or the other. Clearly it didn't matter to Sonia who had told him from the beginning that sex was another transaction, such as eating or talking and, although friendship was preferable, as in talking, it had nothing whatsoever to do with love – assuming there was such a thing which seemed pretty doubtful to her.

Mostly his friends were jealous of the arrangement and a couple suggested a slice of the action, a plan Eddie discounted as 'impossible' although even he could see that was not altogether logical. Henry, however, could not even be jealous because he had a fiancée in Connecticut to whom he was loyal and therefore, so he explained, could only go with a tart.

Eddie jammed the last few leaflets into a narrow letterbox and set off back to Sonia's flat at a run. Fleetingly, he wondered how the old coped with unhealthy bodies. But the idea was too remote to be of much interest.

Sonia looked up tolerantly as he burst into her room. What a lot of pleasure women miss from priggishness and prudery, based on fear, she thought. It would be different if she was married but she had never wished to be subservient to a man, nor did she long for children. Marie Stopes was the most sensible woman around.

'Have you the rubber?

Eddie patted his pocket. Once he had forgotten it and she hadn't even allowed him to undress.

Sonia's bedroom was filled by a chest of drawers and a bed. An embroidered spread half-covered the bed, an exotic note in the dull room. The only other brightness was a NO WAR poster stuck to the wall.

None of this interested Eddie who flung off the cover followed by his clothes. His boots held him up and Sonia was quickest, sitting cross-legged and naked on the bed.

'So how do we start?' she asked admiringly, as he approached.

If there was a drawback to sex with Sonia it was the brevity. But Eddie was young and restless and everything was done at speed. On this occasion, the event was succeeded by a cup of tea in bed and two short arguments, the first about child workers of whom, to Sonia's fury, Eddie declared his approval and the other about excessive use of alcohol of which Eddie also approved. There was never any in her flat.

'I'm driving back to Oxford tonight,' said Eddie. 'I have to see my tutor first thing.'

'I do believe young male undergraduates, particularly those with private incomes, have the most closed minds of anyone in the country.' She picked up one of the leaflets. 'You can look at one of these, hundreds of these, and not see them at all.'

'Quite right,' responded Eddie cheerily. He assumed Sonia's remark was an observation, not a reproach. 'I'm a rower and a flyer, a man of action.'

Sonia stared at him. 'You're not as stupid as you like to seem.'

'On that positive note, I shall take my leave.'

Eddie's feet in their flyer's boots, clattered down the wooden stairs. He swung open the outer door and saw, with relief, that his car was still in the street. As he opened the car door, he noticed one of Sonia's leaflets stuck under the windscreen wipers. He wondered who had put it there and thought, the world *is* in a turmoil but this dire idea scarcely scratched the surface of his lightness of being. He turned on the engine and listened to the roar echoing round the narrow street. He imagined it turning into the super-marine Merlin engine inside the sleek little Spitfire.

His route was across London from East to West. At first the streets were dark, lined with grimy buildings, illuminated at intervals by yellow gas lamps. With an urge to see something more splendid, he changed direction for the river and crossed it at Southwark Bridge, driving slowly enough to enjoy the uncoiling serpent of oily water. Through his open window he listened for the sounds of the Thames after dark: the friendly, low-pitched boom from the barges, the bleat from the passenger boats, the hoot from the police launches.

Eddie pulled up the car and jumped out. He had passed Waterloo Bridge and Westminster Bridge was ahead, behind him the solid grandeur of the Savoy Hotel. He stared at the water, leaning over the parapet, turning one way, then the other. He imagined he was flying along the river, using its gleaming curves as a guide to the heart of the city. Even in this dark night with the lamps strung along the embankment giving little illumination, light from the sky, perhaps stars half-hidden by clouds, spotted any ripples and made them glint. Eddie had never flown at night, in fact the idea frightened him, but it was easy to guess how welcome a shining ribbon of water would be in a blank, black sky.

He sighed, stared so deeply into the river that he seemed to see his reflection. Leaning over further and further, the wings of a plane sprouted above his face, followed by the nose and tail. He saw the black and white swastika painted on the plane's side.

He turned away, walking swiftly to his car. Of course, everyone knew very well that, if it came to it, German bombers could use the Thames to guide them into the city. There was nothing dramatic in that idea, just a fact of war, of geography, just as England is an island and Belgium and Poland and France are too close to Germany for comfort.

Starting up the car, Eddie began to drive very fast, cutting right as soon as he was able and heading for Soho. Oxford could wait. There was a club where a whisky cost no more than a beer and they didn't throw you out till dawn. It would be stupid to waste a night in London.

⋙

Eva lay in bed. She could hear her parents talking across the landing. She got out of bed. It was warm in the upper part of the house and her bare feet padded softly across the wooden flooring.

She stood outside her parents' bedroom and listened to her mother's voice.

'But we need to get out thousands, not tens or even hundreds... People, even the young, children, babies, they take them, often we do not know where... They are herded into areas like animals, poked and prodded, transported into camps... The men taken away. Best if taken, worst if kicked, stamped, shot... Before, we helped all we could. Now it is only the children. I must try to help...'

The Professor interrupted her in a voice so low and soothing that Eva couldn't pick out the words.

Gisela began again, her voice high and trembling, her accent thicker than usual, 'You don't understand what's going on. You can't believe it. You're English ... an island race ...'

A rumble from the Professor.

Eva waited, herself trembling. But instead of speaking, her mother began to wail and sob.

Eva fled back to her room, half aware of the scared faces of Valtraud and Hildegard at their bedroom door. She flung herself on her bed, buried her head in the pillow. The implications of her mother's words were too dreadful to contemplate. In the face of such things, she was nothing. Just another child. But a spoilt, English one.

Eva took her head out of the pillow and listened to her mother's sobs gradually quietening. Eventually she slept. But her sleep was restless, brilliant patterns of red and yellow resolved themselves into a huge trumpet-like flower. At its centre sat her mother. Or maybe the flower was normal-sized and Gisela was tiny.

Eva opened her eyes and saw Gisela sitting at the end of her bed. Her grey face smiled, ghost-like, at her daughter. Eva wanted to put out her hand but she was too tired.

'My *liebling*, my darling. My little English child. Be happy for me. You know how hard is my choice. You will always be in my heart. Wherever I may be.' She began to talk in German.

The soft sounds reached Eva like a lullaby. Although she tried to listen and understand, her eyes closed again and she was asleep.

CHAPTER FIVE
2nd September 1939

Eddie was driving at top speed. Oxford and back in one morning. Although it was the long vac., he'd wheedled another solo flight. No sane person would miss that. Summer-green hills and golden stubbled fields surrounded him; but he was still seeing deep blue sky, clear as paint above a few clouds dangling below. Perhaps he'd try to explain the feeling to his grandmother. Then she'd understand why he was late.

⚒

The terrace at Tollorum Manor was filled with people. Beatrice Fitzpaine, mother and grandmother, watched her family through the tall French windows. There were her daughters, Sylvia married to Fred Chaffey, with their son, and Gussie married to Reggie Gisburne with their multitude of children. While Germany was bombing Poland her family was celebrating her birthday.

Why wouldn't war leave her alone? Her husband had disappeared in the last war, perhaps burned, dead or alive, in the blazing furze at Gallipoli. In 1919 Sylvia had discovered a brigadier's badge on the peninsular that might have been his. Only then had Beatrice given up writing to Turkish hospitals.

Beatrice picked out Fred, for once talking politely to Reggie. After the war Sylvia had swapped her fiancé Arthur Lamb, a clever, high-minded officer, for Fred, maimed, embittered and of the labouring classes. He had grown up on the estate, brought up by his eldest sister, Lily when their parents died. Beatrice's family, titled and snobbish, had refused to come to the wedding or acknowledge the card she had sent to announce Eddie's birth.

Where was Eddie? Beatrice searched for her favourite grandson.

'Lunch is ready m'lady.'

Beatrice swung round and there was Lily, short and sturdy, ageless in her strength and purpose. 'Eddie's not here.'

Lily joined her at the window, although standing a little further apart than a friend or relative would normally. 'He'll be here any minute. He knows it's your special day.'

Beatrice glanced sideways. 'Do you remember, Lily,' she asked suddenly, 'when you first came up to the Manor?'

'With my husband dead and the Colonel at Gallipoli.'

'I couldn't have managed without you,' said Beatrice warmly. 'You were too good to be a housekeeper forever. I thought that perhaps after the war when we were so reduced here, you would go off and do something important with your life. Train to be a nurse perhaps. Becoming Matron, of course.' Beatrice smiled.

It wasn't exactly a question but Lily answered it anyway. 'My girls were still young. I had a good place with you. After the war the men expected the jobs.' She didn't add, 'You needed me' because they both knew it.

'After the war,' repeated Beatrice and the two women looked at each other sadly.

'Young men will always be willing,' said Lily, allowing a pause before suggesting, 'It's lunchtime, m'lady.' She handed Beatrice a bell.

'I told you I couldn't have managed without you, and I still can't.' Beatrice stepped out on to the terrace and rang the bell vigorously. 'Lunchtime, everybody!'

Sylvia was the first to look up. When she moved back to Tollorum with Eddie still a small boy, she'd told Fred that her mother needed her. The truth was that living with Fred, the love of her life, was out of the question. She liked to think he loved her too but was locked into a rebarbative approach to the whole world with no exceptions.

'Where's Eddie?' Fred was beside her, catching her bare arm. Even now she felt a sexual vibration that was surely absurd for a middle-aged woman to feel for her husband. But he'd always been more lover than husband.

She stood up. 'I'm coming. Eddie will come.' Fred had been extraordinarily polite all day. Perhaps it was the approaching war. Now he was whispering in her ear, 'Reggie says Chamberlain will have to say something soon. Perhaps today. Perhaps tomorrow.'

'Not on my mother's birthday!' Sylvia stared helplessly at the younger children racing up to the terrace. 'Reggie's not always right.' Reggie was a regular army officer working in the War Office and would be right about this.

Fred followed her gaze. 'Perhaps Eddie's gone to volunteer,' he spoke with the particular tone of irony Sylvia hated.

'Can't we have just one happy day?' It was typical of him to be unkind when she needed comfort.

'Lunchtime,' repeated Beatrice, ringing the bell again.

Grandchildren ran past her. 'What's for lunch?' a boy called out.

'Pheasant, dear.'

'Not pheasant again!'

Beatrice turned to watch Sylvia walking in with Fred. How badly he treated her! She couldn't think why Sylvia put up with it. After all, her most recent novel, *Smiles Awake You*, had been shockingly independent but there she still was hanging on to his every word. And this was not about class, Beatrice insisted to herself. She had always welcomed Fred, if only for Lily's sake.

Sylvia moved into the dark hallway where heavy Chinese pots stood in recesses. A car pulled up noisily outside the front door.

'Am I late?' Eddie shouted. He was dragging off dungarees as he ran to them.

'You know you're late,' Fred watched as Sylvia kissed him.

'We haven't even started lunch yet.' Sylvia entered the large, panelled drawing-room with son and husband on either side.

Reggie was already settled in the winged chair at one end of the table. His moustache drew a dark line across his red face with its low forehead and full lips. He wore uniform and the tunic strained against his chest.

'I'm flattered the War Office spared you even for a day,' Beatrice was saying, although her eyes were on Eddie.

'Sorry, Grandma,' Eddie grabbed a seat by her and leant across the table to his uncle, 'Whatever's the Mobilisation Branch of the War Office Staff? George says that's where you are. Colonel, sir.' He added as an afterthought.

But Reggie's attention was now at the other end of the table where his wife, Gussie, and his father, the Reverend Euan Gisborne had just entered the room. Gussie was a voluptuously pretty forty year-old. Her father-in-law, although thin, withered and bent over a stick, took hold of a chair and sat down with wiry agility. Behind them came her eldest daughter, Artemis, tall and too stately for her age, with the absent air of someone interrupted from a gripping novel.

Reggie frowned. He said to Beatrice, 'I have to go directly lunch is over. I've told the driver 1430 hours.'

'The cake will be instead of pudding. Sylvia insisted on a cake.'

Sylvia, on Reggie's other side, saw him not listening to her mother and felt momentarily cross. When he'd first come into their lives as the vicar's son and a young soldier, she'd considered him ridiculous and had been shocked that Gussie had got herself pregnant and married him. But after he'd won one of the earliest MCs in the war, survived the Somme and Passchendaele and continued up the ranks till now he was a colonel, she saw that, in the eyes of the world at least, the laugh was on her who had married Fred.

Inevitably, Sylvia's attention was drawn again to Eddie. Where would his life take him? To the war, of course. Oh, the war! The war!

'I'll tell you my plans for the next twenty-four hours.'

Eddie turned reluctantly to his neighbour, his eldest male cousin, George. Why ever was he allowed out of his regiment, in his beastly blazer and cravat? How he'd love all that fighting side-by-side, leader-of-men bullshit which was at the heart of the army. Thank the Lord for the RAF!

'What?' said Eddie ungraciously.

'I'm going to take little brother William out to carry the ammunition and walk round the fields for four or five hours, killing as many bloody rabbits, hairs, pigeons, foxes, rooks, badgers, squirrels and starlings as I can find. It'll be bloody good exercise and bloody good target practice. I know you're not much of a shot but it might be a bit of fun.'

The worst thing about this invitation, Eddie decided, was that George was trying to be kind. He was a year or two older and, ever since going to Sandhurst, had felt invincibly superior to his cousin.

'I might,' said Eddie. 'What about the other twenty hours?'

'Visit to the Fitzpaine Arms,' answered George promptly 'where there's a charming barmaid called Jesmarie.'

'No thanks'. With an ex-village boy for his father, Eddie certainly wasn't going to watch George patronise the locals.

'I plan to stay up all night drinking so when that bloody old buffer Chamberlain finally decides to give us the dire news which we all know anyway, I shall be in exactly the right frame of mind. Then I shall kiss my dear mama and go off to join my regiment.' George sat back in his chair with a satisfied expression.

'What if the PM speaks tonight and you're recalled to your regiment dead drunk?'

'Father says it's tomorrow and his ear's to the ground.'

'Have you got the drink?'

'The best Scotch with chasers of Dorset ale. I've even located the perfect room backstairs.'

George, Eddie remembered, became more bearable when drunk, lachrymose and sentimental, but less conceited. 'Count me in.'

'Good-o!' said George.

Eddie looked round the room at his family. Did he like any of them? Cousin Artemis was still standing, leaning against the Reverend's chair and talking in long sentences. Maybe she reminded him of Eva.

'Artemis!' he called and indicated the empty chair beside him. There were too many men in his life.

'Thank you,' said Artemis flopping down. 'I was trapped by grandfather.'

'You were doing the talking.'

'He asked me what I was reading so I was obliging with the plot of *The Eustace Diamonds*.'

'I bet he knew it already.'

Artemis sighed. 'So I trapped myself.'

As she spoke two girls came in carrying plates already served and put them at each place. Lily followed with more.

'Over here, Lil!' commanded Fred loudly.

'I'm terrified of Uncle Fred.' murmured Artemis. I always sit as far away from him as possible. When I was about eighteen he said I was like a pre-Raphaelite painting without their sex appeal.'

They both considered Fred. 'He's been a bit knocked back by the Soviet-Nazi non-aggression pact,' said Eddie. 'But I can't see it shaking his belief in communism. If it comes to that half the Oxford Labour Party is communist. Where do you stand?'

Artemis blinked. 'I prefer to live in the past. You can see things more clearly.' She turned away to accept a plate piled high with lumps of meat and potatoes and runner beans. 'I wish I wasn't so greedy.'

Eddie began to lose interest.

George, on his other side, interrupted demolishing his own pile of food, to ask Eddie, 'So are you still set on getting your wings?'

Eddie was so surprised at George's interest in his future that he revealed what he'd told nobody else, 'I have an interview for a short service commission on Monday at eleven o'clock.'

'Jolly good,' said George. 'The war will start without you, of course, but you'll catch up at some point.'

This was irritating because true. 'I can already fly a plane.'

'Pottering over the Oxford countryside is a bit different to fighting German aces who've cut their teeth in Spain.'

This was also true. Head down, Eddie concentrated on eating his food. How could Reggie and Gussie produce so many children? When he next looked up he saw his mother watching him. They smiled at each other.

Sylvia was wondering why she was sitting next to the oafish Reggie, instead of Fred. Last night they'd made love, once in the evening and once in the morning. Then they'd slept again. Naked in his arms, she'd felt utterly content. It was always like this, a sense that they had at last become one, each equal and happy in their love. But before breakfast was over, she could feel him pulling away as if something stopped him acknowledging their closeness. Sometimes, it was as if he was punishing himself as well as her but any attempt to discuss it was met with anger or flight. He was one of the few soldiers who had fought through the whole horrible Gallipoli campaign. But she hadn't known him before the war. Perhaps he had always been angry.

Then there was the barrier of her class. But how could he go on being angry at her for being born into the upper class when she'd given him everything? Sylvia knew about Fred's other women, about Sonia. In her low moments, she wondered if he would have been happier if she'd never entered his life. Then she remembered they loved each other, she knew they did.

I am *not* a romantic, thought Sylvia firmly as her vacant gaze rested on the healthy bright faces around her. My last novel was described by critics as 'acid, verging on cruel.'

Beatrice's face swung into focus. She was not talking either but looking happily at her children and grandchildren while leaning slightly towards Eddie. She had been a widow for twenty-four years. That was it, thought Sylvia, her dear father would have expected her to support Beatrice and Tollorum. She could not give herself entirely to Fred, nor, indeed, to her writing.

Eddie turned to Beatrice, 'So how are you, grandmama?

But at that moment Lily who seldom sat down during meals, although there was always a place set for her, carried in the cake. At her command, the girls drew the long curtains, and they all began to sing.

CHAPTER SIX
3rd September 1939

At breakfast the following morning Beatrice announced that the Prime Minister was to address the nation at eleven-fifteen and the wireless would be on in the drawing-room.

Fred responded promptly by saying he was going down to have coffee with the Rector at that very time.

So they were a reduced family group; no Fred, no Reggie who had left the afternoon before and no George who had fallen into an alcoholic sleep so heavy that even Eddie's kicks couldn't wake him.

As the clock on the mantelpiece ticked onwards, Eddie felt his heart pounding the seconds. Lines of poetry came into his head:

'Blow out you bugles, over the rich Dead!
There's none of these so lonely and poor or old
But dying, has made us rarer gifts than gold.'

At school, he'd dismissed Rupert Brooke as an attitudinising sham who'd died from a mosquito bite before he'd got anywhere near the field of battle. He'd even written an essay titled 'A glorious lie or a fatal dream?' But now those lines, '*Blow out you bugles over the rich dead*' pumped through his veins, bringing purposeful drama and, in the immediate present, extinguishing his own hangover.

'Eddie?' Sylvia was looking at her son questioningly.

'Sorry.' He'd spoken out loud. Sylvia squeezed his hand.

Gussie was fussing with her hair, still thick and dark.

'My mother's preparing to be theatrical,' Artemis whispered to Eddie.

A few minutes before eleven-fifteen, Beatrice nodded to Lily who went up to the wireless that had been murmuring about tinned soup and turned up the sound. One of two evacuee boys who were generally kept out of sight, gave a nervous shriek and Gussie, eyes wide, put her finger to her lips and hissed loudly, 'Shssh!'

The boys retreated behind Lily and there was absolute silence.

'I'm speaking to you from the Cabinet room at Number 10 Downing Street. This morning the British Ambassador in Berlin handed the German government a final note ...'

Eddie thought that the Prime Minister's voice sounded like a baleful hermit predicting death and destruction from a dark cave. No Rupert Brooke he.

Before the quavering voice could pronounce the final words of war, there was an interruption as George lurched into the room. 'Have I missed the old bugger? Eddie, you swine, why didn't you wake me!'

'George! How could you!' Gussie lunged at her son.

Encouraged, the evacuee boys came out from behind Lily, and began to yell 'Bugger! Bugger! Bugger!' in high-pitched voices, before continuing with a wider choice of swear words.

Beatrice and Sylvia leant forward in the same praying attitude as they tried to hear Chamberlain's words.

'Why don't you tackle George?' suggested Artemis to Eddie.

Annoyed by George's continuing insults, Eddie launched himself at his cousin who immediately crashed to the rug in front of the wireless which rocked dangerously before righting itself.

Eddie sat firmly on George who went quiet enough for Chamberlain's words to emerge again.

'The situation in which no word given by Germany's ruler could be trusted and no people or country could feel themselves safe, has become intolerable. And now we have resolved to finish it ... May God bless you all. May He defend the right ...'

The Prime Minister's voice now seemed stronger or at least louder so that gradually the evacuee boys stopped bellowing and they all heard his final words.

'... It is the evil things that we shall be fighting against – brute force, bad faith, injustice, oppression and persecution: and against them I am certain that the right will prevail.'

As his words died away, the national anthem was played and everybody stood, including Eddie, thus freeing George. Like a clumsy bear, George lumbered to his feet and his hand came up in a salute. Nobody laughed, even though his fingers wavered round his nose and his trousers were halfway down his hips. He was a soldier. England was at war. George would fight for them, possibly die for them.

⁂

At 10 0'clock the next morning, Eddie was walking along Kingsway towards Astradel House, the headquarters of the RAF. He had caught an early train filled with soldiers coming from a base at Blandford. Over the last few days reservists had been called in from all over England. Eddie, centred on his own aims, had not quite taken in that preparations of all sorts were already underway. Of course, he'd been aware of the evacuees and the black-out curtains but not the sense that everything was changing.

In London sandbags were being piled against shop windows, signs directed to ARP posts or air-raid shelters and, once again, there were soldiers everywhere. After a sober evening and a good sleep, Eddie was feeling particularly active and cheerful. His confidence lasted as he went through the imposing doors of Astradal House and confronted a burly uniformed commissionaire.

'I'm here for an interview with the selection board for pilots in the RAF.'

'Third floor, sir. Room 21. The lift's straight ahead.'

'I'll take the stairs.'

The small waiting room was filling up with other interviewees, his rivals, one of them in school uniform. Another, tall and thin, older than the rest, was boasting loudly about his RAF contacts and the number of his flying hours. A short, stubby fellow with a very tightly knotted tie and ginger hair, nudged Eddie, 'Some chaps take the biscuit.'

At last, Eddie was escorted to the interview room.

'Come right in,' encouraged the central of three men. All were old, and, although in uniform, wore the face of schoolmasters.

'You may sit down.'

Eddie hadn't even noticed the chair. He sat down and listened as he was given the names of his interviewers. Now he could see their wings, their stripes and their sharp eyes.

'Why do you want to join the Royal Air Force?'

'To serve my King and country, sir. In a time of war.' Henry had suggested this answer.

'How old are you?'

'Nineteen years and nine months.'

The man to the right who picked up a bit of paper was slightly younger and more heroic looking with a sun-bronzed face and a sharp little moustache. 'Your father fought in the last war?'

'Yes, sir.' What was that to do with anything? 'I've always wanted to be in the air force, sir.' No reaction.

'We also wrote to your college and your school.' Middle man studied his bit of paper. 'Schools.'

Eddie was prepared for this. 'I've grown up a lot at Oxford. I put my energy into other things.'

'Such as?'

'Flying.'

Suddenly there was a list of questions from the man on the left:

'Which newspapers do you read?'

'*The Times.*' Occasionally.

'What games do you play?'

'Rugger, cricket.' Badly. 'I row.' Well.

'Do you hunt? Do you shoot?'

'Yes, sir.' Sort of. Now if I had a different father...

'How about sailing?'

'Afraid not.' Too late, Eddie remembered that light hands on the tiller suggested light hands on the joystick. Ditto riding. At least he'd lied on that one.

'How many battleships in the Far East?'

'None. They're all cruisers.' Won't catch me out with that one.

'What is the tan of an angle? Sin? Cosin?' Eddie had always surprised himself by being good at maths.

It seemed the interview was winding down. Eddie racked his brain for something that would make him stand out from the crowd.

The man in the middle leant forward, 'Your mother's maiden name was Fitzpaine?'

'Yes, sir.'

'Any relation of Brigadier-General Fitzpaine?'

'Her father. My grandfather. Missing presumed dead at Gallipoli, sir.'

The man leant forward, showing real interest for the first time. 'I met him once. In Cairo. We were both kicking our heels there.'

'He only lasted three days on Gallipoli,' said Eddie.

'A brave death. Churchill called them paladins. Stuck in my mind.' The Air Vice-Marshall, as finally identified by Eddie, nodded to himself before speaking briskly. 'Well, thank you, Mr. Chaffey, for your time. The Royal Air Force hasn't been a fully-fledged part of the armed forces for long but I believe we will have a very important part to play. Take the slip to the commissionaire and he will tell you where to find the medics.'

Repressing an urge to salute (but what was the airman's salute?) Eddie left.

Waiting in another anonymous room, it struck him that things were not as expected at the Royal Air Force. This brave new world was run by old men. His experience at the University Air Squadron had counted for less than the old boy network. How his father would have sniggered!

After nearly an hour, the short chunky chap joined him.

'Two still standing,' Eddie said in an ironical tone of voice.

'Could have knocked me down with a feather,' replied the other cheerily. 'Didn't think I stood a chance, leaving school at fifteen. I guess it was my work with engines that got me in.'

'Where do you learn that?' asked Eddie warily.

'Apprentice is the posh word. Slaving in the garage down the road for six years. Picking up bits and pieces. Doing favours so I'd get taught. Cars, lorries, tractors, boats, I've done them all.'

'Aeroplanes?' asked Eddie.

'There you've got me. I've always wanted to be a flyer.' The man paused, smiled. 'Stupid.'

'It would be easier to be air crew with your skills.'

'That's what they all say. My dad thinks I've lost my wits but I'll prove them wrong.'

'The interview must've gone well?'

'The old fellow in the middle said he admired my sort. Bit rich, I thought. I can read, write, I'm tough, don't give up easily and I can spot a needle on Mars.'

'Good eyesight.'

'Even if I've never been inside a plane, I know how big the sky is. At any rate the old fellow said, "What are aeroplanes but engines on wings?" to which I heartily agreed and then he gave me the blue slip.'

'No maths questions?'

'Need a teacher, don't I. How about it, Chaffey? See, I know your name too. Country name. All city me. Birmingham. Andy Bullit. Don't laugh, it's true. Here's good luck to both of us!'

Bullit stuck out his hand and Eddie took it willingly. It seemed he had maligned the Royal Air Force. They did want all sorts.

'To our high-flying future!'

≫≪

It was nearly eight o'clock when Eddie once again stood outside Astradal House. He had lost track of Bullit or anyone else and was alone with no plans for the evening. It was too early for the Bag o' Nails and anyway he felt too wound up for booze. If he went to the London flat he risked being cross-questioned by his father. If he went to Dorset he'd have to face his mother's sad eyes.

He looked around. The sun had recently dipped below the buildings along Kingsway, leaving a glowing halo in its wake but the facades were dark, the black-out already in place so that they seemed menacing against the bright sky. The streets were dull too, a few cars and buses; they too were dark, their passengers like ghosts, drove by at half the usual speed. Eddie imagined how dismal it would become when all the light from the sky had gone. Most workers had left their offices and on such a fine evening normally would be drinking in the three or four pubs Eddie could see from where he stood. But now there were few takers, people walking fast as if keener than usual to reach their destination.

Hesitating on the edge of the pavement, on his own in a newly strange city on the second day of war, Eddie suddenly had an acute awareness of how alone he was. His body seemed strange as the city, his youthfulness and recent success mere bravado. Yet flying alone in the vastness above the world was where he was most happy. Every minute of the day he longed for that sense of being solitary and beyond reach. So what was it now, in this city filled with people, that made him so aware of being alone and his heart beat too fast as if afraid? The sky, flushed a purplish-pink, pressed down heavily as if warning him of something unknowable in the future. His future was with the Royal Air Force! Why did he feel like this on his day of triumph? Angrily he swung round one way and then the other.

Now he needed company, there was no-one. Henry would have been a possibility. Henry was outside all this war business, but term had not yet started and Henry was still in America with his family. The answer came suddenly: Eva. Eva would understand his mood: the knowledge that he had committed himself, his life to something inescapable, except by death. He who had never committed himself to anything. Yes, Eva would understand.

CHAPTER SEVEN
5th September 1939

Eva wished the summer would end. She wanted the world to be stiff and cold. She wanted the war to be real or not to be. She wanted her mother to come back from wherever she was. She wanted the house to be less full. She'd got used to the two refugees Valtraud and Hildegard and sometimes practiced her German on them which would please her mother, but the evacuees, sisters Ros and Ellie, were a nuisance, always hungry and bored. No mother but still too many females in the house with the only man her father who looked about ninety. What if he died or disappeared? And what of Eddie? Was he gone forever? She couldn't even remember why she had run from him in that horrible café. He had written several times, it was true, with no reference to their parting. Perhaps it had made little impression on him.

Eva, lying in bed, counted off these negatives in a kind of mourning, and only then allowed herself to think slowly and with relish, I am going to The Ruskin! At last her father had agreed. And for that she could thank her mother. The Professor had admitted it, reluctantly. Perhaps he had despaired of her as a classicist – any early promise had not been fulfilled – or perhaps he just didn't care. She stuck her legs out of bed, then slowly went to take down the black-out blinds. It was yet another sunny day and the hard light from the window made shadows from her feet on the shiny wooden floor.

Something, perhaps stones, bounced against her window. Leaning out, Eva saw Eddie standing in the garden. She laughed with surprise.

'Hello Helios!' She cried.

Eddie who had indeed quite forgotten how they'd parted, stared up at Eva's smooth pale face. 'You might at least call me Romeo. Who is Helios anyway? He sounds like a cad.'

'He's a sun god in third-century Greece. My father told me.'

'That sounds all right. Come down!'

Eddie and Eva sat on the stone bench in the unkempt garden. Flowers were turned to stalks, grass to straw.

'I got your letters,' said Eva.

'I've joined the Royal Air Force,' said Eddie.

'Congratulations.' Eva, gazed up at a sky stippled with white clouds, 'A nasty little girl stealing berries at the front of your house stuck out her black tongue at me.'

'That must be Ros. Ellie is quite polite. Luckily Valtraud and Hildegard look after them mostly. Valtraud's very strict and Hildegard very kind. So it works out all right. Although Hildegard is older and cleverer and Papa fears she may be interned as an enemy alien. He tells her to keep in the house.'

'Really.' This was far too much information for Eddie who required a listener. 'I came last night to pack up my things in college.' He paused. 'Last night I wanted to see you. London was very strange. Quite unnerving actually.'

'War is very disturbing, even though it's only just begun. I suppose you won't come to Oxford anymore.' Eva wanted to say, 'I'm going to art school' but she was afraid he wouldn't care. 'Would you like breakfast?'

They went into the house together. Valtraud, Hildegard, Ellie and Ros who sat around the dining room table, stared interestedly.

'What's that man doing here?' said Ros, waving her cereal spoon, so that milk dripped.

'This is not polite,' admonished Valtraud.

'He was snooping around,' said Ros, loudly. 'Then he went over a wall into the back.'

Eva blushed and regretted the Professor's command, stated as his absent wife's wish, that the girls should eat in the dining room in order to learn table manners.

'Little girls should be seen but not heard,' said Eddie, good-humouredly, 'but one more word from you and I'll give you a wallop.'

This provoked a satisfied smirk from Ros who, neverthe-less, preserved total silence from then on.

'I make eggs,' said Valtraud eagerly. It was clear that Eddie's large male presence was a welcome addition to the household.

'We'll just grab something and go,' Eva said, disliking the dilution of her time with Eddie.

'I'd kill for a couple of eggs,' announced Eddie.

Eddie ate cereal, a pile of toast, an apple and drank three cups of tea as well as demolishing the eggs. All this took time. The room became warm with the food and the sun and the people inside. Eddie, not noticing Eva's impatience, felt relaxed and admired.

As soon as possible, Eva led Eddie out of the house and they walked towards the town. The morning was still fine, although the skies' stippling had formed into trails of white. Eva decided it would be exciting to paint in oils where white wasn't such a problem.

'I was in Dorset with my family,' said Eddie, 'when war was declared.'

'Papa called me into his study to discuss the black-out. Since then I've scarcely seen him.'

'I feel I can talk to you.' Eddie didn't say any more but he took Eva's hand.

'Surely you have lots of friends and family to talk to.' Eva considered her own lack.

'Henry's all right when he's not in America.'

'How will we meet now?' Eva tried not to sound pathetic. She thought, how will we get to know each other?

Eddie squeezed her hand. 'I'll write to you.'

Just then Eva spotted her father striding towards them and extricated her fingers.

'Here comes Papa.'

'Oh, where?' asked Eddie politely.

The Professor, only a few paces away, hadn't recognized his daughter and would have walked past if she hadn't cried out, 'Good morning, Papa.'

'Good morning, dear.'

'This is Eddie Chaffey on his way to his college. We met at that lunch Professor Lamb gave.'

'Good morning, sir,' said Eddie. The men shook hands. 'I've just come from Professor Lamb, as it happens. I turn to him for advice. Your tutor, is he?'

'A friend of my parents, sir.'

'I was his tutor. A brilliant classicist. Then he went to war. Supposed to become a banker and make some money but came back here instead. I helped him. Now he advises me.'

'My father served under him at Gallipoli,' said Eddie, adding carelessly, 'My mother was engaged to him briefly.'

'Always seemed a bachelor type to me. Of course, he was very cut up by the war.' He paused while Eddie waited respectfully. 'And here we go again.' He looked at Eddie interrogatively.

Eva noted that her father was more attentive to Eddie than he ever was to her.

'I've joined the Royal Air Force,' said Eddie, as if he'd been asked a direct question.

'I don't denigrate patriotism. There are always hard questions when evil flourishes. Eva's mother is German.'

Eva flushed. Eddie took a step back. The Professor also retreated. 'Good luck, young man.'

'Thank you, sir.'

Eddie, watching the Professor go, murmured, 'I'm glad I'm not old. Old people are so sad. Better to die young, don't you think.'

'He is my father,' said Eva but she was thinking of her mother. 'I wouldn't like to die young.'

'I suppose not. But in war it happens. Anyway, I've got to go to college. Thank you for my breakfast. You seem more real to me than most people. Or perhaps I mean you make me seem more real.'

Eva watched him stride away. She wondered if he made her feel more real. More alive certainly which might be the same thing. She'd been so happy to see him standing under her window. He didn't turn to wave. She began to think of her mother again. It was terrible having no idea where she was.

⇽

Eddie arrived at his college and admired the beauty of the ancient buildings with dispassionate eyes. They seemed like guardians of the past, no place for a young man.

He went up to his rooms where he found Henry, lounging in the best armchair while reading *The Times*. 'Hey champion!' He returned to the paper and read out loud: '*Prepared and quiet. The predominant note in the aspect of London yesterday was quiet and resolute preparedness for whatever may come.*'

'I thought you weren't coming back for weeks.'

'Exciting days or as *The Times* said 'Prepared and quiet'. I don't want to be the other side of the Atlantic when the balloon goes up.'

'Some people thought it went up on Sunday at 11.15.' Although pleased to see Henry, Eddie felt his single-mindedness to his new self would be compromised by his old friend, particularly as he seemed unusually sparky.

Henry got to his feet and began rootling in a sideboard. 'Feel like a drop of cheer?' He held up a bottle of Pernod brought back from a trip to Paris.

'It is ten o'clock in the morning. You're not a boozer and Pernod is well-known for its induction into existential gloom.'

'I see the way the wind blows.' Henry put the bottle down and moved restlessly to the window. 'I was at a cocktail party at the embassy last night.'

'The American embassy,' interrupted Eddie whose mood was hardening. 'Ever heard of Pontius Pilate?'

'I stood in a group with Ambassador Kennedy,' continued Henry, ignoring Eddie's comment. 'In brief, he thinks England is heading down the Swanee fast. He believes the US shouldn't waste any sympathy, let alone aid, whether of arms or anything else on a country doomed to become a part of greater Germany.'

Eddie stood up, found a bottle of whisky, poured two glasses, handed one to Henry, and sat down.

'Interesting, wouldn't you say?' continued Henry. 'An up yours to Mr 'I've-got-an-American-mother' Churchill.'

'What a swine!' said Eddie, 'Not Churchill, of course. Don't you have an English mother? He sipped at his whisky, then stood up and put the still full glass on the sideboard. 'I'm off to the University Squadron to tell them I've applied directly to the RAF.'

'You haven't asked me my plan, you self-centred little island.'

'This little island is going to the rescue of Europe.'

Henry looked into his glass. 'I was bloody ashamed last night. I'm an American patriot through and through but I've spent a year over here and, as you've honoured me by recalling, my mother was English.'

'You can watch and cheer for our side.'

'I've got my Harvard degree already, I've got a job waiting for me back home, I've got Angela. In truth, my whole future's mapped out.'

'No worries then,' said Eddie with friendly irony.

'More or less. But to hear that rat Kennedy speak. Goodbye England, just like that. It made my blood boil.'

'But your blood doesn't boil, Henry,' said Eddie, looking at his friend's frank, clean-cut face for the first time. 'That's part of your charm. My blood boils, usually over the top of the saucepan.'

'Bugger off. Don't you know when a guy's being serious?' Henry put down his glass. 'So I found a friend of a friend. In short, I'm pulling strings to get into the RAF.'

'Pull another.' Eddie was genuinely amazed. 'What about your beloved fiancée?'

'I won't tell her until it's all fixed. I'm just not ready to settle down.'

'If it's adventure you want, how about fighting a black bear in the Rockies or Appalachians or wherever they are?'

'Sure. That's why I'm not telling anybody back home till it's fixed.'

'With all the string pulling in the world, the Royal Air Force may not want to spend the money on training a Yank.'

'Like many Americans who have enough dough and live in the middle of nowhere, I happen to be able to fly a plane already and the friend of my friend is quite a big wheel.' Henry set his square jaw.

'You secretive bastard!'

≫≪

'You're much too young!' Betty was fair and robust, pretty and confident, balanced on the bed where she was sitting with Eva.

'Friends are supposed to be on your side.' Eva stood up.

'Friends give warnings. I don't expect you've even considered life classes!'

'Life classes are an essential part of artist's training.'

'Naked men? Have you considered naked men?' Betty's blushes spread down her neck.

'There'll be naked women too,' replied Eva who was sure neither of her parents had considered the possibility of naked men. 'Many women have babies at my age.'

'Naked men,' continued the remorseless Betty, 'from the front.' Clearly she estimated this a knock-out blow.

'I don't know why you think you know so much about what goes on,' said Eva trying not to imagine her gaunt papa without his clothes. 'You've never looked at a painting in your life.'

'I have brothers, don't forget.'

'But they're all little boys. I've seen Michael Angelo's *Adam* and Donatello's *David* and Caravaggio's *Cupid*.' Eva ransacked her memory for naked males. 'Art makes nudity a quite different thing. But I see you're a cultural illiterate.' Betty's astonished face convinced Eva to follow up immediately. 'All you want is a man in your bed, sticking his thing into you so you can have lots of babies like your mother and never think properly again apart from bossing everybody around and making them miserable. I want something different from my life. Marriage has no interest for me. I'm going to be independent and a painter and Art College is just the way I'm starting.' As she finished this declaration, Eva found she had tears in her eyes and it was that, more than her words which were obscured by emotion and almost forgotten as she spoke, that propelled her from the bedroom. She must not let Betty see her cry.

Once on the pavement, the tears stopped but all the same she felt sorrowfully alone. She imagined her mother's arm pressing her close. Then her mother turned into Eddie. How would he look naked? From the front, of course. Would he be more David or Adam? She had read somewhere that a classical nude was traditionally given a smaller penis than in reality. Was Eddie's very large? She expected so if overall height had anything to do with it.

CHAPTER EIGHT
December 1939

Eddie sat hunched in his Tiger Moth. Ahead was an orange sky fast turning to black. At this far point of North East Scotland the days were short, even if there hadn't yet been ice and snow to stop the planes taking off. You'd think that red sky predicted good weather but he'd seen the forecast and knew snow was approaching which meant two or three days hanging round the little town where he was based. It was just his luck to be in the back of beyond when other chaps were within easy reach of London. He didn't know how he'd stuck it.

Of course he *did* know. Eddie considered the cross-country flight he'd just completed, his first solo since training began. Even after all these months he'd got into trouble. A red light had started blinking, then suddenly the engine cut. He was down to several hundred feet, scanning frantically for a flat place to land among the rocks and furze when his good angel had reminded him that the red light was a warning that he had no fuel. What a dolt! One switch, tanks changed, petrol flowing and Eddie was in business again.

But it wasn't the idiocies that kept him going, it was the ecstasy of flying. None of the pilots training with him knew how to put the feeling into words but he suspected they all felt much the same, even the dullest. It might have been a sobering thought for someone as self-centred as Eddie but instead for the first time in his life he felt himself part of a group who shared the burning obsession.

Eddie who had half-closed his eyes, opened them again to see the red flush replaced by the fast-falling veil of night. He looked round the airfield. As the last flyer out, he should have been the last in but there was one place empty. He turned to see the black mountains silhouetted behind them. They seemed closer and higher in the dusk. Not an obstacle if you kept your eyes half open. The other way there was the sea, not easy to ignore.

Jimmy Stirling was the man still out, the most talented pilot of them all, a Scotsman, never without a glass of malt in the evenings, told jokes badly, played the bagpipes even worse and picked up the prettiest girl in town. Eddie, who had been accused of being a risk-taker, understood that Jimmy, although he could do anything with an aeroplane – landing on his tail, stalling in a spin so he blacked out for whole seconds, tipping his wings at the heather – was a true risk-taker because he didn't really care. Death wasn't a word anyone used but it was a constant presence. Jimmy didn't even care about dying. About death. *O Death where is your sting?*

Eddie got out of his plane and stared at the almost invisible line of light. That was the way Jimmy should come in; it had been the same route for all of them.

'Silly bugger.' A figure had come to stand behind Eddie in the darkness. Eddie turned to see Andy.

'What do you think. Run out of fuel?'

'Never liked coming home, did he?'

Eddie noted the use of the past tense. None of their group had gone, although there were stories about an expected ten per-cent loss during training.

He stared ahead. Surely that was a black dot moving closer. The darkness was already dense and it was difficult to see. The airfield flares glowed brightly, made it even harder. If Jimmy had no engine power there'd be very little noise. He'd be hoping to glide into land just as he'd imagined earlier but it would be too dangerous to put down in an unlit field.

'I think he's trying to come in,' said Andy in a low voice.

There were other figures now, all facing in the same direction. 'He'll never make it,' said Eddie, daring the gods. He'd never liked Jimmy, never got the measure of him. But he was one of them, one of the group.

'He's low,' agreed Andy, 'Jimmy can pull off just about anything.'

The plane was now a visible shape, the spread wings looking too fragile. 'A bird would make it in,' murmured Eddie.

They were both silent. There was no sound from any of the other figures on the airfield. They were all willing the plane closer. They knew well the terrain it was passing over, the walls, the hedges, the stone farm buildings, telegraph wires, a single house. Each one could be a fatal hazard. They knew too that Jimmy would be speaking to the radio controller, estimating the wind, although there was not much, looking for the lights, perhaps even seeing the lights by now.

'Go on, Jimmy, lad,' grunted Andy.

The plane was so low that they could hardly separate it from the land.

Eddie clenched his fists. Andy began a quiet whistling in his teeth. Then humming.

When the impact came it was almost a relief. As there was no fuel, there were no flames, no vast explosion, only a wild shock of metal breaking as something that had seemed living, both man and machine, burst open into a thousand fragments.

It was near enough for half a dozen men to run towards it.

'He must have hit that white house with the red roof. Easy enough to see you'd think. Poor old Jimmy.'

'Maybe the flares muddled him. There's nobody living in that house, is there?'

'Let's hope not. Officially not.'

The two men began to walk towards the buildings at the other end of the airfield.

⋙⋘

It was only when Eddie reached the small bare bedroom in the house where he was billeted that he allowed himself to think further about that sudden death in front of his eyes – even if he hadn't actually seen the feet and arms and head and hands fly about the countryside.

All the pilots had felt the need to visit the pub in town with the best ale. 'Poor blighter' was the nearest Jimmy got to an epitaph. Then Eileen appeared. Had they been drawn to this particular pub not for the ale but because they knew Eileen would be there? Jimmy had called her 'his pretty wee tart' but it was assumed she thought something more elevated about him. Perhaps even love, although none of the young men – only Andy had already reached twenty-one – could speak about such matters with experience.

In the end, Rufus, known as Spots, for his freckles, had been pushed into the challenge of informing Eileen. She had been led away in tears.

Other than that it had, apparently, been an ordinary evening. Andy, who couldn't hold his drink, soon sat with his head on the table, Eddie who was assumed to be richest, paid, although protesting, for more rounds than his due and Spots (after he had delivered Eileen into misery) told unlikely stories about his growing up in Cork. He included the one which always went down well towards the end of the evening, how when out fishing he'd found himself face-to-face with an enormous shark whose villainous eyes had looked him over assessingly before rejecting him in favour of a monstrous dogfish Spots had just caught and was about to throw back into the sea. The story always ended with the same line. 'I knew I wasn't God's gift but never before did I realise that I was uglier than the ugliest fish in the sea.'

They had broken up earlier than usual, early enough for Eddie's landlady Mrs McLeod to accost him as he went upstairs and hand him a packet plus a pile of envelopes. 'Special day is it?'

Eddie thought about saying, 'Yes, actually. I've seen my first war casualty. Death, that is.' But she was smiling kindly so he merely thanked her.

Without even glancing at the mail, Eddie lay on his bed with his hands behind his head. The room was cold but he didn't feel it. For all the three months he had been in Scotland, the war was being fought in Europe. God, it seemed far away. British soldiers, including his annoying but doubtless brave cousin George, were trying to support the French Army. Fighter pilots from the First Squadron were also in France, flying across the Channel and settling on bases often in the North around Rheims or Nancy. Near enough to drop in on Paris or some smaller town with girls and booze.

Sometimes he was anxious that peace would be negotiated and that all his training would be wasted. Would he then return tamely to undergraduate life at Oxford? Guiltily, Eddie thought he should keep up with the news. His mother dutifully posted him up *The Times* but somehow its late arrival dimmed his enthusiasm. Besides, every day brought a new exhausting challenge, new excitement.

Suddenly restless, Eddie got off the bed and, lifting the blackout a fraction, looked out of the window. Sure enough it was snowing. Now it would be lectures and more lectures. Eddie picked up the packet of letters and opened the top one. A birthday card! *His* birthday. His twentieth birthday. It took him a moment to make the connection. A birthday without celebrations, unless you counted the careless death of Jimmy Stirling. Eddie opened the next envelope. It was a letter from Henry.

Henry, doubtless due to his important friend, was training at an airfield in the home counties. At the weekends, or wherever he was off duty, he drove into Oxford or to London where he went to parties with American diplomats and journalists who introduced him to their British and European counterparts. All of them found his present occupation unbelievable, some decided he was having a laugh, but his classy background and open face meant they told him things anyway. Henry knew about the war. Eddie read his letters with a mixture of curiosity and unadmitted jealousy.

The card was from his mother. She had written on the back, *You are still so young, my dearest, but preparing to take on a man's responsibility.* There were also cards from Lily and his grandmother, several bills from his college which had finally tracked him down, two copies of *The Times* and a letter from Eva who didn't know it was his birthday.

Dear Eddie,

Thank you for your last two letters. I agree that Yeats' poem on the airman is quite beautiful if dreadful. I particularly like the lines, 'A lonely impulse of delight/ Drove to this tumult in the clouds.' Tomorrow I am going to London to take back the horrible Cockney sisters – you met them all those months ago ... I am working harder than I ever have in my life ... For the last two days I've done nothing but draw a plaster cast of a foot ...

Will you come south for Christmas? Your letters are different. So perhaps you are too. My mother is still away and Hildegard has been interned on the Isle of Man. Thank the Lord I have Art.

With good wishes

Eddie never read Eva's letters carefully. He could do nothing about the tragedies that surrounded her – it was fairly obvious that if a German-Jewish woman gets mixed up in trying to help escaping refugees and then disappears in Germany, a happy ending was unlikely. As far as internment for Germans was concerned, he called them 'huns' like all his fellow pilots and didn't waste time on some people's bad luck in being born in the wrong place at the wrong time.

Eddie put aside Eva's letter (although, unlike the cards, he would keep it in a drawer) and turned to the most up-to-date copy of *The Times*.

'You find the British Expeditionary Force larger, better equipped, stronger in armament than in any comparable period. You find at the same time a tremendous Air Force, you find a well-found, ceaselessly and vigilant navy.'

≫

Eva kept a tight hold of Ros. Ellie could be trusted and was even carrying her cardboard case. Eva had used her own coupons to buy the sisters new coats and hats at Elliston and Cavell and Valtraud had washed their hair, ignoring shrieks as soap got into their eyes

– or perhaps putting soap in their eyes. Eva was sorry they were going. They had been a bit of life in the dull house and Ellie had even begun to follow her around in an admiring way. Her accent now was a mixture of Cockney, Oxford English plus a dash of Germanic consonants.

'We haven't got to get into *that!*'

Ros's outrage, unusually, was justified. The train was already stuffed with people, standing in the corridors, half out of the windows. In fact, Ellie and Ros tunnelled their way in easily while she struggled apologetically until dragged in by Ellie, shrinking encouragingly, 'Just kick 'em, Miss.'

Standing in the corridor inhaling smoke and other peoples' sweat, Eva suffered a spasm of self-doubt. What was she doing there? Was she always to be the grown-up now?

Meanwhile the girls were worming up and down the corridor just for the fun of it. After the train had been going a while, Ellie re-appeared whispering importantly, 'A fellow's off at the next station. Follow me but don't let on.' It was obvious that, out in the big world, the girls were more capable of looking after her than she of them.

Pushed into the seat by Ellie, with two cases on her lap, she felt calmer. Ros also came to sit on her lap, putting her arms round Eva's neck and announcing loudly for the benefit of the carriage, 'Oh Miss, we'll be seeing our mum after all these months!'

The carriage was unresponsive. Evacuees were well known all over the country. Many were returning to the city they'd emerged from.

'Come on, Ros.' Ellie pulled at her sister. 'Leave Miss Eva to herself.' There was slightly more interest at hearing a name.

As the sisters left, hurdling legs and bags, the young woman opposite who held a sleeping baby, commented, 'Little beggars, aren't they. Still, suppose they miss their mum.'

'I expect so,' agreed Eva politely. Perhaps Ros's bed-wetting was a sign of missing her mum. 'How old's your baby?'

'Four weeks today. He's as good as gold. His dad's overseas. Hasn't even seen him yet.'

Eva thought of mothers and babies and fathers. She suspected it was mainly difficulties and pain, even if the mother opposite smiled very sweetly at her baby.

To her left, a vicar with a small son who had an irritating, possibly invented cough, was reading *The Times* in such a way that it spread across Eva. The train stopped at another station and the baby began to cry. The mother rocked him, jiggled him, held him up against herself and patted his back. The cries increased to wails. The mother looked despairingly at the crowded corridor before undoing the top button of her blouse and thrust the howling baby to her bosom. The silence was abrupt enough for everyone to hear a soft, contented sucking.

The vicar put down *The Times* and stared. He uttered a disbelieving grunt before opening the paper again, this time holding it in front of his son's face. The boy, who seemed utterly cowed, made no squeak of protest. The mother went bright pink but continued to feed her baby with a more defiant air. Everybody else stared straight ahead with the same stoic lack of reaction that they had given the evacuees.

Eva smiled encouragingly at the mother and said loudly, 'Poor you. The war makes everything so hard.' Everybody, including the mother, pretended not to hear.

The train arrived at Paddington Station an hour late. Ellie and Ros reappeared in time to shepherd Eva off the train.

'Where're we meeting Mum then?' yelled Ellie above the station's hubbub.

They met Mrs Brockett under the clock as arranged. A stream of soldiers, packs on their shoulders, separated them, giving time for Eva to note she carried a baby. The girls also looked surprised. The soldiers passed and Ellie and Ros ran towards their mother. As they arrived, both their mother and their new sibling burst into an explosion of tears.

'Come on, Mum!' The girls bounced around her cheerily, just as they had to Eva. Ellie took the baby and began to rock it expertly while Ros kissed her mother into smiles and hugs.

'I'm afraid I've got to catch my train,' said Eva. She had been planning to go to the National Gallery but she felt far too exhausted.

⚬

That evening Eva wrote another letter to Eddie. She tried, without sounding pathetic, to explain how she had no one who understood her or even wanted to understand her.

'Eva! Eva, dear!' Her father was calling from his study.

She descended watched by Valtraud from her bedroom door. Valtraud wore her expectant expression, as if something better probably wouldn't, but just might happen.

'Oh, Eva.' Professor Speke looked up with apparent surprise. He was wearing a plum-coloured, woollen dressing gown. He had been unwell that day.

'You did call me, didn't you? When did you get up?'

'The telephone rang.' The Professor paused. The desk light shining on his bent head made his hair seem more white than grey. Or perhaps it had turned white without her noticing, thought Eva. His bony face reflected a reddish colour from the dressing-gown. Quite like a Rembrandt painting. Eva tried to imagine how she'd tackle such a subject and missed her father's first words.

'I have had a message about your mother.'

'What?'

'Your mother. The news is disturbing. She has been picked up, her passport taken – not her real passport, you understand.'

To Eva's horror, her austere father seemed about to cry. His hooded eyes raised suddenly to hers, were filled with a tragic brilliance. 'I couldn't stop her, you understand. She said it was her destiny and I must not make a coward of her, a little Englander. She did good – we have Valtraud and Hildegard to prove it and so many children in London and elsewhere. How could I have stopped her!'

The tears which had receded with the words now threatened to come again. Partly to stop them, partly because she wanted to know the answer, Eva cried out, 'What about me! Didn't she think of *me*!'

'Yes. Yes. You're quite right.' The Professor ran his hands through his hair in a startled kind of way. 'I'm sure she thought of you.'

'But I was not important enough,' continued Eva out-pacing her father's emotion. 'I was not her *destiny*!'

Father and daughter stared at each other. Both were dimly aware and dimly ashamed that their emotions were entirely selfish. Neither of them knew how to comfort the other.

Sustained by anger, Eva asked boldly, 'Are you telling me she's dead? My mother's died?'

'There is no certainty. But the news is concerning. I can't disguise it. The likelihood is there. The Nazis …' He couldn't continue nor could he contain his sorrow anymore. Bowing his white head, he allowed tears to drip on to the desk.

His helplessness enraged Eva further. How could her learned, distinguished father allow himself to be brought so low! 'I don't believe anything you say.' Her voice was flat. 'In a war all sorts of rumours get around. Mama would hate you to be so – so pathetic.' She heard the cruelty in her tone and made an effort. 'You are not well, that's the problem so I will help you back to your bedroom. Tomorrow things will seem more normal. Here, lean on me.'

Eva stood by her father and helped him up, although his quavering touch was unpleasant to her. Fathers should be stronger.

The Professor allowed himself to be led upstairs. At his bedroom door, Eva said in the professional tones of a nurse, 'I'll ask Valtraud to make you the tea you like.'

Eva did not sleep that night. In her bitterness she hoped her father would die so that she could be an orphan and start her life again. In the grey mist of dawn, she added a note to her Eddie's letter, 'If you do travel south, I would like to meet you. In Oxford. Or I could come to London …'

Her father did not descend for breakfast – she and Valtraud sat silently on either side of the kitchen table – but he appeared just as Eva was leaving for the Ruskin. He was wearing a suit.

'I am better,' he announced, taking hold of his overcoat and avoiding Eva's eyes. 'I shall be back at teatime.'

Eva understood that her mother wouldn't be mentioned between them again and was glad. With all her youthful energy she refused to picture her mother, where she might be or how she might be suffering.

Later, at college, a teacher – the only young teacher who had once confided in her how he dreaded being called up – was giving her advice about scale and the face.

'How do you paint white hair under a bright light?' asked Eva.

'Difficult. There're always shadows of course. Green, grey, purple. White and black don't exist as I'm sure you know.' He stared at her, his eyes painted her pale, oval face and black – no, not black, red, purple, green – hair. 'Why do you ask?'

Against her will, Eva pictured her father's head bent in sorrow and burst into tears.

The teacher who was called Jack Halliwell, came closer and patted her on the back clumsily. 'You young girls all work far too hard.'

'Yes,' agreed Eva while she thought in horror and self-loathing of her cruel behaviour to her father. She loved her father.

But when she saw him at home again, the anger returned and she spoke only polite, meaningless things to him.

CHAPTER NINE
New Year's Eve 1939

Eva and Eddie sat side by side on a bench in Hyde Park. In a small gesture of rebellion, they had taken off the boxes containing their gas masks and pushed them as far away as possible. Eva's gloved fingers clasped a thermos of soup. The sky was bright enough but the air so cold that their breath came out in white spouts.

'This was a terrible idea,' said Eddie, stamping his feet. He wasn't even wearing an overcoat over his pilot's uniform. 'How about we go and find a steamy café?'

Eva looked at him from under her navy felt hat. She unwound her long crimson scarf. 'You can borrow this.'

Eddie snorted.

'I thought we'd be more peaceful,' said Eva.

'It's the coldest winter for hundreds of years.'

That's just another bit of rubbish public information,' said Eva. 'Posters everywhere: *'Freedom is in Peril. Defend it with all your Might.'* What does that mean? *'Careless Talk costs Lives'* makes more sense, at least the picture of two old ladies gossiping on a bus while Goering and Hitler sit listening in the seat behind is fun. Not that Valtraud sees the joke.'

'You do believe that we'll win the war?' said Eddie. It was not really a question.

Eva glanced sideways. He had changed physically since the war started, thinner, his hair shorter and his eyes different somehow, narrower as if used to looking in the distance. She pictured him in the cockpit of an aeroplane, intently staring.

Eddie caught her look and felt an oaf. He supposed he didn't know how to talk to a girl like her. Most young women he met were either working in clubs, bars or the RAF. Or they had families. She seemed so alone. No siblings, no visible mother and a father old enough to be her grandfather.

He made an effort to sound more interesting. 'When war first broke out everything was dark and closed and people were told to stay put. But now all the cinemas and theatres are open again and the place is filled with the usual crowds plus thousands of soldiers. Funny kind of New Year's Eve all the same.' He paused and smiled at Eva. 'Wouldn't it be jollier in a pub?'

'Let's walk.' Eva stood up. 'I've never been in a pub.' Over Eddie's shoulder, she could see a row of anti-aircraft guns, their long dark muzzles pointing to the sky like predatory animals, pterodactyls if those were the fierce ones. She handed him his gas mask. 'The war produces so much paraphernalia here: the guns, the sandbags, the shelters and posters and air balloons. In Oxford hardly anything's changed.' She thought, the air balloons – there were two above the park – were like fat slugs hanging above the city, more threatening than protective in her view. While she'd been waiting for Eddie at the National Gallery she'd done a sketch of one and given it mean little eyes and a round mouth.

They walked quickly, avoiding getting too close to the guns. A few pigeons flew over their heads and when they reached a bunch of sycamore trees, a squirrel ran down the trunk of one tree, crossed their path, and ran up the trunk of another. They stopped and watched him scuttle along a branch.

'Shouldn't he be hibernating?' said Eddie.

'Perhaps London squirrels are different.' She watched the squirrel climb even higher. 'What's the most frightening thing about flying?'

'There's nothing frightening. We scared our Flight Commander though, with our formation flying. Our wings were so close together when we landed, he nearly had a fit.' Eddie sounded relaxed for the first time.

Eva felt happier. She dared ask him now when he would finish his training and become part of the war.

Eddie walked quicker and told her that it was still months to go.

'Even though they've speeded things up, I've still got operational training and all sorts of stuff. Then I won't know if I will get to Fighter Command or Bomber Command or Coastal Command. Naturally I want it to be Fighter Command and in a Spitfire but we haven't lost too many pilots yet – mostly escorting our shipping – so there aren't many free places.'

Eva felt glad that he'd answered her with real information. 'You'd make a good fighter pilot.'

They were now near the edge of the park on the Bayswater Road. The wide space they'd come from, still lit by the remains of the daylight, was brighter than the shadowy city ahead where black buildings cut out the sky.

'I should catch my train,' said Eva. 'There's really no time for a pub.'

'Two thousand pedestrians have been killed since the war started.' Eddie stared into the moving darkness. 'One idiot fought with a threatening lamp-post outside his house. The lamp-post won.'

Eva didn't laugh. 'I've got to get to Paddington.'

'I'll walk you there.' Eddie was meeting Henry later at one of Henry's smart international cocktail parties. He had thought of squeezing in a visit to Sonia but you never knew these days with Sonia. She was always banging on about Finland and how he should understand that the Soviet Union only invaded in order to release them into a truer freedom. Meanwhile his mother was organising knitting circles for '*the poor beleaguered Finns attacked by those monstrous communists*'.

'Do you think it's in human nature to support David over Goliath?'

'Oh, no!' Eva stopped walking in her surprise. 'Big bullies always admire other big bullies as long as they're on the same side. My father says Mussolini won't come into the war until he's decided who's going to win.'

Eddie took Eva's arm and they walked on. The cold was bitter, coming up the pavement into his shoes. He'd certainly have an early drink on the station. 'This war is set for years,' he said, failing to disguise a certain satisfaction.

Only at the station which was already noisy with early home-goers, did Eddie think to ask Eva about herself. She was trying to decode the station boards. 'I know we're trying to confuse the enemy, but we've got to find our way home somehow.'

Eddie looked up at the great glass roof and decided not to be worried about bombs. Apparently, there were plans to take out the glass. He would be high above it all anyway. 'So what are you painting?'

'A self-portrait.' Eva started walking towards the barrier. 'All young artists paint themselves. No one will sit for them and they have no money to pay. They're usually mirror images with a peering quizzical expression.' She opened her shoulder bag and took out her ticket.

'I'll sit for you.'

Eva, who'd been about to leave, stopped and stared. She was immediately seeing Eddie differently, the broad forehead, thick hair, wide eyes, strong nose, well-shaped mouth. 'You might be too handsome,' she said, and smiled.

Eddie smiled too. He liked being admired. 'Next leave. I'll come to your house. You'd better do me justice.'

'Of course I am in my green period.'

They parted still smiling, happy with each other. Neither turned around to watch the other go – they were too young for that.

⧓

Henry had said it was just a few friends at The Savoy because you couldn't really celebrate a New Year during a war but the room was so thick with people and smoke that Eddie couldn't even find his host. Eventually he spotted him by his pilot's blue uniform, always less ubiquitous than the army's khaki. He was standing in a group of mostly suited older men, probably politicians or businessmen with nearly recognisable faces, under what would have been the hotel's famous glass dome except that it was boarded up. A small man with a large watch chain across his barrel chest was lecturing them about the engineering skills needed to build a perfect hemisphere.

'Extraordinary the self-declared experts thrown up by the war.'

Eddie turned to see his uncle Reggie Gisburne standing at his elbow. He was holding a glass of champagne and, judging by his heavy eyes and high colour, had been knocking it back for some time.

'How's George?' asked Eddie.

'Alive, the last time I heard.' Reggie seemed not only drunk but also pugnacious. 'Engineers are all the rage.' He reverted to his theme. 'As if they could win the war. It's men who'll win the war.'

'Yes,' agreed Eddie, although he passionately disagreed. It was aeroplanes that would win the war, not ranks of soldiers. Tanks, guns, machines of all sorts, just as armaments had won the last war. Skilled men were needed, yes, one pilot was worth a regiment of Reggie's men. They were just old-fashioned cannon fodder. '*Into the valley of Death rode the six hundred.*' He recalled a photograph of the grandfather he'd never known, the solemn stare, the full military regalia.

'I haven't said hello to our host.' Eddie tried to edge away from his uncle.

'Those yanks are everywhere, except where they're needed.' Reggie's swollen eyes were now fixed on a point beyond Eddie's shoulder.

Eddie turned to look. He saw a woman wearing a black sheath dress with diamond clips sparkling at her neckline and on her ears. As Reggie moved towards her, Eddie followed. A glamorous young woman might prefer speaking to a shining bright pilot with wings on his shoulders to an obese, drunk old soldier.

On closer inspection, the woman with her red lips and painted eyes and shiny black cap of hair, was not young. Pointing her cigarette in its ivory holder at Eddie, she mouthed, 'Who?'

'My nephew,' responded Reggie reluctantly. 'Moira Lipscombe.' Eddie recognised the name of an actress. 'I've booked a table in the River Room,' said Reggie.

'Darling, you're so clever.'

Eddie now remembered Moira Lipscombe was starring in a film being made about the Royal Air Force.

'Do you know everyone in London, Moira?' It was Henry acting the welcoming host. Eddie stared. How grown-up he sounded!

Moira laughed. 'You're going to need a big table, Reggie.'

'It's for two,' said Reggie, clenching his fists. Moira laughed again.

'Hello there, Henry,' said Eddie. 'I thought we were celebrating with a few friends.'

'Your war seems to lead to chance encounters,' Henry glanced round the room. 'Chance encounters leads to great parties.'

'If you have the money,' sneered Reggie.

Henry looked enquiringly.

'Colonel Reggie Guisburne,' Moira looked up from putting a new cigarette into the holder. 'He's my guest.' She tapped his arm. 'Behave yourself Reggie. And this handsome young man is his nephew.'

'Eddie and I are old chums from Oxford,' Henry shook Eddie's hand vigorously while Reggie glared at Moira, 'I'll see you in the River Room.'

Moira watched him go. She sighed, 'So much energy. These old soldiers hate sitting on their backsides.' The word sounded odd coming from her. 'I expect he'll wheedle his way into some far-flung field of battle and cause a good deal of trouble before getting himself killed.'

'Not much of a loss,' commented Eddie, grabbing a passing glass of champagne.

'Naughty.' Both men were silent as Moira blew an elegant smoke ring before asking, 'When will the US come into the war, Henry dear?'

'Isn't your film going to shame them in?' Henry was serious.

'They tell me that's the idea.' She turned to Eddie, stood very close to him. 'Do you hope to survive the war?'

'*You* will anyway,' said Eddie, becoming bored at this silly film star talk. 'As an American.'

'Born in Hackney Wick,' Moira's accent had suddenly changed to exaggerated cockney. 'Adopted up a class when orphaned at eight. Learnt to sing and dance at ten and off to America to make my fortune at sixteen.'

Eddie thought, why should I want her life story? 'I need another drink.' He walked away quickly and found a waiter. After drinking two glasses of champagne, he began to wonder what ever was the point of a party like this. How disgusting to see his middle-aged uncle lusting after an over-painted B-movie star. He found another waiter and drank two more glasses of champagne.

At the other side of the room, he saw a group of three young army officers whom he recognised from school or Oxford. By now his walk towards them had the floating quality of a ship on smooth waves – the floating even more languorous as he took and drank from another glass.

'Hello Skipworth-Biggs *and* Harley-Smart.' His emphasis of the 'and' suggested they were joined together in some meaningful way. The young officers quickly recognised a kindred spirit.

'Chaffey, old chap,' laughed Harley-Smart. 'Never expected to see you so respectable. What do you say, Skippers?'

'Welcome old boy,' Skippers, who despite being no older than Eddie boasted a flourishing moustache, held out a hand to Chaffey. 'Still owe me a tenner, I seem to remember.'

Eddie entered their company with a mental farewell to sobriety. 'Tell you what, I'm celebrating my wings,' he lied boastfully. 'What's your excuse?'

≫≪

Eva was buffeted by inanimate objects and only too animate people in the darkness of Oxford Station. Nobody apologised anymore. It was ugly too. No painter could have made sense of the bustling, heaving blackness of the station.

'Sorry,' she apologised venomously as she passed through the barrier and a tall figure strode into her path. She edged sideways, resisting the urge to kick.

'Eva!' A hand grabbed her arm. 'It's Jack.'

This introduction failed to register with Eva.

'From the Ruskin. I teach you. Jack Halliwell. You said you were going to London for the day so I decided to meet you. I've been waiting for ages. Perhaps we could have a lemonade together?'

Eva began to walk with Jack a talkative shadow at her side. 'There's the Duke of Wellington just nearby.'

'I have my bike, Mr. Halliwell,' said Eva. Another man wanting her to go to a pub. Was this the effect of war?

'I'll push it. Don't worry about a thing.'

They were out of the station. It was a relief. Jack grabbed the handlebars of the bike the moment she unlocked it.

Eva took a gulp of air and looked up at the sky. There were stars all over the place. Eddie's descriptions of flying had made her aware of the sky as another dimension with its own complicated rules of life. 'I can only stay a moment. They're expecting me for supper.' My father won't notice, she thought.

Eva and Jack sat squeezed in on a bench against the wall of the pub's lounge.

'I'd forgotten it was New Year's Eve,' said Jack, eyeing the crowds disapprovingly. 'You see the thing is, I've been turned down. I just wanted to tell you.'

Eva heard the nervousness in his voice so instead of saying, but you hardly know me, she asked, 'Turned down?'

'For the army. Asthma. Apparently I'm riddled with it. The doctor said painting was the worst possible profession. Ha! Ha!' Jack laughed with more than an edge of hysteria. His black hair joggled around.

'I'm so glad,' said Eva, politely. Couldn't he see she was tired? Yet it was exciting to be wanted, even to be in a pub.

'Yes. Yes. Asthma's no joke of course.' Jack waved his arm before being stopped by the confined space. 'So now I'm thinking of a new direction. The countryside,' he added, shouting above the noise of the crowds. He gazed at Eva appealingly, as if everything was now explained.

'What?' Eva would have liked a glass of lemonade but there was no way Jack could fight his way to the bar.

'I wanted to ask you to come with me on a day trip. With me. Drawing. Even painting...' He paused, gulping.

'Whereabouts?'

'Dorset. Somerset. Devon. Such magic! The light, the space, the swoop of green hills. The dark line of trees. The circular coppices. The views of sea and sky.' The words rushed out. 'Maybe I'll even move there permanently!'

'Heavens!' It did sound wonderful. 'How brave and bold!'

'I knew you'd understand!' Jack clasped his long pale fingers together. 'And I want you to come with me!'

Eva felt herself turn bright red.

'To paint,' added Jack quickly. ' Just for the day. To be free. Art is what counts. You have a talent. And I am a good teacher.'

'I hardly know you.' She thought, does he want to marry me? And tried not to laugh. Then she thought of Eddie. 'I really must be going.'

Jack leapt to his feet. 'Yes. Yes. Of course you must. I will walk with you and be your torch.'

'My bicycle has a light.'

'I am brighter,' stated Jack.

Eva realised she had underestimated the art teacher's strength of will. Or maybe he was just mad. Hadn't she read somewhere that madmen had the force of ten? This time she did laugh.

⌒

Like Alice at the bottom of her rabbit hole, Eddie came back to life.

'Come on, Eddie. They're clearing us all out.'

Eddie looked about the darkness, weakly illuminated by small red lights, and identified the Bag o' Nails. And there was Henry gripping his shoulder in a not very pleasant way.

'Get off.'

'It's going to be dawn soon and I don't know about you, but I've got things to do.'

An image of the Savoy flashed before Eddie. 'Bloody good party.' He frowned and rubbed his eyes. 'Who gave it, do you know?'

'Come on!' repeated Henry, and at his side appeared a large man, blocking out all the little red lights.

Eddie felt himself lifted, carried and dumped. Not ungently. Then he was lying on the pavement in an empty street. 'I feel reborn!' He waved his arms.

'Can you find your way home?' Henry took a long step away.

But Eddie was watching the pale sky unrolling to meet him like a silken carpet. Someone came with it. A slim figure with dark tresses of hair. 'Oh, Eva! Eva!' He muttered, although to his ears it was a clarion call. 'What is love without you!'

'Hey, moron, why are you talking about your sister?' Henry stepped back and shook his shoulder. 'Can't you get up and go home.'

'Only poets like Byron fall in love with their sisters.' Eddie smiled happily and, heaving himself to his feet, he began to walk towards the shimmering figure. 'The apocalypse is nigh and about time too.'

Henry's patience came to an end. This was his last day of leave. He set off decisively in the other direction.

⋙⋘

Some time later, Eddie rang the doorbell to his father's flat.

'I'm working.' Fred, half-dressed and scowling, stared at his son with disapproval.

'If you don't want people to disturb you, you should provide people, me, with a key.' Eddie walked with drunken dignity past his father and into the flat.

The room was filled with piles of books, magazines and paper, some of it scrunched in ragged balls on the floor. On the table at its centre sat a large typewriter, marooned on waves of paper. Lined up were six empty bottles of beer and one half-empty.

'I'm trying to reconcile Communism with Fascism,' said Fred, following him, and sitting at the table. 'But I don't expect you to be interested in that.'

'Hitler has only got one ball.' Eddie proceeded to the kitchen. 'I may starve to death.'

'There's a large pork pie made by your Aunt Lily and brought up by your charitable mother.'

'Thank you kindly, good sir.'

Ignoring his ridiculous son, Fred typed a few words with his left hand. At the moment everything felt difficult which was why he'd sat up all night and downed too many bottles of beer. Ever since Russia's non-aggression pact with Germany, he'd realised that the challenge facing any thinking man who had espoused the cause of communism was to understand how Stalin could line up with Hitler. How simple it sounded put like that! The alternative, of course, which some so-called 'intellectuals' favoured, was giving up on Russia while holding on to the principle of communism. Perhaps this was the easiest answer but Fred found it unsatisfying, as if Marxism had no application except in North London.

Sometimes Fred suspected he was clinging to the last squeaks of belief, terrified that without its stiffening power he'd return to the unthinking classes from which he'd sprung. Ideas, after all, were two a penny, it was the practical application that counted. It was an unadmitted relief that Eddie had come to disturb him.

'Fuck and blast and shit!' Fred thumped the table, using his stump so it would cause him more pain. He'd been a sharp boy once, out for himself, but the last war had done for that, the war, his injury, education and books. 'Books, books, books! Chatter, chatter, chatter! Scribble, scribble, scribble!'

Fred began to throw paper in the air, kicking balls of the stuff on the ground, swearing in syncopated rhythm. It was an impressive letting-go.

Eddie stood at the kitchen door, biting on a very generous slice of pork pie. 'This war has got to you,' he intoned with priestly sympathy. How preferable was Fred's present loss of control to his more usual bitter sniping! In Eddie's view, the world was not bad at all, all things considered. He sat down on a sofa and then lay back against the wall. His eyes closed.

Fred panted to a halt. He stared at his son. 'It's all your mother's fault.' This was not a new thought. Fred sat down, still breathing heavily.

Eddie opened his eyes and swallowed a delicious lump of pork coated with succulent jelly and edged with crisp yet also succulent pastry. Sylvia, according to Fred, had seduced him from the straight and narrow of the working man into the corruption of money, property and friendship. Worse still, she had then lured him into becoming the most bourgeois of all traps, a father.

'Why did you stop working for the W.E.A.?' Eddie raised the point in conversational tones which rather impressed himself. 'Educating the masses would seem just up your... You know.' His eyes closed again.

'You may not have noticed,' said Fred wearily, 'but I am a writer, a journalist, a commentator. There are different ways of educating.' As he spoke, he sank lower in his chair.

'Are you still a pacifist?' Eddie spoke cheerily, although without bothering to open his eyes. It crossed his mind to ask whether Fred preferred marmalade or jam with his toast.

'You, of course, are a Man of Action,' Fred allowed his head to drop on his arms. 'As I once was.'

'Yes, indeed,' agreed Eddie, waking up a bit more. He looked with pity at his father's stump which, owing to all his exertions, protruded from his shirt like the edge of a ham. How right he was to follow the path of a flyer, a clean battle in a clean sky, knights of the air! Of course he had not actually fought yet and the tales coming back from France were somewhat muddled, but any moment now his chance would come. At that thought, or at that moment, with his stomach full and his body comfortably supported, Eddie fell into an irresistible sleep.

CHAPTER TEN
June 1940

Sylvia's rose bush was putting out yet more pinkish-green shoots with tiny drooping buds. It was hard to think they would survive. The plant must be so exhausted, so depleted. It just never stopped flowering. Her pity for the rose extended to herself, trapped on the estate where cows and sheep were the front-line soldiers and she conscripted as their commander.

In her hand she held a book by E.M. Delafield, *A Provincial in Wartime*, a light-hearted frolic about a country lady coming to save London and finding far too many on the same mission, not enough soup kitchens and Red Cross posts to go around. It concluded at Christmas 1939 and Sylvia's publisher had sent it with the suggestion she should do the same for 1940. 'There is always paper for essential writing,' he had advised.

Essential writing? A light frolic? Perhaps in these times it was her duty to amuse the nation as well as commanding the animals. The trouble was she could not separate this war from the last. Churchill, the hero, who had taken over from the despised Chamberlain, was to her the deluded megalomaniac who had pushed through the Gallipoli campaign. She saw this attitude was unpatriotic but it was written in her history – and her mother's and Fred's.

Sylvia had come to this quiet corner of the garden to think about herself and her writing. She didn't want to think about Fred. Not long ago Eddie had telephoned to say his father was having a nervous collapse which seemed to amount to extreme bad temper. She had not paid him a visit. Then Fred had sent her a wild article, attacking the iniquities of fellow travellers within the Labour Party. She hoped, for the sake of his career, it had not been published. Sometimes she suspected they were both trying to work out through their writing what had happened to them in the last war. Her novels were quiet, his journalism explosive. Yet how could Fred believe that now was the right time to rage at the hands that had fed his political beliefs? Such things were irrelevant, even ridiculous as Norway fell, followed up by the invasion of Holland, Belgium and Luxembourg. Even France was only clinging on desperately.

'Sylvia! Miss Sylvia!' A bell rang from the house. It was frustrating that Lily, Fred's sister after all, still had not altogether dropped that 'Miss' – even if it was a sign of respect.

The bell rang again. 'Gussie on the telephone.' Gussie never got a 'Miss' from Lily.

Sylvia stood in the large dim hallway holding the telephone not very close to her ear. Gussie could hardly speak for tears.

'Reggie rang. He was whispering. You know how loud his voice is usually.'

'What is it, Gussie, darling?' encouraged Sylvia.

'He shouldn't have been telling me things.'

'What things?'

'Didn't you hear me?' For a moment Gussie rallied, then the sobs rose again. 'George's been wounded. Wounded! My darling Georgie.'

'Wounded? Oh poor Gussie. But that could be good news, dearest. He'll be coming home.' Sylvia thought, he has only to cross the Channel, unlike our poor father.

'You're not listening, Sylvie. Frightful things are going on in France. Reggie made me swear not to tell a soul. But you don't count.'

'Can't he be flown out?'

'That's what I said.' Gussie's crying became wailing. 'You don't know how lucky you are to have Eddie safely home!'

'Not for long,' said Sylvia, annoyed to find herself sounding defensive. 'You can't fly a plane just like that. They're complicated machines. Pilots die learning.'

'Reggie says no amount of well-trained pilots can stop what's happening in Europe. They fly off for an hour or less then come winging home. Not stuck like our soldiers. Like poor George.'

Sylvia took a deep breath. What seemed like a spiteful attack on Eddie could be Gussie's way of diverting her anxiety over George.

'Why don't you come and stay here for a bit?' She listened as Gussie listed wifely duties, war responsibilities and social events (not easily distinguished one from the other) which made it impossible for her to leave London, despite the heightened threat.

'At least the childrens' schools are in safe areas,' Gussie concluded with the air of a virtuous mother, before suddenly adding, 'And Artemis and I have been invited to stay in a glorious castle in Yorkshire.'

⚓

Eddie looked down and saw banks of undulating clouds which moved and breathed like great white animals. It seemed extraordinary he could dive among them, following canyons and rising above sudden cliffs. He looked again and they changed to the splendid walls and turrets of a magical city. In the midst of them, a castle rose up, decorated with curved battlements, bulking thickly around him. He could see nothing else. Suddenly he was flying blind and the city was circling round him, enclosing him with its whiteness.

Now was the moment to stop looking outwards and fix his eyes firmly on his instruments. Eddie blinked hard and, with a great effort, he pushed the stick forward.

He dropped into the grey world in a rush, registering not just the silk sea wrinkling far below but that he had lost several thousand feet on his too sudden dive. This was foolish, dangerous nervousness. As he set his sights for the airfield, he tried to shake out of his brain images of a white city where he was king.

Andy met him at the airfield. 'How high did you get?'

'Over 20,000.'

'Use your oxygen, I suppose?'

It struck Eddie that he hadn't put on his oxygen mask. Maybe that's where the fairy castle came from. 'Of course,' he lied.

'You didn't,' stated Andy in a satisfied voice. 'I forgot too.'

Eddie was annoyed and refused to smile. 'Since neither of us passed out, clearly oxygen wasn't necessary.'

By now they were in the dispersal room, pulling off their flying suits and fur-lined boots.

'If you want to know, I did.'

'What?'

'Pass out.' Andy looked around, although not with much care. 'Don't tell anyone. It was bloody terrifying. Several seconds in which the plane did what it wanted. Which was to make a dive for the sea. Lucky for me I was so high to begin with or I'd have been a goner. Never fancied a watery grave.'

'Jolly good you got back control. Eddie straightened up. 'It's the pub we need.'

They were down south now, at the same airfield as Henry and all three men near the end of operational training.

As they walked to find transport into town, Eddie knew he'd never have confided such a near-disaster to anyone. If Andy's flight sergeant got to hear, he risked being bowler-hatted. Andy was a good mechanic but as a flyer he had a long way to go. It was a miracle he was there in the first place. Three men had been let go fairly recently and one had crashed doing acrobatics – strictly forbidden.

'Actually,' said Eddie, 'I didn't pass out but I saw a cloud city where I was king.'

Andy laughed. 'And you're telling me you switched on your oxygen.'

'Where's Henry? Kick him out from wherever he's hiding.'

The pub, usually crowded, was jammed. Even such a self-absorbed group as pilots couldn't avoid hearing about the retreat of the Allied army from Dunkirk. As usual Henry knew all the details.

'Over 300,000 soldiers have been brought across the Channel in a mix of destroyers, at least one cruiser and all kinds of smaller boats, civilian boats from anywhere and everywhere. Most of the little boats setting off from Ramsgate.'

'What about our lot?' asked Andy. 'There must have been RAF keeping off the Luftwaffe?'

'Sure. And not many came back.'

'A bloody rout!' shouted Andy who always drunk faster and held his drink less well than the others.

But he was immediately contradicted by equally raucous voices insisting it was a victory. 'Churchill says it's a miracle!' shouted one louder even than the rest.

Somehow the idea of a disastrous defeat disappeared into sweat and smoke and beer.

'I'll tell you what,' suggested Andy after several more pints. 'Let's go and see what's on for ourselves. Probably a lot of hot air.'

'There's nothing doing after we finish tomorrow and it can't be more than an hour's drive to Ramsgate.' Eddie put his arm round Andy and, through the haze, they both peered hopefully at Henry and Andy waggled a thumbs-up. Henry was the one with the car.

Henry who scarcely drank, hesitated.

'Come on old chap, a spot of war-time tourism,' encouraged Eddie.

'I guess it would be interesting to see for ourselves...'

The rest of his answer was lost under congratulatory claps on his back.

⚔

Eddie, Henry and Andy made an unlikely threesome as they got into the car the next morning, two out of the three with hangovers. Andy was driving, given the honour as a treat by Henry who sat beside him while Eddie, murmuring 'hair of the dog' sat in the back seat, swigging from a silver hip flask.

'The point about driving a car as opposed to flying a plane, may I remind you,' pronounced Henry, as a lorry filled with cheering soldiers heading away from the sea, narrowly missed them, 'is that there are often other vehicles on the smallest road. Some of them may have survived indescribable horrors across the Channel so it would be a pity if they met their end on a Brit road.'

'Yessir.' Andy took a hand of the wheel to salute.

'And keep both paws on the wheel!'

The car swerved dangerously as Andy took both hands off the wheel.

'Eddie, I'm joining you in the back,' shouted Henry.

Eddie handed the flask forward to Henry. 'Have a swig. You'll soon feel calmer.'

Henry drank while Eddie stretched himself out. There was a companionable silence, only broken by curses from Andy as first a rabbit, then a chicken, then two rabbits tried to dash under his wheels.

'Tell me, my dear soon-to-be pilot,' perhaps to avoid watching the immolation on the road, Henry turned to face Eddie, 'What have you learnt recently about handling a Spitfire?'

'See here, Hank, old man,' Eddie held up the fingers of one hand. 'One – take the advantage of height; two – coming out of the sun; three – to work as a squadron and obey the squadron leader however much you hate him; four – never follow a plane down after hitting it; five – if forced to break formation, stay in pairs.' Eddie held up his other hand. 'Six – never fly straight for more than two seconds; seven – fire at 200 yards, go wild with all eight guns in bursts of two to four seconds; eight – make the ground crew your best friends; nine – know the weakness of your enemy, a tendency to bunch together and avoid situations when odds are against them.' Eddie paused.

'So what's ten?' asked Henry.

'Thank God you're in a Spitfire!' Eddie shouted and laughed. But they were all serious. They'd flown enough now to picture every manoeuvre, every roll, drop, unexpected cloud or storm, uncontrolled dive or misread petrol gauge.

'I could name dozens more,' Andy swivelled round.

'Just keep your eyes on the wildlife,' advised Henry.

'Put your undercarriage down when landing,' continued Andy.

'I was giving rules for grown-ups, Andy dear,' Eddie took back the flask and shook the last drops into his mouth.

'What about Bill? He was years older than us and managed to forget. Wrote off himself and his poor innocent Spitfire.' Andy sounded righteous.

'You could add more with the Messerschmitt in mind,' suggested Henry thoughtfully, 'Their pilots' way of avoiding an attack from the rear by a half roll and a vertical dive to the ground.'

'Can't blame them when they're sitting on top of their petrol tanks.'

'The Spitfire can turn inside them, that's the main point.' Eddie acted it out like an enthusiastic boy.

On they sped, through the beauties of the English countryside in early summer, talking about how best to bring down the enemies' planes. They didn't talk about death. It was all about hitting and avoiding and the only one killed was the Spitfire or the Messerschmitt.

They swept through pretty pink brick villages with their flint-built churches, through surprisingly dark woods, through elegant coppices, through green or golden fields, passed by rows of chestnut or lime leading up to great houses. By the time they entered the swoop of hills with their glorious expanse of sky, the shadows were long enough to accentuate every elegant rise and fold. There ahead was Ramsgate and the dark blue sea beyond.

They had almost forgotten the purpose of their journey: Dunkirk and the determination to see for themselves. Their imagination took them flying over the hills, heading, of course, for France, but revenge was not yet in their vocabulary.

※

The three pilots, conspicuous in their blue uniforms when everywhere else was khaki, walked along the sea parade. Suddenly a filthy, wild-looking soldier with no discernible insignia grabbed Andy, presumably because he was smallest, and shook him violently shouting over and over again, 'Where were you? Where were you?'

Adding now and again, 'Like to swim the Channel, would you?' Eddie and Henry acting in consort, took hold of him on either side and forcefully sat him down on a convenient bench.

'What is it, old chap?' asked Eddie but the soldier, once seated, seemed to become dumb. Indeed, his head nodded, as if he was about to fall asleep.

'They blame us for not giving cover,' said Henry gloomily. 'But it's no use explaining to a man nearly dead with exhaustion that we kept the Luftwaffe off their tails or they'd never have got to Calais or Dunkirk.'

'And the cloud was low most of the time,' added Eddie.

'Shouldn't he be with his regiment?' asked Henry.

'On a train? suggested Eddie.

It was not comfortable to feel the RAF accused, even if they themselves hadn't yet flown on a single mission. They left the man slumped on the bench and wandered along to the harbour.

The sea, turning to dark emerald as the sun dipped over the horizon, was a rich carpet under layers of small and bigger boats, all shapes and colours, fishing boats, launches and pleasure boats, bobbing together like toys in a child's bath.

'I need a drink,' said Andy.

Eddie thought of the sleek beauty of the Spitfire, very different to this naval higgledy-piggledy. 'Funny sort of victory,' he said.

The first two pubs they found were so full that men over-spilt on the pavement, some sitting as if too tired stand, some bandaged or bruised, some not drinking but grouped close together as if for comfort.

'I suppose it's far worse at Dover,' said Eddie. He was angry at the muddle. It made him feel as if life on an airfield was a privileged bubble. He began to regret their visit. Again, he thought the soldiers should be on a train by now. There were no more to arrive. It was all over now. He didn't want to admit that he felt a little ashamed of their voyeuristic jaunt.

The third pub, The Cock and Bull, was different, no-one outside and the men inside quieter. 'They're French,' said Eddie.

'*Comment allez-vous?*'

He was immediately surrounded by a gaggle of men, some French and some Belgian eager to speak their own language. '*Ou sommes-nous?*' enquired one to which 'Ramsgate' seemed an inadequate answer. But at least the French and Belgians didn't seem to blame them for the men who didn't get away. '*Enfin, j'ai vu des avions Anglais de temps en temps mais je n'ai pas vu un avion Francais.*'

After several pints of the strong local ale, where even Henry joined in, all three pilots felt more able to answer any questions and speak freely in most languages. They also had begun to refer to themselves as Eddie, Hank and Andy, the three Musketeers of the sky.

'You Tarzan, me Hank,' Henry beat his chest in a most un-Henry way.

It was then that Eddie noticed a group of young British officers eating in a recessed alcove. 'I'm starving,' he nodded in their direction.

'It looks like pies,' encouraged Andy greedily. 'Go on. Ask them where they found them. You're the posh one.'

Eddie wandered over. 'Sorry to interrupt...' As he spoke, he recognized his mission was doomed to failure, if not worse.

The officers looked up with bleary faces, no energy left for expression. The leg of one was wrapped in stained bandages.

'We just wondered where you obtained your pies.' Eddie's voice wavered. He put down his empty glass and began to back away.

'Pies you want to obtain, is it?' A loud voice, probably Scottish, mimicked Eddie.

'Leave it, McDougall,' suggested a weary drawl.

Eddie turned back again to see a very angry, unshaven man raising his fists. Was it his imagination or had the rest of the pub gone quiet?

He felt Andy pulling his arm. 'You've had too many pints to take on that one.'

'You desire our pies, do you?' growled McDougall.

Eddy held his ground, after all these were British officers, his kind of people. Defeated, it's true … His mind, befuddled by good local ale, got no further before a fist landed in his midriff, followed up by another slammed into his face. He staggered, fell backwards, knocked over Andy close by him and they both fell onto the floor. There were a few cheers.

'Fucking wee flyers.' The Scotsman stood over them, looking down.

Andy scrambled to his feet and put up his fists before the new Hank, a foot taller, grabbed him. 'Don't be such an idiot. This lot's got an excuse for a fight.'

Eddie, still flat on the floor, felt curiously unwilling to leap up and smash the Scotsman's head against a wall. Not because of the pain in his stomach and face but because the uneasy feeling he'd had ever since they'd arrived in Ramsgate had sapped any anger. If anything, he felt like crying. Was England beaten? This McDougall the last man standing? He'd drunk far too much, that was the trouble.

'Fucking coward!'

Could that be true? Strangely, none of the other officers had even risen from their chairs. Perhaps this was McDougall's business, not an argument between the services.

Eddie's head cleared further and he saw Hank's bulk placed protectively between him and his fiery antagonist. 'Let's get moving, Eddie. Here.' Eddie allowed himself to be heaved up.

'Just don't look back,' Andy advised as the three airmen pushed their way to the door. The crowd closed round them, as noisy as before.

'Call me Orpheus,' muttered Eddie. But speaking was a bad idea. 'I'm going to throw up.'

'Hold it till we're outside.'

Outside was cool and fresh and smelled of the sea. Once Eddie had finished vomiting, without saying a word, they headed down to the beach. Pebbles rolled and crunched under their feet.

They turned away from the harbour and the town and when

the pubs let out their customers, it was only a distant din. They scarcely looked at the multitude of boats stretching out to sea which had so amazed them earlier. They walked and walked until they were in a no man's land, beach below, cliff beside and sky ahead.

'This is better,' said Andy. 'Too much going on back there. Poor buggers. Feeling alright, are you old mate?'

'Never better,' said Eddie. There might be blood on his nose, he thought, but it wasn't broken. The night seemed infinitely expandable. He wanted to walk forever. Sometimes as they moved ever further into the darkness he had the strange sense they were floating through a black sky.

'Pity we've got to go back and pick up the car.' said Hank. He thought, I am Hank now and I like it.

They still walked on and on, until by the time they turned the summer night was thinning and the sea gave off an unearthly sheen.

'It'll be dawn next,' said Andy.

But it was still dark when they collected the car and set off back to London, this time with Hank at the wheel.

For a long time there was silence, then Andy announced suddenly. 'Soldiers are different. Stamina. Weeks and months fighting. Look at the last war, months even years in stinking trenches. Give me an aeroplane any day, no sortie lasts over an hour.'

Half asleep in the back of the car, Eddie produced his first words for what felt like hours. He spoke carefully, 'I hope you're not suggesting soldiers are braver than pilots.'

'Don't be like that. We're braver. Of course we're bloody well *braver*. But we don't have the *stamina*.'

'Different worlds,' drawled Hank, 'don't mix well.'

It was only as they entered the patchwork of fields and woods that outlines became visible. A wan light gradually coloured in lozenges of green and gold but the woods remained dark, waiting for the sun to cast brighter rays. There was no-one around, not even an animal.

'Lazy sods in the East,' commented Eddie, pulling himself upright. 'In Dorset they're up with the lark.'

'Seen any larks?' asked Andy. 'In Birmingham they get up with the factory hooter at two in the morning.'

'In Pittsburg,' said Hank 'the guys never go to bed at all. Saves the trouble of getting up.'

'Hard to picture you in America,' said Eddie. 'Were you always a little rich boy?'

'My father made rivets,' said Hank good-humouredly, 'a small business which went wild in the First World War, but crashed spectacularly in the 'Twenties. So I guess I was a little rich boy between the ages of one and six, then dirt poor till eighteen when my dad found a different kind of rivet. It was scholarships for me all the way.'

'When did you learn to fly?' asked Eddie

'A Southerner friend of my dad's, a rich man from the first rivet phase, took me up. He owned his own plane. It's his daughter I'm engaged to.'

Eddie yawned. Life the other side of the Atlantic was a stretch of the imagination too far just at the moment. He sank down again. 'Wake me up when we reach London.'

The sun came up behind the car and glittered in the rear-view mirror. 'When are we getting mirrors for our Spitfires?' Hank half turned to Andy.

'Maybe a Spitfire mirror can make my fortune like your dad's rivet?'

'Depends whether Beaverbrook gets wise first.'

Eddie woke up properly as they drove over Albert Bridge, a sleepy soldier at either end. He stared at the elegant struts suspending it over the water and thought of wings that suspended a plane in the sky.

'How about breakfast?' suggested Andy. 'Bacon, fried bread, sausages, black pudding, sunny-side up eggs... I might be gone tomorrow, don't let's forget.'

Eddie woke up further. 'How about we go to my parents flat?

My mother's visiting so there's sure to be food. My Aunt Lily does a pie to die for...' His voice tailed away.

'A pie! Did you say a *pie*!' Andy who despite his drinking habits, was always insufferable bright in the morning, gave a huge guffaw.

Hank laughed too.

'You buggers!' Eddie smiled. 'Why can't you do something useful and tell me if there's blood on my bloody tie.'

CHAPTER ELEVEN
July 1940

Everyone grumbled as Eva and Jack struggled to get their bicycles out of the train. An old man in dungarees and a cap muttered self-righteously, 'Don't they know there's a war on!' Eva began to suspect that this whole trip was a frightful mistake. It had taken months to set up and she would have ducked out except that Jack had been so insistent and when she asked permission from her father he hadn't cared enough to give the expected refusal. Did no-one realise how young she was? No-one did realise because she'd had her eighteenth birthday two days ago without a comment. Her mother used to bake her a special cake with apples and put one candle in the middle. Perhaps she had cut Betty out of her life too readily. Betty would have remembered.

But here they were on a small country station. The day was fine – gauzy white clouds over a blue and gold sky and Jack was in high spirits. She watched him critically as he mounted his bike, signalling her to do the same; his long legs and even longer torso came together at an uneasy angle. Eddie was handsome and well put together. Eva suspected some of this was to do with 'class' but she hadn't been brought up with such a luxury commodity so she probably couldn't judge. On the other hand, she appreciated Jack's knowledge of art and his need for her company, and, after all, Eddie was mostly far away pursuing the war, even if he did scribble her a note now and again.

Eva tied the strings to her white panama hat tight under her chin and bicycled so fast that she overtook Jack who shouted 'Hey!' She waved and her mood rose. Jack shouted 'Hey!' again and she cycled even faster.

The hedges whizzed by and the birds burst from them and sang odes to the sun. This is my birthday present, thought Eva: minutes of nature's glory and, when we arrive, I shall get out my notebook and draw.

After a while, the shouts behind increased and, reluctantly, Eva slowed down and looked round. Jack stood at a narrow turning which Eva hadn't noticed in her happy flight. 'I think we head left here.' He waved a map.

The road was only roughly made up and led upwards into small hills and coppices, sometimes perched on top and sometimes filling in the bottom of slender valleys. The uncut hedges became higher so it was harder to see where they were and other roads, some no more than tracks, came and went. The sun, unveiled now from the stratus clouds, shone directly on to them.

'Not very long now,' said Jack with unconvincing confidence.

'Are we going anywhere special?' asked Eva cheerfully. 'I thought we were merely seeking freedom.'

The land was gradually becoming more open; on either side appeared wide fields, most grazed by cows or sheep, some planted with crops. Up till now they hadn't seen one village but, as they reached the top of a long hill where they paused for breath, they saw below them, half-hidden by trees and two descending hills, the roofs of a small village. There seemed to be a large stone-built house, a church, a few other buildings and a scattering of cottages. It was hardly more than a hamlet.

'We can ask them where we are?' suggested Eva.

Jack stared at his map, then leapt on his bike and began to free-wheel down. Eva followed, bumping and skidding over loose stones. Their progress was abruptly halted at the bottom by a wall of sandbags and an old man pointing a shotgun.

'Where do you think you're off to?' He growled.

'That's just what we'd like to know,' Eva smiled and pushed her hat off her face.

Jack, to whom the gun was pointing, reacted less positively. 'We don't need to be treated like criminals.'

'Are you saying you're not spies, nor Huns nor other unwantables?'

'Do we look like whatever you call them?' asked Eva happily.

'That's it, isn't it. Would you look like them if you was them?'

Eva laughed but decided not to say she was half-German.

'Did you read that, see?' the old man lowered his gun and indicated a printed sheet of paper nailed to one of the sandbags.

'*In case of invasion,*' Eva began to read out loud, '*you must remain where you are.*' But we haven't been invaded!' She managed not to laugh again.

'Be you sure of that? Fifteen miles from the sea, as the crow flies, that's what we are. How do I know you're not part of the scouting party?'

'But we're coming from the inland direction and you're the only one with a gun.' Jack was exasperated.

Eva's good humour continued. 'Can we pass now?' she asked cheerfully.

'It's him, Miss.' The gun returned to point at Jack. 'I know his type.'

Eva was surprised that Jack should inspire this level of respect. But now a small stocky figure with a basket over her arm, approaching briskly towards them.

'Now Mr. Ham, who have you got there?'

'There you are, Lily Chaffey.' Mr. Ham propped the gun against the sandbags. 'Bringing a bite to eat, is I may ask?'

'And who are you?' asked Lily, smiling at Jack and Eva.

'That's it,' muttered Mr. Ham. 'Who are they?' But his eye was on the basket.

'We're on our way to the sea,' said Jack with returning dignity. 'There's an ancient by-way ...'

'We're painters,' announced Eva.

'And Mr. Ham held you here. He's a very conscientious member of the Home Guard.' Her look softened and she extracted a large cheese sandwich which she placed into Mr. Ham's somewhat shaky hand. 'Now how can I help you, assuming you're not spies?'

Mr. Ham's eyes raised for a moment, then returned to his sandwich.

Eva watched as Lily Chaffey and Jack inspected the map. After a bit she sat on the sandbag wall and half shut her eyes. Lily's voice had a country sound to it, not as pronounced as Mr. Ham's but gentler than the hard Oxford vowels.

'I'm afraid your map is nothing like detailed enough.' said Lily, after a while. 'It doesn't even have Tollorum on it.'

Half-asleep – she'd been up since six – Eva heard the name with a faint sense of recognition.

'You'd better come up to the Manor and we'll sort you out with a better one.' added Lily. 'There're shelves of maps there.'

Along they walked, pushing their bicycles into the village, past a pub called *The Tollorum Arms*, past a Victorian schoolhouse with fish-tailed tiles and down a driveway lined with chestnut trees that met in a roof above their heads.

'That's the church,' said Lily proudly, 'Fourteenth century.'

'It's so pretty.' Eva looked about her in a wondering way.

'We're in a hurry,' said Jack, 'or the light will go.'

The house was big but only two floors high and an old oak and beech beside it were taller.

They were a hundred yards away when a woman straightened out of a flower bed and stared at them in a surprised way. Lily went to her quickly.

'I wanted you all to myself,' muttered Jack regretfully.

The lady who was elderly and did not tell them her name, led them to the house and into a hallway which seemed black after the brightness outside. A woman's voice said, 'Hello, mother,' and Eva made out pale hair and a pale face.

Sylvia looked at Eva and, her eyes, accustomed to the darkness, recognised her at once. After all, Fred, Eddie and she had discussed her after that lunch in Oxford.

'You're Eva, aren't you? Do you remember me? Sylvia Chaffey.'

Jack sighed. Eva understood he felt the day, his day, was slipping from him. She felt sorry but now she knew where she was.

'Yes, I'm Eva Speke. And this is Mr Halliwell. He's my art teacher.'

'They're looking for a better map,' said Beatrice.

Talking about the Colonel's love of maps, Sylvia led them through two airy rooms to a study and from there into an alcove where several shelves were piled with maps, although even more held brass figures of a shocking ugliness.

'I don't much like them either,' Sylvia smiled. 'My father was killed in the last war and he loved them so we can't get rid of them. Of course proper maps might have saved his life. The army hadn't bothered to find out about Gallipoli where he died.'

Sylvia wondered why she was talking like this to the girl. Perhaps it was the war again. Now that the Nazis had taken the whole of Europe and obviously would make plans to cross the Channel, she found herself thinking a lot of her father. She gave Jack a map, then took down a many-limbed statuette of Shiva before handing it to Eva. 'No accounting for tastes.'

'No,' agreed Eva.

'This is a great map!' exclaimed Jack. 'The way through the hills is called the Dorset Gap.'

'It's quite a distance and not easy on a bicycle. Most people walk it. Are you planning to stay somewhere overnight?' Sylvia looked at Eva doubtfully.

'My bag's got my painting things in it,' said Eva, seeing where Sylvia was looking. 'We've come to paint.'

'We're going back this evening,' said Jack gruffly.

Eva felt herself blushing and saw Sylvia noticing.

'Such a hot day. You must have a drink before you go.' Sylvia's voice was wistful. She wondered that Eva's mother would let her go about with this older man, even if he was an art teacher. Perhaps that was about war too. A few days ago Eddie had rung and told her with exultation in his voice that he'd been sent to a front-line station, 'In the thick of it.' Mr. Halliwell wore no uniform.

'We're very grateful,' Jack was still gruff. 'But we should push on. You can never be sure of the light.'

Eva longed to ask about Eddie but, for reasons she didn't want to understand, also wanted to keep their friendship secretive.

'I think you met my son Eddie at Professor Lamb's luncheon,' said Sylvia when they were out in the bright light again, collecting their bicycles. 'He's a fighter pilot now. All that stands between us and the enemy, as the saying goes.'

Jack stood astride his bike.

'That's so brave,' said Eva. The girl and the woman stared at each other. They were close enough for Eva to see that Sylvia's pale hair was more grey than blonde.

'I'd love to see you again,' said Sylvia impulsively. She felt there was something special about this girl. She remembered that Fred had felt it too. 'Would your mother let you stay here sometime?'

'My mother...' Eva seemed unable to speak for a moment then began again determinedly, 'My mother is away. She went to Germany last year and we haven't seen her since.'

'Oh, my dear!' Sylvia wanted to clasp her tight. 'I'm so sorry.'

Jack began to make whirring noises with his wheels.

'I've got to go.' Eva shook her head to clear the tears from her eyes.' Sylvia did clasp her and kiss her on her cheek. Her body was stiff like a child's.

'I'll tell you what,' said Sylvia, going impulsively to Jack. 'I don't expect you'd stop if I suggested you painted in our garden but I know a beautiful place which would be just the right spot. Only a twenty-minute ride from here, over beyond the village. On the estate but very secret. A lovely wild place with an old barn in the middle of the field. 'I'll show you it on the map. Wait. No-one would bother you.' She held out her hand for the map.

Ungraciously, Jack pulled it from his pocket and handed it over.

'There you are,' Sylvia unfolded the map and pointed. 'You'll have sun or shade there the whole day.'

'Oh Jack, do let's!' Eva suddenly realized that her legs were trembling and that all she wanted was to sit down and think. And paint. Of course.

'We'll see.' Jack mounted his bike with an obstinate expression and Eva followed.

As they rode off, Sylvia called out, 'I'll find your address, dear, and write to your father!'

Eva turned her head and smiled. Jack stared determinedly forward. Now she had to work hard to keep up with him. He had told her that bicycling was good for his asthma. She thought about Eddie up in the sky which was better than thinking about her mother.

After twenty minutes or so she really didn't want to bicycle much further.

'I'm tired,' she shouted. She stopped and took off her hat, pushing at her hair so that the air cooled her head.

She was wiping her sweating face with her hat when Jack noticed and raced back to her.

'Sorry,' he said, all at once caring and sympathetic. 'I've been pushing you too hard. I'm like that. I get carried away. Won't accept defeat.'

'I just want to paint,' said Eva, not liking to think she had accepted defeat.

'We'll search out this lovely secret place,' said Jack, just as if it was his idea.

The barn was surprisingly easy to find, very large and in the middle of a field that sloped away from it. The field was filled with long grasses and a multitude of wild flowers. As they pushed their bikes towards the barn, Jack bent down and picked bunch of pink flowers for Eva. 'They're wild orchids,' he told her. A white owl stared at them from a row of bars across the barn's entrance. He seemed to look them over before flying off in a slow, unfrightened way.

'We still have plenty of time,' said Jack.

They sat down where they were, unpacking their pencils and paints and jars of water.

'We'll eat our sandwiches in an hour,' decided Jack, handing Eva tea from a thermos.

As they worked, only talking when Jack advised Eva about a line or a colour, the sun changed from yellow to gold and the shadow of the barn reached out towards them. The owl returned and there was a receptive squeaking within the barn.

'Another time we'll explore the whole area,' promised Jack.

Reluctantly, Eva found her bike. A dark rush of rooks heading for a group of tall elm trees made her stop and stare upwards.

'We don't want to miss the train!' called Jack, already on his way. 'I'm coming!'

As they paused to pant at the top of the first hill on the return journey, Eva murmured, 'It's like being in a faraway country where there's no war. Just flowers and birds.' She felt her face glowing with all the sun and pulled her hat down lower. From under its brim her eyes searched for Tollorum but it was too far away, over a long ridge. Thin clouds coloured by the lowering sun, were forming above. Gradually they shaped themselves into feathery plumes. 'Look!' she cried, 'Just like an ostrich feather fan!'

But Jack was already bent over his bike, spinning down the hill.

Eva followed him recklessly, so fast that the wind pulled off her hat which, held by its strings, followed behind like a miniature parachute.

CHAPTER TWELVE
July 1940

Eddie woke up the moment before the cup chinked on the saucer.

'I hope it's bloody whisky this morning, Capwell.'

'Four o'clock, sir. Call for four-thirty.'

'I know it's bloody four o'clock. Put it on the side. Filthy stuff.'

It was pitch black in the bedroom. No point in opening your eyes. Eddie heard Capwell retreating. 'Cheers, you old bugger.'

He put out a naked leg and kicked the bed next door. There was no response and all of a sudden his heart shot along as he imagined that Andy had copped it yesterday. What rot there was in his head! Andy was always up before Capwell made his entrance.

Eyes still closed, Eddie stood at the basin and shaved. His face felt big and solid.

This was the eighth day of Capwell, of the tea which he never drank, and four-thirty standby. *O Lord preserve thy servant.* That was a line that came into his head every morning now. Most unlike him. Although what was he now but a flyer waiting, called out, up there in the sky, trying to kill and not to be killed? No time for anything but expectation or action. Even hard to stay awake long enough for a beer or two at the end of the day.

Dressed now, flying suit, over his uniform, silk scarf to soften the crick in his neck – the crick in his neck which might mean he saw the Hun before the Hun saw him – Eddie reached under his mattress and took out a bottle. One swig, that was enough.

First day, there'd been call-outs twice, second day three times, third, four times. On and on. Probably five was the limit. That was yesterday. His mother wrote and told him it was being called 'The Battle of Britain'. *For* Britain, surely?

There was an airfield at Warmwell, not far from Tollorum. But he wouldn't want to be there guarding Portland shipyards, battling with barrage balloons and British anti-aircraft guns as well as the enemy. Besides, being too close to home might undermine this new man he felt himself to be. He could imagine Sylvia's heart in her mouth every time a plane went over, convinced it was her only son on his way to his death.

Nobody used the D-word. Spots had got it yesterday. Uglier than the ugliest fish in the sea. And actually in the sea now. The English Channel. Eddie had seen it happen – one hit and he'd fallen so fast there'd been no time for a parachute. He'd only arrived in the squadron the day before. Probably didn't know where he was.

Best not to dwell. Eddie walked along to the mess. He was always the last, although not late. No one was ever late. No-one who survived was ever late.

It was still dark but the darkness had that eerie feeling of something lurking behind, waiting to emerge. He glanced over to where the aeroplanes waited too, dispersed round the perimeter of the airfield in case of bombers. He tried to pick out his own. Jones and Jenkins would be there already, a Welsh fitter and rigger team who spoke gibberish to each other but looked after the plane and its pilot as lovingly as a nanny with a baby.

Wow! Sentimental. Some baby. Some pram. Eddie went into the hut. Smoke already hung in the yellow light, adding to the fumes of stale smoke and stale beer from the night before. Men were variously occupied; eating, drinking, smoking, writing, reading, playing board games, apparently engaged but Eddie knew all they were really doing was waiting.

Andy looked up from a game of Patience. 'The weather forecast's good.' Andy knew things before anyone else. Maybe they were all like that in Birmingham.

'When isn't it?'

'When it rains.'

Eight days of sunshine in July wasn't so odd. Every day the dawn smoothed away the night.

'You don't want it to rain, do you?'

'I've never thought about weather so much in my life.' But he looked out of the window. A paler shade of black. Indigo. Changing as he watched. He could see the aeroplanes now. Actually, one day of rain would be welcome.

'Not even when you were up rowing every morning at dawn? Rain and wind must have meant something then.' Andy knew all about Eddie. His 'posh life on a tributary of the Thames', as he referred to the Oxford days.

'We went out in snow,' said Eddie. The past was another country. All sorts of half-remembered quotes popped into his head, as if his mind was trying to find a new language to cope with it all. What would his mind say when he had his first kill? Most people had at least one already. No idea how he'd react. Just glad to be alive, probably.

Andy had gone back to his Patience. He was right: chit-chat didn't help anything much. Hank was at the other end of the mess reading *The Times*. Probably *pretending* to read *The Times*. Sometimes it was not so good to have old friends in the squadron. Hank was even in the same section and yesterday Eddie had noticed he was slow in the turn. Speed in turning was the one real advantage the Spitfire had over the Messerschmitt 109. They told each other that over and over. It didn't do to be slow in the turn. You've got to turn so fast that the plane nearly stands on its tail.

Friends could worry you. Make you lose concentration. Restlessly, Eddie picked up a cup of tea and walked over to a different window. Other people seemed better at coping with the waiting than him.

A steward appeared at the door. Everyone looked up immediately.

'Buzzard transport outside, sir.' On to another stage of waiting.

The dispersal pen always made Eddie's heart leap, no talking in the tumbril, then at the dispersal checking the order of battle, red section, blue section, Eddie was junior still but that day he was Number Two to the leader, Sean. Sean was a dark horse, didn't mix much, but was totally trusted. Trust mattered more than anything.

Gathering their helmets and parachutes each pilot walked the fifty yards or so to his own plane. Love of its sleek lines gave them confidence.

'Morning Jenkins, morning Jones.' The fitters and riggers weren't ghosts any more, already one by one starting up the engine until the airfield vibrated with the roar of twelve Merlin engines at 1200 revs. Of course, they were not going anywhere yet but the horses were ready, snorting blue flame from their exhausts, their flanks trembling with curbed power.

Gradually, the engines were reduced to idling and then cut out altogether. As the light brightened into a blue tinged with lemon, the airfield became silent again.

Eddie hung his parachute on the port wing and walked back to the dispersal hut for more waiting. Even worse this time. He could never understand how people managed to sleep. Or *appeared* to sleep. There were camp beds provided but he might have been lying on a bed of nails.

The telephone sat on a table covered with a green cloth, perhaps to soften the noise. If so, it didn't work. Everybody jumped out of their skins when it rang. Same every morning. The telephone orderly always listened with the same lack of expression. He handed the telephone to Sean, 'Squadron Leader for you, sir.'

Sean, also expressionless – he had a big flat face, good for that sort of thing – listened, said 'Cheers old boy' to the Ops Controller. Eddie thought, you wouldn't get that sort of thing in the Army or Navy. They were a cozy crowd in here.

Two pilots were detailed off to catch a German plane doing an early recce which happened most mornings. So, more waiting for the rest of them.

It was after six now. The sun from a glorious summer's morning streamed through the windows.

The telephone rang again. 'Squadron scramble base angels one four.'

Fourteen thousand feet. Eddie put on his Mae West and ran for his plane. All the pilots ran for their planes. Not very high, 14,000 feet. Should be easy to get above them. 'Beware the Hun from the sun.' Not a very elevated line. But he wondered how many. No point wondering how many. Either he'd be told or he'd see for himself.

The nannies were there, Jenkins and Jones, to put him in his seat. They checked his harness, watched closely as he set up everything as it should be. Thumb passed by the firing button on the stick. That's what it was all about, he knew that now, but he could still love the flying. Now he needed to get behind Sean. This was the first time he'd been given the Number Two spot which said more about the number of pilots lost than his prowess. On the first day he'd flown with the squadrons, two planes, out for the same German plane, crashed into each other, twirled downwards in a loving embrace before exploding into flame and finally smashing into a yellow corn field. He'd been told off for watching that. 'The second you lose concentration on what's around you, by which I mean the enemy, you're a sitting duck. Just one second is enough and you watched that bloody stupid pair for at least three.' 'Yes, Max. Never again, Max.' Two days later Max, the most experienced leader in the squadron, had been shot down trying to break through twenty circling Dorniers.

Now Sean was CO. Eddie had located him, already picking up speed, and began towards him, weaving slightly so that he could see round the raised nose of the spitfire. Once it was in the air, it was straight enough. Securely tucked into the cockpit, not an inch to spare around him, he had that absurd feeling of safety, coupled with heart-throbbing anticipation, that came to him each time he flew.

He was going faster now, bumping over the ruts. Sean was off the ground and another second he was too, lifting gracefully into the expansive blue.

How happy he was on his own, no gunner at the rear or navigator behind him. He was connected by his radio of course. One mad afternoon he'd forgotten to turn it on. Another bollocking from

Max. Today there were two new pilots; he supposed Sean would do the bollocking.

Sean was turning south. 'Bandits at angels one two. Thirty plus.' From the controller a pause. 'Forty plus.' Then Sean's voice, 'Where are you, Lennie?' That was one of the new pilots. 'Keep close to Hank.'

They said if you got through your first day or two, your chances of survival went up but Eddie didn't believe in that. What about Max? Eddie believed in flying, the sky, the sheltering clouds (if there were any), the Spitfire. *O Lord preserve thy servant.*

Black shapes ahead. Everything so quick when you're hurtling together at 300 miles per hour.

'Tally Ho! Buzzard. Tally Ho!'

Even a few days ago, the whole squadron would have stayed closer together but they'd learnt to hunt in pairs, and even then they would eventually break apart.

Softly in his ear, Eddie heard Andy humming. He often did that, usually some patriotic song, sometimes when he was extra stressed, something dirty.

'Follow me up.' Sean's voice. And he was right: the bombers were nearer 18,000 feet. They'd need to get up quickly. As he gently pulled back the stick— the Spitfire was a sensitive lady – he saw out of the corner of his eye that one of the planes was lingering. He hoped it was one of the new guys, not Hank. No time for finer feelings.

They were higher, just a bit when the first Me 109s arrived. Below would be the bombers, heading for some unlucky convoy. But that was for the Coastal Command to worry about.

The sun still cut across from the east. Not ideal.

'Go for it!' shouted Sean.

So now it was pick your prey and stick to him. Tense muscles and the Spitfire would react any old way: bucking and rearing like a horse. Best to shout 'View Halloo!' and enjoy.

Eddie pushed up his goggles and immediately spotted a plane that didn't know what was what. But before he could act Sean was there, tracer flashes, real bullets, hitting the plane almost along its length. One less Nazi.

No time to pick and choose now.

'Look behind you, Eddie!' That was Hank; hooray for lingerers. Eddie turned so steeply that the Me 109 at his tail nearly ran into him. That wouldn't do. But Hank was after him. They must be one to four, so plenty to go round.

Eddie sent the Spitfire upwards in a steep curve, before coming down almost randomly on a 109. Like two birds, they swooped and swirled around each, sometimes closer, sometimes further, always looking for the advantage, the moment when they could press the button and tear the other apart. Other flyers left them alone. Eddie recognised an experienced adversary who could throw his plane about with skill and strength. When they were in close, he could see the way he sat, jutted forward, still and concentrated. But Eddie trusted in the superiority of the Spitfire and something made him certain this plane was his. Perhaps the man was arrogant, had swept through France, attacked helpless convoys along the Channel for weeks, too sure he was invincible. Too many swastikas along the side of his craft. It would be good to get a first kill like this, to make up for the long wait.

Sweat poured off Eddie as he pursued the fight but he only noticed when it trickled into his eyes and he wiped it away quickly. He half-heard the excited voices of the other pilots over the radio but merely as background to sounds of battle, the Merlin engine, his own breathing, a stray bullet that hit his wing. Close, but he felt his enemy tiring. He could *feel* his enemy tiring.

And suddenly the moment came. Instinctively, he depressed the firing button. Four full seconds which felt like an hour. A trail of smoke, a puff of flame. The pilot tried to escape but there were no clouds and his twisting was already laboured. Another moment. Another four seconds. Long enough. The plane was falling away, steering badly, losing. There was nothing down there for him but the sea.

A few days ago, Eddie had watched one of Buzzard Squadron

hurtle into the sea. There'd been no parachute and the plane was on fire. They had all heard the man's screams. Eddie watched his 109 pick up speed until it was in a vertical dive. Perhaps the pilot had been hit. He had no pity, only pride.

Sean's voice came over the radio. 'I'm low on fuel.'

Eddie looked round. Suddenly there was open sky. Just the tail of Hank's plane still just visible. As if the whole scene had been a demented nightmare. Yet he had killed a man. An enemy, a Hun, a Nazi. He checked his own gauge. Time to head home. Return to the base. But now he longed to sail the high seas, victory roll over the waves, the cliffs, the cornfields.

Turning steeply, he looked for the other planes, increased his speed, overtook Hank, swung in behind Sean. He'd land with the rest, whoever remained, swap stories, modestly make his claim, grab a deckchair if he could, because it would be waiting again for the next mission.

If the sun was still out, which it probably would be, he'd shut his eyes, as if protecting them from the glare while taking a little doze, and he'd relive his moment of glory.

CHAPTER THIRTEEN
August 1940

Eva received a letter from Eddie. Underlined and in capitals at the head was written, 'O LORD PRESERVE THY SERVANT.' She stared in wonder. She didn't think Eddie had ever been religious.

She had bought a second-hand radio so that she could listen to the news without her father's active gloom and Valtraud's downcast eyes. She pretended it was to encourage herself as she painted, although why she pretended she did not know. Nobody cared. Jack cared but he cared too much.

Her studio that she had created for herself at her home, was very small and contained a laundry cupboard so it was very warm too. On these hot August days, unless she was actually painting, she sat on the window ledge above the garden. There she looked at the sky and listened to the news telling about the battle being fought up there. She heard phrases like 'Knights of the Sky' and blushed with excitement when the German losses were greater, sometimes far greater, than the British, not forgetting Poles, Czechs, Australians, New Zealanders, French, Belgian, even a few Americans who fought with them. She knew the Luftwaffe had far more planes and pilots which only made it more of a storybook adventure with Eddie its hero.

She only wished she had a photograph of him to pin on her wall. In its absence, she painted a portrait from memory. It was unsatisfactory in every way but improved as a painting, although no more like him, when, in despair, she messed about with it, putting the yellow paint on his hair, over his face and letting the blue from his eyes leak down his nose and mouth. She forgot who it was and began to enjoy herself. She thought that just at the moment it was hard to have much of a grip on reality.

She supposed if she lived nearer the coast, she would have seen the planes in action, been able to tell the Spitfire from the Hurricane, the German bombers from the fighters. Occasionally, a plane or a group of planes did fly over but there were no fighter stations near Oxford.

Eva held Eddie's letter out into the bright air. Where was he now? Up in the celestial? Odd questions flitted about her mind. Why should he be a hero while she struggled with her earthly paints? Could she ever join him up there in the sky? Was he a bird and she an earthworm? Didn't birds eat earthworms? 'O Lord preserve thy servant.' What was happening to Eddie? She had never truly understood him but was he further from her than ever? She felt closer to his mother. Why was there always so much to think about when she should be concentrating on painting?

She peered at her easel, with its half-finished painting, at her paints set up on a table beside it. But here she was, holding Eddie's letter out of the window and doing nothing, not even reading it!

Jack thought he was leading her towards Art. He was ten years older, her teacher, her mentor, so he told her. But she knew he really wanted her, herself and she had to keep herself free. Free for Art. Free for Eddie. Free, simply to be free. She had imagined Eddie free. He had always described flying in ecstatic terms. He didn't want to pinion her or come down to earth himself. Eva waved the letter in the air and wobbled dangerously. She edged further back into the room. What would her father do if she fell into the garden, hit her head on the stone bench and died? He had cried over her mother.

Eva slid inwards and downwards on to the floor. The bare wooden planks were agreeably cool. She began to read the letter.

'Only out three times today. Myself, Hank and Andy all back safely. Seems like a bit of a miracle at the moment. We lost two pilots, one drowned, one missing. Maybe he'll be found. The drowned one had trained with Andy and me.'

As usual, it was written more to himself than her.

> *'Of course we don't talk like this, but the call for a jaunt to the pub doesn't have many takers. The Mess is good enough for a celebration. They all knew I'd got my first Hun today. Jones and Jenkins can hold up their heads again. Jones said, "First one's hard, after that it's easy, sir".'*

She was his witness.

> *'I didn't think of the man I shot down. He was wearing a helmet, goggles, oxygen mask and a scarf so I couldn't see his face. But I guess by the way he handled his plane, he was older, experienced so I've a right to feel proud. One less Jerry to knock our lot down. Simple.'*

Eva paused. Here was a glimpse of something more thoughtful, edging in against his will.

> *'Sean is a great leader. We're lucky. He went up twice more and I took part share of another 109. Jenkins and Jones were right. This one crashed over land and I saw the parachute so some happy farmer probably picked him up on the end of his pitchfork. We treat them properly, of course. Hank is even promising to visit a wounded Hun in hospital. But Hank's going through a hard time. He's flown since he was a boy so it's not that. I expect it's hard being the only non-English in the squadron.'*

Eva remembered the American (but surely not called Hank?) from the brief visit to the toxophily club. She could picture his open, friendly face, his broad shoulders. She couldn't quite see him in a cockpit which Eddie had once described to her as the size of a dog kennel. He had added that its constrictions made you feel part of the plane, which he obviously reckoned a good thing.

Eva wondered how she should answer his letter. The Ruskin

was closed for the summer so there was nothing to say about that and, even if she did have the confidence to talk about her painting, she didn't think he was interested. He certainly wouldn't want to know about her home life, even duller since Hildegard, after being let out of the internment camp, had discovered friends of friends and moved to Manchester. She was a big city girl, she'd told Eva and Eva had felt reproved. She didn't know what she was.

What she'd like to tell Eddie about was her visit to Dorset and to Tollorum, his home. But that entailed all kinds of complexities. Jack's interest in her might be disguised under the word 'teacher' and she certainly didn't expect Eddie to be jealous but Sylvia Chaffey was another matter. Why had she not revealed her friendship with Eddie? Why should Eddie mind? Possibly she was just being secretive, like her family.

Eva let the letter drop to the floor and shut her eyes. Her father was taking her out to lunch with his friend, Professor Lamb. There would be too much drinking and eating and nobody of her own age.

'Eva!'

Oh, no. Could it be time already?

※

The lunch party was not as Eva expected because there were two young men, students of Professor Lamb's who had joined up at the start of the war. One was on three-day leave from the army and the other was a pilot who had just emerged from hospital.

Eva sat between them, wearing the same red dress she had worn at the lunch party where she had met Eddie. The soldier preferred to talk about golf with the man on his right so she was left with the pilot whose face was so horribly scarred that she could hardly bear to look at him. He seemed content to eat his chicken, albeit with some difficulty.

Eventually, the silence became worse than anything and, noting her father was well away down the table, she said softly, 'I have a friend in the Royal Air Force.'

111

The pilot leant his head towards her, 'I'm out of all that now.' His voice was hoarse and he paused while she stared at her plate. Then he said with what was probably supposed to be a smile, 'The doctors say it will look a lot better than this when they're finished with me. Even my hands.' He held them up and they were like chicken claws.

'That's good,' said Eva weakly.

'Yes. If you believe them. The medics went on about how I had to get out in the world which is why I'm here. I'm sorry if I gave you a shock. My sister fainted when she saw me.'

'Poor thing,' said Eva. 'I mean she must love you very much.' But that sounded no more consoling.

'Having a pilot friend, I expect you know all about it. Burns and drowning, that's what pilots fear most. Secretly, of course.' The hoarse, rasping voice now seemed unstoppable while all the time the bright young eyes with no eyelashes to shield them, held her gaze appealingly.

'It was my fault, of course. It always is. On my first op. That's what's worse than the pain and the scars. All that training and no use to anyone. I wasn't even wearing my goggles or gloves.' He stopped abruptly as a college servant lifted away their plates.

'Do you live nearby?' she asked. Was it her duty to befriend him?

'Yorkshire. Farmers for generations. I'm heading up north now to wait for the next op, hospital op, and I'll only shock the sheep. After the war, I'll meet a plain girl who doesn't mind my face and will have children with smooth faces and no one will think about the war, except for me and I'll know I wasn't a hero.'

'You *are* a hero,' said Eva as a dollop of some terrible pudding landed on her plate. With its lumpy grey and red jam squiggles it reminded her of the pilot's face.

Again, he attempted to lever up his mouth into a smile. 'I can't talk to my family about this.' He touched his face with fingers twisted with burns. 'I never shall. It's too dreadful for them. So I picked on you. Sorry.'

'I hope things turn out better than you expect.'

'It all happened in a few minutes,' said the pilot, 'from hero to has-been.'

Neither of them spoke again. In fact, no-one spoke much to her at all until she and her father were leaving when the Professor suddenly asked, 'What do you make of this war, my dear?'

Eva thought of her mother's disappearance, her father's ageing, of Hildegard and Valtraud, of the confident cockney evacuees, of Eddie in his airman's uniform, even of Jack with his asthma, and didn't know how to answer.

'I am a painter,' she began bravely. But her words crossed with her father's farewells and she stopped.

'It probably hasn't changed your life very much,' the Professor said, more kindly than before.

When they were back in the house, Eva found a new canvas which she placed hopefully on her easel. She painted pink, grey, more grey, streaks of red. After a while she had to admit she was painting the pilot's burned face. She couldn't even remember his name.

✂

Sylvia wrote to Arthur Lamb asking for Eva Speke's address. The Professor was surprised by the contraction of his heart when he recognised Sylvia's writing on the envelope. How they had loved each other! But that was before the last war.

✂

Jack led Eva into the Ruskin's solemn entrance hall. It was quieter than a church.

'Isn't it closed for the summer?' Eva looked around nervously.

'I have special permission.' He wore the irritated look she had come to recognise when his authority was questioned.

He went forward into one of the studios and when he was at the far end, took a large canvas from a pile of others.

'I want you to see this because I've sold it so there won't be another chance.

113

Eva looked. At first it seemed to be mostly pale coloured patterns: pale grey, a little dark-grey, lemon-yellow, blue soft-beige, winding delicately over the canvas. Then she saw there was a girl's flat, upturned face at the bottom and that she was watching fighter planes in the sky, grey crosses with white smoke trailing behind. 'It's beautiful,' she said. 'Where did you see them?'

'Near Portland. I bicycled there one day. I stood on a headland and as I watched, I thought of you. So I put you in the picture, also watching.'

'Who bought it?' Surely he couldn't know about Eddie.

'Someone from the War Artists' Advisory Committee. Pure chance I was here when they came.' He smiled. It was a simple smile of pride. 'I'm in danger of becoming a war artist.'

'Wouldn't that be wonderful!'

'But I might be sent to Scotland to watch for convoys or to the dockyard in Liverpool.' Jack suddenly clutched Eva and cried out desperately. 'I don't believe you have any idea what you mean to me!'

Although he didn't attempt a kiss, his arms were tight around and his angular face, with its male roughness very close. She stayed quiet as one might with a boisterous dog in case worse befell.

'I want to marry you. You do understand, don't you? I want us to live together in the Dorset countryside.'

'I'm going there soon,' murmured Eva, as a diversion from marriage.

'Where?' asked Jack, immersed in his emotions.

'Mrs Chaffey wrote and asked me to take pity on three old ladies and stay at Tollorum for a week or so. She thinks it will do me good.'

Jack dropped his arms. 'She's asked you on your own.'

'She'd met me before. My father, too and my godfather.' She edged away towards the painting. It really was beautiful.

'Perhaps you can come down one day and we can paint together.'

Jack stared at her. Her calm lightness in the face of his passionate proposal, baffled him. Perhaps he had underestimated her and she was not worthy to be the object of his love. But, seeing her gazing admiringly at his painting, herself watching herself watching the fighting aeroplanes, she seemed almost divine. Perfection was in her smooth skin, gilded now by the sun, her graceful neck, raven hair, plaited today around her head. The lightness, he told himself, was just a youthful response to something she didn't understand.

'I love your painting,' said Eva warmly.

Jack came to stand beside her, nobly resisting the impulse to put his hand on her shoulder.

'I'm sorry you sold it,' continued Eva. 'Is that the point of painting?'

'Of course not. But everyone needs money and encouragement from an appreciative audience.'

Eva glanced at Jack. She had never heard him say something that sounded so sensible.

As they walked out of the building together, an aeroplane flew high above them, a small dark cross in the blue sky. They both looked up and, finding nothing to say, parted.

≫≪

'Sir! Sir'

Eddie hadn't even woken to Capwell's entrance, the well-known chink on the saucer.

'My legs are made of lead.'

Sir?'

Twelfth day running? No tenth. Or thirteenth. Lucky thirteenth. Hardly worth shaving. Feel his way to the mess and pour tea down his throat. Be all right once he was in the air.

'Don't even remember getting to dispersal.' Eddie nudged Andy who grunted.

'Open your eyes, damn you.'

'Not till I'm called.'

'How many days have we been out?' Why did it matter? 'Would you say it was twelve or maybe thirteen?'

'Give it a rest, can't you?'

Eddie sank into the kind of coma that passed for rest. Once he started up, mumbled, 'Coming in from the east...' then sank back again.

The telephone rang. Voices in the haze of his exhaustion.

'OK Buzzard. Don't all run at the same time. Bandits flexing their wings at Angels ten.'

Men ran, stumbled, parachutes suddenly heavy, tangling their legs.

'Is it the thirteenth day in a row?' Eddies asked Jenkins as he helped him into the plane.

'Fifteenth, sir. Not surprised you've lost count.'

'So where did thirteen and fourteen go?' muttered Eddie as he checked through the instruments.

'Turn off your blasted R/T if you want to talk rubbish,' shouted Sean into his ear.

CHAPTER FOURTEEN
August 1940

Eddie was lost. Or rather he felt lost. You couldn't be lost, he tried to tell himself, when you'd come out with your squadron, eleven planes and pilots vectored to the sky where thirty or forty bandits, Huns, that is, waited for them. Not bad odds or not as bad as usual. They'd been over land too, just drawing the opposition out, probably, but dangerous for them.

What a fight! Eddie's feeling of being lost didn't stop him remembering the 109 he'd brought down and another one he'd damaged. The thing was, just after that, when his blood was still up, heart pounding like a drum, a great white swathe of cloud, which he hadn't noticed coming had swallowed him up. It felt like that, like entering a whale, entering darkness, although actually it was whiteness.

'Pull yourself together, Eddie.' He spoke aloud. You're connected by radio, aren't you? Of course he was. And you're flying on instruments, he added to himself. You're not blind or lost when you've got instruments. Was this the panic that has no name because pilots don't like to mention it?

Eddie did pull himself together and checked his panel. Why was he flying so fast when he didn't know where he was going? He slowed down to 150mph. His heartbeat slowed too. He spoke into his radio transmitter.

'Red Two. Heading South.'

'Where the hell have you been, Eddie? Don't ever turn off your R/T!'

Had he turned it off? Why would he do that?

He listened to Sean shouting co-ordinates. It seemed the

party had been going on without him. He could hear explosions, screaming engines, screaming men.

'I'm with you.'

'I should fucking hope so!'

The cloud was thinning as he turned and built up speed. He had only been lost for a few minutes. Perhaps only seconds. A few minutes is a long time in the sky. In a cloud.

He burst out into light so strong it cut into his eyes. He must have pushed up his goggles. He pulled them down quickly.

'Atta Eddie!' shouted Sean. He was a good leader.

But there was no need for encouragement. Eddie's heart was banging at his ribs again and he'd already spotted a Hun who'd let himself get separated. Limping a bit too. Time to finish him off.

'Take this you bloody fucker!' yelled Eddie who didn't usually yell imprecations, in fact rather despised men who did. Those lost few minutes or seconds had just been tiredness. Or maybe lack of oxygen. He hadn't checked his height.

Eddie's Spitfire whirled downwards and, like an avenging angel, poured a stream of glittering lead into his victim.

Without stopping to watch its screeching, flaming descent, Eddie wrenched round his plane to look for another target. But suddenly the sky was empty. He'd seen that happen too often to be surprised. Time to go home. He checked his fuel tank. Somewhere behind him over the sea, he sensed the cloud and turned his back on it with a confident flip of his wings.

He came in to land so fast that he saw Jenkins and Jones running from him rather than towards him. He bounced down, nose settling at the last minute.

'Keen to get home, sir?' yelled Jenkins, although Eddie couldn't hear him above the noise of the engine.

'How many?' shouted Jones.

Eddie held up two fingers and a third bent. Two definite and one shared. It was strange, he thought fleetingly, that he'd got such a bag on a day that had given him such a fright. Then he pulled off his parachute and allowed Jenkins to heave him out of the cockpit.

'Good show, sir. Clouds coming in now. You might get a break.'

Eddie didn't look where he pointed. 'I never count my chickens.'

'Unless they're dead Jerries,' Jones cracked.

An hour later the clouds did arrive, bringing heavy rain. By six o'clock the pilots were stood down for the rest of the day.

'Come on Andy, Hank. The Barley Mow will think we've abandoned them.' Eddie had started drinking more in the evenings. It seemed the only way to relax enough for sleep.

'Dead, you mean.' Andy pulled off all his clothes except for his underpants. He sat on his bed with his arms dangling between his legs. His hair stood up in sweaty tufts. He was about a stone lighter than he had been a few weeks' earlier.

'I thought we didn't use the D-word.' Eddie stood somewhat belligerently between the two beds.

'You can drink in the mess if you want,' said Andy, 'I'm done.'

Hank, still in his flying suit, lay on Eddie's bed, reading a letter.

Eddie pulled on his arm. 'What do you say, Hank?'

'I say I'm reading a letter and tomorrow I'm on 48-hour leave and going off early.'

'How early do you think we'll be up?'

'Forecast very bad, in other words, or, as some might say, very good.' Andy spoke without raising his head.

'Then you *will* come?'

'Make it worth my while.'

'All rounds on me.'

'And I don't have to dress?'

'I love your naked little body. There'd be some who wouldn't, but I'd knock them over.'

Andy raised his voice to Hank. 'D for desperation, would you say.'

Hank stuffed the letter into his pocket. 'I'll come.' He swung his legs off the bed, groaned, and stood up.

'There you are, you little squirt,' Eddie slapped Andy's bony back. 'You can come or not come as it suits you.'

The three men, all properly buttoned into their uniforms got into Hank's car and drove away. Only Eddie cast a backward glance at the airfield, the planes spaced around the edges, the rainwater sluiced backwards off their up-tilted noses, hammered on to their wings, swirled round their undercarriages. Two aircrew, wearing tent-like Macintoshes, shouted incomprehensible instructions to each other.

'This isn't such a bad idea,' shouted Andy curled up in the backseat of the car.

The pub was only half full, room enough for the airmen to find chairs and a table to themselves.

'The rain's kept them away,' commented Andy who was always keenest for action. 'The girls too. Shame that.'

Then silence fell. Even if they hadn't been so exhausted, it would not have been easy to talk about the last days. Too many men had died, gone missing or been injured. There came a time when it was too difficult to joke among the men you knew best when they could easily be the next to go. The beers in front of them went down slowly.

Hank took the letter from his pocket. 'No good news from America,' he said.

'Not planning to ride in on their white horses,' Eddie tried to sound facetious.

'Angela's had enough,' Hank's voice was steady. 'She reads reports from some American commentator over here who stands on promontories and watches dogfights. She's decided I'm unlikely to survive if I carry on.'

'Clever woman,' commented Andy who had started to do better with his beer than the others.

'Not our war. That's what she says.'

'Sensible woman,' Andy raised his glass in salute.

'Bugger off to Birmingham, can't you?' Eddie leaned closer to Hank. 'So what are you going to do?'

'I don't know. We've been engaged since I was twenty-one. Four years.'

'No hurry, then.' Andy avoided a clout over his head from Eddie.

'I'll think about it over my leave.' Hank picked up his glass. This time he drank with more conviction.

'Going to London, I suppose?' Eddie also drank. He turned round and saw rain running down the small window behind him. The light was green and eerie.

'I guess so.'

'Pity you can't go somewhere quieter.'

'Yeah.'

They all began to drink seriously. After a while Andy left them for a friend. 'You're like zombies, tonight, you two.'

When he was gone, Eddie and Hank looked away from each other. They felt like zombies. Their glasses were empty and when Eddie returned with two more pints, he said abruptly, 'Let's drive to Tollorum.'

'Your family's place?'

'Yes. You need somewhere quiet to think.'

Hank laughed. 'You're not on leave.'

'You heard Andy. Pissing rain forever.' Eddie sat down.

'That doesn't mean you can do a bunk,' Hank still wasn't taking the suggestion seriously.

'I need a break.'

'Apply for leave.'

'I won't be given it.'

'Exactly. Your eyes aren't jerking, your hands aren't shaking, well, not much. You can still deliver a pint.'

'I can't sleep. I had a bad day. I want to see my mother.'

'You're such a liar.'

Eddie stood up again. He didn't want to admit how scared he'd been in that cloud. He went to the bar and came back with two double whiskies. 'Cheers! It will be a great little jaunt. I'll be back before it's stopped raining.'

≫≺

It was only just light when Hank and Eddie drove off the

airfield. This time Eddie didn't look back at the planes. It was too early and too wet for Jenkins and Jones but he was still afraid some instinct would bring them out. In an uncomfortable flash, he remembered running away from school. He'd been drunk at the time, one o'clock in the morning and expecting to be thrown out that day. A bit different now but perhaps it meant he was the running-away sort. The CO might point out that if all the pilots ran away when they thought they were at the end of their tether, how could the RAF manage? Why did he feel at the end of his tether? Because of a minute or few seconds lost in a cloud? Perhaps he wasn't at all. Merely needed to get Hank to Tollorum and himself too for a day while it rained. The clouds were still low and it was still pouring, he observed. Unfortunately, his head ached owing to the amount of beer and whisky poisoning his body.

'How do I proceed?' asked Hank, his first words.

'Head west. Away from the rising sun.'

'There is no rising sun.'

'Thank God,' Eddie took two slices of his Aunt Lily's fruit cake from his pocket, handed one to Hank and bit into the other. The sense of his desertion, his Spitfire spreading her wings unadmired, lessened. He pictured Tollorum in the summer, the lanes shimmering with morning dew, the fields stretching away, utterly peaceful except for the trilling of larks rising skywards without a thought of killing.

Hank drove very fast which was fine because there was nothing on the road, not even animals, except once when they had to wait for a herd of deer to cross the road. A dignified stag led them slowly by as if a furiously revving car was of no more concern than a boulder.

It stopped raining briefly but the clouds were dark and thick. Sometimes they joined with a white mist that clung around the trunks of the trees and swathed the lowest hills.

After two hours they had emerged from Hampshire, entered Wiltshire briefly and come into Dorset.

'World speed record,' commented Eddie, looking at his

watch. There were no signposts of course, which made it feel as if they were travelling through one magnificent country. Eddie's spirits rose higher. It was just a day out, he reassured himself, a day to help a friend.

They dropped down off the heights, lifted into one side of a valley, slipped down the other. The light came pale and ghostly, tinged with green. It was infinitely restful. They were moving more slowly now.

'Did you tell Andy?' asked Hank.

'Left a note for when he wakes. Told him I'll be back forthwith.' He glanced at Hank. 'I'll pick up my own wheels so you're free.'

'Free,' repeated Hank ironically.

Eddie suspected he wasn't progressing with his decision-making. He pictured Angela, matronly, prim, favouring white collars and gloves.

As if reading his thoughts, Hank reached into an inner pocket and handed over a photograph. 'Angela. Miami Beach.'

Eddie looked at a girl in a two-piece bathing suit, slender, deeply tanned with long blonde hair. It was harder to see her face but that looked pretty good too.

'Bloody hell!' exclaimed Eddie, 'and that's an under-statement.'

'There're two other things I haven't told you.' She's a journalist and she's on her way to England now.'

Eddie digested this. 'I thought she disapproved.'

'She wants to see for herself. She wants to take me home with her.'

'However is she getting here? You can't just cross the Atlantic for fun.' Eddie focused on this aspect of the news. 'What about U-boats? The Nazis think American ships are fair game now, even if they're not in the war.'

'She's hitched a ride on a military plane.'

'Left here,' instructed Eddie, feeling threatened. 'We're only five minutes away.'

Soon Tollorum was spread below them and, like Eva and Jack, a few weeks' earlier, they went bumping and swerving down the steep hill. They were going too fast for Hank to stop at the sandbag wall which he only noticed at the last minute. Instead he crashed through it, sand flying from split bags. Mr. Ham was not in attendance.

'Right at the pub, past the church and we've arrived.' Eddie pronounced without even looking back.

CHAPTER FIFTEEN
August 1940

Sylvia and Eva were having breakfast at a round table set at one end of a pretty chintzy room.

'It's cosier in here,' said Sylvia. 'Such a miserable morning. Until now we've had nothing but sun.'

Eva preferred this room with its two matching sofas, to the immense dining-room where they'd eaten with Eddie's grandmother, Lady Beatrice, daughter of an earl apparently, and an old, talkative rector the night before. 'I don't mind the rain,' she said politely.

'Do you see many people in Oxford?' asked Sylvia, pushing away her plate.

Eva saw she wanted to know her better and tried not to feel nervous. 'Not really.'

'There was that friend you brought here?'

'Mr. Halliwell's more of a teacher than a friend,' Eva felt a blush spreading. 'Although what he most wants to do is live in the countryside and paint.'

'I see.'

Eva understood what she was thinking. 'He can't fight. He's got asthma.'

'Well, he'll have to have a job or he'll be called a shirker and given the white feather like in the last war.'

'Oh, he's not a shirker,' said Eva defensively. But why was she defending Jack? 'He's very serious.'

'I could see that.' Sylvia smiled. 'Of course there's a real need of schoolteachers with so many young men gone to the war. In our local school, they're desperate. Perhaps he could teach art and English? Then paint in his time off?'

'I don't know. I expect so.'

'He could camp in the barn you told me you both admired so much until he found somewhere better.' Sylvia seemed to be enjoying her planning. 'You can ask him and I'll write a note. It's sad how unused the land is. Until we get more help, we haven't even sowed all the usual fields.' She paused and looked at Eva who was fiddling with the cutlery she hadn't used. 'I'm sorry. I've got used to running things. But I will write that note just in case.'

'Thank you.' Eva wondered why the prospect of Jack living so close to Tollorum depressed her. After all, she wouldn't be living at the house. Nor would Eddie. 'I did wonder whether he could visit one day while I'm here. Then we could paint together.'

But Sylvia had stopped listening and was looking out of the window.

'Now who's that coming?' She hurried out of the room.

Eva heard men's voices. She picked up her plate. The countryside had been so empty when she and Jack had visited and Mrs Chaffey had seemed lonely. She put the plate down again.

'I'll dash to the kitchen and find you something to eat. Go through to the breakfast room.'

Eva heard Mrs. Chaffey's voice and noticed that her usual calm tones had changed to excitable happiness.

Two tall blue-clad men came into the room. Eva came out from behind the little table. She stared from one to the other, then held out her hand to Hank. 'I'm Eva.'

'I guess I know who you are: Eddie's sister. We met in Oxford.' Eva noticed that Hank's face was tight, his eyelids swollen, the whites tinged with red. He smiled at her.

'Hello sis,' Eddie lightly touched her shoulder. 'Some surprise.'

Eva blinked. 'Would you like to sit down?' She pointed to one of the sofas, then felt silly because this was Eddie's home.'

'Not yet.' Hank stretched his arms over his head. 'I was the driver.'

Eddie sat down and stretched his legs across the carpet.

'I'm not really his sister,' said Eva earnestly to Hank. 'I'm staying

126

here with Mrs Chaffey so I can paint.' She held up a sketchbook and pencil as if to show her credentials.

'We won't be here long,' said Eddie. He shut his eyes. He wasn't up to all this. He couldn't begin to imagine what Eva was doing there and didn't want to try. He said, 'I've just come to collect my car.' He would have a few hours' sleep and drive back to the base. That's where he belonged now. What if the clouds cleared? He must have been mad to leave. He had been mad. Temporary madness due to exhaustion. Hank must have been mad to let him leave.

Hank and Eva talked politely about the beauties of Dorset until Sylvia returned with Lily and trays of food. 'Just don't ask us where it came from!' Lily was as excited as Sylvia.

Eva found it difficult to look at Eddie and noticed he didn't look at her.

Eddie knew he couldn't eat. He couldn't drive yet either; his hands were shaking. He stood and began to prowl about the room, picking up and then putting down again ornamental objects that he'd known from childhood, mother-of-pearl boxes, silver bowls, porcelain figures,

'Your food will get cold, Eddie,' said Lily reproachfully.

Eddie gave her a fleeting smile but didn't sit down.

'I'll tell you what, darling,' said Sylvia, 'why don't you take Eva into the garden. The poor girl arrived last night in pouring rain so she hasn't seen a thing and I think it's easing off now. I can quiz your friend about America.'

Eddie turned to Eva. To her his look said, I'd rather be alone but you are the price of my freedom from this situation which is unbearable. She stood up.

⤝

The garden smelt strongly of wet grass, sodden flowers, dripping trees. There was still a murky drizzle. Eva shivered. Eddie, his increasing thinness making him seem taller, strode ahead. They reached a pink wall, darkened by the rain to a deep rose colour.

Eddie pushed open a small door and headed down one of many narrow paths between beds of potato, cabbage, peas, carrots, beans and more potatoes. He reached a bench.

'I need to rest.'

'It's so wet.' Eva placed her hand on the soaked wood.

'So it is.' Eddie went over to one of the two long greenhouses at each end of the garden. He came back with two canvas sacks. 'One for each of us.'

It was his first friendly overture. 'What a lot of vegetables!' she said, sitting down beside him.

'It is a vegetable garden.' He looked round unwillingly. 'Dull stuff. Part of the war effort, doubtless. There used to be beautiful things here.'

'There will be again,' said Eva. She thought, all he wants to do is close his eyes so I won't bother him with anything. Then she thought, I spend my life not bothering people with things. Is that because I'm cowardly or because there's a war on?

Eddie did close his eyes. In a second he was asleep. His head dropped on to his chest. He slept silently.

Eva opened her sketchbook which she'd brought with her. She stood up and moved away so she could see the vegetables at Eddie's feet and the wall behind him. She was glad to see no sky. The painting would be called, 'An airman rests'. The drizzle fell away leaving a wet haze. Dissatisfied with one sketch, she started another, this time, adding colour notes: Rose pink for the wall, blue-brown (what was that colour?) for the bench, blue-grey for the uniform, grey-green for the vegetables. Her heart picked up speed with the intensity of her concentration.

Eddie fell sideways but didn't wake. Eva put down her pad and went closer to him. Perhaps she should stretch him out. The bench was quite long enough, a big, old bench. Deciding to risk it, she gently eased up his feet and turned his head until it rested comfortably on the sacking. His soft, rhythmic breathing never changed.

Eva returned to her pad, drawing, detailing, making

decisions. The clouds receded upwards and as the garden grew warmer, a delicate steam rose from the earth and the walls.

'I thought we'd lost you.' Sylvia came through the wooden door. She carried a basket.

'I'm so sorry, Mrs. Chaffey.' Eva closed her pad, guiltily. Of course, she wanted to see her son. 'He fell asleep.'

Sylvia looked at them both. 'I'm sure he needs it.' She smiled. 'And you must call me Sylvia. I've brought coffee and cake. You've been drawing have you?'

'Trying.'

'I won't ask to see it. I hate talking about a new novel. Not that I'm writing one.' She turned to Eddie. 'Did he say anything to you?'

'He just fell asleep. I suppose he's exhausted.'

'He shouldn't be here, you know. Hank told me. He isn't on leave.'

'Hank was Henry in Oxford.' Eva stopped abruptly. Would Mrs. Chaffey, Sylvia, guess from this that she had become a friend of Eddie's?

'I hate to wake him,' Sylvia lightly touched her son's hand. 'But he's had a couple of hours' sleep and Hank says the sooner he gets back the better. His car's being filled with petrol at the farm; they'll bring it round.'

Sylvia crouched down. This time she kissed Eddie's hand. It was a very beautiful hand, young and burnt golden-brown from the waiting on the sunny airfield. Sylvia laid her cheek against it.

'I hate sending him back,' she murmured.

'Yes,' Eva was moved but also embarrassed by her emotion. 'Oh, yes!'

The urgency in Eva's voice didn't wake Eddie but her hand, rising suddenly to her mouth, disturbed a passing fly who, buzzing loudly, flew directly at Eddie's warm body. It spun jerkily round his face.

Eddie opened his eyes. 'Damned flies.' He was right: another fly had appeared and another, as if given permission by the first to break the calm.

'Hello Mother.' Eddie sat up.

'Hello darling.' They looked at each other. 'I've brought you coffee and cake.'

'I've hardly seen you. Sorry. I just had to sleep.' He took the cup Sylvia held out and drank thirstily. She handed him cake and he ate that too. He looked like a hungry child.

Eva watched them both, glad she liked Sylvia too much to feel jealousy. She held the sketchbook close to her heart and when Sylvia offered her coffee she came quickly and drank from the same cup as Eddie.

All three looked up as Lily appeared at the door. 'Your car's ready for you, Eddie.'

Eddie stood up stretching. 'Dear Aunt Lily, you remind me of my rigger and fitter, Jenkins and Jones.'

'Don't you Jenkins and Jones me, young man!'

'It's a compliment. They're the two people who care about me most on the airfield. Or about my Spitfire anyway which comes to the same thing.'

There was a silence. No-one wanted to put their thoughts into words. Then Lily patted Eddie's shoulder, 'Come along now and I'll find you some more food to take back.'

At the house, Eddie went inside for a wash. He found Hank wandering about. 'I'm off in a moment.' He glanced at his friend. 'You seem very at ease.'

'Your mother's invited me to stay tonight.' He waved his hand appreciatively. 'This house must be centuries old.'

'Half a millenium,' agreed Eddie. 'Always owned by the Fitzpaines.' He went up the wide stairways. Is that why he fought, to save his family home from the Nazis? But he knew it wasn't true. He flew and fought because that was his life, his mission, as if flying had chosen him, not the other way round. Somehow it made sense of things.

Sylvia, Beatrice and Lily hovered in the hallway.

'In the last war, the house was filled with wounded officers,' said Lily. 'Do you remember, m'lady, one of them presented you with a bouquet of flowers when he was leaving?'

Beatrice smiled. 'Flowers from my own garden. Most of them going over.'

Sylvia suddenly gave a gasp and ran to the open door. They watched as a car drew up and a WAAF driver got out briskly and opened a rear door. 'Oh, Lord! I'd quite forgotten. A Wing Commander is coming to discuss whether he can billet some men from Warmwell here. I'm sure he'll realise it's too far away. But what about Eddie, home without leave?'

'Will he know?' said Beatrice.

'If he meets Eddie, he'll want to know everything. He thinks anyone in the RAF is his business.'

The Wing Commander got out and stared up approvingly at the old house. He was old himself and walked towards them with an obvious limp.

'Put him and Hank together in the drawing room,' suggested Lily, 'and they'll swap stories while Eddie slips away.'

Hank and the Wing Commander sat in the large drawing room. The light had now changed from grey to white, shining on the embossed wallpaper and the highly polished wooden tables, the wood-framed chairs and sofas.

The Wing Commander surveyed Hank. 'Very rare to find an American in the RAF. Pilot before the war, were you?'

'I flew, sir,' answered Hank. 'I was studying at Oxford.' Why did the man make him feel as if he was muscling in on someone else's show. 'My mother was British, sir.'

'Jolly good. Can't fly myself anymore. Bailed out at 10,000 feet in 1916 and the chute only partly opened. Lucky to be alive and have one leg to call my own.'

The RAF didn't even exist when he was flying, thought Hank, while nodding politely. The Wing Commander settled in even more when Lily came in with a decanter of sherry and glasses.

'I expect you know what the Nazis are up to now?' He sipped contentedly as if he was reporting on a race at Ascot.

'They don't tell us much. Just call us out when we're needed.'

'Was ever thus. Talk is the Hun is turning his attentions from the air to the airfields. Duxford got it this morning. How long's your leave?'

'Forty-eight hours. The cloud was scarcely off the ground and it was raining heavily when we – I – left the base this morning.'

The Wing Commander glanced at his watch. 'A fine old house.'

'With permission, sir, I'll check if Mrs Chaffey's been held up.'

Outside, Eddie was coming down the stairs whistling cheerfully. Hank was about to tell him about Duxford and the bombing of airfields when he stopped. He'd find out soon enough if it was true.

'See you later, old chap,' said Eddie, slapping Hank on the back, before turning and heading quickly for the back door.' His peaceful sleep in the walled garden had induced a benign mood, yet the brightness of the light outside disconcerted him. So did the sight of Beatrice, Lily, Sylvia and Eva lined up to see him off. He kissed mother, aunt and grandmother but stopped when he reached Eva who was standing apart from the others.

'I didn't come here to say goodbye.'

'You were tired. You didn't expect to see me.' But she couldn't help continuing, 'I wish we'd talked just a little.'

He looked at her reproachfully as if she should have understood him better. 'I'll write. Are you here long?'

'A couple of weeks. I made a drawing of you.'

'Asleep. Not much fun.' He kissed her cheek abstractedly and got into his car.

Everybody waved but nobody said goodbye.

⤢

Eddie drove impatiently, longing to catch up with his real self who was waiting for him at the base. It hadn't rained now for an hour or more. Firstly, he had to negotiate all the ups and downs, twists and turns of the road. At one point when he was flashing off the crest of a hill, he felt he was in his Spitfire with the sky all around him. Then he saw crossing below him bunches of white sheep, like substantial clouds. Crying Tally Ho, he sped towards them, defying their dignity and scattering them into a bleating, urinating, defecating rout. If only a *Staffel* of Messerschmitts was as easy to disperse!

He looked in his rear-view mirror and, seeing a boy running hither and thither in a desperate attempt to gather the flock, he slowed down to a more sensible speed, passing quietly through villages, skirting round towns.

It was around three o'clock when Eddie heard a heavy load of aeroplanes passing overhead and stopped the car. He got out and watched them retreating. They were German medium bombers, Heinkels escorted by Dorniers, acting as fighters but perhaps loaded with bombs too. He had heard nothing as he sped along but he noted that the formation was ragged and one of the Dornier engines was on fire. He'd be lucky to make it back over the Channel. All the same, it was the sight he feared most, making it clear that, even if the cloud was still low and unbroken above him, there was enough visibility for enemy attacks.

An hour more and the sun blazed through, creating hard shadows under trees, walls and buildings. Again he drove as fast as he could.

⊰⊱

Eva sat on the bench where Eddie had slept, fiddling with her drawings. They didn't please her but she remembered that Jack told her every artist worth his salt was hypercritical of his own work. The trouble was that Eddie had looked so monumental, lying there, when everything about his waking self suggested action.

It was hot now that the sun had come out and an old gardener who was digging up potatoes kept stopping to mop his face with a large red handkerchief. Eva turned the page of her sketchbook and picked up her pencil. She started on the parallel rows of vegetables stretching in front and beyond the old man.

Hank had been given a shotgun and told by Sylvia to walk round the fields looking for pigeons. She had advised him that he couldn't make a decision about his future before talking to Angela the next day. This was a relief but when he looked up to the trees, he was not searching for pigeons but noting how the sharp rays of the sun squinted through the leaves and imagining a plane come hurtling towards him.

Lily was on the telephone in the hallway. 'No, Gussie. Miss Sylvia is holding her WVS meeting. I cannot bring her out.'

Sylvia sitting at the head of the dining-room table with six local ladies, noted the sun was out and worried about Eddie.

Beatrice, as so often, in the herbaceous border pulling out ground elder, stepped out on to the lawn. She had seen Eva go alone to the walled garden and now decided to follow her. Such a young, lost girl. She pulled off her gloves which were soaked through by the wet plants and looked up at the sky; she took off her cardigan and draped it around her shoulders. She was trying not to remember the day her husband left to fight.

CHAPTER SIXTEEN
August 1940

Eddie saw the black smoke blowing gustily into the sky before he heard any noise. The bombers would have headed for the Channel once they'd dropped their load, the fighter escort not far behind.

The smoke was enough to tell the story. That was petrol tankers going up, aeroplanes ready- fuelled if they'd been on the ground, lorries and cars. There was no point in hoping it was coming from anywhere but his airfield.

Eddie had never seen bomb destruction first-hand before. Anything he *had* seen had been from the air, far below and hardly real. He stopped his car before the perimeter fence because now he had seen flames nearly as high as the smoke, and the smashed buildings, the tossed lorries, the planes, not too many, he estimated, reduced to smithereens.

He ran forward, determined to check his own Spitfire but such were the craters, the spreading about of objects in the bombers' paths, that he lost his bearings and started out in the wrong direction. The all-clear sounded and he became aware of aeroplanes circling above as if looking for somewhere to land.

He stopped, identified them as RAF and tried to count how many were coming in, too many perhaps for the undamaged part of the landing field. Figures were already running across the grass and behind them a single lorry loaded with debris to fill in the holes. Some of the figures were women, WAAFs, seen in the canteen and offices, driving transport, and now emerging from shelters to help restore the airfield.

It was perfectly clear what had happened: an unexpected raid flying in under the radar, planes scrambled but too late for some to get airborne and probably too late to catch any invaders. The result: the airfield smashed, in shambles and who knows how many dead.

Uncertain which way to go, Eddie set off once again for where his Spitfire usually rested. As he walked across the airfield where men and women worked with grey, shocked faces against a background of crimson flame and purple smoke, he had a curious sense of invisibility. It seemed as if he had not only betrayed those he cared about most but also cut himself off from them so completely that they could not even see him.

It was fresher on the outskirts of the airfield, the smell of burning petrol less enveloping. And there, standing quite as usual were Jenkins and Jones. Eddie hesitated. A Spitfire was coming in nearby. He turned to watch it land, bumping dangerously over holes but, almost miraculously, missing the biggest which would have tipped her nose over a tail in an instant. Jenkins and Jones watched too until she slowed to a standstill, then ran over. Eddie recognised his own plane. His kills marked on the side with the RAF insignia.

The pilot pushed back the cockpit cover and leaned out. He began to vomit violently. Jenkins stood back until he'd finished, then helped him out, lifting off his goggles gently.

'You did well, sir.' He yelled above the noise.

Eddie didn't recognise the pilot's face and, even from where he stood, could see his legs were shaking as if he might fall.

Eddie walked over slowly. For a moment he thought he would remain invisible but then Jones saluted, 'Afternoon, sir.' The irony was cool and cutting. 'Missed the show, did you, sir.' Then he went to the plane.

The young pilot, still held up by Jenkins who was stripping him of his parachute, didn't seem to notice anyone much.

'You're all right, sir,' said Jenkins either in reassurance or as a question.

'One minute he was there in front,' gasped the pilot, 'joking to me over the radio that I'd be up for a DFC on my first sortie, the next he'd gone. So quick, just a flash, I couldn't believe it. Then I heard his voice, his screams, his...' He broke off. 'I only saw a flash, like a red torch in the corner of my eye. It was the screaming... over the radio... into my ears – on and on... It's in my ears now...'

'Come on, sir,' encouraged Jenkins, as the pilot stammered distress without words.

This time the young man responded and, looking round, took a deep breath. He stood straighter before saying in a quite different voice, 'Plane's okay, I think.' He saw Eddie. As did Jenkins.

'Afternoon, sir,' he said in exactly the same voice as Jones. 'This is Flight Lieutenant William White. Arrived midday in the nick of time. Took the plane up like an old pro.' He didn't attempt to introduce Eddie.

The pilot's face was pale and smooth as a girl's.

'Who was the pilot who went down?' Eddie calmly asked the pilot.

'Andy. He was called Andy. I don't know his surname. I only knew him an hour or less but...'

Eddie turned quickly and walked away. He didn't want them to see the absolute horror which must show on his face. He stood on his own trying to control the shaking that threatened to take over his whole body. He would have liked to lie on the ground and howl.

All for one and one for all! So much for that bit of romance. Andy becomes a human torch while Hank muddles about whether to go back to America or not and he, Eddie Chaffey, fearless Spitfire fighter, takes a kip in his mother's garden.

Ignoring the chaos all around, Eddie went looking for the Wing Commander. Having his wings ripped off his shoulders, the pilot's biggest punishment and worst fear, seemed of little importance. It was only what he deserved. He remembered the look on Jenkins' face.

There were three buildings left standing on the airfield. In one of them the Wing Commander sat at his desk as if all was usual. However, when Eddie knocked and entered at his 'come', he put a hand to his head wearily.

'Oh, God.'

'Sir.' There was nothing to say.

'Everything depends on getting things up and running.' The Wing Commander who encouraged his pilots to call him Les, continued. 'I can't deal with you now.'

'No, sir.' Eddie turned to leave.

As he reached the door Les spoke again, 'If you were in the Army, you'd be shot.' There was exasperation but no rancour in his voice.

'Yes, sir'.

'But the Army runs hundreds of thousands of men and we only have a few hundred. Come back here.'

Eddie came back.

'Sit down.'

Eddie sat down, still holding his cap; he didn't expect to be there long.

'I heard about Andy. In your section, wasn't he?'

Eddie heard the past tense with sickening dread. There was no hope of expecting him back. Burning men don't return. He pictured the young pilot vomiting over the side of the plane. 'Yes, sir. We trained together.'

'A new pilot got your plane out of the way. Couldn't do much more.' Les looked at Eddie questioningly, 'I suppose you're going to blame yourself for Andy.'

'I wasn't with him. I'd buggered off.'

'Bloody fool on all counts. You, not him. If you want to do something useful and a bit of penance, write to his parents.'

'I didn't know his parents.'

Les looked angry for the first time. 'Nor did I and I'm writing to them. Say something nice, if that's in your nature.'

'Sorry, sir.'

'That's a start. Now get back on the job.'

There was a knock at the door. Eddie stood up as a face blackened presumably by smoke, appeared round the door. 'You're wanted, sir. Two reserve planes flying in.'

The face left. Les reached for his cap, then opened a drawer in his desk and took out a bottle and two small glasses. He poured and handed a glass to Eddie while raising his own, 'To our brave pilots!'

Eddie raised his glass too but couldn't speak. He felt tears in his eyes.

Les put away the glasses and bottle. 'Best way to remember Andy is by shooting down Jerry.' He stood up. 'Incidentally, where did your bunk take you?' He came round from behind the desk.

'Home,' said Eddie.

Les clapped him on the shoulders. 'They all say that. Now get out there before the Luftwaffe's back to finish the job.'

✂

The Luftwaffe did come back – twice more. Eddie who had believed his life as a flyer had ended at the same time as Andy's, found himself with no time for such considerations. Jenkins seemed to share this approach as he handed him up to the cockpit, draped the parachute round him and made sure he was properly buckled in. Perhaps his face was a little more impassive than usual but whenever did either of them show emotion as they sent him off? All the same, he'd felt the warmth. 'It's just another job.' That was the message their faces conveyed now.

'See you in an hour, sir.'

Eddie himself did not change his tactics. Men who became reckless did not last long. He wasn't put in the Number Two spot on either operation – perhaps a small punishment. But it pleased him, leaving him free to chase after his prey. He was surprised to find just how cool he felt, not a tremor as his finger pressed the trigger. He took a dive under his adversary, so close he could see the scratches on its blue belly. Sometimes in the past, in the middle of a fight, if it went on for more than a few minutes, he found his knees knocking uncontrollably, even though his head seemed clear. Now his mind and body felt in tune with each other and with the Spitfire too. It was no surprise to see two

139

aircraft spin away from him to the ground. He didn't even stay to watch.

The first time he flew back to the airfield for refuelling, not one bomber had got through but there were still flames flickering round a couple of buildings. Jenkins handed him out silently.

On the second occasion, the bombers had again been deflected and the only casualty was a herd of cows and a cow-girl bringing them into milk. The airfield seemed astonishingly calm, all the craters roughly filled and a new hangar being erected.

Jenkins nodded at Eddie, 'Good job, sir.'

Jones patted the side of the Spitfire, 'Not a scratch. How many, sir?'

Eddie took off his gauntlet and held up two fingers. He had been forgiven.

The long summer's day at last gave up to a glowing sunset which suggested perfect flying – bombing – weather the next day. Although it was unlikely they would be called out again that evening, Eddie went over to the Dispersal Hut and found a deckchair outside. Oddly, the area had escaped the bombing. Other pilots came, with cigarettes, a newspaper, cards. Whether by chance or design, none sat near him. Eddie was glad of it.

He tried to write a letter to Andy's parents in his head but soon realised it was impossible. Miserably, he remembered their last evening together when he'd told him to go back to Birmingham. It didn't seem like a joke any more. The next morning he and Hank had left with only a scribbled note to explain, 'See you later if you survive.' Another joke.

What could he tell his parents? There was no hurry, at least, because the Wing Commander and probably the Squadron Leader would write with the news. His exhausted mind wandered and he found himself thinking that Andy should never have been a pilot at all. If he'd stayed on the obvious pathway for him he'd have been a rigger or fitter like Jones or Jenkins and would probably be alive now. He jerked further awake as he realised, with shame, that was to demean Andy's talent as a pilot. It struck him then that he might pay his parents a visit on his next leave instead of writing. The idea calmed him.

As the light turned to purples and blues, the order came to stand down and the pilots began to drift away – no transport so they were walking to their quarters. Philip, an older pilot who Eddie considered dull, came over to him, 'Sorry about Andy.'

'Thanks.' Philip moved on. What did one say? With so much death around, Eddie had never been given special mourning rights before. It made him agitated again, almost angry. No one should try and sum up Andy in a few words of sympathy, even if they were heartfelt.

A second younger pilot, Doug, came strolling by. He nodded at Eddie, 'Bad show about Andy. I'll be at The Barley Mow later.'

'Thanks.' This was better. A road-map for a public future: the pub.

With still some light in the sky, Eddie got into his car. He soon found himself giving a lift to Doug, Ernie and Willie the new young pilot. 'Some wheels!' shouted Doug, 'Where've you been hiding them, old chap?'

Eddie knew about this. He'd been part of it when someone had died: the effort to carry on, be cheerful, help the man closest to the dead pilot to be cheerful too or at least not be maudlin. It had seemed perfectly natural, and necessary, but now he saw it was more complicated because it depended on co-operation and trust from the one who was shocked and mourning. 'What this old banger needs,' he shouted, 'is a fitter and rigger.' He was glad to get a shout of laughter.

It was harder to pretend in The Barley Mow. He didn't want to talk and he didn't want to get drunk. He did his best to display the expected high spirits but after an hour, he stood up, 'Need to make a telephone call.' Doubtless they were relieved to see him go.

⋙

Hank was watching Angela undress. The lights were low, the curtain silky over the blackout, the bed behind them large.

'However did you get this room? I'm told Savoy bedrooms are guarded like chests of gold.'

Angela who had just stepped out of her dress, didn't answer. She wore a salmon pink slip, heavily embroidered in cream. Her breasts swelled above it.

Hank forced himself to sit still on the chair. It was what she wanted: admiration, desire. The actual sex that followed came with more reservations, 'I do not want a baby. Prophylactics are dreadfully off-putting.' He hoped it would be different on this night. She had come all the way to find him, to seduce him home.

Angela lifted the edge of her slip and undid the suspenders one by one. The silk stocking slivered down her thigh. She turned to the other leg.

They loved each other, of course. Just as important they understood each other. She understood his restlessness, the riches-to-rags, rags-to-riches family history which made him insecure and volatile. His English friends, even Eddie, didn't understand that; they just saw a well-connected Yank from the most powerful and prosperous country in the world.

'Do you want to take off my slip?'

Obediently, Hank stood up and eased it over her head. He kissed her neck under the heavy blonde hair.

'Now sit down again.'

Angela pretended this show was for him and it certainly made his body excited enough but his mind was too tired for games. She didn't understand that. Nor had she travelled to England just for him. Over dinner, she had described her busy day following up an assignment from *Philadelphia Observer* to write about the wives of England. She had already interviewed a politician's wife, a fireman's wife and the wife of a serving soldier. Tomorrow she had lined up the wives of a naval captain and of a farmer whose husbands had been called up. Angela took a step towards him, posed in her pink bra and cami-knickers, raised her arms above her head, twisted sideways. She was as beautiful as any film star.

He had been surprised and relieved by how little she'd asked him about his life as a pilot. But then she wanted him to leave it behind which he would, wouldn't he? She had made him feel ridiculous, quixotic, not serious. 'If there was an American squadron, that's another thing. Or if we come into the war. But now, darling, it makes you seem, let's face it, crazy in not a good way.'

'Darling!' He stood up, still fully dressed.

There was a knock on the door. Automatically, he turned to it.

Angela pouted in protest, 'Henry'. She put her hands on her breasts and squeezed them.

No-one called him 'Henry' any more. 'What is it?'

'Bell boy, sir. With a message.'

'Put it under the door.'

A piece of paper slid under the door.

'Oh, Henry.' Angela sat on the edge of the bed and crossed her legs.

Hank unfolded the paper. He read the words while one part of him remained concentrated on Angela and what they would do next.

'*Andy copped it. Eddie.*'

Hank went to Angela, pushed her gently backwards, and kissed her. He unclasped her bra, slid down her knickers and felt all over her soft, sweet body. Quickly, he took off his own clothes.

He held her close then raised her enough so that she could lie above him he pulled her down, pushing her legs apart.

She hesitated a moment, then seemed to make up her mind.

It was too quick, thought Hank, after all those years of waiting. Angela lay beside him, slowly stroking his face. Even if it had been quick, it had been good and he was grateful to her. She got out of the bed and went to the bathroom.

Hank realised he didn't want her to come back to him. It was a sobering thought considering he'd just decided to go back to America with her. It struck him for the first time that the RAF might not let him go so easily. They have invested a lot of training in him, even if he was an American citizen.

Angela returned, wound in a towel, and sat near him. 'I gave myself a douche. We don't want a baby until after we're married.'

'No,' murmured Hank, with his head still on the pillow. 'Perhaps I feel as I do because my mother was British.'

'I suppose that is some explanation.' She sounded unconvinced.

'I was ten when she died.'

Angela said nothing. She took off the towel and got into bed. 'I'm so tired after the flight.'

'Yes,' agreed Hank, thinking she didn't know about real tiredness. He wondered how Andy had died. They lay together quietly. 'One of my section died today. A friend. That was the note. 'I'll have to go back to the base tomorrow.'

'I know that. You'll have to extricate yourself from the RAF. I'm sorry about your colleague.' She touched his chest, moved her hand down. 'Do you want to again?'

Hank thought, that's very generous of her when she'd have all the trouble of a second douche. 'I'm exhausted.' He thought hers might not be generosity but desperation.

'You've had a shock,' she said.

'Someone gets killed most days.'

'Not always a friend.'

That wasn't the only point; he didn't want to argue now. How more important was a friend than a friend's friend? The friend of a friend of a friend? It was true that someone on the base was killed most days.

'I need to try and sleep. I'll be up at five but I'll try not to wake you.' He kissed her warm shoulder. 'Thank you, darling, for everything.'

He did sleep for a couple of hours and woke feeling sorry for Angela. He could not go back home with her. He put out his hand and touched her cheek; it was wet, Could she cry in her sleep?

He decided not to wait till five and got up, washed, dressed quickly and left the room.

As he closed the door, Angela sat up and said 'Good luck, darling.'

Capwell put down the cup of tea and said in his usual voice, 'Four-thirty, sir.' Footsteps receded. They came back. Eddie kept his eyes closed. Another cup of tea was put down. 'And you, sir. Good morning, sir.'

Eddie opened his eyes. Willie, the new pilot had been put in Andy's bed. Andy had always been up and away long before Capwell brought tea. Willie's bedclothes were pulled over his head. With that attitude, he'd never last.

Eddie put out a long leg. 'Come on, old man. The local ale's not that bad.'

Capwell watched tolerantly from the door. 'Give him a chance, sir.'

'That's just what we pilots don't have.' Eddie sat up, stretched and yawned. He'd slept better than he expected. It struck him that if you can survive the death of one of your closest friends, plus a fair amount of guilt, then nothing much else can get you. Capwell left the room. The electric light hanging from the ceiling cast a greenish light in the darkness.

'You'll feel better once you're up. Here.' Eddie pulled back the bedclothes and thrust a cup at Willie's face. Obediently he sat up and drank.

Eddie went to the wash basin. That was enough molly-coddling for one morning. He looked forward to getting to the Mess, seeing the old faces, not talking much, waiting for transport, then to Dispersal, waiting time while the light spread across the airfield – they'd done a great job getting it up and running – then the telephone ringing and off to the good old Spitfire with Jenkins and Jones in attendance. No point in thinking about the rest – what will be will be – but he'd be up in that vast beautiful sky with the perfect machine in his hands. You couldn't ask for more than that.

CHAPTER SEVENTEEN
August 1940

Valtraud called up to Eva, 'A man at the door for you!'

Her accent had improved, Eva noted. Time was passing. She put down her brush and was about to take off her overall when she pictured herself greeting her visitor whoever he was in a paint-stained overall. Then she thought, how childish, and pulled it over her head.

It was Jack who stood at the open front door.

'So you're back from Dorset.' To Eva's surprise, Jack had grabbed at Sylvia's plan for him. Eva was conscious of Valtraud hanging round the staircase. Recently she'd showed signs of wanting to play mother. Jack wore a black beret and a belted mackintosh which made him look like a French painter.

'I'm in Oxford to fix a few things. Can I come in?'

'My father's not well. He's in bed.'

'I want to show you something.'

'Will it take long?' It didn't really matter how long it took. It was not one of the days when she'd allowed Betty (back in her life for want of anyone else) to persuade her into helping with toddlers' groups while their mothers worked in factories.

'You'll need your bike. It's out near Cowley.'

'Cowley's where the factories are.'

'I thought you'd be interested,' said Jack impatiently.

'You haven't told me what it is.'

'You'll see when we get there.'

⋙

Jack threw down his bicycle and spread his arms wide. 'Just look!'

Eva held on to her bicycle for support. They were standing on the edge of a vast unending dump. At first, she assumed it the wrecked detritus of modern life but as she focused more clearly, she saw every piece of metal, however tortured and twisted into macabre shape, was part of an aeroplane. 'It's a graveyard,' she said. She saw propellers, blown apart like dandelions, a wheel crowning a jagged point or flattened under a still shining flank. A nose peered out from under a mountain of metal. Wings, attached to nothing clung to each other, rising upwards into a deformed pyramid. 'I hate it!' she cried.

Jack didn't seem to hear her. He was staring as if mesmerised. 'Do you see?' he spoke in a reverential voice. 'They're making waves. Waves of metal, beautiful waves in a rough sea. I've already made some sketches. I wanted to share it with you.'

Eva looked and saw his waves but she also saw swastikas, black and white slashes, even in their death throws, frightening, and elsewhere the colourful circles of the RAF. 'There were men in there!' she whispered. 'Human beings died in your beautiful waves of metal!'

Jack turned to her, his face almost comical in its lack of understanding. Then he understood. 'Of course! The whole place is a memorial to the dead. My picture will be a memorial to the dead.' He came over to Eva and put his arms round her.

She held on to him. He must be right. He was a true artist who would create something lasting out of this horror. She was just a silly girl who reacted with her emotions, who thought about one individual, Eddie, asleep on a bench, flying in the tumult of the clouds. She'd lost all sense of something wider. More important. More lasting. Tears began to trickle down her cheeks. She wiped them away angrily.

'I'm so sorry. How stupid of me.' Jack held her gently.

Eva wept harder. Jack was so kind, so clever, so tolerant, so imaginative. He was able to interpret this grim life while she allowed herself to be submerged.

Jack looked over her head at the metal, shadows changing now as the sun rose. He had his sketchbook, a small paint-box, brush and a jar of water in a canvas bag slung over his shoulder. It was irresistible. He put Eva aside and opened his bag.

Eva watched. Gradually her tears stopped.

Jack sat on the grass at the edge of the dump and Eva sat beside him. After a while, she asked, 'Can you spare me a piece of paper and a pencil?'

He handed them over frowning. Eva began to scribble but it was all such a mess and she was far too impatient to untangle it.

She stood up and climbed down to the bottom of the metal mountain range. Close to, she saw the sharp edges, like guillotines raised to the sky. The danger of one falling, slicing through her body – off with her head! – made her heart beat faster. Perhaps Jack wouldn't care; he'd just put her in his picture, like the one he'd painted of the planes above Portland. He might be thrilled that the flowing scarlet blood gave a lift to all that hard grey.

Eva stroked a smooth piece of panel and touched lightly its torn edge. A slight roughness caught her finger and a pinpoint of blood appeared. She put it into her mouth. To her left there was a jagged-edged shard, like a vicious sword, or the teeth of a vast shark. She couldn't think how Jack had turned these vicious remnants into beautiful waves. There was nothing beautiful here, only memories of a hideous death. But Jack was staying at a distance, making charming patterns, noting the light and the shadows. Whatever he might say about 'a memorial' was a sham. This here in front of her, this sharp-toothed fang which tore apart its occupants and blew them into the sky, that was the real truth.

Eva flung up her arm in protest and whether purposefully or by chance, caught it on the serrated metal. She gave a cry. Blood welled out and ran down her bare arm. Far more then seemed reasonable. In a moment it had reached the white blouse at her elbow and soaked it red.

For the first time since the conversation with her father, she allowed herself to imagine how her mother had died – if she'd died – whether she'd been tortured, killed maliciously or by some accident or even by her own hand, protecting some of those secrets. Standing there in the macabre graveyard, with blood spreading through her blouse and to her heart, seemed an appropriate time to think of her mother.

'Eva! Eva! What's happened!' Jack's voice, high-pitched with fear interrupted her thoughts.

She glanced at him casually, watched him slide down towards her, take her by the shoulders. Under the bright sun, his face was pale and stricken. 'I had an accident,' she said.

He led her up, found a clean rag in his bag, and tightly bound her arm.

'I'm fine really,' she said. She heard a faint mewing high above her and, screwing up her eyes, spotted two large birds, wings spread wide as they slowly circled.

Jack followed her gaze. 'Buzzards. There're a whole lot in Dorset. You need stitches. We've got to get you to hospital. But you can't ride a bike.'

'No,' agreed Eva. She had never felt so calm. The blood was still moving under the makeshift bandage but not so fast.

'I'll wheel you to the road on my bike, then flag down a car.'

'I hope no-one steals mine,' said Eva. 'They might think it was part of the dump.'

It took nearly two hours to get to the hospital and when they arrived the doctor was busy. A nurse re-bandaged the arm and they waited in a small room.

'What happened?' asked Jack as he had at the beginning.

'I don't know.' Eva looked away from him. 'But I feel better for it.'

'What a ridiculous thing to say!' Jack was so shocked his face flushed deep red.

'Don't you ever feel weird that horrible things are going on all around us and we're quite comfortably doing what we like.'

'I suppose you mean because I'm not a soldier. But you know I'm going to be a teacher, in a school where they'll be little children as well as older ones. Teachers are essential if the next generation are to make less of a mess of things than this one.' Beginning on the defensive, Jack sounded angry at the end.

'I was thinking of myself.' Eva's arm was beginning to hurt badly and she didn't want any more discussion with Jack. 'I'd like to be quiet, please.'

Jack went away and marched up and down.

When the doctor came, old and kind, he lifted up her good right arm saying, 'I hope you're right-handed.'

'Oh, yes.'

'That's lucky.'

But when he heard how she'd done it he became gruffer and told her she'd need a tetanus injection and clearly wanted to say she should have known better than to climb around that dump. Instead he merely grunted, 'Enough people have suffered there already.'

He does understand, decided Eva, even if he's too rushed to think about it. 'I'm sorry,' she said several times but she wasn't really. She was glad to feel pain, even if her suffering was so small compared to others. Compared to whatever had happened to her mother or might happen to Eddie. Perhaps at this moment he was lying in a mangled plane just like the one that had cut her.

≫≪

Hank said very little to Eddie about his day in London. Nor did either of them talk about Andy. He was gone. What more was there to say? Two days later, their squadron leader, Sean, was gone. It was rumoured that he had been too close to France, been shot down, parachuted into the sea, before being picked up by a German boat. He might be dead or a POW. Either way, he was gone. Not as gone, possibly, as Andy. Sean had been a nice man and a good leader so they hoped he was a POW. But, even then, he might be wounded or burned or blind. It was better to stick with gone.

Eddie and Hank were either flying, waiting to fly, hanging out in the Mess or trying to sleep. Against the odds, their airfield was not bombed again, although reports of other airfields were grim. The talk was that German tactics had changed to more bombing and less fighting but it didn't seem to make much difference to them. At least one front-line airfield had been closed after it had been smashed to pieces four or five times. The lesson was learnt that if you were too near the coast, there was not enough time for the fighters to get up and score a hit.

The pilots talked about such things in the mess, lying back in their chairs, pretending to relax. One man disappeared. They all knew he'd lost his nerve and felt glad their squadron leader hadn't pulled off his wings and made him scrub the bogs, as had happened in one squadron, according to rumour. In the couple of days before his disappearance he'd chattered excitedly about the Nazi menace and the heroic Englishmen so that the Mess had withdrawn from his chair. Too much talk was always a bad sign. When a new intake came in, they always talked too much for the first few days, until they settled in. Every day was like a week, each short flight, a day. Like automatons, they woke to their tea, walked to the Mess, got on the Transport, waited at Dispersal, ran to their Spitfires – *charged* to their Spitfires.

It was only in the air that they felt truly alive, all senses alert, their finger on the button, their eyes darting all around, their feet braced against the bar.

Eddie and Hank were still friends even if they were often silent together; they sat nearby in the Mess and on their deckchairs outside. They looked out for each other but without Andy, they felt incomplete; it was easier to be part of the wider group.

Then Hank caught an eye infection. His eyes went bright red. 'I can see fine,' he assured everyone. 'I've always had sensitive eyes. It doesn't mean anything.' But the CO arranged an appointment with a specialist in London. 'A pilot flies with his eyes,' he told him, 'A fighter pilot needs the eyes of an eagle not a rheumy old man's.'

Hank quoted this to Eddie who looked round the room. 'We all look like rheumy old men.' It was true that they were slumped forward or back, scarcely able to tap the ash off their cigarettes. They seldom went into The Barley Mow now.

'Maybe it will rain tomorrow,' said Eddie. Hank's red eyes stared at him and Eddie felt compelled to ask more. 'You never really told me how it worked out with Angela?'

'She's still in London, writing a series for a paper back home about wives in war-time. It could run and run.'

'Does she still think you might go back?'

Hank drew up his legs so he perched on the edge of his chair. He might have been in a cockpit. 'I guess I'm here for the duration, even if I can't fight just now.'

'You'll be able to see Angela now.' Eddie felt tired and incurious to hear more.

'She's good in bed. Or rather she's got a terrific body. She's worked out that's her best means of attack.' Hank shut his hot eyes for a moment, 'That's unfair. She's clever and strong and she loves me. We love each other. Have done for years. But I'm only in London for the day.' He paused. 'Can you give me your Dorset address?'

Eddie was surprised. 'Why?'

'I've been meaning to write and thank your mother. For having me to stay. Your place got under my skin.'

'I don't like to think of that day.'

'No. Sorry. Seems an age ago. You couldn't have saved Andy wherever you were.'

'Maybe not. But I'd have been with him. I'd have tried. Is it the devil who has red eyes?'

'I'll ask the consultant tomorrow.' Hank stood up. 'Good hunting. I'll see you in the evening.'

Hank did not come back in the evening. The consultant was unhappy with his eyes and almost everything about his physical condition. Hank tried to explain that all the pilots were in much the same shape, bar the red eyes, and that, if they were all grounded, you might as well invite Herr Hitler to bring a flotilla across the Channel.

The consultant, also tired out, faced with this large American reached for philosophy, 'The graveyard is filled with indispensable people.'

To Hank, trying not to rub his eyes which had begun to itch, this was a practical truth he'd seen every day on the airfield. Pilots were indispensable and they or their smashed bits and pieces lay in all kinds of graveyards but very seldom with a headstone.

He telephoned Angela and went along meekly to the hospital.

Eddie found he missed Hank, another man gone, even if temporarily. On the day he left, Eddie had his nearest escape. He was leading blue section when they found themselves confronted by a formation of more than a hundred German planes. Other squadrons came to join them but the odds were still eight to one and some of the English pilots were employing the tactic of head-on attack, which was almost suicidal and very dangerous in such a crowded sky for everybody if planes collided. Eddie had always considered it a crude method of attack, even if it did require a good deal of skill and daring negotiating the last-second pull away.

It was a game of chicken in the sky, while he preferred the subtler unwinding of a duel. But this time the Dorniers were forming a great circle in the sky, round and round, each covering the other's tail and something had to be done to break them up.

'I'm going in!' He shouted into his radio above the screech and whine of other battles.

'Good luck, Eddie.' He hardly noticed the response from Mike, his second.

He'd done it before: dive straight through, lure a plane after you, fight or flee, leave the circle open for others behind him to pick up a target. But this time, because there were so many planes involved, just as he dived, a plane from the other squadron did the same, as bad luck would have it, in much the same place.

They smashed apart the circle alright but were heading for each at over 300mph. Eddie pulled up as the other man pulled up, then down as he went down. They seemed drawn together in some kind of magnetic dance of death. Eddie saw the man's face, a mirror of his own, distorted with effort. Their wings brushed, a moment of friction which he felt like a shiver through his body, then, suddenly, he was untied, free to carry on. He even got a burst in on a Dornier five minutes later.

But it had been close and left a mark on him. Also on his Spitfire.

'What have you been doing with your wing, sir?' grumbled Jones when Eddie landed. 'Might need more than tonight to put that right.'

'Talk about the bloody enemy. It was one of our own, from Tangmere, I think.'

'Don't do to be brought down by your own. What was he, a young'un?'

Eddie got bored of the conversation. 'It was just bad luck.' After all, he was only twenty himself. 'Do what you can for the old girl.'

'Yes, sir!'

The airfield was filling up with returning aircraft. He had given up counting them in or looking for spaces. The news came soon enough. With such a force of invaders, there were sure to be high losses.

The sun had already dropped behind the horizon but still threw brilliant ribbons of colour across the sky which brightened the grass and made the aeroplanes glow. Eddie walked over to Dispersal. Although it was unlikely they'd be sent up again, they had to wait to be officially stood down. Besides, he felt like watching the sunset. He chose a deckchair a little way apart, pulled it round to face west and sank down. He could feel the sweat drying on his skin, his face tightening. Perhaps because of his near miss or the awesome extravagance of the sky – yellow, apricot, crimson, purple, navy – he found himself thinking of Andy or at least his habit of humming at the critical moments of a fight. He had liked the sound of it, a cheery, no-nonsense sound, like the man himself. But Willy had described Andy screaming as he went down in flames. The Lord hadn't preserved that servant. The thing was he couldn't imagine Andy screaming: humming louder and louder, yes; shouting imprecations, yes; but not a victim's screaming.

The sky was scarcely darkening but the balance had changed, more lime and lemon, muddy pinks, diffused violets. The lines were blurring, the ribbons winding into each other.

Willie had probably got it wrong. Poor chap was on his first flight, first day and hadn't a clue what was going on, saw a man going down in flames and, quite understandably imagined he heard screaming. But he could have got it wrong; it might even have been someone screaming in victory. People made the oddest whoops and squeals in the height of battle.

Eyes still fixed on the sky, Eddie determined that Andy had been humming as he went down, or maybe even singing, 'When you wish upon a star makes no difference who you are ...'

The night was rising now, overwhelming the sunset colours with a thick greyish-purple. Eddie smiled; Andy was out there somewhere, singing still. Humming. The Ops controller put his head round the door of the Dispersal. 'You're off, gentlemen. Wheels on their way for those with buckled knees.'

Eddie walked slowly across the dark airfield. He was due leave in a few days and he would use the time to visit Andy's parents.

≫≪

'I'm so glad you're up again, Father,' said Eva, entering Dr. Speke's study with a smile. She'd just had a note from Eddie: '*I'm going to Birmingham in a few days. Why don't you come along. We'll drive if I can steal enough petrol ...*' She knew it by heart already.

'Come in. Shut the door.' Professor Speke seemed nonplussed by his daughter. Perhaps he was surprised by her youth or her beauty or perhaps her resemblance to her mother.

'Shall I stand?' asked Eva gaily. 'Do your students stand?' She was surprised by how wild was her father's white hair and how long and bony his face. He wouldn't look very different dead, she thought cruelly.

The Professor coughed and plunged in recklessly, 'Valtraud tells me you were picked up by a man, stayed away the entire afternoon and came back with your arm in a sling. It's still in a sling, I see,' he added rather piteously.

Eva felt sorry for him. 'It's healing so quickly. Only a scratch really. I can't think why the doctor insisted on a sling. Look, I can take it out, no problem.' Eva took out her arm which was bandaged and waved it in the air.

The Professor gave what appeared to be a groan. 'Do sit down.'

'But Papa, what is the matter? You never worry about me.' Eva did not sit down.

'Tell me, how did you acquire your wound?'

'I fell off my bike.' Eva opened her eyes wide which if her father had known her better, he'd have recognised as the sign of a lie.

'I see. Yes.' He put his hands together on the desk.

'People fall off their bikes all the time.'

The Professor resisted putting his head in his hands. He knew he had forgotten something. 'The man, who was the man, Eva? At your age,' he paused, struggling to remember her age. Eva did not help him. Another reckless plunge. 'Who is this man?'

'Oh, that's easy. He's a teacher from the Ruskin who gives me occasional private tutoring. Free. He's very kind. He wants to meet you but you were unwell. He's called Mr. Halliwell and one of his paintings has been bought by the War Artists' Advisory Committee. We bicycled out to a particular landscape he believed would inspire me.'

Eva decided to sit down. She felt that she had answered all questions satisfactorily and now they could be comfortable again. But the Professor was not comfortable. He leant forward.

'This is no life for you. I'm writing to your Cousin Phoebe to see if she will have you to stay with her in Scotland. She has several children, perhaps four or five, and her husband is away in the East so I'm sure she'll be glad of help.'

For a good minute Eva sat silent. All her confidence vanished. Once more she was a child or, worse still, a piece of baggage to be disposed of as convenient.

'I don't know Cousin Phoebe,' she said eventually in a wavering voice.

'She's my cousin's daughter who married into a Scottish family. She sends me a Christmas card each year.'

Obviously he didn't know her either. Eva tried to marshal her defences: the Ruskin, Betty's toddlers, her role as a companion to her father. But her heart was not in it. By the Professor's anxious, even guilty expression, his wasn't either.

'We'll wait and see how Cousin Phoebe reacts to my letter.'

Eva went back to her studio room and took up Eddie's letter. It seemed even more significant now, a summons from the world outside. '*We've hardly seen each other and now we'll have a whole day together.*'

CHAPTER EIGHTEEN
August 1940

The Commanding Officer looked at Eddie sitting the other side of the desk. He had grown rather fond of him since his brief AWOL and he noticed sadly that Eddie's hands were shaking and he had a twitch in one eye. It was the end of another eighteen-hour day. He had not yet heard how many men and aircraft they'd lost.

'So you're going to see Andy's parents after all. His father works in the Post Office.'

'Yes, sir.'

'You certainly deserve your leave. Get some sleep.'

'I'll try, sir.'

The CO, who was just fifty but often felt ninety when faced with twenty year-old pilots who looked fifty, sat back in his chair. 'Good. Good.' A thought struck him. 'Birmingham, isn't it?' He opened his drawer in what seemed to be a reflex action and took out glasses and the bottle of whisky. He poured out two substantial shots and pushed one towards Eddie, 'Cheers!' He smiled. It was so seldom he could give pleasure; it was one desperate assignment after another. 'I've been asked to get a Tiger Moth two-seater up there. You can fly it can't you?'

'I trained on it, sir.'

'There you are then. First light tomorrow. I'll give you a bit of paper to make it official.'

⬦

It took Eva nearly two hours to bicycle to the Oxford University Squadron airfield. Her arm was mostly healed but felt weak so she rested often, looking up at the bright sky. She imagined Eddie flying over her head like a giant bird and soon she would be up there with him. After his telephone call the night before about their change from wheels to wings, she'd laid awake all night, watching the clock, watching the black curtain that wouldn't remind her when it was dawn, listening to her heart throbbing.

The airfield was on the main road but there was no sign and she might have ridden past except that suddenly an aeroplane really was above her head, circling round and round, dropping lower all the time. Stopped, although still astride her bike, she stared upwards and, to her delight, there was Eddie's face, blonde hair flying, leaning over and grinning at her. The plane whisked over a hedge and disappeared.

Eva rushed after it, pushing her bike through a gateway just in time to see Eddie jumping out. She dropped her bike and ran towards him.

'Ace timing!' he yelled.

Eva was even more astonished by the sight in front of her. From the way Eddie wrote about his plane, in an almost awestruck way, she had imagined that it would be huge and very obviously a modern machine, but this one, with four wings, two per side, reminded her of a child's toy.

Eddie hugged Eva. She looked so pretty with her dark hair loose about her and her face flushed with all the bicycling and running. 'I'm not supposed to be here,' he said, 'We can't stay long.' He led her towards the plane, still talking. 'I heard the field wasn't being used. So, hey presto! Your personalised air service. It's a Tiger Moth. Needed in Birmingham. We'll get this parachute on you, then you can hop in the back. You'll find helmet, goggles, straps. I'll help you fix them.'

Eva was far too excited to say anything but did what Eddie told her, looking up into his face as she finally sat in the seat and he pulled the leather helmet over her hair and clicked her belt.

Leaning over her attentively – everything must be just right – Eddie was reminded of Jenkins and felt a sudden rush of tenderness for the girl sitting there with her bright face.

The flight to Oxford, short enough, had been weirdly enjoyable because he was flying away from the usual paths of the enemy. In fact, the only other plane was an RAF spotter who flew round him in a baffled way so that Eddie felt compelled to perform a victory roll, strictly forbidden in Buzzard Squadron.

He had remembered what it had felt like to be free and flying before the war and, although the spotter had gone, he performed a few more acrobatics. The Tiger Moth was no Spitfire but it rose to the challenge nobly, took him back to when he had flown from this very airport and had nothing more pressing on his mind than where he'd get his next drink. Could that really be scarcely over a year ago?

He glanced back at Eva, sitting there so trustfully,

'Right! You OK?'

Eva nodded and smiled. She thought she was putting her life in Eddie's hands and wanted to laugh.

'We can communicate through this speaker,' said Eddie and Eva nodded again. She thought of asking if they were likely to meet enemy planes but she didn't care.

Eddie jumped down, swung the propeller, jumped into his own seat, put on his own leather helmet, and soon they were off, bumping along the grass, before swooping upwards.

The morning was still fresh, the sun spreading slowly all around them so that Eva felt as if she was at the centre of heavenly rays. The air rushing by the open cockpit seemed filled with benign energy. She saw Eddie lift a hand to his face and realised he had removed his goggles. She quickly did the same. Now everything felt even closer, more thrilling.

'It's amazing!' she shrieked.

'It's a biplane,' shouted Eddie.

'Four wings and two people,' giggled Eva. The giggles turned to laughter. 'Why didn't you tell me how *glorious* flying is!'

Eddie smiled but didn't answer. He was plotting their journey to Birmingham on a map, following roads and villages. The RAF airfield was close to the city and he didn't want to overshoot. At least he was on the expected route now. That spotter plane might have reported him, if he had nothing better to do. The Tiger Moth had no radio connections so he was out of reach till he landed.

All too soon, the airfield appeared below. Eddie circled lower.

'We're coming in!' he shouted.

'But we've only just set off!' yelled Eva.

Eddie looked at his fuel gauge: very little left. Perhaps the CO hadn't fully trusted him. How tempting it would have been to fly to Scotland or Dorset!

'No fuel to go further.'

Eva didn't answer. She was extracting every last moment of joy from this flight. Unsurprising, that 'flight' also meant 'escape'.

They were near enough to see the carroty hair of a man guiding the plane in. I'm coming back to earth, thought Eva, but I still have Eddie.

Eddie made a perfect landing, rolling up to the signaller's feet.

'Got a passenger, sir?' The man stared at Eva who had taken off her helmet and was shaking out her hair.

Eddie grabbed a bag he had beside him and hopped out. 'I never could say no to a lady.'

The aircrew smiled. 'They're expecting you inside.' He went to help Eva who was already unfettered and half out of her seat. 'Better than a train, Miss?'

'Better than anything!'

They walked across to the office where a harassed officer produced papers to sign and asked, not very graciously, 'I suppose you'll need a lift into the town?'

Eddie agreed and went outside to find Eva. This was a training airfield and there were Tiger Moths in every direction. Eva was watching as one took off tentatively.

'They're getting us transport into town.'

'Don't let's hurry.'

'I haven't told you why we're here.'

Hearing something different in his voice, Eva turned to face him.

'I'm visiting the parents of a pilot friend. He died.'

'You want me with you?' Eva stared. Eddie's face had lost all its careless confidence.

'I'm a bit of a coward where the emotions are concerned. Frankly, I've been in a funk about it.'

Eva took his arm. It felt taut and strong. The image of defeat was replaced by a rush of love which surprised her so much that she dropped his arm and took a step away.

'It's a bit pathetic, really.'

'Oh, no! Of course I'll come.' Eva's face was earnest but she hid her love, distrusting what it meant. 'It will be easier for me because I didn't know him.'

'So many people die ...' began Eddie, then stopped. He didn't know nor want to know what he had been going to say.

They were interrupted by a WAAF who arrived with an influx of energy. 'I'm your transport, sir.' She looked as if she could carry them on her back. Both Eddie and Eva were relieved. 'Mabel, sir, but call me Mabs.'

They sat behind Mabs, close together, while she talked. She had discovered that he was a fighter pilot – she even knew how many planes he'd shot down – and wanted both to impress and look after him. She had short fair hair, a pink neck and a pert nose.

'Quite a poor part of the city you're going to. Respectable, which matters a lot round here. I'm desperate to get a posting south. Have been for months.' She laughed. 'What you'll need is a watering place. Only one worth your pennies: The Star and Garter. Might be there myself later.'

The sun shone on the rows of red brick houses and Eddie was a warm presence beside Eva. She wondered what it would be like to have a man in your bed, skin to skin. She took his hand and lay back.

Andy's home was no different to any of the hundreds of others they'd passed.

'Here you are, sir.' Mabs opened the car door.

Eddie got out and stood looking at the front door. Eva followed him.

'Star and Garter, don't forget, sir. And you can walk to the station. Might see you there if my luck's in.'

'You're very kind.' Eddie put on his cap absentmindedly.

'Sir!' Mabel saluted smartly.

The front door opened and a man and a woman looked out expectantly.

'Mr. and Mrs. Bullit.' Eddie went forward with a charming smile. He took off his cap and realised he'd forgotten to return the WAAF's salute. He'd already forgotten her name.

Eva lingered. Eddie suddenly whispered, 'I'll say you're my sister.'

Mr. and Mrs. Bullit were small, the house was small, the front room where they were led was small and Eddie remembered Andy had been small. He had stopped noticing it almost immediately.

Tea and cake were produced. 'No eggs,' said Mrs. Bullit apologetically. 'I got time off from the shop, when we heard you were coming,' she said. 'The Post Office was good to Fred, too.'

'Fred?' repeated Eddie. 'My own father's name.'

'Is that so. Quite a common name, of course.' Mrs. Bullit stopped with a nervous gasp.

Mr. Bullit was silent but watchful. When Eva's plate slipped a little on her lap, he leant forward as if ready to catch it.

'Andy was one of my best friends,' announced Eddie. 'We met at our first interviews.' He put down his plate and stood up. He towered in the little room. 'He was a good friend and a very good pilot. No-one better. The sharpest eyes in the squadron. We all mourned his loss.' Eddie sat down again abruptly. He was suddenly terrified he'd bawl like baby. He looked at his knees in desperation. There was a long silence with the only sound as Eva put down her plate very carefully.

Mr. Bullit cleared his throat. 'Andy worked for that job. Wouldn't hear no.' His Birmingham accent was much thicker than his wife's or Andy's had been. 'He was like that, our boy, didn't take no for an

.wer. His fiancée says the same. She would have come today but work wouldn't let her off. Not Andy's wife, you see. They were waiting till after the war. Andy knew what he wanted even though they all said he wouldn't make it. Had enough with playing with engines, he said. And when Andy wanted something he got it.'

'Fighting for his country,' murmured Mrs. Bullit. 'We had a service for him, even though …' She did not complete the sentence.

'He died in a second,' said Eddie firmly. 'No suffering,' he added even more firmly.

'He was doing what he wanted,' said Mr Bullit with heavy finality.

Eva wondered if there was a hint of reproach.

They stood up to leave soon after but, as Eddie picked up his hat, he stopped and opened the bag he'd brought from the aeroplane. He held out a large notebook. 'I pinched Andy's log book for you. His flying history. The RAF can do without.'

'You mean it's not ours to have?' asked Mr Bullit.

'Andy wouldn't like us to have something we shouldn't,' said his wife without waiting for Eddie's answer.

He stuffed the notebook back in the bag and pulled out an RAF tie, 'You'll have this?'

Mrs. Bullit took the tie, wound it round her fingers, unwound it and let it dangle.

'That'll do,' said Mr. Bullit.

They all walked to the door and the farewell seemed the worse thing to Eva. How could they not remember how their son had left, jauntily wearing that same uniform as Eddie, *to do what he wanted*. Eddie hadn't even bothered to ask whether there were other children, it seemed so obvious Andy was the only one.

Eva and Eddie walked down the road. The moment they were out of earshot, Eddie said, 'That was appalling, frightful, shocking, disgraceful.'

'They were obviously suffering.' Eva was taken aback by his vehemence.

'That's what I mean. They were suffering, but so quietly, so politely, so respectfully! Why wouldn't they be angry, full of accusation? Why do they accept death so easily? It was all nonsense. I couldn't begin to tell them about his humming. They wouldn't even take his log book which held everything about what he was. That tie could have belonged to anyone! In fact it probably wasn't his at all. They should have been filled with hatred for the RAF, for the war, even for Andy. He didn't have to be a fighter pilot. And then the fiancée who didn't even show up.' Eddie strode at a great speed.

Eva struggled to catch up. 'Did you know he was engaged?'

'No. I need a drink.'

Eva remembered another occasion when he'd rushed along ahead of her. It was in Oxford going to see Hank do archery. She stood still and wound her hair back from her face.

Eddie walked back to her. She said, 'I thought they were dignified.'

'Death isn't dignified.'

'What did you want them to do? Scream and tear their hair?' Eva thought her own mother had almost certainly died and she hadn't even cried. She shivered and took Eddie's arm. 'I expect they can't imagine what happened to him. He's just gone.'

'Death should be more than that.'

'I don't know.' To her horror, Eva felt as if she was about to burst into tears.

'His mother mentioned a service. Do you believe in God?' Eddie didn't sound totally serious.

'My father's an atheist.' Her tears disappeared.

'Your mother's Jewish. Jews believe in God.'

'Not necessarily.'

Two workmen in overalls, one carrying a bag of tools, passed by. They looked at them curiously.

'I need a drink,' repeated Eddie. He shouted after the men. 'Which way to The Star and Garter?'

'Number 134 bus at road's end!' one shouted back.

'Can't we go somewhere quiet?' murmured Eva. But when

they arrived, the big light room was almost empty. Eddie ordered a beer for himself and lemonade for Eva. He put his hand over hers. 'I'm sorry I got upset. My life at the moment is not normal and Andy was a good friend.' He drank his beer first. 'Also, I'm exhausted. Actually, that is my normal.'

Eva wondered if her life was normal. 'I crept out of the house soon after five,' she said.

'I'm so glad you did. What I would really like would be somewhere dim and cool where we could rest. Our train's not until four.'

Eddie went to get another beer. 'They've got a room upstairs we can use,' he said. 'It's the light in my head. It goes right through my eyes into my head.'

'But you took off your goggles,' said Eva. She thought how she loved light and how she wanted to make her paintings filled with shafts of sunlight, going this way and that, across the sky and the ground.

'What do searchlights look like?' she asked.

'I don't do night flights.' Eddie considered Eva carefully. 'Why do you want to know?'

'I might try a painting.'

'At dusk they seem ethereal, misty, waiting for blackness before they show their full strength. They search the sky as if they know exactly where to look, which of course they don't. All the same, if I was a bomber pilot, I'd be frightened of them because once they have you in their sights, they don't let go and the ack-ack send up their nasty chatter. Bomber crews are incredibly brave. Fighter pilots are in command, desperately engaged for a short time, but a rear gunner in a bomber sits in a coffin hoping for the best.'

'Isn't he shooting?' said Eva.

'Oh, yes.' Eddie fell silent, before saying, 'I'll have to lie down. Sorry.'

'I'll sit here a bit,' said Eva.

Soon after Eddie had gone, Mabs arrived with two other WAAFs. She was disappointed but understanding on hearing that

Eddie had gone for a rest. All three ordered gin and tonics. 'Tonic's good for you,' said Mabs laughing. 'Quinine. Believe me, I grew up in the tropics. Lord, it's dead in here today.'

'I thought I'd explore Birmingham,' said Eva. 'But I don't know where.'

The three WAAFs conferred, while admitting that they hadn't got much further than The Star and Garter. 'The Cathedral has splendid windows,' suggested one eventually, 'or so I've heard.'

So Eva set out on the hot streets. The Cathedral was splendid indeed but the windows had been removed by the Birmingham Civic Society in case of bombing or so she discovered from a pamphlet. There were photographs of a crucifixion showing a strong man, white-skinned, nailed to dark wood. She thought about Eddie and wondered what she was doing away from him.

All the same she continued to sit in the pew in the vast empty church. Eddie had asked her if she believed in God. Well, she could believe in Him, sitting alone in the Cathedral. Even without the stained glass. She could believe in God when she was at Tollorum or just in the countryside. She hadn't believed in Him at school services. She decided to take the pamphlet for Eddie. She looked at the crucifix again. So much suffering. Such beauty.

CHAPTER NINETEEN
August 1940

Eva arrived back at The Star and the Garter. The WAAFs had gone. 'No, your bloke hasn't come down,' the barmaid told her.

She went upstairs quickly and found the room. Eddie was fast asleep, flat on his back, still fully dressed in his uniform. He must have flung himself down on the bed and gone straight out.

Going closer, she saw his hair was darkened with sweat. Sun poured through a window that was tight shut. Blackout material lay crumpled on the floor.

Eddie woke to the rattle as Eva struggled with the latch. He'd been dreaming of flying, not a bad dream as those dreams go, no cruel deaths but the usual sense of encroaching danger. Eventually the sky had cleared – as bright as this place. Wherever he was. Disorientated, Eddie closed his eyes. When he opened them again, he recognized Eva.

Her hair was too dark for an angel but she seemed angelic to him all the same, her outline defined and slender. The window shot open. Startled, Eva turned round, fingers to mouth; she saw Eddie's open eyes.

'Sorry.'

'Come and sit down. Wherever are we?'

Eva smiled. 'I've been to St Philip's Cathedral. You've been sleeping.' She sat on the bed.

'I never expected to see you when I woke up. More likely a 109 or a Dornier.'

'You're so hot.'

'I can't move. Undo my buttons, would you.'

Eva undid the buttons. 'You'd better take off your jacket.'

'You're so right.' Eddie sat up suddenly and pulled it off. 'Do you think there's a bathroom somewhere?'

'I passed one on the corridor, I think.'

When Eddie was gone, Eva lay back on the bed, feeling the pillow damp where his head had laid.

'That's better!' Eddie came in bouncily. His hair was wet and flicked back; he dangled his pilot's silk scarf from his fingers. 'You look sweet lying there.'

'So did you.' Eva opened her eyes.

'Two babes in the wood.' Eddie sat down and picked up the pamphlet. 'Not sure about the crucifixion. Not just now. I'll give my vote to the nativity. Did the stained glass glow exquisitely?'

'They'd been removed.'

'There's the war for you. Spoils everything.' Eddie stroked Eva's forehead. He felt protective of her and remembered that rush of love when he'd strapped her into the Tiger Moth.

'When you were angry after visiting your friend's parents, you asked me if I believed in God,' said Eva. 'Well, I've decided I do, but not all the time and I'm not sure about Jesus.'

Eddie moved his hand from her forehead to her cheeks and, for a second, her mouth. Then he took it away. 'I bet they'd be surprised downstairs if they thought we were talking about God. For what it's worth, I only believe in God when I'm flying in an empty sky which doesn't happen often these days. When I was coming to pick you up in Oxford, I expect I believed in God. I was happy at least. I was more than happy. I was in another, better place.' He smiled. 'Luckily for me, it had you at the end of it.'

Eva blushed. She felt embarrassed that Eddie would see it. She sat up beside him and shook her hair over her face.

Eddie turned her round and gently kissed her. Eva's blush spread through her whole body. She put her arms round him and kissed him back.

'We can't do this.' Eddie stood up. The sun shone around him. 'You're so lovely. So young.' He stepped away from her.

'I'm only two years younger than you.' Eva stared at him, at the dazzle surrounding him.

'Oh my God!' Eddie looked at his watch. 'It's five past four.'

Eva got up lazily. 'No trains run on time.'

'I'm more used to planes. They always run on time, even ahead of time.'

Eva trailed her arms round his neck. She couldn't think where this person had come from who wanted to twine herself round Eddie and never leave him.

'We'll have to go. I've got to pay for the room too.' Eddie separated himself firmly.

It was cooling down outside but once they reached the station, the heat and smell and noise of hundreds of would-be travellers, mostly soldiers, sent the temperature soaring.

'I don't think I'm fit for the ground anymore,' shouted Eddie, 'How do soldiers bear it! Always in crowds of people. And then expected to fight.'

'Yes, you're of the air.' Eva was sad at his irritation. Obviously men were different. One kiss was not enough for happiness. 'Some people prefer being squashed in with others. It makes them feel safe.'

'Then they're fools.'

It was hard to tell when their train was leaving or even whether it had arrived. Groups of men ran or sometimes marched hopefully from platform to platform. Eventually, Eva found the corner of a bench and sat down.

'O, Lord protect thy servant,' said Eddie standing above her.

Eva stared upwards. He seemed unaware he'd spoken.

A soldier shifted his pack and Eddie sat beside her. 'I'm worried about getting you back to Oxford.'

'Nobody else will be.' Eva laughed.

'You're very carefree.' Eddie took her hand. 'You're the loveliest girl in the world.' But he wasn't thinking of her. Ten hours of his forty-eight-hour leave were gone. He'd promised to go to Tollorum. He *needed* to go to Tollorum.

'Does that include in the sky?'

'There you have a rival.'

'I knew it! The Spitfire is the loveliest girl in the sky.'

There was a rush of people to the right. A train hooted. Eddie jumped up and a young woman immediately took his place. She was crying so hard that the bench shook.

'Can I help?' asked Eva.

The woman turned, eyes bulging with tears. 'Nobody on earth can help.' She considered Eva not altogether kindly. 'You'll know what I mean when you're older, Miss.'

As Eddie came dashing back and pulled her away, Eva glanced backwards. The woman had stopped crying and was staring blankly ahead.

'This might be it!' shouted Eddie. He was tall and forceful enough to push his way on to the platform, then the train and into seats.

'I hope this is the train,' Eva smiled as every space was filled in behind them, 'because we'll never get off.'

Three hours later they arrived in London. During the journey, Eddie hardly talked, except to comment once, 'Reeking humanity' and later 'I'd rather be in a Spitfire with four German planes attacking,' before shutting his eyes.

In London he discovered the last train West went in ten minutes.

'You don't have to wait for me,' said Eva. 'I can look after myself. Did I tell you my art teacher, Mr. Halliwell, asked me to marry him.'

At least this gained Eddie's attention. 'You never told me that. Is he fighting?'

'He's a teacher. And he has asthma.'

'That explains it.' Eddie sighed. 'Crowds and crowds of people everywhere.' He glanced at Eva. 'I'll tell you what, why don't I take you to Tollorum? My mother obviously loves you.'

Eva tried to see if he was serious.

'We could telephone your father.'

Eva remembered how Sylvia had kissed her son's hand when he was asleep in the walled garden.

Eddie's train was being announced. It was delayed for ten minutes. Eva ran to a telephone box but there was a soldier inside and another waiting. 'Please. Please!' She took his arm and opened her eyes wide.

Eddie watched her from a little distance. He wasn't certain he wanted her to come with him. She was a distraction. What was all that about her art teacher? She distracted him from his job in the war. But why would he not want to be distracted? Because he had to get back. Because you never really left the airfield. Maybe she could be a distraction for his mother. From him.

Eva came back from the telephone box giggling like a naughty child. 'I spoke to Valtraud. She told me I was 'not controlled.' So now I can do what I like.' Eva spread her arms.

Eddie, rattling coins in his pocket, waited for the soldiers, before going into the telephone box.

'My mother's expecting us,' he told Eva. They bought sandwiches, lemonade and an illustrated newspaper called *The War*. The cover showed a photograph of an aeroplane.

'A Lancaster bomber,' commented Eddie. 'A fine plane.'

'It's very big,' said Eva doubtfully. She pictured with affection the little Tiger Moth that had skipped over hedges and whisked them across the countryside. 'It hardly looks as if it could get into the air.'

'It does. Loaded with five hundred pound bombs too.'

The train was curiously empty. 'It'll probably give up the ghost at Woking,' said Eddie. Why was he rushing to Tollorum when he could have had a good time with Hank in London? He might have been able to pick up a real woman too, not this, this girl. He looked at Eva almost with hostility.

Eva sat blithely staring out of the window. Even though she sensed Eddie's darkness, her own happiness was intense. He would come round, she decided, when they arrived at Tollorum. She allowed herself to remember a train journey she'd taken with her mother about ten years ago. They were going to the seaside. She had looked out of the window then and shouted '*thalassa*', as her father had taught her, when she first saw a strip of darker blue below the sky. Her mother had hugged her and told her she was a proper scholar already. They had spent five days away and her mother who was usually so studious, so remote, was apparently content to spend hours with nets in rock pools or paddling along the edge of the sea. She told Eva that she couldn't swim because Germany, the country where she was a little girl, had no sea round it. Eva had found this confusing and later they had studied the world together in a map and her mother had pointed out Germany. Eva had thought it looked big but dull compared to England. 'I'm glad we live here,' she said and her mother had smiled and agreed.

The train bumped and Eva decided to change the subject in her head. Eddie was closing the paper. 'What's it like?' asked Eva quietly. The other three occupants of the carriage were all sleeping, heads lolling with the train.

'Rubbish. There's an article about propaganda saying how bad we are at propaganda compared to the Germans. They might as well say we've got to get better at lying.' Eddie lowered his voice. 'It's like chaps in the squadron who report they've downed a plane when everyone knows it was already hit. I *hate* lying.'

'Who would lie about things like that?'

Eddie changed tack and became defensive. 'Not many of course. We all have to turn in our reports after an op. Worst part of the whole thing, trying to remember precisely what happened in a few minutes of mayhem. Quite often several chaps claim the same plane. It's not always easy to tell.'

'So it's not exactly lying.'

'It is when the propaganda fellows get hold of it. They should know better.'

Eva glanced out of the window. Already they were far outside London's sprawl, the fields glowing gold with their ripened crop.

'Then there's an article about, I quote, 'a small British steamer' bringing down two Nazi planes. Fat chance of that. Turns out that one of them ran itself into the ship and the other was most likely invented.' Eddie opened the paper again, 'Listen to these headlines.' He read, scornfully imitating a newsreader: 'Italian empire is doomed', 'They're laughing in Malta', 'US pilot has fun fighting Messerschmitts.'

'It's only headlines.'

'That last one goes on, "I wouldn't have missed this for all the Japs in China." What does that *mean*?'

'Nothing.' agreed Eva. 'Let me have a look.' As she took the paper, one of the sleepers, a woman in ATS uniform, opened her eyes, sighed gustily, then shut them again. 'Surely Eddie, you like this picture of saucepans being turned into Spitfires? That's Beaverbrook's idea, isn't it? And this diagram of the German Heinkell 113?'

Eddie frowned. 'I'm tired.' He shut his eyes.

Eva went on reading and she found stories which were not victories for the Allies, however cheerily they were written. The word 'grim' recurred. By the time she reached the sinking of *The Lancastrian* on July 25th where 2,800 soldiers, women and children had drowned, she was could bear no more. Many of the men clinging to the sides of the ship were singing 'Roll out the Barrel' and 'They'll always be an England.' How could they *sing*? And such silly, hopeful songs.

For about half an hour she inwardly cried about war and the world and, after a while, she realized she was mourning for her mother. The setting sun was bright outside so she pulled down the blind as one might in the house of someone who'd died and sat quieter in the shade. Not long, afterwards her eyes closed too.

Eddie woke feeling calmer. The movement of the train had been soothing. Gently, he took 'The War' from Eva's lap. He rolled it up and put it in the luggage rack above his head. Someone else could find it and attempt to make sense of the world. He tried to recognise where they were – surprisingly close to Tollorum, he realised. The train was going through most stations without stopping. He needed to find a guard at once.

Eva opened her eyes. She had just noticed Eddie was gone

when he reappeared. 'Quick! Quick! The train's only stopping for a minute.'

Eva found herself dragged into the corridor, out of the door, on to a platform.

They stood and watched the train leave. It had never really stopped at all.

'That was a close run thing!' Eddie was radiant.

The silence bounced and surged around them. After a few seconds individual noises rose: the last birds crying out before bedtime, insects singing, the slight crackle of leaves in a row of tall lime trees.

Eva looked round and sniffed the cool fresh air. 'I'm so glad to be here.'

'Let's start walking.' But almost at once they saw lights approaching. A trap appeared drawn by a fat pony. Lily was driving it, not very expertly. Eddie waved his arms happily.

'Hello Lily! Hello Rosie!'

Eva remembered how magical Tollorum and the countryside around it had seemed, when she first came with Jack. She pictured Jack intensely painting in the field with the barn and briefly wondered what he did with himself when darkness fell.

Eddie drove the trap at high speed while Lily brought him up to date with Tollorum news.

'There's Madame Gussie here in a great state because George's leg might have to be taken off, poor lad. They've given him two weeks' grace to see if it heals so there's a nurse, a right tartar, and your father is living down at the Reverend Gisburne's so he's up for every meal and her Ladyship's poorly and taken to her bed, although it's the best place for her whether she was poorly or not. Then there's a surprise visitor for you, came down especially this afternoon. And he's invited another visitor tomorrow, a movie star, he says, and that Wing Commander can't keep away. He was quite put out to find your mother had a husband more or less in residence.

'However are you feeding everybody?' interrupted Eddie. He slowed Rosie's mad progress.

'There's two willing girls from the village ...'

Eddie gave a roar of laughter. 'As long as I've lived, you've found two willing girls from the village. What do you do, kidnap them?'

'I pay them,' said Lily in a dignified voice.

Eva listen to their chatting, half jealous of such a big cast of characters when her own family was so very small. Had Eddie expected it, she wondered, this hurly-burly awaiting him?

A moon rose over Tollorum, escorted by stars far brighter and clearer than any searchlight. Eddie, standing now like a charioteer, guided the little trap up the driveway to the house. It was dark of course, like an empty house on the lit stage.

'Here we are then. Home sweet home.' He had not expected to be home again. His expectations went no further than a day.

CHAPTER TWENTY
August 1940

Eddie stood at the sideboard in the dining-room and poured himself a cup of tea. By Tollorum's standards, there were not so many people at the breakfast table. But too many for his comfort. As he'd come in, Aunt Gussie had clawed at him, murmuring 'George', before bursting into tears.

Eva stopped making polite conversation to Hank who had been the surprise visitor and watched as Eddie took his cup and slid quietly out of the room. Hank was in uniform but Eddie was wearing a cricket sweater, baggy shorts and battered gym shoes. A streak of sun across the floor lit up his pale legs and the glint of blond hair. Hank, also watching, commented, 'I guess it is his home.'

Eva wanted to go and sketch in the walled vegetable garden. 'Dig for Victory.' That was a Great War slogan but it would do as well for this war. Yesterday she'd seen a poster commanding: 'Eat potatoes not bread.' Eva turned back to Hank to ask what it meant.

'I guess it's to save on imports so sailors don't have to risk their lives bringing them in. You could add, so airmen don't get killed trying to protect shipping and save the lives of sailors.'

Hank seemed the friendliest person in the house. Eva knew he wasn't flying because of an eye condition and wondered if that was the reason he was relaxed enough to give her time.

≈

The curtains were drawn in the big front bedroom where George lay. Eddie had no wish to feel sorry for his cousin; he'd come seeking refuge with someone who understood what war demanded.

'It's like a morgue in here.' He pulled wide the curtains and threw open a window. 'Smells like one too.'

'Oh, bugger off,' muttered George. He lay in bed with one leg protected by a bridge of raised sheets.

'You're not sick are you?'

'Bloody hospital infection.'

George raised himself slightly. 'I wish you'd go away. I enjoy lying here feeling

furiously sorry for myself.'

Eddie laughed. 'Just like my old dad.'

'He came in here the other day. Waggled his stump and gave me advice about what to do if the leg went. Want a bet on what he said?'

'You are an ass. How about "Better put a pistol to your head."'

'Blast you, know-all.'

Pleased that he'd annoyed George out of his gloom, Eddie came back from the window where he'd been enjoying the sun on his back and sat down. He picked up a copy of *The Times*.

Neither man spoke for a long time. George seemed to be dozing as Eddie turned the pages slowly. Outside there was the sound of voices on the driveway.

A uniformed nurse put her head round the door. 'Time for your medicine Captain Gisburne.' She came in and Eddie stood up.

'I'd better go and join the crowds. Whatever possessed my mother?'

George opened his eyes. 'She's trying to dilute *my* mother.'

Eddie laughed. Perhaps he did quite like his cousin. Walking downstairs, he remembered what his father had said the night before. He'd come out and helped unharness the pony. 'If I'd had the education and was young, I'd become a politician and set the scene rather than be carried along. But the young man wants to be a hero and the old soldier's learned to rely on obedience.' Eddie had supposed Fred was talking about himself and his grandfather, the Brigadier General, although it was hard to believe Fred had ever valued heroism.

Before they'd reached the house, Fred had looked up at the sky, the sharp-eyed moon and trailing stars and whispered intensely 'What do you think about while you're up there?'

'Staying alive and sending down a few blasted Huns.' Did his father believe he'd tell him more?

'God. You don't think of God?'

Pretending not to hear, Eddie had hurried on. Neither of them had referred to his words again.

This morning the house was quiet as Eddie reached the bottom of the stairs. Lily appeared at her usual brisk pace.

'Everyone's walked down to watch the cornfields being cut. It's being done the old way, with horses.'

'Everyone's gone?'

Lily smiled. 'Don't look so pleased.'

'I'll walk in the other direction.'

Lily watched him go. She couldn't understand his sort of fighting, lazing around on an airfield for hours on end, then up in the sky for the time it would take her to lay the table before back to the deckchairs. Being able to come here seemed strange too, popping home for a day. When Fred had joined the Army, he was gone for nearly two years and she didn't know whether he was alive or dead. Lily supposed Eddie was part of a new war.

❧

Eddie stepped into the walled garden and immediately saw Eva at the far end. For a moment he wanted go to her, hold her in his arms. He paused, but she remained totally concentrated so he turned, in a way relieved. More than anything, he needed time on his own.

Eva lifted her head from her sketch book and saw him go. She jumped up, then hesitated. He must have seen her. She ran after him.

Eddie was passing by the front of the house towards the stables.

'I suppose you want to be alone?' Eva caught up with him.

Eddie stared at her. She had coiled her hair and stuck it up with a couple of pencils. Her face was fresh and clean, her neck very white in the blouse, the same blouse she'd been wearing the day before when they'd kissed. Well, she had no other clothes. Eddie thought of the hay in the loft above the stables and how it would feel to lie with her there, how he would undress her, taking his time with the buttons.

'Why are you looking at me like that?' One part of Eva thought she knew why but another wanted to ask the question and even sound a little indignant.

'Do you want to take a whirl in the trap?' asked Eddie.

⪼

The noise of Rosie's hooves on the driveway, made a loud rhythm and suddenly Eddie began to spout poetry in time with the beat:

'... barbarous in beauty the stooks arise
Around; up above, what wind-walks! What lovely behaviour
of silk-sack clouds! Has wilder, wilful-wavier
Meal-drift moulded ever and melted across skies?'

Eva clapped her hands; she felt they were beating up joy, daring the gods to extinguish them. Now and again Rosie neighed, indignant at being taken from home, and shook her head.

'Where shall we go?' shouted Eddie. He waved a stick in one hand. He was Apollo. He was Helios driving his chariot across the sun.

'Where shall we go?' Eddie slowed for a moment. They were approaching the end of the long drive.

'Right!' Why did she say right?

'Left!' directed Eva a few minutes later.

They were dashing on at quite a pace and Eva knew they were heading for Jack. Jack sitting in front of his barn painting in the field with the barn. Jack who understood she was a painter, who wanted to marry her. Who was always there waiting. Quite soon, they'd pass by the wildflower field.

'We should turn back.' Eddie reined back the pony who dropped her head and snatched grass from the verge.

Eva could see the barn. Then she saw Jack walking across the field towards them, carrying his canvas painting bag, swinging his easel.

'That's a friend of mine,' she said, pointing.

'How odd!' Eddie frowned and stared. 'We can't stay.'

Jack couldn't see them over the hedge. 'I'll say hello.' Eva hopped out of the trap and ran towards him.

Eddie, still standing, watched the surprise of the long, skinny man as he dropped his bag, then his easel. He heard his welcoming cry, 'Eva!'

'We were passing by. I'm staying at Tollorum.'

'I know. Did Mrs. Chaffey tell you she's invited me to lunch?'

'Not, actually.'

'I'm glad your arm's better.'

'Oh, yes.' Eva waved it in the air.

Eddie sat down. What was Eva up to? He didn't care. He was very tired. The trap was pulled along inch by inch as Rosie looked for sweeter grass.

Eva came back. The dark man slouched beside her. Eddie thought, I don't have time for this.

'This is Jack. I told you about him.'

Eddie nodded. 'Good morning.'

Jack nodded, 'Jack Halliwell.'

'I'm off. Get in, Eva.' Eddie picked up the reins.

Eddie drove sitting on the bench, a heavy, huddled figure. The trap sped dangerously towards Tollorum. Stones pinged and rattled against the wheels and Eva clung on with both hands.

'Jack's coming to lunch,' said Eva.

Eddie muttered as if in pain, 'Don't you understand. There's no time.'

'But I love you!' cried Eva. Eddie made no sign he'd heard but she felt brave and happy. She did love him and he should know it.

Eddie drove straight to the stables at Tollorum and handed down

Eva carefully. He led her inside. He kissed her with the pony's warm head pushing and shoving at his back.

'I just want you to know.' Eva put her hand on his face, eyes, nose, mouth. I love only you.'

He kissed her again. He didn't consider saying he loved her. He just wanted this moment, even if he couldn't undress her in the hay. How close they were! He put his hands under hair and pulled her even more tightly against him.

Outside the stable, there were loud voices of returning walkers, then a car arrived, followed by an extremely loud noise.

Eddie broke away and hurried out, the pony trotting behind. An aeroplane was landing in the field at the front of the house. Rosie whinnied and cantered away. The trap rattled and bounced behind her. Lily appeared at the front door of the house and shouted, 'Eddie!'

A spruce old man in RAF uniform was helped out of the Tiger Moth.

A woman who Eddie recognised as the actress from Hank's New Year's party, stood by her car and laughed. Even in the bright sun, her lips were vermillion and shiny. Fred and Sylvia and Hank appeared from the house.

Eva came to the stable door, shading the glare with her hand. She was in time to see Jack, some way down the drive, throw aside his bike and grab Rosie.

Ignoring anyone else, Hank walked briskly to Eddie. 'Here you are, old chap. I thought you'd be off or I'd be off and we'd never talk at all.'

'Nonsense,' said Eddie, 'I was going to ask you to drive me to London.' His voice became awestruck, 'Is that Angela?'

'If you mean the beautiful blonde talking to the well-preserved and glamorous film star, bingo! Angela came down in Moira's posh car. She's been pumping Moira about this RAF film she's in. Honestly, I don't know who's pumping who. Beware, Moira is sure to get at you.'

'I'll look for cloud cover if she's any-one near.' The two men smiled at each other.

Hank spotted Eva hovering indecisively outside the stable. 'Hi there! Had a good morning?'

In the sunlight, Hank's eyes were pink, Eva noticed. 'Lovely, thank you.'

She saw Jack approaching up the drive, trying to lead both his bike and Rosie. Perhaps he thought that retrieving Rosie would make her love him. What did she care! She didn't care about anything. She was happy. No, joyful. No, filled up, brimming with love.

Fred was welcoming Angela and the actress. He was making them laugh, saying something outrageous, Sylvia guessed. Sylvia watched her husband. He was wearing a greenish tweed jacket over a white shirt. His skin was sun-darkened from his stay in Dorset and his hair more black than grey. He looks so young, she thought. Am I too old for him? Too responsible? Too serious? She turned away and went to meet the Wing Commander who was walking across from the field.

The aeroplane's engine cut abruptly and all of a sudden the light was clearer and she could even hear the birds.

'Mrs Chaffey. Mrs Chaffey.' Jack blocked her way. 'I've brought back your pony.' He seemed distressed.

'Hello Jack. How very kind.'

Lily appeared at Sylvia's side. 'Have we enough food for so many?'

'Those two won't eat much.' Sylvia indicated Angela and the actress.

'Sylvia noticed Eddie. 'He's still wearing those dreadful shorts.' She began to feel happier.

'Someone needs to put that pony in a field,' said Lily.

'But the aeroplane's in the field.' Sylvia began to laugh. 'And here comes the Wing Commander. Uninvited, I may say. What fun it is to have the place filled for once!'

Jack led the pony and trap towards the stable.

Seeing him approaching, Eva fled towards the house in a

cowardly fashion.

'Thanks.' Eddie came back and took the pony from him. Briefly, both men looked towards Eva who disappeared through the open front door.

Hank appeared again and said, 'Now I want to introduce you to Angela, Eddie. Can't have your father monopolising her.'

A gong, rung exuberantly by one of the girls from the village, with five beats, a beat of silence and five more, echoed from the house.

'I need a drink,' said Eddie but actually he felt quite cheerful and even rather sorry for this Jack person. How could he stand being a non-combatant? 'I bet you could do with one too.'

'Thank you.' Jack looked at Eddie in his shabby clothes and thought what a fine painting he'd make. Jealousy made him curl his fingers. He tried to overlook the fact that Eddie had not introduced him to the tall American.

At lunch Sylvia put the Wing Commander on her right and Eddie on her left. Soon they were talking across her about the failings of barrage balloons. She stared at Fred and sighed.

'What is it, Mother?' Eddie asked suddenly.

'I'm happy you're here.' Sylvia smiled at him.

'You were looking at Father.' He looked too and saw Fred was recounting some anecdote to the actress. 'Last night, when I arrived, he talked about God. He was quite serious.'

'Your father is a seeker. He had to do his growing up in the war.'

'Oh, the war. *That* war.' As Eddie spoke, he pictured himself back in the Mess, slumped down, perhaps with a crossword puzzle. You could stare at a crossword puzzle for a long time without doing anything. Then you were off. Out and up and off.

Angela was on Eddie's other side. Catching his words, she began to describe to him her series of articles about the war-time wives. Her voice sounded far more American than Hank's. Beyond her, Hank listened without speaking and beyond him, Eva heard nothing. Eddie had kissed her properly. Perhaps he loved her.

Jack sat opposite Eva. The light from the tall windows was behind him so she couldn't see his expression but she suspected he was watching her, even though apparently paying proper attention to the Reverend Gisburne.

The Rector pronounced loudly, 'As Ovid would have it, 'Art clothes all things with beauty.'

Fred, sitting between Gussie and Moira, was amusing himself by winding up Gussie. 'So your husband Colonel Reggie VC MC DSC DSO OCDC you say, dearest sister-in-law, is far too busy at the war office for the likes of us, or even the likes of you, I suppose.'

'Oh, Mr. Chaffey, dear man, do pipe down.' Moira assumed a loud, actressy voice, 'While others sow peace, you sow discord.'

'A false witness that speaketh lies and soweth discord,' Proverbs 6.19,' contributed the Rector.

'Forwardness is in his heart, he deviseth mischief continually and soweth mischief.' Proverbs 6.14,' quoted Fred with a smug expression.

'You disgust me!' Gussie's voice rose. 'You are neither patriot, nor gentleman! Do you never consider the feelings of a mother whose son lies suffering and alone, one leg less in the service of his country!' She turned her back on Fred and began an animated monologue with a bemused Jack.

'Has her son really lost his leg?' The Wing Commander asked Sylvia gravely.

'He'd still got it this morning. My sister enjoys a scene,' Sylvia was brisk, signalling for the attending girls to clear away.

Fred poured himself more wine and leant close to Moira. 'My dear sister-in-law and I have always brought out the worst in each other and Reggie's such a pompous brute. I don't know how you stick his company.'

'Actually he's moved on to pastures new. He told me quite seriously that, on consideration, I was not his type. What an old goat! Doesn't his wife realise?'

'She's far too convinced she's the centre of the world.'

Fred put down his glass and stared round the table. Sylvia was looking at him with the considering expression that he knew so well. Foolishly, he'd once asked what it meant and she'd answered, 'I ponder whether you'll ever learn to like yourself.'

'Who is that young woman?' Moira asked Fred, indicating Eva.

'A stray,' said Fred, 'picked up by Sylvia. Her mother is lost in Germany.'

'I had the impression she was a friend of your son's.'

'Perhaps that too.' Fred glanced again at Eva.

'She's very pretty. And the man without a uniform?'

'Another stray. A teacher, I think. Sensible chap.'

⚭

The lunch continued. Fred was quieter. Coffee, a rare commodity, was offered sparingly in the drawing room but with the splendour of a silver pot and gold-painted china. Afterwards, Sylvia asked Eva to visit Lady Beatrice. 'She's in bed. She can't bear to see men in uniform. I'm afraid her mind is not quite right.'

The curtains were closed in Beatrice's bedroom but she was sitting up, her hair in a long plait and her fingers scrabbling with something under the bed clothes.

'What is it, Mother?' Sylvia gently revealed a brass Hindu god with many gyrating limbs.

Eva remembered it from the display in the study downstairs.

'It was his favourite,' said Beatrice, in a calm voice. 'I never could see why. In my view, it brought him bad luck. You shouldn't love alien gods. Please, take it away.'

Sylvia took it without comment and placed it out of Beatrice's eye-line. 'I've brought Eva to see you. You remember Eva.'

Beatrice smiled. 'Sit down, my dear. That's right, nice and close.' She continued without a pause. 'You see his body was never found so I can't help thinking that nasty god might have got him, dragging him down like an octopus in the ocean.' She looked at Eva appealingly.

'If I had someone I loved die, and his body was never found, I would imagine the worst things. But I would never give up hope he'd come back.'

Sylvia made a small movement of protest but Beatrice brightened. 'Oh, my dear.' Her fingers grabbed for Eva's hand and clutched it hard.

Eva put her other hand over the bony fingers. 'I wouldn't ever be consoled. Not in my heart. Not my body. I might be able to in my mind, I suppose.'

'Yes. Yes. In the heart. In the body. How could I ever accept it? However much I prayed.'

'No one ever taught me how to pray,' said Eva thoughtfully.

Neither Eva nor Beatrice noticed as Sylvia went out of the room shutting the door behind her. She couldn't understand how a girl as young as Eva could have a conversation with her mother which she herself would quail and avoid. But on the other hand, Sylvia thought sympathetically, the poor girl has had to deal with the disappearance of her own mother.

'I'm not saying God hasn't been a help,' continued Beatrice, 'but the forces of darkness are very strong and when I'm tired, they drag at my poor brain. For the first years it was very bad when every night I imagined dearest Bingo lying naked and alone on the fields of Gallipoli, so very, very far away. Then it was better. I had so much to do, so busy – Sylvia and Gussie and their children. The forces of darkness couldn't get me. But now I'm old, they've come back again.' She paused. 'They say we're fighting another war. Is it really true, dear? Can it be true?'

Eva wondered what to say. So this was why Beatrice refused to see men in uniform; not fear for their safety, but a wish to believe there was no war. Eva considered and decided that this seemed a perfectly rational choice.

'I'm a painter,' she said. 'I came before and you worked in the garden and I painted. I don't expect the two jobs are so different.'

Beatrice looked reflective. 'Touching flowers has always been a consolation. God made the flowers so it is a form of praying. I once said that to the Rector and he was not pleased. Do you paint flowers?'

'I did a drawing of the vegetable garden.' Eva got out her sketchbook and held it up.

'God made the vegetables too,' said Beatrice peering in a kindly way. 'I think I'll rest now. Bring me some flowers when you visit next or a painting of carrot tops. Carrot tops are very pretty.'

Eva walked down the stairs, carrying the odious brass effigy. Now she must find Eddie. Dumping the god on the desk in the study, she ran out to the driveway where she could hear his voice. Surely he wouldn't leave without her?

Eddie and Hank were escorting the Wing Commander to his aeroplane but he seemed unwilling to leave. The pilot who had being lying on the grass behind the plane jumped up as the three men approached and saluted smartly.

'We're not so busy this side of the country, you know.' The Wing Commander seemed defensive. 'Have the naval bases to defend of course but, mostly you lot catch them before they get to us. Going back today, are you?'

'Yes, sir.'

'Better leave you to it, then. All hands to the joystick.'

Eddie and Hank watched the plane make a doubtful take-off, bumping half a dozen times on the grass before finally getting into the air.

'Poor old buffer,' commented Eddie. 'I suppose we'll end up like that.'

'If we survive.' Hank was still watching the plane, now making a graceful arc before straightening to the north-east.

'Do you mean you're coming back?'

'I've finally persuaded the medical powers that my pink eyes are a congenital disorder and in no way threaten my vision.'

'What about Angela?' They began to walk back towards the house and Eddie saw Eva standing at the door.

'Angela's become a war groupie. She's got herself into a crowd of journalists who enjoy war more than anything.'

Eddie's attention was on Eva, walking slowly towards them. She seemed to fit into Tollorum so well, better than he did. Perhaps it had become a female preserve. He tried to imagine how it would have been in his grandfather's day, with huge hunters in the stables, teams of all-male gardeners and a butler bossing everybody about in the house.

'I was afraid you were leaving,' said Eva. She took hold of Eddie's arm.

'In my shorts?' said Eddie, laughing at her.

'When do you want to go?' asked Hank.

Eddie stared up at the sky. Already there was a hint of yellow in the blue. Time for a couple more ops, he thought automatically. 'Half an hour?'

'Yes, sir!' Hank gave an exaggerated salute and walked away to find Angela. From the open window to the drawing-room he could hear women's voices.

The chauffeur who had brought the actress, got out of his car and stretched.

'Have you been there all this time?' asked Eva, still holding on to Eddie.

'Just the last hour for a kip, Miss. Found a welcome in the kitchen, didn't I?'

Eva looked at him again. He was young, thin, with a foxy face, below slicked-back hair. She imagined he was a Cockney. 'What's it like in London?' she asked.

'Same as usual, Miss. He who has, gets and he who has not, takes.'

'But there's enough food and things?'

'Same rule applies. Got my ma some onions from the kitchen, didn't I.'

Eddie unhitched himself from Eva. 'I'll see if Miss Lipscombe is ready to leave.'

The actress lay on a sofa in the drawing-room, eyes closed.

'All on your own,' commented Eddie.

She stretched languorously and opened her eyes. 'I haven't had so much fun for years. Your Dad's quite something.'

'Your driver's waiting.'

'That's what drivers do.' She rose not very gracefully. 'Got to make decisions. Back to America or risk my life in the old city.'

'Aren't you our one woman mission to bring in the Yanks?'

'No comment,' the actress took out her lipstick and deepened the red on her mouth. 'Just be pleased I didn't ask you to join the team. Actually, I did ask and they said you were too busy saving England.'

'No comment,' said Eddie.

As they reached the hall, Sylvia appeared with Jack behind. Eva had quite forgotten his presence at Tollorum.

'I was showing Mr. Halliwell the house,' said Sylvia. 'I told him there're quite enough bedrooms here if sleeping at the barn becomes too uncomfortable.'

'He likes it there.' Eva frowned. 'There's a tap and everything.'

'I'll be off, then,' said Jack. 'I enjoy painting in the evening light. Sometimes the shadows are as substantial as buildings.'

Eva frowned more.

Jack tried to reach her but she attached herself to Sylvia who accepted Jack's thanks politely while putting an arm round Eva.

It crossed Eva's mind that whereas Eddie loved her when she was there, his mother was prepared to love her all the time. Possibly Jack was as well. They went together outside.

'Too many people all day long,' murmured Sylvia. They stood and watched Hank hurry out to say goodbye to Moira and then Jack on his bicycle being narrowly missed by the actress's car which took the driveway at speed.

'Apparently that young driver sneaked things from the kitchen without permission,' commented Sylvia. 'I suppose one must forgive everything in a war.'

Eddie, now in uniform, came from the house. 'Where's Hank? We should be off.'

'And what about Eva?' Sylvia gave Eva's shoulder a squeeze.

Eddie, who in his mind was already half-way to his airfield where his Spitfire waited for him, glanced at Eva and again felt a loving warmth which each time took him by surprise.

'Can't she stay here?' As if that was decided, he walked past both women calling 'Hank! Hank! Where the bloody hell are you!'

'Of course she should stay here. We can find her anything she needs. My dear Eva, please stay.' Sylvia watched Eddie who was going back to the house in search of Hank. 'Everyone hates goodbyes and if you stay at least we'll be here together.'

Eva thought, I could have more time with Eddie if we travel together. Except there is Hank and Angela too. And Eddie wants me here. She remembered their kiss.

'I'd love to stay.'

⋙

Hank drove his car at a moderate pace which led Eddie to believe his sight wasn't perfect after all. Angela sat in the back scribbling into a notepad. When Eddie asked her what she was writing, she answered that she was noting down points of particular interest from their visit. 'I had so many enlightening conversations.'

'Enlightening?' queried Eddie.

'Angela asks questions,' explained Hank, 'Journalists are like that and American journalists especially so. Nobody told them not to be a bore.'

'Then you can explain to me what's going on.' Eddie paused. 'That is, if I want to know.'

Hank laughed. 'You can't pretend to be brain-dead every moment of the day. The talk in London is that we're downing far more of the Luftwaffe than they're getting of ours and we're also quicker at turning out new planes. On the other hand they started with a huge numerical advantage and we can't train pilots quickly enough. They can still put up a few hundred or more if they want to. We could never equal that.'

'But we're still winning.'

'It's all about not losing.'

'So we're not losing.'

'Correct. On the other hand, they're knocking out our airfields at a dangerous rate.'

'I'm not keen on your other hand.'

'I talked to Sir Hugh Dowding's number two a couple of evenings ago,' Angela leant forward, 'and he's much more worried about the loss of pilots than planes.'

'Quite right too,' said Eddie.

'If they knock out our airfields we've had it.'

'This guy told me,' insisted Angela, flicking back in her notepad, 'that on one day recently Fighter Command lost forty aircraft which isn't good. But far worse was the nine pilots dead and eighteen seriously wounded.'

'Do you see what I mean?' drawled Hank in an exaggerated southern accent, 'She asks questions and gets answers we don't want to hear.'

⋙⋘

Sylvia and Eva sat on a bench in the rose garden.

'It's very pretty here,' said Eva, 'and peaceful. I'm not used to so many people.'

'I suppose with your mother away,' Sylvia hesitated.

'We were always quiet. I don't think my parents understood the need for people. Funny, really, that my mother gave her life to save others when she didn't seem to care before. She loved me, I suppose.'

'Oh, yes. Are you sure she won't come back?'

'We don't know anything but I find it easier to believe she's dead and not suffering.' She leant forward and lightly touched a curled rosebud, white with a hint of pink. 'I was always a bit of a disappointment.' She sat back and looked down. 'I'm not very clever and I can't play the piano. She taught piano, you know.'

'But you can paint,' suggested Sylvia gently.

Eva who had been talking in a monotone, turned to Sylvia with more emotion. 'She did understand that. She persuaded my father to let me go to the Ruskin. I only found that out after she'd gone.'

Sylvia smiled, 'You see she did understand you.'

'But she's still gone.' Eva frowned and stood up.

CHAPTER TWENTY-ONE
7th September 1940

Eddie undid the harness to his parachute with extreme care; the RAF had been known to charge for bits of parachute left behind. It wasn't easy because his fingers were soft and shook. He supposed he was lucky it wasn't worse since he'd just jumped from an aeroplane at several thousand feet. He sat up and shook himself free and stood, noting his legs were soft too. No sign of the plane; it might have crashed miles away. Thank God he'd been over land.

The grass under his boots was very smooth, far smoother than their airfield. His vision cleared further and he saw a red flag. Automatically he thought danger, then he saw the bunker.

Two stocky men in plus-fours came running towards him.

'You all right, old chap?' The first puffed out.

'Lucky it's you landed not the plane or there'd be hell to pay.'

'Not broken anything?'

Eddie shook his head which still seemed to be whirling somewhere in the sky. The sky was quite empty now. He thought with sadness of his Spitfire, mortally wounded, then abandoned to a death of mangled metal.

'Jolly good show. I expect you could put back a double.'

The men led him towards the clubhouse. It was a longish walk – he had landed on the thirteenth green – 'Lucky for you!' the men told him, chortling – and he didn't know if his sense of an undulating grassy carpet was the true lay of the course or his wobbly legs.

In the bar, he was given a warm welcome as well as a large brandy.

'We'll have to put a sign up, 'Evacuating pilots welcome. Fees waived,' boomed an old fellow who'd obviously enjoyed several doubles. 'A couple of days ago we had a Polish lad sail down on the sixth fairway. Three vodkas later and he'd got some kit out of us and was on the course. Never played before. Never missed the ball. Had to give him credit. Gave us a bit of his plane for a thank you. There behind the bar.'

Eddie politely looked where the old man pointed. But he thought, they'll be hanging up an arm or leg next. He said, 'I need to telephone the base.'

After being told rather grudgingly that someone would pick him up, he went to sit in a deep leather armchair, away from the bar. Everybody noticed it, the Poles' superior levels of energy, as well as their skill and bravery, which arose out of their violent hatred of the Germans who had destroyed their country. There were no Poles in Buzzard Squadron but a couple of days ago a few of them joined in the same fight and Eddie had seen a Polish pilot deliberately cross the strings of a parachute so that the Hun dangling below plummeted to the ground. If an Englishman had done it, he'd have been truly shocked – but how could you blame a Pole?

Eddie sat in his chair until a very pretty WAAF collected him. As the men at the bar shouted, 'One for the road,' she looked him over.

'You seem in one piece, sir. If you're not careful, they'll have you up again in a tick.'

She thought she was joking, but when Eddie arrived back, he was sent urgently to the Wing Commander who only seemed slightly shamefaced as he announced: 'Lee got it in the foot but his plane's patched up. Can I put you on standby?' As an afterthought, 'Get a cup of tea first.'

Eddie went up. He was even grateful. Once he was in the air, his trembling fingers and wobbly legs behaved themselves and he managed a shared hit on a 109. But in the darkest hours of the night, he felt Willie shaking his shoulder. 'Wake up! Wake up! You're dreaming.'

He had been dreaming, reliving the moment his Spitfire had been hit and he'd lost control of the rudder bar and stick. He'd believed his exit had been easy. The hood hadn't stuck, the flames were moderate and well away from him, the parachute had opened with no trouble and he'd landed without a scratch on the thirteenth green.

'What was I doing?' he asked Willie.

'Shouting.' Despite the darkness he picked up Willie's embarrassment.

'You mean, screaming in a cowardly fashion.'

'Of course not.'

Eddie didn't push it further. He would be a pity to spoil Willie's tendency to hero-worship him – principally based on Eddie's record weeks of survival. Lately, he'd not been getting so many kills. Could he be losing his edge or even his nerve? He didn't think so. It was just exhaustion. Or not enough hatred.

Wide awake now, Eddie decided to go for a midnight stroll. It was a cloudy night with only the dimmest lights marking the airfield which made it difficult to walk without blundering into wires or sharp edges or tin canisters which rattled together and might bring a guard running. Instead he sat in the Mess and wished that Hank was around. He'd been posted up north to a sector with less action, either to give him a chance to get up to speed or because they were still worried about his eyes. If Hank had been around, I might have opened up to him, thought Eddie. Then again, I might not. It doesn't do to depend on anyone outside yourself.

With nothing else to do and no chance of sleep, Eddie picked up a pad on a nearby table, perhaps used to score Scrabble, and wrote: *2.30 am, September 7th*. He thought for a while, then added: *Do I want to die? Today could have been curtains time and of course I don't. That wasn't why I joined the Air Force at all. I don't feel sorry for myself, just amazed that it should have come to this. Death so close, I mean I've done more ops than most and never had a scratch*. He paused to remember Andy. How long was it since he went? He couldn't even remember that. *I've had too much luck for one person. I'm twenty years old. I'm young, although I don't feel it. The worst thing is we all know that Fighter Command is on its last legs. The airfields are still being bombed to smithereens, despite all our efforts, and each time we go up some of our best pilots don't come back. And that's not to mention the lads who come in who've had no real experience. You see the look in their eyes and you weep. You know the odds. Soon they do. Then you stop looking.*

Eddie put down the pencil. The CO had him in the other day and told him that there were reports that 11 Section couldn't hold out beyond two days.

'So what next? 'Eddie had asked.

'Ring the bells and rely on the Home Guard,' came the ironic answer.

Eddie began writing again: *How will it feel to risk your life for months, see your mates killed around you and then have the Nazis walk in? What's the point of it all? You might be forgiven for enquiring.* Eddie stopped writing; this time to consider the nature of patriotism. At once he heard his father's voice. 'Patriotism, my little soldier, is the last resort of the fool and the braggart.' Fred had found him marching round Tollorum with a stick over his shoulder. He must have been about eight years old, an ordinary, noisy little boy who didn't have enough friends. Naturally he hadn't understood what his father meant but the words stayed with him. Five years later, when he was thrown out of school, his father had said, 'You know you won't rule the country now' in a way Eddie understood was praise.

But surely patriotism didn't only exit for the top dogs? Love of country. He loved the Tollorum countryside all right – 'from the vantage of a landowner', he could hear Fred's mocking voice. He'd told Eddie two or three years ago when drunk – both of them drunk, as a matter of fact, that he'd joined up in the last war to get away from his fucking country – and the fucking countryside, if it came to that. 'You ask the man in Stepney,' he'd said furiously, 'if he's fighting for his country!' He'll tell you, "I leave that to the toffs. I'm fighting for my mates, for money, to avoid my missus,

196

the kids, work, starvation...'" He'd gone on a rant and Eddie had walked away, bored and wondering how his mother stuck him. But he still remembered his words.

Eddie picked up his pencil: *My father learnt to read in the war; he was taught by an intelligence officer who was blinded by shellfire and eventually died. He told me that once. He continued his education with boring old Gisburne at the Rectory. Then he worked for the Workers' Education Association who paid him, although my mother gave him everything he needed. This country did well by him. Very well. So why isn't he a patriot? It was the enemy who took his arm.*

Eddie lay back and held the pencil which now needed sharpening, in the air. He thought he could scribble all day and not find out why he was fighting. Why he was prepared to die. Prepared? No, not exactly, but ready.

He remembered that day when he'd run away to Tollorum with Hank. He'd felt he was at the end of his tether. But actually he'd only been at the beginning. Like a child, he'd merely been a bit tired and overwrought. He was a thousand times more tired now and strung up so high that he was sitting in the dark Mess looking at the ceiling but he would no more run away then he'd screw the barmaid in The Bag of Nails, the skinny one with the spots and greasy hair. He was here that was all he could say about it. Here he was.

Here I am, wrote Eddie. *Soon it will be time for Capwell to bring my tea and he'll be concerned when I'm not in bed but not very. He knows his pilots, does Capwell. He might even find me here and remind me to wash and shave. Where does the RAF find men like him? Ugly as they come, never opened a book in his life. Jones and Jenkins are clever but they have the same kind of dedication. Dedication! There's a grand word.* For a moment Eddie shut his eyes but it was too late – or early – to sleep so he started writing again.

So it's tea and toast in the dining-room, transport to the Dispersal Hut, the telephone which sets of the charge to the planes. Angels 15, Angels 20, bandits 100 plus. Coming over Dungeness. What does it matter? Put on parachute, hobble across to the plane, watch Jones finish up in the cockpit before he drops me in place, fix the shoulder to the leg straps. Insert the pin and yell, 'OK.' Door closed. Helmet on, mask fixed, R/T on. Nearly ready to taxi. Wave. 'Chocks away' and there they go, any old direction. Brakes off, open throttle and we move, Jones and Jenkins holding the wing tips.

'Okay Buzzard,' that's your leader over the R/T. 'Here we go.' Brakes off with a hiss of escaping air, ease throttle open, more acceleration, racing across the ground. We fly. Wheels up, throttle back, pitch back to 2,850 revs. Climb up and turn to port.

Over the R/T, 'Hello, Sapper, Buzzard Squadron airborne.' Four minutes from leaving the Dispersal Hut … 'Eddie!' Willie stared down at him.

'I must have dozed off.' Eddie sat up, blinked and stuffed the pad into the pocket of his flying suit. He must have put that on last night. Capwell hadn't come. He hadn't washed or shaved. But the adrenaline was running already. Tea and toast in the dining-room. Out to Dispersal.

Time passed. Nobody talked. Hours passed, well past the time Jerry usually came. Eddie's beard prickled. His eyes prickled. It was another golden clear day. What was holding them? They were all thinking the same.

'Perhaps they're missing their Wiener Schnitzels and gone home,' suggested one wit. There was half-hearted laughter.

Jim settled by Eddie. 'The new lads have got the wind up.' Jim had arrived recently from another squadron. Older than Eddie. If he'd been asked, Eddie couldn't have described him. What was the point of knowing?

'Join the club. What do you think?'

'It takes a long time to collect a massive force. We'll be facing that every time now.'

'That's what I'm afraid of. Although naturally I've forgotten what fear is.'

They both attempted a smile. There was a longish pause. Then Eddie said, 'I've heard there's hardly any telephones functioning in the emergency sector ops rooms.'

'I've heard Goering thinks were down to our last fifty Spitfires,' said Jim.

'Aren't we?'

'If you're going to be like that.'

'Didn't get much sleep.'

'New plane OK?'

'Very good. Runs even smoother than the last. RIP.'

'Good you jumped.'

'Aren't you hungry? I'm glad I jumped too.'

'I'll see if I can get some sandwiches brought over. It's after one.'

Eddie watched Jim go over and make arrangements. All the pilots watched him.

He came back and sat down again. 'Maybe Goering thinks he can wipe us out in one sweep if he gets enough planes.'

The two men were not looking at each other but now Eddie sat up and turned to Jim. 'But he can't. Silly bugger.'

Jim smiled. He sighed. 'You're so bloody right.'

Eddie flopped back in his chair, then wondered if he had enough energy to go outside. He could feel the adrenaline, there still, but bottled up, giving him a headache, a backache, a pain in the arse. You'd never do it to a dog. Not a greyhound anyway, straining in the slips. *'Cry God for Eddie, England and St. George!'* Waiting took the biscuit. He reminded himself it always had.

The call finally came at four. Word got about as they ran for their aircraft, it was a vast force. Bombers, fighters, all sorts, hundreds of them, perhaps a thousand, two miles wide. Approaching the coast between Deal and North Foreland. This was the worst. Only for a minute or two because then they were in their planes, in their routine, watching carefully because all the squadrons on the base had been ordered aloft and you didn't want to have an accident before you got in the air. They made a pretty impressive sight themselves, smart formations, heading to the coast, assuming the Huns were aiming for the oil terminal at Thames Haven or on the usual factories. Squadrons raced to guard them.

But suddenly the orders changed. When the bombers reached

the Thames Estuary they'd swung west and headed directly up the river.

Eddie understood at once. Many of the pilots did. Geography was etched into their brains and this was a no-brainer: the vast force of bombers escorted by double the amount of fighters was going for London, up the river, in a direct line to the East End, its docks and factories. Their job was to stop them. Try and stop them.

Buzzard Squadron, two flights of ten elegant Spitfires, along with any other squadron who could answer the call, soon enough found themselves confronted by an awesome sight, the stuff of nightmares: they were on the edge of a tidal wave of aircraft, towering above them, rank upon rank, more than a mile and a half high.

What to do? There was only one way and that was to attack. Like a small vessel again a tsunami of water, he flung his Spitfire into the first wave, circling, hurtling, diving, firing whenever he got the chance. His knees shook, sweat rolled off his face but he was exhilarated too, shouting, cursing, battle cries as old as the centuries. He might have been alone in his plane but his R/T surrounded him with other men's voices as they yelled taunts and jibes.

Soon the sky over the Thames estuary and London, that beautiful sunny sky, was a seething, shrieking mass of aeroplanes swooping, swerving, in and out of the vapour trails, tracer lines, bullets – *Oh Lord protect they servant*.

No time to make sense of it. Keep moving. Look behind. Across his flight, a Hurricane, transformed into a flaming beacon hung for a moment, before falling to earth. Black smoke, white smoke, red flame, flashes of silver, blue sky almost lost in the fog, the white bloom of parachutes falling at their own dignified pace. What chance did a man have dangling in the middle of such mayhem? There a foolish 109 showing his side, here a Spitfire, was that Willie? Being too brave.

So many squadrons attacking now. Who knew how many?

But the bombers kept on. No hope of stopping them. Pity the poor buggers below. Pity poor old London. The Jerry fighters were leaving now. Out of fuel. Nearly out of fuel himself. Eddie wondered how The Bag of Nails was faring. Strange, that he should think of it, but at least it meant there was a little more time to think. Perhaps he'd have one more shot at catching a bomber on his way home. He'd been careful with his ammunition.

It was luck that gave him his kill, a bomber straggling, flying low, probably hit already. At least it didn't take much to bring him down in a long, low, shrieking dive over a marshy part of the estuary. It was lucky too that it didn't fall on a built-up area.

Going back to base now with just enough fuel for safety, Eddie could only watch the bomber long enough to be sure he was crashing. In his own sudden security, heartbeat slowing, knees still knocking but sweat drying, he pictured for a flash the eight men inside the Dornier. None of them had jumped. Perhaps they were dead or wounded. Perhaps the plane wouldn't burn in the marshy land and they would survive, stumbling out into the lovely evening.

This was too much. Who knows how many men, women and children their bombs had killed? Who knows how many had been lost from Buzzard Squadron?

Sailing gently in the nearly empty sky – only a few other aeroplanes in the distance, birds returning to roost – Eddie thanked God for his survival and was surprised to find himself doing that. He thought too of Eva. She would be glad he was alive.

CHAPTER TWENTY-TWO
7th September 1940

Eva arrived at Paddington Station from her stay at Tollorum. She was on her way home, commanded there by her father who informed her over the telephone that Cousin Phoebe had written and a discussion about her future was urgent. Since Eva was planning to return anyway for the start of the Ruskin's term, she conceded graciously, although inwardly determined that her future should never coincide with Cousin Phoebe's.

It was 2.30 in the afternoon and the next train from London to Oxford wasn't due till 5.30. The station was packed as usual and swelteringly hot. Her stay in the country had made her less able to cope with the oppressive noise and smells of smoke, sweat and food. When a drunken soldier tried to barter a kiss for a place at the free forces canteen, she slapped him away and headed for the exit.

The streets were nearly empty, people either at work or had evacuated the city. The air was heavy and the sun brilliant, as if it hadn't noticed the arrival of September, but it was still fresh compared to the station.

She swung her gas mask case provided by Sylvia; she had also provided sandwiches and other necessary bits and pieces. Eva had brought nothing when she arrived at Tollorum with Eddie. She stopped and stared upwards. If she lowered her eyes a little, she could see the giant silver blobs of barrage balloons but, directly above her head, the sky was empty. She imagined it filled with roads, on one of which Eddie might appear, winging his way towards her. She pictured the roads crisscrossing, making patterns, the way their trails did if there were enough of them. But it didn't really work. The sky was a free space.

She continued walking briskly until she passed Marble Arch and reached Oxford Circus. She looked up again and heard a plane but too high to be more than a silver flicker where it caught the light. She decided to head south towards the river and make a circle of her walk.

She was standing on the top of a flight of stone steps when she began to hear something else: a loud insistent drone which, although it was far away, must be loud because otherwise why would she hear it? It grew into a great, rumbling roar, a little like an approaching storm. But she still couldn't see anything. Storms sometimes gave up and went away but it felt as if this noise would never retreat or deflect.

Nervously, she turned to man in uniform standing nearby, 'Where am I?'

He looked nervous too. 'Down them steps there's Pall Mall and Buckingham Palace.'

Then the siren began to wail.

'Oh lor!' The man plonked a tin hat on his head.

She nearly laughed. He looked so silly and surprised. They ran down the steps together to find a shelter at a the bottom.

'There you are, love.' She went in but the man dashed away muttering 'East End, East End,' reminding Eva of *Alice in Wonderland*'s White Rabbit.

Eva suspected she was becoming hysterical. All alone in the city she didn't know, in a shelter near Buckingham Palace (which she'd never seen) with bombs falling somewhere – on the East End which was obviously not here. But were the bombers on their way, that ominous rumbling advance, followed by the vast blackness of explosions? Not here. Not yet. Quickly, the shelter filled up with the oddest assortment of people. A fat old lady handed out toffees. 'Very good for the nerves,' she repeated each time she offered the paper bag. An even older woman replied, 'It's not my nerves I'm worried about, it's my teeth – what's left of them.'

'You should be wearing your gas masks,' said a suited middle-aged man in a bowler which went very oddly with his gas mask.

Eva sat on a bench, invisibly small and quiet, a country mouse, she imagined, obediently wearing her gas mask. Her hysteria subsided. Two boys, perhaps fourteen or fifteen, stood by her. They were restless, talking in disconnected words. 'Go on… 'I am…''You…''My nan…''Don't say…''Me it is…' Perhaps it was the toffees getting in the way. They weren't wearing gas masks either. Eventually, Eva realised that one of them, small and sharp, was trying to persuade the other, large and placid, to go the East End where their Nan lived. It seemed they were delivery boys, come up west on their bicycles which were outside. Even in the dim, now crowded shelter, she could feel the small boy's excited energy, no anxieties, but jigging feet and snapping eyes. Giving up on his friend, the first boy tried another tack.

'Want to give a hand out there, Mister?'

The suited man grunted through his mask, 'There's people for that.'

The boy's sharp ferret eyes landed on Eva. 'How about you, Miss?'

Eva waved her hands in a negative.

'Take off your mask and have another toffee, dear. It'll be All Clear in a few more minutes.'

This finally propelled the boy outside. Why should he miss it all? As Col went, elbowing people in his rush to escape, he reminded Eva of Ros and Ellie, the evacuee sisters. They'd come from the East End.

But just then another siren went and there was a general standing up and dusting down and a move outwards for those already on their feet. So this was the 'All Clear'.

'Hardly got the weight off my feet,' grumbled the old lady, without moving from the bench.

'Half an hour,' announced the suited man in the bowler. He had a long grey face with a grey moustache. Eva stood by him outside the shelter. 'Yes, this is just the start of it. Incendiaries. The pathway for night fighters.' He seemed to be talking generally, while staring intently into the distance.

Eva stared too. Against the darkening sky, she saw the paler smoke and soon waves of red, billowing upwards like a sunset out of control.

'It's the docks alright,' said an elegant woman wearing a green hat with a long pheasant's feather.

'Let's hope our boys got a good lot of them,' said a man tied into a long apron and carrying a basket. It seemed that now the All Clear had sounded, they were not quite ready to re-join everyday life. The two old ladies sat together complaining about the price of tinned sardines.

Eva wondered whether Eddie had been one of 'our boys'.

'There must have been hundreds of those swastikas coming up the river,' commented the bowler-hatted man. 'I should be getting back to the office.'

'Where there's life, there's hope.'

Eva glanced again at the white smoke and red flame, noting that now some of it was black.

'Oil,' said the man in the apron, still lingering. 'The docks have all sorts. That's where it comes in, doesn't it? Timber, sugar, rum, oil, that's flammable goods, not to forget the gunpowder storage bins at Woolwich, without even mentioning the factories and the people. Ever been to the East End, have you?'

'No.' Eva took a step backwards and looked at her watch. 'I've got to catch a train.'

The man hadn't spoken unkindly but it was suddenly all too much. Eva burst into tears.

'Oh dearie me. Not that I blame you.' The man brought his reddish face topped with thin gingery hair close to hers. 'Which station is it? I've got my van round the corner. Purveyors to Royalty. Get you there in a flash.'

Eva stopped crying as suddenly as she'd started. 'That's very kind of you.'

It was a butcher's van, baskets of nicely cut flesh and a few bigger joints hanging on hooks. They swung together and made strange clumping noises when they turned corners. Haunch against haunch.

'Call me Bob.' The man began to talk and didn't stop. 'I've lived in London all my life, all my working days, and now I've got to see it reduced to ashes and ruin... Jerry's no fool. Look how he dealt with the Frogs. Big army. Cut through it like a sharp knife through tenderloin. Just softening us up, isn't he? Thinks he'd done for our air force. Brave lads. Not much you can do about defending a city... And that's not even to begin on the markets. What would we do without Smithfield? Or has it already been done for? Didn't like the look of those flames. Never fancied charred meat myself. Takes the taste away. A bit of pink that's what I like to see. High-class clients... Bob, they'll say, or their butler will say, make sure we can enjoy a touch of pink. Came in from France. Funny that when their meat's nothing like roast beef from good old England. But mustn't speak ill of the dead...'

By the time Eva jumped out of the van at Paddington, the smell of flesh and Bob's conversation which circled round meat, knives and death combined to make her feel horribly near vomiting.

'You alright, love?' A young woman with a bright face and a child in one hand, patted her shoulder. 'Nasty things, butchers' vans. That's why they call prisoners' transport meat wagons.'

This was too much. Eva was sick, carefully, into the gutter. It would be a relief to get on the train.

But the train was nearly as bad. The five-watt light bulb made it impossible to read and condensation from cigarettes and sweat trickled down the windows, plastered shut against bombs, and soaked into Eva's thighs. Tollorum seemed like another country.

Even returning to Oxford, to her quiet road and her quiet house, made her experiences in London seem unreal.

The following morning when the first light was softening the darkness, Eva got out of bed and went to her studio. There she filled her sketchbook and began a painting to reflect the shapes, and even the sounds and emotions, of the day before. The people would come afterwards, she thought, tight-rope dancers between the conflagration and the blackened sky.

When it was breakfast time, Valtraud turned from making toast and said sadly, 'They've been bombing London. Now Germany will be bombed.'

Eva snatched two pieces of toast and went to her father's study. 'What did the radio say?'

'The bombs fell all night long but the damage was confined and casualties far less than expected. I suppose you were lucky to get a train.' The Professor looked at his daughter seriously but without emotion.

Eva sat on a chair. 'What are you writing?'

'A few thoughts for a PhD student. He's not too bright, I'm afraid. He'll make a fine soldier.'

'May I make a telephone call? I promised Mrs Chaffey to let her know I'd arrived safely.'

The Professor pushed away his papers. 'You've reminded me. Cousin Phoebe.'

'Can we do that later?'

'Certainly.' He seemed relieved. Perhaps he would forget again.

As Eva dialed Tollorum, Valtraud appeared in the hallway. 'The heart of your father is not good. He see a doctor and the doctor say go to the hospital but he not go.' She went back to the kitchen.

Sylvia answered the telephone. 'I did worry about you, Eva dear.'

'What about Eddie? All that mass of planes…'

'We haven't heard anything bad.' There was a little pause. 'Would you like me to pass on any message about Eddie, should there be one?'

'Please.' Eva felt tears in her eyes. Sylvia understood about her and Eddie. She put down the telephone, hot from her clutching hand. Valtraud appeared again.

'I have a little egg,' she said. 'Yesterday I worry all evening.'

Eva hugged Valtraud and went into the kitchen. She could enjoy the little egg now she knew that Eddie was safe. Afterwards she went up to her studio. She must prepare her work for the Ruskin tomorrow. She tried to look at her sketches critically. But she was too excited by what she was doing to see them objectively. The teachers might hate them: 'running before you can walk' or something cutting. But really, she didn't care.

Eddie was alive. In the afternoon, she'd sit in the garden and write to him. She'd tell him she'd caught a glimpse of him leaning out of his Spitfire. Like the morning at the Oxford airfield.

She didn't think of her father's heart. He always seemed so old and tired lately that it hardly seemed important news.

That night Eva lay in her bed and smiled into the night. Eddie was alive and she loved him. She'd told him so and he'd kissed her. She slept suddenly, deeply, without dreams.

CHAPTER TWENTY-THREE
September 1940

Eddie's squadron was rotated to the north for a rest. It was the first time they'd been out of the front line since July and they all felt disorientated. Since their dreams made sleep unobtainable they didn't feel they were resting.

On the first night, Eddie replayed over and over again his conversation with Jim on the afternoon of 7th September. Jim, whose face he'd never committed to memory, had not returned from that op. No one had seen him go: he might have been shot dead, wounded, crashed into another plane, burnt, tangled in his parachute lines while burning, caught his parachute on another plane's wing – Eddie had seen that once – had a faulty parachute or swooped, still in the cockpit, to the ground in a swift annihilation, which was the best option. Whatever way, Jim was gone but his words on the afternoon of 7th September wove a continually repeated chorus in Eddie's head, whether awake or more overpoweringly, when he'd lain down to sleep. *It takes a long time to collect a massive force. That's what we'll be facing every time now.*

Eventually, he confided in Hank. The only positive in this posting, as Eddie saw it, was that Hank who'd already been on the base, re-joined Buzzard Squadron.

'You're just exhausted all the way through,' Hank said. They were sitting in a country pub, The Hare and Hounds. Eddie found Hank useful as a drinking partner, although Hank himself had reverted to his original abstemious ways. 'Think of something else,' continued Hank.

'You didn't know Jim. He said Goering was planning to wipe us out with massive force and he was right.'

'He didn't wipe us out.'

'You didn't see them. Hundreds, seven deep. Two miles wide.'

Hank looked at the walls of the bar for inspiration; they were covered with colourful prints of huge horses, ridden by men in red coats jumping huge fences. Occasionally a fox with a face like a man ran out of the picture. 'They didn't wipe us out,' he repeated. 'Tally Ho.'

'They wiped out London.'

'No, they didn't.'

'Well, they are now.'

Hank sighed. He stood up to get himself a drink, then he sat down again. He took a folded letter from his pocket.

'Angela checks in regularly. Two nights ago she stood on one of those hills in south London and watched the city blazing, not just the East End. She was horrified. She thought it was the end of a beautiful historic London she'd grown to love. But do you know what?' Eddie didn't look up from his pint. 'She went into town and everything was much as usual. There was destruction, even the palace was hit, but people were still going to work. All that panic the higher-ups were predicting, 40,000 dead on the first night, a vast exodus, none of it's happened and it's been nearly a week.'

'Eight days,' said Eddie.

Hank went to the bar which was full of British servicemen and came back with two whiskies. He sat down.

Hank had been looking at the letter again. 'Then Angela had lunch with a contact in the War Office.'

'I sincerely believe Angela's running the war,' Eddie gulped his whisky.

'She does too.' Hank smiled. He was pleased that Eddie looked more relaxed.

'Her contact said it's still touch and go with the air force but the concentration on cities have relieved the pressure on the airfields, making its survival possible. Which means, QED, there'll be no invasion. Goering loses. Hitler loses.'

'Cheers to that.'

Later that night, Eddie thought it odd that all the inside information came from an American whose country wasn't even in the war. Or perhaps it was a case of the War Office trying to get the US on-side. Or could it be the effect of Angela's rippling blonde hair and long legs.

For the first night he slept without hearing Jim's voice and set off for the op of the day – German bombers were reported approaching Liverpool docks – with a renewed sense of purpose.

'If you're not careful,' Jenkins winked meaningfully as he tipped him into the cockpit, 'You'll be made Squadron Leader.'

At about five o'clock that afternoon when he'd been bullied by Willie into playing Racing Demon, a message was brought to him. 'Your father is waiting for you at The Hare and Hounds.'

'Some joker,' he commented to Willie.

It was another fine evening as he set off for the pub but as the middle of September approached, the sun had already set and a blue mist crept out from under the hedgerows. A group of planes passed overhead. Eddie had only night-flown during his training and never enjoyed it. It was bad enough using instruments in a deep cloud but at night they were all you had. Everything he liked about flying, the vast expanse around him, his own glorious mastery of the plane, as he flung it around in swirls and dives, was reduced to digits on a panel. He tried not to think of that overwhelming cloud any more but on random occasions his alienation had made him believe he was hanging, unmoving in the air. Or that he was going backwards or that he had only just avoided the infinite vacuum from which there is no escape. Yet it was clear that bombing raids, night bombing, would increase on Germany and that there would be a corresponding greater need for night-time fighter escorts. His turn would come. Not yet, perhaps while the Luftwaffe tried to pound London and the big cities into submission. Now he was needed at home.

It was a relief to force his mind away and consider who could be pretending to be his father and why.

Fred was sitting in The Hare and Hounds; he had been there since opening time. On the table in front of him were his glass and a book which he kept open with his stump and consulted regularly. An old man with a greasy cap and a brown mackintosh sat by him and occasionally Fred flung a few words at him – received with an appreciative nod and a grunt.

Fred and Eddie caught sight of each other at the same time. As usual, each was surprised by the other. Fred saw a tall handsome young man, with dark circles under his blue eyes but also confidence that was obvious from his leather jacket slung around his shoulder and the way he stared through people.

Fred waved.

'I didn't believe it was you.' Eddie came over and sat down.

'I never said goodbye to you at Tollorum.'

'Who needs goodbyes.'

Catching Eddie's eye, the old man looked away respectfully and edged a little further away from father and son.

'We didn't speak.' Fred's glance flickered to the book and Eddie realised it was a bible.

'There were too many people there.'

'I need a drink.' Eddie brought back two pints and set one in front of his father.

'However did you get here?' His tone was warmer. His father had come to see him, not easy in wartime.

'That old Wing Commander who's in love with your mother gave me a lift most of the way. Bumpy old landing his pilot made. Then I caught a train. Then I walked and felt happier. Can't think how you get into those tin things every day.'

'The pilot was no better at taking off, assuming he's the same one I saw at Tollorum.'

'If the old chap hadn't been on board too, I'd have thought he was trying to kill me off. Leave the coast clear with your mother.'

'Your first time up, was it?' Why had Fred come to see him? Obviously not for the flight.

'First and last. Love, now there's a subject. A lot of people set a lot of store by it but I've never found it the answer.' Fred stopped and drank.

'The night I arrived at Tollorum, God seemed to be on the agenda,' said Eddie. Perhaps he should try and enjoy his mad father.

'God and death. Love and eternity. Probably the last is most important.' Fred looked nostalgic. He tapped the book between them. 'That's why I carry the Holy Book.'

'You used to carry Marx's *Das Kapital*.'

'God is very unpopular with intellectuals. I've never liked intellectuals. I'm looking for answers, that's all I'm doing.'

This was too much for Eddie. Didn't Fred realise how he lived his life? 'Why do you have to be so serious? Why can't you just let things happen, let things be, like other people do?'

To Eddie's surprise, Fred laughed. 'You could ask that? Don't you know I'm a boy of the trenches!'

'There weren't so many trenches on Gallipoli,' said Eddie sulkily. He felt as if he were being made a child again.

'Enough. Quite enough.' But Fred still smiled. He seemed genuinely cheered by Eddie's obstinate response. 'You're a creature of the air. A creature of light.'

'Oh, Dad. How can you spout such rot!' There had been those days though, remembered through the haze of a hundred ops.

'Quite. But do you ever think what it all means?' Without waiting for an answer, Fred continued. 'You're so young.' He looked at Eddie with kindness. 'I was young too. I was always angry. I expect I was born angry and life proved me right. I suppose I'm trying to work from anger to understanding. You've never been angry. Why should you be? You've always had everything.'

So his father overlooked all that teenage rage, thought Eddie. Or, more probably, he just hadn't noticed. The thought gave him reason not to explain how being part of the RAF, facing death every day, willingly, had given him a certain familiarity with one of Fred's big questions. It hadn't bred contempt – he still wanted to live – but he had overcome fear. Death was his daily companion.

O, Lord, protect thy servant. But make him useful too.

'Did you travel here for a theological discussion?'

'Is that bad?'

'Other fathers come with love and offers of hot meals.'

'I've already given you my view of love. Insubstantial at best.' Fred tapped the book. 'At least this lasts.'

'You're bringing me God? Or the Bible? I was baptised you know. The Reverend Gisburne poured holy water over my head. God and I are on good terms.' As he spoke, Eddie felt that this was true. He couldn't give anyone, not even God, more than he was already giving. He believed in a purpose, although it wasn't clear what it was but he was perfectly happy for it to be God's purpose. Perhaps if he died, he would understand. Any day now. 'I believe in God.'

Fred looked at him with interest. 'I used to believe the world was about politics: Marxism, Fascism, but none of it really added up.'

'You can't ever have believed in Fascism,' said Eddie firmly, 'Not even you.' He was beginning to feel tired, the day's flights replaying back to him, interfering with his father's words. He needed to be calm, he thought, and remembered Eva, their kiss in the stable, her joyful face.

'You're not listening to me,' said Fred, patiently.

'I'm frightfully tired. I'd better eat something. I missed the Mess dinner and they make good chips here on Friday night. Is it Friday?'

Fred, the eternal seeker, who'd come to the north with his Bible, like a travelling salesman with his wares, stared at his son and thought he had nothing to offer him. He thought it gently, with love, perhaps for the first time. He said, '*My beloved is like a roe or a young hart; behold he standeth behind our wall, he looketh forth at the windows, shewing himself through the lattice.*'[1]

'You always did know the Bible by heart,' said Eddie.

'I found it in the trenches when I was learning to read.' Fred

[1] Song of Solomon, 2:9.

stood up and went to Eddie, put a hand on his shoulder. 'We'll eat now. Tomorrow morning I'll be gone and you'll be fighting for your country.'

Eddie wasn't sure whether this was a commendation but the hand on his shoulder felt warm and approving.

≫

The day after Fred's visit, Eddie's Squadron was ordered to return south again, back to their old airfield. That afternoon, their latest squadron leader, an affable New Zealander who had fought in France, crashed his plane for no obvious reason.

They flew south in elegant formation, except that they had no leader. From above and as he landed, Eddie saw the airfield had been transformed in the few days he'd been away; there were three new hangers, a runway, new offices, a new building for the WAAFS who were more and more in evidence as drivers, waitresses and in the Ops room. Even that building which had survived the bombing without being seriously damaged, had been given a face-lift.

'I thought you said it was smashed to pieces,' Hank commented to Eddie as they strolled across to their accommodation building.

'Amazing what you can do if you bring in the Army.' Eddie was non-committal. He didn't like looking backwards – or forwards, if it came to that. He had dumped his bag on his bed when a servant, not Capwell so he didn't bother to look up, told him he was wanted by the CO. On his way across the airfield, Eddie spared a thought for Capwell. He had been killed in a raid on Reading while on home leave. No-one had thought to inform Eddie until he asked, and yet Capwell had looked after him every day of his life on the base.

It was the same CO as before, Les. It was a surprise to see a face he recognised.

'Good evening, sir.'

'Had a good rest, did you?'

'Went up every day but not much luck. One Heinkel.'

215

'What's your tally?'

'Don't know, sir.'

'You expect me to believe that!'

'No, sir.'

The two men smiled at each other. Then the CO pulled a paper towards him as he always did when he had something to say. 'Should have put you in for an award days ago. Can't have a squadron leader without an award.'

The words sank in. Eddie stared at the CO's smiling face. 'I haven't had my twenty-first birthday. I can't vote.'

'Don't share your excitement too obviously, old man.'

Old man, that's what I am, thought Eddie. 'I know I've had the experience.'

As usual, Les opened the drawer to his desk and took out a bottle and two glasses. 'It's good to have you back, Squadron Leader. Well, let's be honest, Acting Squadron Leader.'

They drank and Les poured another, 'I'll be an alcoholic before the war's over.'

Eddie thought Les probably was an alcoholic already. So why not? They drank again. Eddie felt a pleasant glow. It might have been pride or it might have been the whiskey hitting an empty stomach.

'Incidentally, it seems Goering is up to his tricks again. We're not told a thing of course but the indications are he's planning another 7th September or bigger. Just thought I'd mention it.'

≫≪

Eva suddenly found herself with a girlfriend. Jack had been replaced as a teacher by a famous old painter, iconoclastic in his youth, who brought with him a daughter about Eva's age who enrolled as a student. Salome, known as Omy, had long yellow curls, blue eyes, a large bust and a small waist, accentuated by a tightly clasped belt. Her paintings, like herself, were exuberant and original.

In her first conversation with Eva, after they had looked over each other's paintings, she'd said casually, 'I suppose you're still a virgin. It's such a bore. I felt much better when I got rid of it.'

Eva, too taken aback to speak, merely nodded.

'Have you read any Freud? Most of it's horribly dull but when The Great Artist,' this was how she referred to her father, 'began leering at me, a friend recommended I read it. It opens your eyes,' she laughed. 'A good thing for a painter. What's your father like?'

'Old,' said Eva.

'So we both have old fathers.' Omy sighed. 'But I expect you have a mother. My father can't stick with one woman. But somehow he sticks with me.'

Eva hadn't felt it necessary to tell Omy about her own mother but she wondered whether her virginity could really be a barrier to progress in her painting. Omy pointed out, in a phrase that stayed with Eva, that you paint 'with your body not your head'.

On her side, the side of virginity, she invoked the kiss with Eddie which had seemed so wonderful, so perfect. There had also been that brief kiss in Birmingham which had not been enough for perfection, but Eddie had turned her away saying, 'We can't do this.' Omy would have said, 'Why not?' She took to calling Eva, 'Eve', to encourage the seductress in her.

Eva had tried to laugh but Omy had tossed her curls scornfully saying, 'So who's the better painter, you or me?'

Eva didn't answer. The Ruskin placed huge emphasis on drawing and she was glad of the discipline and the exactitude. Omy took very little notice of lessons and because of her father's position, no one tried to make her. It struck Eva that she might never become a better painter than she was at the moment.

At night, lying awake in bed, Eva sometimes thought angrily (she was never angry with Omy in person) that she did paint with her head and that she loved Eddie – Omy never thought of love except to ridicule it – and that one day they would *make love* and her virginity was neither here nor there. She tried to see less of Omy who was too busy balancing one admirer against another and slapping the canvas with yellow paint to notice.

Eva was in her studio at home, making a careful study of two spoons in a glass, when the telephone rang. It rang and rang and no one answered it so she went downstairs.

'I thought you'd been spirited away. The ring seemed to echo into emptiness.' It was Eddie. 'Or worse still, you'd been kidnapped by Cousin Phoebe.'

'Oh, no. I'm here.' Eva sat on the bottom stair. 'I was doing a miserable little drawing.'

'Of what?'

'Two spoons in a glass.'

'That just about sums us up. Are we heads down or looking out?'

'How witty you are!' Suddenly the drawing was filled with interest. She remembered a Picasso still-life of a jug and apples where they'd all seemed utterly human.

'Are you still there?'

'Yes. Do you remember you promised to sit for me?'

'Did I? How conceited.'

'I could come over to the base and make preliminary sketches next weekend.' There was a pause. 'I could stay somewhere. I'd keep myself busy all day.'

'You know I can't make plans for the future.'

Eva was about to say, it's only next week, when she understood what he meant and needed to stay quiet for a moment, breathe quietly before she spoke. Then she said lightly, 'Maybe I'll just turn up.'

'My father turned up a few days ago. Talking about God.'

'I won't do that.'

'He came by aeroplane. As if he was trying to get close to me.'

This time the pain was in Eddie's separation from her, a sense of his drawing further away. 'We talked about God once.'

'The bible got left behind. On purpose or by chance.'

Eva's sense of heaviness increased. 'Have you been reading it?'

'No time.' He paused. 'It's scribbled all over with comments and exclamation marks.'

'That sounds like your father.'

'He's better confined to the page. I've got to go.'

⋙

Eddie went to his quarters. The bed next to his was still unoccupied. Willie had gone the week before in the predicted massive raid on 15th September. He had tried to break up a great gaggle of Heinkels and had been hit by one of them, both exploding in mid-air. It was his first recorded kill. Eddie had seen it all in the shutter second of such sights during a big fight. In another second he'd been miles away.

Someone had taken Willie's things. That was thoughtful, probably the new servant whose name he found hard to remember. It was surprising that no new pilot had yet arrived, suggesting there was still a shortage. New aeroplanes, on the other hand, now arrived quite regularly, often flown in by a woman pilot.

Hank had also gone but only as far as London and the eye hospital. 'With all the bombing, you're safer here,' he'd told Eddie which they both knew was a lie. Odds were odds, after all.

Eddie realised for the first time that the servant whose name he couldn't or wouldn't remember, had left behind Willie's bedside clock. His mother had sent it for him. The night before the 15th September, Willie had asked Eddie, with respectful diffidence, whether, in the event of, well, you know, he had any plans for his car and, if not, could he have it. 'To use for all the chaps,' he'd added. Eddie had laughed and said he'd write his will in the morning. But now he had Willie's mother's clock. It was not worth being sad. No more visits to bereaved parents.

Eddie undressed, washed in the basin and lay down on his bed. He allowed the darkness to soothe him. The last few days had been relatively quiet. Perhaps the gigantic attack of 15th September which still had failed to destroy the RAF had finally broken Goering's resolve. Hank had telephoned and told him that Churchill had been watching the battle unfold at Air Marshall Park's side at his Uxbridge headquarters.

'That man always gets to the centre of things,' Hank had commented. Eddie supposed that he himself was at the centre of things but with Willie's clock ticking nearby, it gave him no sense of pride. Angela had been full of pride, so Hank said, as she described the scene at Uxbridge, 'Every red bulb on, not a squadron in reserve.'

Eddie considered himself as a red light bulb or a part of a bulb. Not so bad. Worth remembering that the Americans had come in at the last war and saved the day. Turning over on to his side, Eddie settled down for the semi-conscious dream-filled state that passed for sleep. He surfaced again to find himself wondering if Eva really would come to find him.

CHAPTER TWENTY-FOUR
October 1940

Eva stood on Orpington station, a tan case at her feet. Eddie had said he would meet her but she supposed his squadron could be called out as easily on Saturday as any other day. The few other passengers had gone and she felt surprisingly peaceful. The sun shone as usual and the only sign of autumn were plump blackberries on a long tangle of brambles. This was Kent, with its neat patchwork of small fields, stitched together by woods in herringbone patterns. From where she stood she could see at least three villages joined by roads, and several oast-houses.

'Great view, isn't it?' A railway worker stood beside her. 'Crowds used to come up here to watch the dog-fights.'

They turned as the noise of aeroplanes rapidly approached. 'Speak of the devil.' The man watched them tolerantly. 'Brave lads but even they can't stop what's happening in London.'

The planes, four of them, flew lower so that they were only a few hundred feet above their heads. 'Coming into land,' commented the railway man. When the leading plane was directly overhead it waggled its wings.

The man looked at Eva. 'They never do that for me. Friend of yours, is he?'

'I'm waiting for him to collect me.'

'Won't be long then, a cheeky beggar like that. Their airfield's only down the road.'

⤜⤛

Both Eddie and Eva were disorientated by finding themselves

together in Eddie's working space. Eva recovered quicker and looked about curiously. 'Where are we driving? Are we going to the airfield?'

'Absolutely not. There's a pub that might have a room.' Eddie wondered why ever he hadn't ever tried to put her off. 'It's in the next village.'

'I'd never been in a pub before I met you.' Eva laughed.

Eddie gripped the steering wheel. It was odd for him to see his hands without gloves. It was odd not to be wearing headphones or goggles nor sitting on a parachute. Why had he waggled his wings when he'd seen her below? He'd felt happy then, heading for home, now she seemed a responsibility when all he wanted was to lie down and sleep, except he wouldn't sleep.

It hadn't been a bad op, as ops go these days. Unusually, three Dorniers had got out of formation and lost contact with all but one of their Me109 guardians. It had almost been too easy to get him. Either he or Red, his new Canadian number two had got him, perhaps both of them. He wasn't arguing. Probably, they should have gone for the bombers and left the 109s. It had come down very slowly, glycerol streaming in a controlled crash landing. He might be captured or dead. Eddie didn't wish him dead.

'What are you thinking?' asked Eva.

'Sorry,' said Eddie.

A misty dusk was shrouding the countryside, merging the golden of the cut corn fields with the grassy meadows. There was no sunset.

'Perhaps it will rain tomorrow.' He hadn't meant to speak out loud.

'So you can't go up.' Eva was pleased to understand this. 'Then I can sketch you all day.' She added lovingly. Longingly. She wanted him close to her.

The pub was smart. There were cars outside and men and women jauntily dressed, the women in short dresses or slacks, the men in uniform, all smoking, drinking, talking loudly.

'Wait here.' Eddie went inside. He pushed his way through the crowds. 'My sister's visiting me,' he said to the woman behind the bar. 'I've heard you have rooms.'

'Just for her?' The woman's face, homely enough, was surrounded by sausages of dark hair, held in place by heavy grips.

'I won't be staying. I'm at the base.' He resented a sense that he was being interrogated. He was too tired to be interrogated.

'There's a room over the back.' The woman relented. 'Not so noisy. It has another room attached. You can meet there. Come in round the side.'

Both rooms were very small. There was a bed in one and two leather chairs and a table in the other. The moment they were alone, Eva began to lay out her sketching things on the table. Her movements were jerky. She was nervous but excited.

'Sit down,' said Eddie, watching her from one of the chairs. 'She'll be back with the sandwiches.'

Eva sat down and immediately felt better. 'I love you, Eddie,' she smiled at him.

Eddie smiled too. She looked so pretty, sitting there, rather upright, like a child behaving well.

'How long do you have?' Eva asked. It crossed her mind suddenly that Omy wouldn't be able to understand this scene at all. How filled with love she felt and how she trusted Eddie to love her, even if he didn't say so.

'There's no hurry.'

'Except you're tired.'

'I like looking at you.'

'I expect I'm quite dirty after all that travelling.'

They smiled at each other.

'My mother's best friend was very ugly.'

'You should say plain, not ugly.'

'She had hairs on her chin. Anyway, her husband was blind when they met. He'd been blinded on Gallipoli. Nothing very heroic, I think. But he'd been gloriously handsome, titled, rich, a great catch, loved beautiful women – before he was blinded, that is – then he married Hilda.'

'I suppose going blind changed his values.'

'But would he ever have married Hilda, an old maid from Birmingham, family makes rods or something?'

'I suppose love always depends on circumstances,' said Eva uncertainly. She didn't want to believe her love depended on circumstances. 'I suppose you mean you could never love an ugly woman. But she might have a beautiful voice or hands or skin. Or do you mean you only love me because you think I'm beautiful?'

Eddie didn't know what he meant. He lay back in the chair. 'Hilda was his nurse. I could never love my nurse. Anyway, she's dead now.'

'Oh, Eddie,' Eva clasped her hands together and leant forward, 'Are you worried because so many pilots get horribly burnt – I met one at Professor Lamb's – that if it happened to you I might be like a nurse? But I'm much better at loving than nursing, I'm sure I am. I had no wish to nurse that poor young pilot. In fact I found it quite, well… The point is I shall always love you!'

Eddie had shut his eyes. He didn't think he *had* been talking about burnt pilots – best not considered – he'd been trying to talk about the spell of beauty that Eva cast over him.

'Just look at you!' Shirley came in with a plate of sandwiches and glasses of water. 'Not too tired to eat I hope. I made these myself. And you, Lieutenant, can get yourself a beer.'

When Eddie came back, he stood at the door and said, 'I suspect I'm rather odd.'

'It's not surprising.' Eva held a sandwich in the air.

'It's partly the not sleeping. But I'm fine in the air. Sharp as ever.' He sat down, then took a gulp of the beer.

Eva placed her uneaten sandwich back on the plate. 'Can I do a few sketches?' She picked up her pad and pencil.

Eddie drank his beer without speaking. The noise of voices from downstairs became louder but in the little room the only noise was Eddie drinking and Eva's pencil zig-zagging over the paper. Sometimes it performed long zig-zags, sometimes tight little ones, heavily scored. Eddie watched until his glass was empty.

'I suppose if I came over and kissed you, Shirley will burst in and accuse me of incest.'

'Do you think she really believes I'm your sister?'

'On further thought, why don't you come over here and sit on my lap.'

Eva put away her pad and came to him. Her expression was demure but her body was hot and her heart thudded.

He pulled her on to his lap and held her tight. 'You can't escape.'

'I don't want to escape.'

When they broke apart, Eddie said, 'Kissing you is better than falling asleep. That's my highest compliment.'

Eva stroked his cheek. Then made her fingers bounce lightly over his face.

'What are you doing?'

'Just testing.'

'I shaved fifteen hours ago.'

'I like it.' Eva put her fingers on his mouth, on his eyes. She closed his eyelids.

'What are you doing?'

'Research for my painting.'

'Do you always research in that way?'

'At the Ruskin, we're not allowed to touch the models.'

'I'm glad to hear it.' Eddie smiled lazily. He wanted to touch her differently but she was playing with him like a child would with an adult. Or was she daring him? Exhaustion? Desire? Love? Which was strongest?

Eva put her hand in his shirt. She felt along his chest.

'I thought you were only painting my face.'

Eva removed her hand. 'I suppose you've made love with lots of women.'

'What do you want me to say?'

'I don't know.'

'I can't make love to you properly because I'm too tired, you're too young and I haven't got a French letter.'

'I see,' Eva dropped her head on his chest and felt the thump

thump of his heart. Was she his heart's desire even if he couldn't make love to her? She had never heard French letter pronounced out loud.

Eddie stroked her hair, spread over them both like a dark cape. 'I'm sorry if that didn't come out lovingly.'

'Omy would be ashamed of me.' Eva's voice was muffled.

'What?'

Eva moved her head a little. 'There's a girl my age at the Ruskin who told me I'd paint better if I lost my virginity. Her real name is Salome.'

'You mean I could be any old male?' Eddie sounded incredulous.

'I'm sorry if that didn't come out lovingly.' Eva sat up and swivelled round so that her face was close to his. 'I try to make you see me.'

Eddie stared into her dark eyes and found his own face reflected. 'Oh, my darling. I see you in the brightest sky, in the earth below, in the black waves of the sea.'

⚭

Later, Eva couldn't remember anything they'd said that evening, except that one sentence from Eddie. As their kisses grew more passionate, the words echoed in her head until they disappeared and gave way to visual imagery, sky, earth and waves.

She knew he loved her but how was it they undressed and made love on the floor in that little room? She didn't remember how that happened, how, at one moment, they slipped off the chair and onto the floor.

Shirley did not appear as they lay entwined among the table legs.

'Oh God.' Eddie sat up, banging his head.

'I think you fell asleep.' Eva was curled up away from him. She'd been watching him. She touched his toe. Even his toe seemed beautiful to her. 'I suppose I seduced you.' Eva smiled. She thought, my love has seduced him.

Eddie sat by the table rubbing his head. 'I don't know what

happened.' He thought about apologising, but first dared to look at Eva.

'I shall always be yours,' she said solemnly.

Eddie came to himself a little more. He realised he felt very well. He smiled at Eva. 'You're a witch.'

Eva accepted the compliment complacently. She hoped life would never be ordinary again. He had seen her. He was looking at her now.

'You're so pretty.' He grabbed at his trousers hanging down from the chair. 'I suppose you'll want to paint the whole of me now.'

Eva thought once they were dressed he might want to leave. He couldn't leave while he was naked. Perhaps if she didn't dress he wouldn't dress. But she was beginning to be cold on the floor.

'Come on, my darling.' He eased her out from under the table and dressed her before he began on himself.

Every place his hands touched was precious to her. But his body went into his clothes far too quickly. 'I wish you would take more time dressing.'

Eddie said, 'Pilots are quick at everything. It's part of the job.' He felt great tenderness for Eva. 'It's why we drink, to slow us down. Talking of which I'll go and get another beer.'

How happy Eva was for that beer! He'd be gone for five minutes but his presence would still be in the room, then he'd sit with her while he drank. She curled up in the chair and waited.

Eddie went along the brown passages and down the steep staircase to the bar. It was very crowded and he almost turned back. Why had he left Eva? He was surprised at the thought.

Shirley smiled at him from behind the bar. Before he'd asked, she drew a pint, pushed it over to him.

There were three RAF officers, he saw, making their way towards him, friendly young faces he scarcely recognised. He took the drink and hurried out but not quickly enough to avoid hearing, 'Got other fish to fry, have you?' accompanied by jolly laughter. He didn't blame them; he'd have done the same himself.

'What's the matter?' Eva held out her hand.

'Nothing.' He sat in the other chair with his drink.

Eva picked up her pad but she didn't want to turn him into a picture just now. 'Was there someone down there?'

'No one that matters. I should have brought you a drink.'

Eva laughed. 'Yes. You should have.'

'The thing is,' began Eddie, struggling to choose delicate words for what he wanted to say. 'Over these months, I've changed. At least my attitude to flying has changed. At the beginning it was all about the excitement of the Spitfire, the chase, success, survival. I never thought or even believed in the idea of death. That was for other people. Then Andy got killed and too many others to name and I understood only too clearly the danger and risk to me personally. In fact, sometimes it felt as if the Luftwaffe knew all about me and had a special mission to snuff me out. It wasn't the sort of fear that made me unwilling to go up, I still ran to my plane as eagerly as ever, but I had caught on to the reality of my life and there was no going back. That's when I stopped sleeping. But now it's different again. I'm still not sleeping but I'm not afraid anymore. I don't really know how to describe it. I just seem to have accepted my fate, whatever it is. I was angry about Andy's death – you remember I was angry with his parents' lack of anger – but I feel quite different now.

'When my father came here and talked about God, I even found myself wondering whether I hadn't been given some sort of grace, strength, courage – I like the idea of grace – because, after all I am trying to do my best for others. Oh, there's so much more I could say and this isn't even why I opened my mouth in the first place.' He looked up at Eva. 'I expect I'm talking nonsense.'

She smiled but said nothing. She wanted him to go on talking.

'So I can manage now. One day, one or two ops – not so many now – but I don't make plans for myself, for the future.'

'Do you mean I am only part of this one day?'

'I mean I can't ask you to marry me or be engaged to me.'

'But I'll see you tomorrow?'

'God willing. The weather willing.'

Eva felt old and young and happy and sad. 'You didn't have to say all that. I didn't expect a proposal. Don't you know? I am wedded to my art!' Eva lifted up her pencil and smiled at him as if it was a joke. But all the same there were tears in her eyes.

Eddie sipped his drink seriously. He still had more to say. 'If I do have a future, it's in the hands of the RAF. They may decide to send me off to fly as a night-fighter. There's a desperate need, now the bombers come mostly after dark; at some point they may even get airborne radar working. Meanwhile only a few fighters and Blenheims have it, and the rest of us are doing the best we can which is bloody nothing. Spitfires hate the dark. Or they may send me abroad, to Europe, Africa. You see what I'm getting at?'

'Yes.' said Eva. 'But you said you'll come and see me tomorrow.'

Eddie put down the empty glass. 'That's my plan. I'll try to get over by midday.'

'We'll go out into the countryside.' Eva uncurled her legs. She could see he was going. 'I'll order a picnic. Do you like eggs? The pub might keep chickens.'

Eddie took Eva's hand and pulled her up. 'I'll see you soon.' He hugged her and left.

Pilots don't say goodbye, thought Eva, and you don't say goodbye to them.

⋊⋉

Eddie arrived at lunchtime. They took a picnic and walked, although the weather was cool and drizzly. At four o'clock Eddie said, 'I'll drive you back to London. It'll save you one train journey. But we should go now. I'll need to get back before there're any problems.

'I'd love that,' said Eva. Problems meant bombs. They'd hardly talked all day. They had kissed carefully, without too much passion. They were preparing to part, that was how it seemed to her, gathering strength by walking quietly in the countryside. Although even that was not quite possible: too many planes went overhead and each time Eddie looked up to check out whether RAF or Luftwaffe, whether fighter or bomber or something or other, whether Hawker Hurricane, Supermarine or Messerschmitt Me109, 110, Junkers Ju 87 'Stuka', Dornier DO17, Heinkel He 111, Junkers 88.

Eddie listed the names. Then they started on the journey into London.

Eddie drove her over the river and into Chelsea. The King's Road still seemed untouched, the Town Hall sturdy as ever with sandbags up to its waist but as they continued some of the shops had no window panes, piles of glass glittering on the ground.

'Must have been a big blast somewhere,' said Eddie.

They reached Sloane Square or rather saw what remained of it. 'Peter Jones has gone,' said Eddie. 'My mother loved to shop there. She said it made her feel secure. We'll have to go round. South or North.'

So they turned back and went the long way, through Knightsbridge, Hyde Park Corner, near enough to Buckingham Palace. Eva stared out of the window and saw strong stone buildings with no obvious damage, although she knew many had been hit. Even when they passed jagged ruins or piles of rubble, she had to concentrate to believe that this had been a place of death. Yet she knew that in the three weeks after that first bombing which she'd witnessed, hundreds had been killed and injured each night. It took time, she thought, to really believe in death. Then she thought of what Eddie went through each day and felt like a foolish child.

'I won't get any closer to Victoria,' Eddie said. He stopped the car at a traffic light just outside the station.

She was about to kiss him, not saying goodbye, when she suddenly laughed.

Eddie looked at her with surprise.

'My train goes from Paddington Station!' How happy she felt as they drove on.

'We're both mad,' said Eddie, without surprise. 'We'll go along Park Lane.'

There had been a bomb or bombs in Park Lane. Again Eva stared out of the window, wondering about the dead. Or if there were any dead.

'The West End's getting hit then.' Eddie wound down his window and drove slowly. He hadn't been to London recently either. The evening air carried the smells of burnt bricks, whiffs of gas from broken mains and somewhere under it the dusky autumnal odours from the park on their left.

'I'm glad I'm not a bomber pilot,' commented Eddie.

'I'm glad too.' Eva remembered when they'd walked through Hyde Park to the station. It had been bitterly cold and Eddie, despite being dressed only in his uniform, had refused the offer of her red scarf. It felt like an age ago.

This time Eddie drove right up to the station, even though it was very busy. 'Hank's in town,' he said. 'Eye trouble again. Actually, I think he does more good here, talking up the British cause with his powerful American friends. Perhaps I'll see if I can find him.'

Eva tried not to feel jealous. 'I thought you needed to get back.' She sounded jealous.

'Yes, I do.' Eddie tapped his fingers on the wheel.

Eva kissed him. Eddie had explained to her how he felt after they'd made love under the table in that little room.

'I'm so happy I came, even though I didn't draw much,' she said. This time they kissed more tenderly. She got out of the car and went briskly towards the station. When she turned to wave, he was still watching so she waved again.

Eddie drove slowly to the Savoy Hotel. As a fighter pilot, it pained him that the city could not be saved from attack. But he was also impressed by the orderliness of roped-off destruction, of signs, sandbags and uniformed men and women, ATS, ARP, AFS, NFS painted on their helmets. He imagined it must be more confused in the East End where the houses and shops were often closer together. Vaguely, he wondered about Sonia; he hadn't seen or even thought of her for months. She could hardly be handing out anti-war leaflets. Maybe, now Russia had come in on the right side, she'd change her tune. He wondered if his father still saw her. Perhaps God had taken her place.

The foyer of the Savoy was very full. How odd it seemed that people didn't flee the city! Encapsulated in his own world, Eddie hadn't given much thought to London. Now he realised that of course the city had to go on, in the same way as he had to go up into the air. It was all part of the simple demands of war.

He was making his way to the reception when he spotted Angela coming towards him. She was wearing dark slacks and jacket which made her yellow hair glow even more brightly than usual. Press I.D. hung round her neck. At first she didn't seem to recognise him then she started, cried 'Oh, you!' and flung her arms round him.

'What is it?'

'I'm on my way to hospital. Have you got your car with you?'

'Yes. I've …'

'Can you drive me to see Henry?'

Somehow they were in the car together. 'I thought I'd have to fight for a taxi.' Angela took out a compact and lipstick from her bag. She tried to apply red lipstick with shaking hands. 'You're my fucking saviour. Sorry. I'm upset. Of course I'm bloody upset! You know the way to Saint Thomas's? Not far.'

'I didn't know Hank's eyes were bad enough to put him in hospital,' said Eddie.

Angela gasped, 'Oh, Eddie!' she clapped shut her compact and put it away with the lipstick. 'I thought you'd come because you knew.'

Eddie didn't look at her. 'What happened?'

'We were having dinner out last night. In Piccadilly.' She stared straight ahead as she spoke. 'We were just finishing when the sirens went. We were heading for a shelter but the bombs came too quickly or we went too slowly. Henry, sorry, Hank, was right beside me. A great lump of ceiling crashed down, hit him full on, missed me altogether. He's been unconscious all last night, all today. I only left him because I needed to get some of the plaster dust off me. Oh Eddie, I'm so frightened.' She turned suddenly and clung to his arm so he had difficulty steering.

'Which hospital did you say?' Eddie kept his eyes on the road ahead, not blinking, scarcely breathing. Hank would be all right. Angela would naturally fear the worst.

'St. Thomas's,' repeated Angela. 'We'll have to fight our way in. Last night's was a bad raid.'

Eddie and Angela stood on either side of Hank's bed. His normally brick red face was grey, his eyes closed. He seemed already gone. Another one gone, thought Eddie dully, and he could say nothing to console Angela.

'He's still breathing,' she said, putting her face close to Hank's.

Eddie went downstairs where a WVS woman gave him a cup of tea. He stood drinking it slowly and was just thinking of leaving when Angela reappeared. Her face was distorted with crying.

'He's gone. He passed as soon as you left. A doctor came. I've got to get away while the nurses do their thing. You know. It's so horrible. Please drive me.'

Eddie led her to the car. He walked like an automaton and opened the door like a chauffeur. Angela cried all the way back to the Savoy.

'Please come up with me just for a moment,' she begged. Eddie sat on a chair still and silent while Angela went through the whole story of her life with Hank. She sat on the bed and sometimes lay down for a moment and sometimes sat up very straight. She cried as she spoke. Her father had always been rich, she told Eddie, old rich, not like Hank's father. Everybody thought Henry was so easy-going. 'Such an affable man,' people said, but he was a bundle of anxieties. That's why he preferred it over here where nobody knew him and he was free of baggage. 'But I always knew his worth. I loved him!' she cried out, 'I knew we'd have a future together. And now what? Now what! Why did he ever come over here!' She wailed and sobbed.

Eddie's stomach was hard like a rock, his neck rigid and his heart jerking. Angela's extreme grief helped him to hold himself in like a spectator. He'd loved Hank too and probably understood him better than Angela realised. They had grown up together. Another friend gone. His last close friend. But he was on duty the next morning. He couldn't afford to let go. He needed a drink. He needed to get back to his base. He could sit in the Mess and pretend to play solitaire.

'Angela, I've got to leave. Let me know when…'

'Not yet!' She interrupted him, her voice rising. 'Please. I'm going back to the hospital but stay just for a few minutes more. I have no real friends here.' Her face was blotched with red, her eyes small, with swollen eyelids.

Eddie looked at his watch. It was lucky there'd been no raid yet. He went to Angela and put his arm round her. 'Is there anyone I can get to be with you?'

Angela grasped his hand. 'Please! Please! Don't go! ' She pushed her head in his chest like a child looking for comfort.

Eddie knew he mustn't share her panic. He felt her hot trembling body before pulling away.

Angela held out her hands as if to drag him back. 'I never really wanted to make love but I did it for him. Why ever did I hold back? What a waste! What will I do! What will I do!' Her total lack of control made her seem another woman to the cool, efficient Angela Eddie had known. He tried to make himself deaf. For a moment, he remembered his meeting with Andy's parents and their stoic acceptance. Why had it angered him? He wished Angela would show some of the same dignity.

As gently as he could manage, he sat her down on the bed and started toward the door. The further he was from her, the calmer he felt. 'I'm so sorry. I know how much he loved you.'

She shouted, 'I've known him all my life! He's the only man in my life! I would have let him fuck me all the time if I'd thought it would keep him alive!'

'He loved you,' repeated Eddie, desperately searching for a way to escape. 'Why don't I ring your embassy? Is there a friend there?'

'The embassy?' Angela stared at Eddie. She became silent. She smoothed her tear-darkened hair from her face. She sat up straight and put her hands together. 'Yes. Yes. I can call them myself.'

Abruptly, she stood up and pointed to the corner of the room. 'I keep that can of petrol for people who drive me around. Take it please.' Her voice was quite different, although her hand shook.

Eddie went over to the can, at least three gallons, he estimated, and picked it up. 'Thank you. That will be very useful. I'm so very sorry ... I'll phone you tomorrow.' But he thought, I can't promise anything about tomorrow, not even to Eva, and he pictured her naked on the floor. He continued to think of Eva as he went down the corridor.

When he got out into the street, he looked up and saw a thick carpet of cloud. There'd be no bombing that night.

CHAPTER TWENTY-FIVE
October 1940

Eva went up to her studio and took out her sketches of Eddie. It struck her that a face would be much easier to paint if it mirrored the personality of the sitter. Perhaps old people were more fixed. She stared at it for some time and noted that the warmth of the little room was comforting now.

Crossing the landing to her bedroom, she took off all her clothes. She tried to catch her nakedness in the small mirrors on the wall. She stood on a chair and eventually took down the mirrors for a better view of her body. Now that it had been touched by Eddie, she was much more interested in it. She touched herself and imagined her hand was Eddie's but soon she stopped. He would be her only lover.

⊰⊱

Professor Speke's study was dimly lit. Eva unwittingly felt herself sucked into its darkness. Her father stared at her, his hair white, his eyes black holes.

'You called?' He could not know about Eddie but, if he did, she didn't care.

'My dear. My dearest. Sit down. Was your weekend, your weekend with...' he paused, clearly his mind was not on his daughter's weekend. He seemed nervous but not, Eva thought, distraught. Nor did she believe he was thinking about Cousin Phoebe. This was not a Cousin Phoebe face with the intimation of boredom. This face, despite its aged angles, had an intensity. Irritated with herself for thinking so carefully about her father when she only wanted to contemplate Eddie, Eva sat passively waiting for the Professor to speak again.

'See for yourself.' He pushed a small slip of paper across the desk.

Eva picked it up. She read '*Meine Lieblinge* I am well. I am in a camp. Tomorrow we travel. I will find you.' It was her mother's handwriting, different from anyone else's because she was German. At the bottom of the paper there was a sketch of a violin.

Muddled emotions of fear, love and anger kept her head down. 'She doesn't play the violin.' She heard her voice, bitter and low. She knew her mother was dead.

The Professor dragged the bit of paper back to him and stared at it eagerly. 'It is her writing.'

'It could have been written any time. She's been away a year.'

'Oh, please.' The Professor flapped his hand. 'Why are you being so hard?'

'We know she's dead.' Eva's voice was flat. 'You know better than me what's happening over there. I can't see how you can believe in that scrap of paper.' Eva watched her father's misery with cruel and pitying eyes. 'What camp? Where are they travelling? Who are *they* indeed?'

He knows nothing about me, thought Eva. He doesn't know that my lover risks death every day and every day friends die in the most horrible way around him. Why did her father want to play games with a silly scrap of paper?

'You know she's dead.' She watched her father put his head in his hands. Eventually, he said, in a dignified voice, 'It has given me hope. I admit I had lost hope but now it has come again. Hope costs nothing. The merest speck of hope is better than nothing. Perhaps you don't understand that.'

Eva didn't answer but she thought, no, I don't understand. Hope when it is false is self-deception, muddle, new suffering. 'I'm sorry, Father.' Her anger was gradually fading away, leaving a wider gap between them than ever. 'I'll pray for her.' Why had she said that when her father didn't believe in God and she probably didn't either? Perhaps it was just a form of politeness.

'Thank you.' He seemed to accept it as that.

She went over and kissed his dry cheek. 'Good night, Father.'

It was weeks since she had gone into the living–room but now she opened the door. It was dark and cold, unused. She went over to her mother's piano and opened the lid. She played three notes. Couldn't her father understand that she needed her mother to be dead, not probably or possibly or almost certainly but absolutely. A spurt of anger re-emerged. Her mother had wanted to go, knowing the risks, abandoning her daughter. But it was a worn–out anger. She loved her mother. Her mother would have understood about Eddie. Eva lowered the piano lid carefully. She would ask Valtraud to dust it.

⤜

The CO found Eddie in the Mess. He had only just arrived and was gobbling a cheese sandwich.

'Thought you might have done one of your runners,' he said jovially.

'No such luck.'

'Come to my office before you turn in.'

'Right, sir.'

The CO already had the bottle and the two little glasses on the desk when Eddie walked in. 'Sit down.' He poured two very small drinks. 'I'm cutting back.' He took a sip. 'I've heard that Hank's been badly injured. Did he make it?'

'No, sir.'

'I'm Les, tonight. Hank was a hero. No need for him to fight, although more Americans are joining the force. But to be killed in a London raid. Ironic.'

'Worse than that.'

'Makes you think.'

'About death, you mean.' Eddie thought that at least Hank deserved the forbidden D-word. The two men looked at each other. Eddie guessed he hadn't been summoned here for a chat and a drink, although that was sometimes the case. 'How were things this afternoon?' he asked respectfully.

'We didn't need your squadron. That leads me to my question. How do you like being Squadron Leader?'

'Because I'm no good?' Eddie sipped his whisky.

'You're one of our best pilots...'

'Surviving pilots.'

'As you say.'

Eddie stared into his glass. The war seemed to have taken away choice, likes, dislikes; you did what you were told. 'I'd never thought of myself as a leader. More of a loner. Good at thinking for myself.'

'You were on your own in the Mess.'

'Was I?'

Les sat back in his chair. 'I knew I was taking a bit of a punt on you. You're far too young for one thing.'

'Some of the chaps are even younger, inexperienced too. They hardly stand a chance, like ghosts already, and I can't save them.'

'Isn't your job to get the enemy?'

'I'm good at that.'

'Your award, incidentally, is progressing through the system.' Les paused to put the bottle away. Out of temptation, Eddie thought. 'I've got a new chap coming in. Shot down a couple of months ago. In hospital but OK now. In France at the time of Dunkirk. Senior to you.'

'I was only Acting Squadron Leader.'

'That's true. I've seen men lose their way. You remember Mel?'

'Can't say I do.'

'One op. He never came back. It transpired that a member of his squadron had seen him heading out to sea, not chasing the Hun, just flying, without much fuel. Neither he nor his plane were ever seen again.'

Eddie drained his glass, 'I enjoy success. Winning.'

'All the same I'm going to move you to Warmwell. South West. Fresh start. They've had a tough time trying to stop bombers getting to Portland Naval Base and further afield.' The CO stopped talking and looked at Eddie warily.

Eddie knew several things about RAF Warmwell. Pilots' gossip, which was usually accurate, claimed that it was too close to the coast for fighters to get into the air above an Me 109 or 110. It was a satellite airfield with Middle Wallop at its hub. It was over a hundred miles west of London and it was less than twenty miles from Tollorum. Was that why the CO was sending him there? Did he think he was cracking and might need to hide his head at home?

'When do I go, sir?'

'No time like the present.'

'I suppose you mean tomorrow.'

'Good man!' The CO tapped the table.

It was time to leave. Eddie saluted and went to his room. There was an unknown man asleep in the other bed. Willy's mother's clock ticked beside his own bed. He began undressing, then sat down. After all, what was there to miss here? Jenkins and Jones certainly. He was as reliant on Jenkins and Jones as he was on his Spitfire. No dawn was too early, no dusk too late for them. Even in the days of the airfield bombing they were on the apron, checking, ready to hoist him into the cockpit, steadying the wings and invariably asking on his return, 'Any luck, sir?' Modestly proud if he held up a finger, sympathetic at a shake of the head which was more usual now.

Perhaps he should have got to know them better, some pilots did, but he'd wanted them all to himself with no personal details, pregnant wife, frail mother, to get between them. He had been happy to see them as one identity, Jenkins and Jones, his devoted ground staff, Welsh but you can't have everything. He should get them a farewell present. But how could he when he was leaving the next day? He could buy them a bottle but he didn't even know if they drank.

Eddie bent over and pulled off his boots and socks. His feet were long and pale. They didn't look strong enough to control the control the rudder bar in the tumbling, swirling cockpit.

Eva sat attentively in a life class. Omy, who had arrived late as always, was dabbing pink on the paper plus an occasional dark squiggle to indicate nipples or pubic hair. The Professor, not her father that day, glared at her, advising the other students that he had spent five years in the Uffizi gallery making pencil studies of marble busts.

'Colour is treacherous,' he hissed, 'and can turn against you.'

'Is it true,' asked a student, in a squeaky voice, 'that life classes have only been recently allowed at the Ruskin?' His squeaky voice was due to an injury to his windpipe sustained during the retreat from France. He'd confided in Eva that the injury was a small price to avoid fighting in some faraway hell-hole.

The Professor ignored him too. 'Regard your pencil as a bridge between your imagination and the figure in front of you. Beware of the line. A figure has no lines. If I see a containing line, I shall react mercilessly.'

Omy gave a theatrical giggle but the rest of the thirty or so students, including Eva, took a more respectful hold of their pencils.

At a break with tea and buns, when Eva was standing on the white stone steps outside the Ruskin, Omy appeared. She was carrying her oil painting which had smeared her smock bright pink.

'Why doesn't the old goat love my work? I never use containing lines. Why hasn't he noticed? Because he never looks at me. He's scared of my youth and sex appeal. I've a good mind to seduce him.'

'How could you!' protested Eva feebly.

'At least there's no chance of getting pregnant with a dried up old stick like that. My ma was only just seventeen when she popped me.' Omy leant her painting against one of the steps and stood back consideringly. 'Has that man never heard of Impressionism?'

'I think he's more of a classicist,' Eva glanced at Omy's painting. It really was the most revolting pink.

'Although I must admit, this is disgusting.'

'I suppose you only did it to annoy him.'

Omy kicked her painting which fell on its face. 'How's that artist lover of yours, the one living in a pig-pen in Dorset?'

'A barn,' said Eva. 'He's not my lover.' In order to avoid talking about Eddie or her mother, she had offered Jack to Omy.

'I might visit him.'

'I'm sure he'd love that,' said Eva politely. But Jack was *her* territory, even if she didn't altogether want him. 'It's started to rain.' She stepped past Omy and went back to the studio. The model, robed in scarlet, was smoking a cigarette by the door. Eva scrutinised her drawing with the new curiosity of a fresh eye. The buttocks were nice and round, without being outlined, she noted with satisfaction. Rounder than her own buttocks, she suspected.

⊰⊱

Eddie drove through Oxford. It was term time and there were a great many students dashing in and out of the stone colleges or huddling in groups on the pavements. It felt like a long time since he'd seen so many young men out of uniform and it was very was hard to believe that he had been one of them only a year ago.

Although it was a grim kind of day, Eddie stopped as he approached the centre of town and put down the hood of his car. He, of course, was dressed in his RAF kit, including a flashy silk scarf as a cravat. Eddie was pleased with the stares, even if he did feel like an alien, driving through an ancient world.

It was a surprise when he saw a face he recognised. Oz had been on the walking tour with Hank. He waved. Eddie hesitated. He didn't know the man any more. He stopped.

Oz leant over the car, 'Glad to see you're still with us.'

Eddie remembered he was a medic, which would explain why he was still at university. 'Not enough bodies to cut up?' Why had he said that when he should have told him about Hank? Too late now. Hank was gone.

'Want a cup of tea?'

'Perhaps later. Off to persuade my college to give me a berth for a couple of nights.'

'The colleges take any old riff-raff now. Brasenose is filled with thuggish soldiers.'

'A step up from the usual rugger buggers.'

'I'll look out for you.'

The interchange cheered Eddie. He found himself fantasizing about being wounded, parachuting out, and coming round to see Oz's long, clever face peering concernedly.

It was a surprise to see the same old porter at the lodge of Eddie's college.

'Of course I can find a room for you, sir. I'll talk to the boss. Glad to be of service to one of our young heroes. Why do you think Oxford hasn't been bombed, sir?'

'Give it time, Plush.' Eddie smiled. The man hadn't been so friendly in the past. More of a running battle to get him punished for his misdemeanours. And what were they? Drink, noise, late nights, arrogance. They seemed not so serious now.

'We shut up shop at eleven.' Plush called as Eddie walked away.

He drove along the Banbury Road towards Eva's house. He stopped and looked at his watch. Three o'clock. He'd missed lunch. A short woman with a pretty cat-like face, came along the pavement and turned into one of the houses. Eddie recognised her as the German Jewish refugee. He got out of the car and closed the roof. He was still standing undecided, when he saw Eva, riding her bicycle towards him. Something flew out of the basket and she stopped, dumped her bicycle and ran back to pick it up. She was full of vitality, bending with supple ease to pick up a piece of paper. Eddie remembered how he had first noticed her for the pool of calm she spread about. This girl was different.

Still not noticing Eddie, Eva stared at the paper. She frowned and made a shape on it with her finger. It was not difficult to guess she was looking at one of her drawings. He wouldn't have been surprised if she'd taken a pencil out of her pocket and started on it then and there.

'Eva!'

'Eddie!' She ran straight for him, threw herself at him, bound him in her arms. 'Oh, Eddie. I didn't think I'd see you for ages!'

This was why he'd come. 'I've got two nights leave before my next posting.'

'You have to spend it all with me!'

They sat in the car and kissed, then lay back to breathe, although tightly holding on to each other's hands.

A passerby knocked at the window. He had a mild, apologetic face. 'Do you know whose bike that is? It nearly caused an accident.'

'Heavens!' Eva jumped out and pulled her bicycle off the road. She didn't even look for the paper which had taken flight once more. She returned to Eddie. 'What do you want to do? Do you want to come in? I warn you, it's very gloomy.'

They went to the house, the door already opened as they arrived by a curious Valtraud. 'My father's in bed,' Eva whispered to Eddie.

'We could go somewhere else,' he whispered too.

Valtraud offered tea and a voice, rather feeble from upstairs called, 'Eva, is that you?'

Eva who had taken Eddie's hand again, dropped it. 'Yes, Papa. I have a visitor.'

'Later, then, later.'

Eva led Eddie into the dark living-room, and stood in front of the piano. 'This was my mother's. She played beautifully but, despite all her teaching, she had to admit I didn't have any talent.'

'You're a painter.' It was a statement to remind himself.

'My father had a note, perhaps from my mother, perhaps from a camp, sent we know not when. He wants to believe she is still alive but his heart tells him otherwise. So he is ill. He was already but now he's worse.'

Eddie put his arm round Eva. Her body was quivering. 'I'm sorry.' He knew he should have said more but it just wasn't possible. He thought of telling her about Hank but that wasn't possible either.

Valtraud came in with a tray of tea and biscuits. 'You are in here.' She put down the tray and switched on a light.

'I was showing Eddie my mother's piano,' said Eva, a little defiantly.

'It is sad.' Valtraud lifted the lid of the teapot. 'I hope it is strong.'

'My mother arranged for Valtraud to leave Germany,' said Eva. She sat down, and poured tea carefully into the two cups. Milk and sugar?'

'I met her before,' said Eddie. He felt he was being tested. Before, Eva had simply admired him. 'Two spoons of sugar if you've got enough.'

Eva saw he was uneasy but couldn't stop herself. She wanted him to be at least a little bit part of her life. 'None of us take sugar so there's plenty.'

Valtraud watched them for a moment and then left. She was twenty and had had a boyfriend at home. Who knows where he was now. In the goodness of her heart, she wanted Eva and Eddie to be happy but in a dark corner, she was jealous and angry. Besides, Eddie was a pilot, trained to kill her countrymen. They were not all Nazis.

'We'll drink our tea, I'll see Papa, then we'll leave.' A brighter thought struck her. 'Would you like to see my studio?'

Eddie waited in Eva's studio while she visited her father. He looked at the sketches of London being bombed, of the various portraits of him, of neat drawings and wild paintings. Now he had to accept that she had a life away from him. Perhaps that was good. It made her seem stronger and him less responsible.

As they left the house, Valtraud stood in the hallway. 'Often at night I hear the bombers going over. Very high. Very heavy sound. They are going to cities not so far, I think?' She looked at Eddie.

He nodded. 'Birmingham. Coventry. Sometimes we stop them.'

'So sorry.' Valtraud shut the door carefully behind them.

'I can see why you like coming to Tollorum.' Eddie smiled.

'I'm lucky really.' Eva smiled too. 'Valtraud is very kind to me, you know, and she doesn't moan in her sleep anymore. She even has a few friends.'

'There's only a certain amount of sadness anyone can feel.' For the third time that afternoon he thought of Hank. He put Eva's arm in his and began to walk faster. 'How about the park? It's not cold.' He wondered whether he had a room in college yet and, if so, whether he could smuggle in Eva.

'I don't mind where we go as long as I'm with you.'

They walked over damp grass by the fast-flowing river and, looking into the water, like a dark sky with its sudden depths and swirls, Eddie began to talk about Warmwell.

'I'll be so near the sea, over it before I'm properly in the air. Sometimes pilots fly backwards first to get a run at it. I could almost live at Tollorum but that wouldn't work. Think of poor mother getting up at four to wave me off. It wouldn't be allowed anyway. They'll be new aeroplanes, new chaps to get to know, new fitters and riggers, new Mess customs, new quarters, new pub. Everything, even the flying, will be different. We all need sleep, that's the problem. Not so bad now, of course. Now the bombings are mostly night time. We're nearing the end of the Battle of Britain, so we're told, and it must be true because quite often we go up only once or twice in a day.'

As Eddie talked the exhaustion that lay in wait for him every minute descended like a heavy cloud. They both began to walk slower until they found a bench and sat down. 'Sometimes I feel as old as that chap over there.' He was staring at a bench where a large man in a long overcoat, scarf and homburg sat, head down.

Eva didn't feel old. She felt as if her life was just bursting open. She looked across at the old man. 'That's Professor Lamb,' she said.

'So it is.'

The Professor stood up, recognised them and raised his hat. 'A little chilly now.' He moved away.

'He wasn't very friendly.' Eva commented.

'I suppose he prefers books to people. I can't imagine living so long.' Once again Eddie thought about Hank. This time he took

Eva's hand and said, 'Hank was killed by a bomb in London.'

Eva saw he was flushed and his eyes shining with pain. 'I'm so sorry. He was kind to me. When we were altogether at Tollorum, he explained a poster to me. '*Save Bread, Save Lives, Serve Potatoes.*' It was to do with our Navy.'

Eddie took Eva's fingers and laid them out on his knee. 'Hank liked explaining things. He was clever and unselfish and fought for England because he loved it.'

'I'm very sorry,' repeated Eva. What could she say to help him? He was still playing with her fingers.

'The RAF might want a funeral but I wouldn't put it past Angela to get Hank's body transported back to America.' Eddie let go of Eva's hand abruptly. 'I'm frightfully sorry but I think I've got to get my head down.'

'What?' Eva didn't understand. Was Hank's death a way of pushing her away?'

'If I have time, I'll telephone in the morning. We could meet. Maybe.'

Of course there was nothing she could say. He was exhausted, mind and body. She could tell that by the way he walked. Eva watched him go. She thought she did that a lot. He was right, he did look old.

CHAPTER TWENTY-SIX
October 1940

Eva was reading a letter from Jack:

My dear Eva, I trust you are working hard and your skills are beginning to match your imagination. Dorset has never been more evocative, early morning mists rise up and dissolve, revealing grass strong with pearly threads of dew. The chestnut trees gently turn from brilliant green to crinkly gold and the birds gather like gossiping old ladies in the hedgerows. The drawing I enclose features a tribe of bullfinches.

Eddie had not telephoned yet. But it was still only eight am, she looked at her watch, eight ten. Soon she would have to go to the Ruskin.

The village school is a success; it is firmly run by Miss Woolly, a spinster who, although not above thirty, dresses like a matron. I hope to draw her in one of her long hand-knit cardigans, the heather mix, preferably. I teach English and drawing to fifteen pupils aged from five to fourteen.

Eva put down the letter. Why did Jack assume her interest? Then she remembered how she'd shown Eddie her life the previous afternoon, her mother's piano, Valtraud's woes and kindness, her father's failing heart. She supposed that if you were in love with someone you wanted them to understand everything about you.

The bad news is that a herd of cows appeared in my field two days ago. They tear and trample the grass, then nose inquisitively at the barn and leave huge slimy pats wherever I walk. If I try to settle anywhere and paint, they circle round me like Red Indians about to charge. When I bearded the ancient tenant farmer in his filthy lair, he banged his spade – he was shovelling muck – and shouted 'Cows are in the frontline of the war, not that you'd know!' This morning a massive, bad-tempered bull joined the cows. I write this from the cottage Miss Woolley shares with her mother. Can Art survive with so much bellicosity around us?

≫≪

Eva was standing with Omy on the steps of the Ashmolean when she saw Eddie. Omy gasped, 'O my Lord! A god has come to visit us!'

Eva ran down the steps. 'Say I'm ill!' She called over her shoulder.

≫≪

Eva sat demurely in Eddie's room. A servant was laying plates of cold meat, bread and glasses on a round table, while Eddie lounged on a leather chair, his hands clasping its arms. Eva guessed he wasn't as relaxed as he looked.

'Thank you, Trendle,' said Eddie, as the servant left the room.

'It's early for lunch,' said Eva.

Eddie stared at her. The room suited her. He wondered if he could fix this image among the swirling clouds, the drifting cirrus, the twirling vapour trails in his mind. 'I've decided to stay the night at Tollorum before I report in.'

'So you'll go this afternoon?'

'It's getting dark earlier in the evening.'

Eva sat even straighter. Eddie watched her being brave. He needed to turn her back into the picture he'd seen at their first lunch-time meeting.

'I'm not very hungry,' said Eva.

'We're in no hurry.' Eddie lit a cigarette. He noticed Eva's surprise.

'You're right. I'm about the only pilot who doesn't smoke.' He stubbed out the cigarette.

They sat on either side of the little round table. Eddie poured himself a glass of wine. 'It's strange you're still so young.'

'Plenty of girls marry at eighteen.' She immediately regretted the reference to marriage. 'But not many drink.'

Eddie didn't notice the word marriage. He poured water into her glass. He was imagining the drive west to Tollorum. He would go down through the Wallops. Over Wallop, Middle Wallop and Nether Wallop, before heading across the Salisbury plain with Stonehenge on his right. Perhaps he would drop in on the Middle Wallop airfield. It was headquarters of Sector 10, of which Warmwell was a part and its CO was his mother's admirer. The war wouldn't have changed the beauty of the countryside, apart from the thunderous roar as one or more squadrons gave their aeroplanes full throttle and swept into the air. Eddie took a first sip of his claret – provided by the college to welcome a hero – and felt the noise of a Rolls-Royce 12-cylinder Merlin engine surge through his body.

Eva, peering at him over the rim of her glass, noticed the change in his expression. She wanted to sit close to him, to feel their bodies heart to heart, but he seemed remote. They had only kissed once when she had come into the room. She supposed they couldn't make love here. There was Trendle on guard.

They both ate little, talked little. It was a relief when Eddie walked Eva out of the college into a quiet autumn afternoon. There was no wind and an undecided sun far away. He stared with professional interest at the thin clouds.

'Altostratus. Shall I escort you back to the Ruskin?'

'No. No.' She wanted to ask piteously, *is there nowhere we can be alone?* But instead she cried, 'Just look at that magpie!' They'd been holding hands without really knowing but now Eva broke apart to point at a large magpie on the roof of the Porter's Lodge. 'Wicked creature.'

'You're not superstitious, are you?'

'Of course not. Anyway, I can see her mate further along.' This was a lie but, as Eva kissed Eddie on the cheek, she painted the second magpie in her mind's eye. Then she ran away. After several steps, she turned and called, 'Give my love to your mother!'

Eddie watched her go but only for a second, before turning back into the college.

'Nice sister,' commented Plush from his post at the gates. 'We're very close,' replied Eddie, firmly. It was reassuring to be downgraded from hero to his old disreputable status.

⚖

Sylvia saw Eddie's car arrive from her mother's window. She ran out of the room and down the stairs but slowed as she crossed the hall. A mother must be calm in wartime, accepting of all eventualities. Nevertheless, she called out, 'Lily? Eddie's here!' Lily, acting under the same loving duress, arrived in a hurry, then took off her apron, carefully folding it, before commenting, 'Bottling done for another year.'

'That's good.' Sylvia kept her eyes on the door. But Eddie surprised them by coming in through the drawing-room windows. They turned at his footsteps.

'Sorry I didn't let you know. I'm posted to Warmwell. On my way there.' The close attention of the two women unnerved him.

'So near!' said Sylvia, failing to disguise her emotion. She pictured an aeroplane overhead, an aeroplane falling in one of Tollorum's fields, the smashed body of a pilot being lifted out and carried into the house.

'Well then, you'll always know where to get a hot meal.' Lily did better.

'Funny, you should mention that,' Eddie smiled at her. 'I've got to leave early tomorrow. I'll bring my bags in.'

Darkness had fallen completely. Eddie took out his bags, pulled across the roof of the car, then stood quietly. Everything was quiet now, even the wood pigeons. The sky was enormous, the evening star already bright, others winking their way into visibility. It would be a bright, clear night. Perfect bombing weather.

'Come in, darling. It's getting cold.' Sylvia put her arm through his.

Eddie turned and gave her a quick kiss. 'I was tempted to go on now.'

'It's kind of you to come.' Sylvia wrapped her cardigan around herself. She could see he was nearer the brilliant sky than the dark earth. 'Of course, I wouldn't stop you.'

'No. You wouldn't do that. Where's father?'

'He was here two days ago. He's restless. He will be angry he's missed you.'

'He visited me and left behind his Bible. It's full of angry comments.'

Sylvia smiled. 'Let's go in.' She felt the cold night stabbing painfully. How awful, how unbearable that every meeting might be their last! She turned to go in.

'What does he do here?' Eddie didn't seem to notice she had turned.

'Since he's found God he comes more often. He sees a lot of the Rector. Of course the Rector more or less saved his life when he came here after Gallipoli. He taught him how to learn, that's when I first met him. He was like a wild man. He *was* a wild man, living in the Rector's shed, boozing in Weymouth. He joined my studies of the Classics. Now they read the Bible together.' Sylvia smiled suddenly. 'I'm not sure they've reached the New Testament yet.'

'Forgiveness not his strong suit?'

'He's been kinder recently.' Sylvia forgot the cold. It was true. She only realised as she said the words. Lately, it was as if he was trying to reconcile as much as to disturb. 'I just hope the dear old Rector doesn't drop dead before the process is complete.'

Sylvia and Eddie walked into the house together, arm in arm.

CHAPTER TWENTY-SEVEN
October 1940

'For Christ's sake, A Flight, get off the deck!' Eddie hadn't even heard the telephone ring and here he was, rudely roused from a sunny doze outside Dispersal, sprinting towards his new Spitfire. New design Spitfire. It was his leader, Beaky, who'd shouted and now he could see why. Surely this was supposed to be a quiet posting!

Even as a new hand helped him with his parachute and he went through the usual routine, he became aware of a huge force of bombers approaching from the south. It was far too high for Warmwell to be a target but it was their responsibility all the same. So the daylight raids hadn't gone out of fashion entirely. Just his luck. First afternoon. Where were the fighters? No time to look. Check R/T on; it certainly was, Beaky giving a blasting to the controllers who'd allowed the formation to get so close without informing anyone. We should have been scrambled ages ago. Check oxygen. If they were going to get above this lot, heading to Angels 30 or higher they'd need plenty of that. His job was simple enough: follow Beaky, follow orders. The bombers were going over them now. First job would be to catch them up.

Off they went, Eddie in starboard 'V' formation, rising upwards on full throttle at three thousand feet a minute. The usual exhilaration made his adrenalin soar with the plane. Noticing black petrol vapour pouring from the planes ahead, he decided to use his own energy boost. He sat back as the plane rocketed forward, the engine vibrating the whole machine. At sixteen thousand feet they could see the bombers, eighty of them, and above them, at something over twenty thousand feet, twenty escorting Me 109s. What next?

Sometimes he didn't envy the squadron leader. They certainly couldn't attack from behind with all those rear gunners, fingers on firing buttons.

'We'll take them from the front, boys.' shouted Beaky.

All well and good old chap, thought Eddie, but we're not ahead of them yet.

But soon they were, although only by a few miles.

'Prepare for head-on attack.'

Four of them against eighty with twenty fighters above. Not brilliant. Beaky did a steep turn to port and, since they were playing follow my leader, the rest did the same. Finger on the button. Coming straight towards them, a great wall of flying metal. Not easy to miss, you'd think. If you held your nerve and kept your finger steady.

Ahead Beaky finished firing and slipped deftly beneath the first bombers, followed by his number two. In all the months of attacking, Eddie had never done anything quite like this before; he'd considered head-on attacks a crude kind of fighting, depending more on steely nerves than skill. But now he felt magnetically drawn ever closer to the bombers while his fingers fired in an unbroken stream of bullets. The third Spitfire turned sharply away and Eddie was staring at an ugly Perspex nose of a Heinkel 111 coming straight at him.

'Oh my God!' As Eddie screamed, he was already wrenching round and down the poor Spit with all his might. The force was so great that he blacked out for a moment. Then he was dashing away towards the ground. The Heinkel was still far above. In a passion of relief, he imagined he spotted Tollorum and began to laugh manically. What a sight his Spit would make, buried head first in the field in front the house. 'That's my son,' Sylvia would comment benignly to a visitor.

Calm. He needed to calm himself. He must be well below five thousand feet by now. Oh, lovely brand-new Spitfire! Just push forward the rudder pedal anti-clockwise to the spin and she's happy to oblige.

Next moment the dive had ended and Eddie was sailing forward in an empty sky. His heart was still pounding, his face dripping with sweat and his knees knocking but what of it? He was also down to a thousand feet but that was easily put right.

Now he slid back the hood and looked down. He was nowhere near Tollorum, in fact that seemed to be the Bristol Channel to his right. He'd survived again. When had he started thinking like that? Time to let the sweat dry and head gently back to the base.

Eddie was last back but not by much. After reporting that he used up all his ammunition at nearly point-blank range with absolutely no idea whether he'd damaged or shot down a single plane, he went straight to the Mess, where he was met by loud voices and laughter. Often, he'd seen men silenced by their struggles with life and death, wanting a bit of solitude to recoup – he'd felt like that himself. But this lot seemed to be enjoying themselves. Perhaps things felt different when you were not going up four or more times a day.

'Eddie, old chap!' Beaky welcomed him. 'We thought you'd go straight through that Heinkel.'

'How did we do?' asked Eddie.

'Six confirmed and three probables for the squadron. Our flight got three confirmed, a Heinkel 111 and two Junkers 88. We chased them beyond Bristol. Cheers!'

Other pilots were crowding round now, smiling, raising cups of tea. Eddie wondered whether they were mocking his lack of success – he'd arrived with a fighting tally that gave him a reputation – but he didn't think so. Beaky had seemed genuinely pleased to welcome him back.

'I was scared rigid,' Eddie said. 'Must be getting old.'

The men laughed, chaffed him about being a has-been and that evening they drove to Rat Inn, named, as he was informed, for the rats that leave the sinking ship. Two or three squashed into Eddie's car, as usual filled up with aeroplane fuel, and set off in the direction of the sea. The smell of salt air was strong as they passed over a windy headland and arrived in a sheltered cove. Eddie felt confused. Over the last few months, the sea had been the place where he dreaded losing his life, dragged to the bottom by his heavy flying boots like a weighted corpse. The Channel was full of men unwillingly pulled into the wet underworld. In his worst night's dreaming, he had heard their pleading, their screams, their silence. But this was the sea of his childhood: long hours spent on Chesil Beach, clambering up the cliffs, finding fossils with never-failing amazement. Two hundred million years old! He counted in days now.

'Come on old thing.'

'Still seeing the ugly mug of that Heinkel?'

'Moonstruck, I'd say.'

Eddie became aware of friendly voices. How long had he stood at the door of the pub? He pushed it open and was met by a heavy blue blanket and then by another. The blankets smelled of smoke and booze and damp salty wool plus a heavy dose of dog. It dispelled images of deep, dark wetness and made certain that no predators outside on the sea or in the sky would be guided by the tiniest chink of light. In the bright gas light through clouds of smoke, two large lurchers' hairy inquisitive noses checked over the newcomers.

'I'm buying first round!' called Beaky. He wore an old tweed overcoat over his uniform. Besides him stood a pilot called Hoby, with a small terrier peering out of his arms. A large ancient clock on the wall, weights dangling, struck nine.

It seemed the safest place in the world.

⋙⋘

Early next morning, the whole squadron was vectored towards Southampton, codename 'Dustbin', at about 10am.

'It's not usually so busy,' complained Hoby, who was washing the terrier, named Terror, in a basin. 'It's got to be your fault, Eddie, you've brought the action with you.'

'I was sent here for a rest,' protested Eddie, as if it was a joke.

They'd only just been put on standby when they were scrambled.

'They're making up for yesterday's cock-up,' shouted Beaky. They were already running.

Eddie was beginning to admire this squadron. They could fly all right, but they were more individual, freer. Perhaps it was something about their situation on the edge of the sea or that they were such a small set-up, with authority mostly over the hills in Middle Wallop.

He clambered into the cockpit with no help, fastening his own straps.

Up in the air, with the usual exhilarating speed, he was flying Red 2 to Beaky. It was a blue-sky day, but filled with puffy white clouds, some of them based in grey. If they grew together they'd be big enough to hide a plane. Make the game more exciting.

Beaky was calling him on the R/T. 'Close up, old man. Let's give them a fright, two by two. They won't be expecting a whole squadron.'

'Angels right,' shouted Hoby excitedly, 'coming in over the sea. What dimwits! Don't they think we can see them?'

'Maybe they were caught earlier,' suggested another voice.

Eddie stopped listening. He could see them now. A surprisingly small group of bombers with a single squadron of Me 110s above them. For once the odds would be equal, with the fighters anyway. In a few seconds they would be over them and could come in with the sun above them.

'Red section, take out the fighters,' shouted Beaky above the noise of the Merlin engines, above the noise of ten hearts thundering. 'The rest of you get to the Heinkels. Tally Ho!'

How strange to hear 'Tally Ho!' shouted high above land that had been hunted over by generations. In the old days by his own family.

It was a copybook operation. Beaky and he went straight for the 110s who broke up immediately. For once they seemed a little hesitant, seeking comfort from these puffy clouds that still were too small for hiding. They would be near the end of their range, longing to get back over the Channel. He picked out one of the fighters, circled him acrobatically, firing sporadically, playing with him, eventually driving him inland in a north-westerly direction. He must be a beginner because he was now in a one-way, one-ending direction. Perhaps he was wounded because he didn't try to turn and flew at about seven thousand feet. It was a chase game and then they were back over Warmwell where some gunners opened fire in a random way.

Eddie closed in, kept his finger on the firing button. He saw the tracers, felt in his finger the bullets as they hit a wing, then the body near the black swastika. The pilot was moving, probably unclipping himself, pulling back the hood. Smoke and flame spurted with shocking violence. Finally, he'd hit the engine. The plane dived steeply. The pilot jumped.

Eddie wrenched open his hood and watched the plane falling towards the Dorset hills. Some way back now, the pilot's parachute bloomed, dropping gracefully through the little clouds, another puff of white. Eddie turned his attention back to the 110, fast nearing the ground. He looked again, scarcely believing his eyes. The plane was about to smash down on the great Cerne Giant, a gigantic naked man, including phallus to match, cut into the grass. Standing back from him, armed with what looked like pitchforks, danced small figures triumphantly. Clearly they were planning a warm welcome for the Jerry. Their enthusiasm was catching and, as if he was an over-excited novice, Eddie found himself performing victory rolls over their heads. Although he couldn't hear the cheers, he could see the outstretched arms until they ran away as, with a great crash of metal and flame, the aeroplane fell among them.

Eddie turned round then, imagining with a smile, their disappointment at the empty plane. If the German pilot had made a good parachute landing, less bellicose men would pick him up and, if he'd fallen badly, he'd find himself in Dorchester hospital, only a few miles from Warmwell. How many Heinkels had got through to bomb Southampton, Eddie wondered, and how many people on the ground had been killed or maimed?

He stopped feeling sorry for a young pilot in a hospital bed.

That evening Eddie set off again with a full car for Rat Inn. Terror, the terrier, yapped in his ear, as Beaky and the rest yelled encouragement to go faster. He shouted the story of the Cerne Giant to appreciative roars.

≫≼

Reggie Gisburne had come to Tollorum to collect his son and escort him home to be with his mother. Reggie seemed far younger than George, red-faced, energetic, impatient.

'You'll be glad to get rid of one patient, Sylvia, I have no doubt.'

Sylvia looked at him warily. She had offered him coffee while George made his final preparations for departure and they sat together in the study. His loud voice and his way of sitting with his head jutted forward, perhaps in Churchillian imitation, unnerved her. He should have been allowed to fight, she thought. His body was still strong but his brain had never been big enough to flourish behind a desk.

'So, how's the war going?' she asked. 'We only get a very sketchy picture here.'

'Better than it was.'

'Eddie has been stationed not far from here,' she said.

'Great chaps, those flyers,' said Reggie heartily, 'We must never assume invasion is right off the cards.'

'I was wondering about the wider war?'

'There's a great deal of that. They're threatening to take me off Europe and put me on the Middle East. I suppose it's better than Greece. At least there's a good fight going on in the Sahara. Have you heard of this new lot young Stirling's got together? SAS they call themselves. Yes, Egypt wouldn't be such a bad option.' Reggie paused briefly, before adding gloomily, 'I'd swap London for Cairo any day.'

'London must be hard. The bombs. No sleep.'

'I'm not the sedentary type. You know that, Sylvia.'

This seemed to be an appeal in his plummy dark eyes.

'Is something wrong, Reggie?'

'Whenever I do see Gussie, she moans or shouts or weeps. It's not surprising, is it?'

'What isn't surprising?' asked Sylvia.

'The trouble is the friend, the female friend concerned has got the wrong end of the stick.' continued Reggie bitterly.

'The female is threatening to tell Gussie?' Sylvia was taken aback by Reggie's unprecedented wish to confide in his sister-in-law. Was this another effect of war?

'More or less. More more than less.' Reggie gave an aggrieved smile.

'Then you'll have to tell Gussie first. Throw yourself on her mercy,' Sylvia warmed to the scene. 'Insist this woman was nothing but a passing fancy, created by your beloved Gussie's absence. Implore her instant return to London...' Reggie's face of doom caused Sylvia to slow up and stop.

There was the sound of a crutch, knocking at the door. 'That's George!' cried Sylvia gaily. She turned back at the door. 'Your friend's not that actress, Moira Lipscombe?'

Reggie raised his heavy head. 'No such luck. She knew the score.'

Sylvia held out her arms to her nephew. 'Dearest George, I am going to miss you.'

The young man leant on his crutches. Pale and delicate as a flower when before he seemed to take after his father, he smiled wryly. 'It looks like the war will go on forever now that Germany, Italy and Japan have joined forces.'

'Oh dear. Japan. The Rising Sun. Are you still hankering to fight?'

Reggie joined her. 'Of course he is. Got two legs, hasn't he. Another couple of months and he'll be fit as a fiddle, won't you George?'

Sylvia watched father and son going out together and thought she'd never understand men's desire to fight. She hadn't in the last war and she didn't in this. Of course these two were regular soldiers – as her father had been. She supposed she must allow them pride and joy in their chosen profession.

'Come on, old girl,' Reggie called to hurry her. 'Got a few hundred miles to drive before dark.'

Sylvia caught them and kissed each in turn. As the car raced away, she hoped that it was action they liked, not killing.

CHAPTER TWENTY-EIGHT
October 1940

Eddie's squadron was called out often, but usually too late, too low or asked to take on fighters who were provoking rather than important. They faced the first of the fighter-bombers, Me 109s with a heavy bomb slung under them. In fact they were more of a threat to sheep than planes, since the moment they were attacked, their pilots jettisoned their bombs and made a run for it. There were fewer heavy daylight bombers coming over but the squadron was sent up just as often. Life seemed almost routine.

When the controllers did warn of a big force coming over, it could be fighters as high as 35,000 feet which took some reaching and yet the squadron still lost men. Hoby went and Eddie found himself Terror's new owner. The dog changed his allegiance remarkably quickly, following Eddie everywhere and sleeping on his bed.

One evening in the Rat Inn Eddie was bet a total of twenty pounds that he wouldn't take Terror on an op with him. Early the next day, Eddie smuggled the dog into the Spitfire. He had been sent off to chase for a solitary reconnaissance plane flying very high somewhere near Bournemouth. It was the sort of op where most times nothing would happen, least of all finding a single plane in a sky heavy with clouds. Indeed, the only movement came from three Hurricanes heading towards Salisbury. Terror had just poked his nose out of Eddie's jacket inquisitively when he heard a thickening in the sound of the engine, then a stuttering, prolonged into silence. He knew the routine, of course, if the plane had truly broken down, he should glide down on to a flat field. Someone had once managed to land on a road. Just another experience and not an enemy in sight.

Eddie turned on his R/T and gave the glad news to Warmwell. 'Cheers,' came the laconic reply. 'Try and bring her down in one piece but don't leave it too late to jump.'

'Good to know you care.' acknowledged Eddie.

'Any time. Did you find that reconnaissance?'

'Bugger off.'

Meanwhile the sky seemed very wide and the ground still far away. He'd been up at over 20,000 feet so it really was a long way down. They were still at 10,000 feet.

'Right, Terror, you close your eyes and I'll tell you when we're down.'

Eddie couldn't think how he'd been oaf enough to take another creature up with him. It must be like having a child to look after. 8,000, 6,000, 5,000, 4,000, they were coming down fast and soon he'd have to decide whether to jump. They were through the clouds now and he could see there were plenty of fields below, as well as woods, villages and roads. Unfortunately, they all seemed to be on hills or below hills or between hills or high stone walls. Not a nice big cricket pitch in sight. 3,000, 2,500, 2,000; it was now or never and the Spitfire's nose which was generally supposed to be turned snootily upwards was definitely pointing down.

'Sorry, Spit, discretion is the better part of valour.' Buttoning Terror securely into his jacket with his documents, he checked his parachute, slid back the hood and jumped. 'Right, pooch, more than you bargained for, I know, but put it all down to experience.' Then they were out, tumbling, falling, rip-cord pulled, floating, landing surprisingly calmly, in a field of turnips. It was raining. Eddie lay on his back and contemplated the bunched layers of clouds.

With a strong sense of unreality, he sat up and let out Terror who ran round and round in small circles, yapping loudly. Perhaps he'd lost his marbles or was furious or celebrating their safety. How did one tell with animals?

Wanting to see if he could spot the poor abandoned Spitfire, Eddie stood up just in time to hear a loud bang from somewhere over a high ridge of hills – or perhaps on it. He really had no idea where he was. In a moment he'd get out his map. Terror had stopped chasing his tail and was peeing over a large white turnip.

Eddie watched him rather vacantly, before following suit. He'd have to start walking, find a house with a telephone, get back into the world again. But there was no hurry, even if the rain was pelting now.

※

It was four hours before Eddie made it back to Warmwell. His means of transport included a very old horse and cart, the back of a motorbike and, only for the last twenty miles, a jeep from the base which he'd met by chance on the road.

'I'll give you a ride, sir,' said the driver, a groundsman, 'if you don't mind going by the hospital.'

'No problem.' Eddie hopped in, followed speedily by the terrier.

'Hey,' said the groundsman, 'that dog's followed you in.'

'Always popular with dogs,' agreed Eddie.

'But...' began the groundsman, before deciding life was too short. 'I'm Corporal Samwell.'

At the hospital, Eddie had an idea. He shut Terror into the Jeep and followed Samwell. It wasn't difficult to track down a German pilot fitting the dates when he'd shot down the plane over Cerne.

'He's got two broken legs,' said the receptionist. 'A very polite gentleman everyone says.'

Eddie found the pilot easily. He was sitting up in bed reading. His legs were covered in a cage.

'You speak English?' asked Eddie.

'The pictures are good but not that good,' said the pilot with very little trace of an accent. 'My mother is English. I was studying the Golden Age of Shakespeare at Hamburg University.'

'May I sit down?'

'Please.'

Eddie found a chair and sat down. He took out a full pack of cigarettes he'd just bought off Samwell, 'I think I owe you these?'

The pilot looked at him with new interest. 'Yes?'

'I shot your plane down.'

'Is that so. I expect you're an ace. I wouldn't have bet on my chances of surviving the war so you probably did me a good turn.' He stretched out his hand. 'I'll take the cigarettes anyway.'

Eddie handed them over. 'What happened to your legs?'

'They met a bloody stone wall.'

'Dorset walls are notorious. I've just bailed out myself. Engine failure.'

'You couldn't put her down?'

'Bloody stone walls. But I was lucky enough. I landed in a turnip field.

The two men looked at each other. They were very similar: same age, same build, both fair, even-featured. They could have been brothers.

Samwell appeared noisily at the door of the ward. 'If you don't mind, sir. I'm in a hurry now.'

Eddie stood up and shook hands with the pilot, 'Good luck.'

≈

Back in Warmwell, Eddie was in the Mess scrounging some food when a sergeant ran after him with a packet.

'Here, sir, this was left for you earlier.'

Eddie took it with him and forgot about it until he'd eaten two rounds of cheese sandwiches. He took off the brown paper: the Bible was back again with a note from his pa. *I left it for you. I am now on the New Testament which proposes many ideas I find difficult. The Road to Calvary strikes a chord, however. We are all on that, you more than most. But I've done my time too. You told me you were on good terms with God which I've thought about a good deal. Well, I'm glad I'm not young any more. Sylvia watches every plane that goes over with loving eyes. She is a clear-sighted woman. From your respectful father. May the Lord protect you.* Had he told him about that saying too?

Eddie hid the paper in the Bible just as he was called with the rest of Red Section to Dispersal. As he walked across the airfield he supposed Fred would declare he was walking the Road to Calvary. He thought of writing to Eva. But what could he say to her?

'I don't know how you got away with that pesky dog.' Beaky clapped him on the shoulder. 'How much will you clean up?'

'That depends on the honesty of my fellow pilots.'

'And their survival.' Beaky laughed merrily.

⚌

'What is that, Miss? A sky? Perhaps you see yourself as a Mr Turner?' Eva looked up with alarm as a throaty voice boomed in her ear, and saw The Great Artist, Omy's father. His bushy white hair with a hint of fierce red, his thick, pitted skin and prickly beard, made her feel soft and vulnerable as he leered over her. She kept her head bent close to her work. He continued, clearly enjoying himself. 'Or maybe that overrated decorator of the Sistine Chapel, Michelangelo? Visited Italy, have you?'

As he swayed away a little, Eva dared to look up. 'I'm trying out something.'

The Great Artist placed a large finger on her painting. 'Tell me, if you can, why is your sky so *moderate!*' The last word was bellowed so that several other students who had used this break period to pursue their own ideas, looked up nervously. Just possibly he was a genius, but most fled before discovering.

'The sky is not moderate. Never ever moderate. It is in a state of constant war! As desperate a war as the one we hear so much about on the wireless. Rain fights the clouds. The clouds fight the sun. The sun fights the mist. The mist fights the wind. The wind fights the clouds who fight each other which is not to mention the terrible attacks by lightning, thunder, gales, hurricanes and tornadoes. The sky is a battlefield! Not the limp, pretty thing you are choosing to show us. Yours is and forever will be a *moderate* sky. Why is that, I ask myself?' Here the Professor paused to tug on his beard, perhaps to imitate Jupiter, the God of war. 'Oh no! Can this mean you are a *moderate* woman? My God! Have you ever

266

heard of a great painter who is *moderate*? A moderate man – or woman – will never rise above a moderate painting. He is stuck, fatally, because he is so moderate he has not even noticed the battle. Then he – or she – paints with a pallid pallet to match his pallid mind. Despair. Should we despair of such a person?'

Now he took a few steps back and threw his arms wide to embrace the room whose inhabitants could hardly fail to pay attention. Eva breathed a sigh of relief as one captured and at last released.

'Exaggeration! The painter's best friend. Note what you see, what your mind's eye sees and exaggerate. *Exaggerate!*'

Despite her nervousness, Eva noted this word with interest. She appreciated the Professor had been giving a performance all along with her playing the part of unknowing stooge. She looked at her sky with a different kind of critical eye. She could see that her flowing lines and pastel colours would never fulfil The Great Artist's criteria. Was that because she didn't want it, because she was striving for calm, elegance, yes, even beauty? Or was it as the ancient professor judged that she was a moderate woman, scared of drama, striving for moderation? And, if that was true, that she was deliberately striving for balance which he could call moderation if he liked, why was that?

Ignoring the Professor's voice as he moved among the students, ruthlessly demolishing any inner confidence they might have been lucky enough to acquire over the last year of study, Eva placed her hands in her lap and examined her heart.

There was Eddie. There was Eddie at war in the sky. There was courage (his), terror (hers) and everyday exaggeration of life and death. How could she let that out and bear whatever might come next? She must hold Eddie and his war wrapped tight in her love and keep it safe. If she painted a pink and golden sky, she was helping to make it so. War was too real, too terrifying.

Now she remembered how charmed she'd been by Jack's painting of her face uplifted to a sky filled with a pattern of aeroplanes, criss-crossing white smoke trails and the occasional scarlet spurt of flame. Her own attempt at painting the bombing of London had been equally fatuous. She had turned death and destruction into charming patterns, nothing more. The Professor was right to scorn her!

Then she remembered how angry she'd been at Jack drawing that graveyard of planes at Cowley. She had refused to be turned into a voyeur, even sliced through her skin in protest. That had been honest.

Eva sat quite still, calm and pale while all these thoughts raged in her mind.

A large hand with a piece of charcoal descended on to her pad. It scrawled a few lines, squiggled once or twice. 'You cannot expect a Eureka moment overnight, my beauty.' Eva saw that the Professor's charcoal had breathed life into her picture. He supposed he was trying to cheer her now. It was an unexpected kindness.

'I would like you to sit for me.'

So that was it. All along the predatory male. She pushed back her stool and stood to face him. 'No thank you. I'm busy.' She enjoyed his shocked expression.

'Only a head, my dear. I work so quickly.'

She knew about a head that became shoulders, that became breasts. All the female students had learnt to avoid his old seeking hands. Perhaps Omy had dared him.

'No!' Eva gathered her belongings quickly and walked briskly from the room. Then she ran half-way home before remembering her bicycle and returning. Her 'No', forcible and independent, cheered her spirit. She bicycled home, telling herself that it was not to flee but to give herself time to consider.

Once in her studio, she flung herself onto her chair. It did not matter whether Eddie wrote, she must be part of his life, the suffering and the joy, not just the off-duty bits. It was no longer enough to peer through the narrow slits he opened for her. She would explain all that to him, go to Warmwell and they would talk. And kiss and make love. Eva smiled to herself.

Sylvia returned from a meeting in Dorchester and found Fred sitting in the hallway with the telephone in his hand.

'I didn't know you were back.' She hurried towards him and gave him a kiss but without putting too much enthusiasm into it. Fred took what he wanted and didn't like to be asked.

He put back the telephone on the cradle. 'Eddie called.'

'I missed him!' Sylvia felt tears ready to come.

'He thanked me for my bible and said he and a terrier called Terror had just had a lift from a parachute when his Spitfire's engine conked out. Came down in a turnip field. He said it was a surprisingly soft landing. The turnips must have been rotten. He seemed in high spirits.'

Sylvia tried not to imagine Eddie's jump into thin air. 'Now that he's left that terrible South East corner he seems more like himself. Have you noticed, Fred?'

'He doesn't go up so often. It's not so dangerous.'

It makes me nervous when you say that. You do love him, don't you?'

'I love him more than the Hun, the Dago or the Nip. Come to think of it, more than the Frog or the Yank or the Gyppo. Although my Christian studies tell me I must love all men equally.'

'Oh, Fred!'

'Oh, Fred!' He mimicked her then, stood up. 'Come here.' He kissed her, holding her tight against him so that she could feel his heat. 'And I love you, my darling Sylvia.'

For a moment, Sylvia's intolerable burden of anxiety over Eddie shifted.

CHAPTER TWENTY-NINE
October 1940

The clouds swirling around a pale sky opened and closed like a camera shutter. For one second Eddie could see the plane, a Messerschmitt Me 109, its belly the same blue as the sky, the next it had vanished. He assumed it was the same for the enemy as he saw the Spitfire fly in and out of the clouds. You'd expect the clouds to be neutral. Although as they were fighting over the English Channel, they should have supported the Allies, if anybody. Indeed, sometimes it felt as they were players in this dance performed by men – the dance of death.

It had been a surprise to spot a single fighter over the sea.

Should be easy prey this one, unless it was a trap. It didn't feel like a trap. It felt more like some idiot out for an adventure. Well, he'd found one, all right.

For a full three seconds Eddie did not see the Me 109. This cloud was bigger, that was it. The dance would end if the Hun found enough cloud to cloak his escape to France. Now was the time to head home himself.

But there was the 109 again. The clouds, a curtain now, had parted to reveal him centre stage. One on one. Almost too good to be true. How could he resist after a week of daily blanks or planes so high you'd need to be a spaceman to reach them. Eddie felt his knees knocking as they sometimes did in the excitement of an approaching fight. He had the advantage of height, about twenty thousand feet to the other's nineteen thousand, but enough, and the sun was behind him. If only the clouds would hang in the air just as they were, he would have a clear view of his prey.

He was diving now, closing in for the kill, like an eagle, with talons outstretched, beak thrusting. One more second and he'd squeeze his forefinger and let loose the streaming lance of lead. He could already picture the spurt of flame, the gorgeous burst of fire, the twist, the turn, the screaming corkscrew descent. He'd seen it all before. A kill. One more kill. How bloodthirsty he felt today!

The Spitfire shuddered. It shook. It slithered. Clouds whirled above and below. They had become malignant. Eddie blinked, then stared. The sweat, in droplets on his forehead, turned to ice. He thought, I'm so tired. Even though I've been flying much less, I'm still so tired. And he saw the tracer lines and the bullets from a second Me 109 which had crept up on his tail. They fired into the flesh of his Spitfire, into the heart of his stupid pride. The plane sped passed him and disappeared into the cloud ahead. The two of them could do what they pleased now.

Two of them. The oldest trick. One engages, the other sneaks onto your tail. How could I fall for it? 'Because I'm tired and I'm on my own.' Eddie spoke out loud and a terrible loneliness took hold of him. *I chased him because the others turned for home and I saw the 109 and I thought I'd be clever but now I'm hit and soon I'll be on fire.* Liquid splashed across the windscreen, thick tears of glycol. The engine had been hit.

The Spitfire gave a wobble and seemed to sigh as if in sympathy with its pilot's pain. Shame and pain. You never allow the enemy to surprise you from behind. Number One Rule.

Eddie pushed up his goggles, rubbed his eyes, put them back down again and pulled himself together. He was not alone. He spoke into the radio telephone. 'Red 2, Red 2. I've been hit. Two bandits. I've been hit.' But nothing came from the headset and the plane seemed to sag in his hands.

Only bullets, he told himself, a spray of bullets. He realised he was still heading towards France. Desperate to see the English coast, he pushed up his goggles again and tried to swivel his head. But it would only move so far. Had he been injured too? How far had he chased that German?

Turn, he needed to turn and that's what he'd been trying to do automatically since he was first hit, turn for home. But his head wouldn't turn, nor would the Spitfire. Nothing was happening. The Spit continued on. All you need are wings and an engine or if that fails and you can reach land, wings on their own will do. *As long as you are going in the right direction.*

Eddie pictured the green fields around the airfield where he and his Spitfire lived. Any strip would do or even one of those green fields. He'd done that before now. Where exactly had those bullets hit, he wondered. But none of this mattered if he couldn't turn.

He glanced round and realised with a shock that all the clouds had gone, leaving him in an expanse of empty blue sky. So they had been *Boche* clouds guarding their friends as if some Wagnerian opera had taken to the air.

His eyes returned to the front but not before they'd caught a bright flicker. The sun glinting on his wing? He knew better than that. The flicker grew into a flame which he could see without moving his head. It hurt to move his head and anyway at last he could see the coast ahead. The end to another perfect summer's day. Both shoreline and water were burnished by the lowering sun. They merged into a mysterious, vibrating, probably unobtainable line.

No! No! It was the wrong coast. 'Get out, Eddie!'

If he was a bird, he'd land on the water, fold his wings and rock gently on the waves.

'Jump out, now!' Who was shouting at him?

Eva's pale oval face stared at him with dark luminous eyes.

The wind that had so impatiently burst him into the sky also blew the scarlet flames around his head. They danced mockingly around him snatching at his shoulders. Was that an explosion?

But he was free, tumbling headlong, falling too fast. Space above and below. Below was the sea with its high-crested waves. *Pull it, Eddie!* Just in time he remembered to pull his ripcord.

Now he was floating, legs swinging. He shut his eyes.

Not so far away, he heard his dear old Spitfire roared down into the sea, hissing and shrieking and sizzling angrily, just as he'd imagined the Me 109. He opened his eyes but he couldn't see her.

He shut his eyes again.

How silent it was. Not a sound. Not even wind. How peaceful!

CHAPTER THIRTY
December 1940

At seven o' clock in the morning it was very cold and dark in the hallway of Eva's house. She buttoned up her coat and put on her hat. Although she was standing in front of a mirror, she didn't look into it. She was thinking how odd it was that in Eddie's absence he was more present than ever before. He was in the brush that she filled with paint and laid on the canvas, in the brush that untangled her hair and sometimes made it rise into the air; he was in the wind that blew into her face as she bicycled to the Ruskin; he was in the steps of the Ruskin where she'd seen him come to collect her, so dashing in his blue uniform. But their times together had been so brief. She preferred this sense that he was with her everywhere and in everything. In the two months since Sylvia had rung and told Eva that Eddie was missing, she had thought about him every moment of the day.

She kept the two places in her heart that held Eddie and her mother entirely separate. She could not deny that they both were declared missing but otherwise there was no link. Her mother, she knew, was dead. Eddie still alive, not only in her thoughts, but somewhere in the flesh. Perhaps he was thinking of her too.

Today she was travelling to Tollorum. She'd said her goodbyes to her father and Valtraud the night before. Now she looked into the mirror and straightened her hat. She would be part of a family Christmas, so Sylvia had said.

⋙

Sylvia, opening Beatrice's bedroom window, paused to admire the view. The old trees around Tollorum, the chestnuts lining the drive, the yew by the church, the limes and oaks around the house, the single grand oak, the sycamores further out in the fields, all seemed sprayed with silver.

It seemed strange to be admiring trees when her heart and mind, body and soul was completely taken up with the refrain, 'Eddie is missing.' Two months now and no news. How odd it was that she could still stand here admiring without resentment the dazzle of a frosted countryside.

'Sylvia, dear.'

'Yes, Mama.' She could still turn to her mother with a smile and find out what she wanted.

'What are you looking at out there? Is someone coming?' Beatrice sounded both anxious and hopeful.

She now lived before and mostly during the last war. She was probably hoping that her husband, the Colonel, was coming up the driveway. Perhaps she imagined him on his black horse, Balaam, who had gone to war with him.

'No one, Mama. I was looking at the trees turned silver in the frost.'

It was a relief that Beatrice no longer had any memory of Eddie's existence. Questions from her would have been unbearable. Talking to most people was difficult because quite soon she saw by the depth of their pity that they assumed Eddie was lost forever. She could not argue with them because there was no argument except a mother's love that refused to believe he was gone. Sitting with her own mother reminded her painfully of those times in August 1915 when her father had been posted missing and Beatrice had refused to believe it.

This sad history of her father's loss didn't affect Sylvia's own conviction that Eddie lived. Some people she refused to see. The Wing Commander, making it obvious that he assumed the worst, had come to give sympathy and she had turned him away immediately, pretending she was off to a meeting.

Unexpectedly, Fred was the only truly consoling presence. He came to the doorway now, waiting for her to join him.

'I'll see you a little later, Mama. I'm going to have breakfast with Fred.'

Beatrice said nothing, but gave a half smile; she liked the sound of her daughter's voice. Sylvia smiled back, trusting she was in a world of happier memories.

≫≪

A thin slice of light pierced Jack's face like an icicle. He opened his eyes and stared at the walls of the barn. Even dark stone was persuaded to shimmer by this winter spirit. If it hadn't been so cold, he'd have crawled out of his bag and grabbed his pad and pencil.

In fact, he had to get up for the last day of the school term before the Christmas holidays. He'd spent most of the previous week in the warm cottage of the head teacher, Miss Wooley. But he didn't want her to think he'd moved in permanently, particularly after she'd rejected some minor overtures with such distaste that he'd wondered how she managed to work so closely with him day by day.

It had been foolish of him, certainly, when Eva was the only women he cared about. Eva would be at Tollorum soon, so Mrs. Chaffey had informed him. Eva just over the hill!

Avoiding thoughts of Eddie, Jack jumped up so suddenly that the sleeping bats in the rafters swung nervously. He ran to the great barn door and pushed one side of it. Slapping himself and swinging around, he surveyed his domain. Never could any sight be more beautiful! Around the edge of the field and in a copse, every tree had turned to tinsel, glittering in the rising sun.

Grabbing his clothes, boots and bike, he was soon crunching across the grass and out into the road, slippery with ice. The cold air entered his lungs as he sped along, pumping the blood in great waves through his body. Oh the joy of being alive with the prospect of two weeks when he need do nothing but paint, paint, paint!

≫≪

'We're in the kitchen,' called Lily as Sylvia and Fred came down the stairs together. Kitchen life was quite new and consoling, the freshly baked bread and the homemade jam, blackberry at the moment. 'And the Rector's here.'

'However did he get up the drive?' Sylvia asked Fred. 'He's so frail and it must be icy.'

'I picked him up in the trap. Rosie has a better grip now we've given up shoeing her.'

'I hope her feet don't split.' This kind of chat was all right. How glad Sylvia was that she didn't live in a country where grief was celebrated, terrors paraded! Perhaps that stoicism was learned from the last war. If there were no wars, would men and women become soft and pampered?

'Lily's planning what she calls a Christmas pow-wow,' said Fred, as they entered the corridor leading to the kitchen.

'It will be good to have the house filled again.'

Sun from the kitchen spread into the dark corridor. Fred watched Sylvia go in with half-appalled admiration. How could she be so brave! He knew that Eddie was never out of her mind. She had described how she saw him, quite often, at the end of a room or walking across a distant field. If love could keep a person alive, then Eddie wasn't dead. Sometimes Fred felt a little flicker of hope for, after all, nothing had been discovered of Eddie's aeroplane or of him.

Sylvia kissed the Rector. Her extreme thinness and pallor reminded Fred of the days in when they had first become lovers. Then, her father had been missing and he was still fighting her love. Fighting the whole world in fact.

'Now I'm going to be a nuisance,' said Lily who had a pad and pencil at her elbow.

The Rector put more jam on his bread and took a large bite. He didn't hear very well and preferred talking or eating to listening.

'No butter today?' asked Fred.

'You know we don't have it on Wednesday,' said Sylvia, not very reproachfully. Fred's unimportant demands were part of carrying on.

'Butter brings out the taste of jam better than anything,' pronounced the Reverend. Clearly 'butter' was one of the words he could hear.

'Now...' said Lily firmly. She began to list the bedrooms needed if all Gussie and Reggie's family appeared, and then there was Eva arriving soon and perhaps her father, if he was well enough, and his refugee housekeeper and that odd painter Jack from over the hill and poor Angela of course, if she hadn't gone back to America. 'That,' she said, 'is just for starters.'

No one in the room even pretended to be listening as she moved on to food. 'The home farm still has a few chickens but we don't want to eat them because of the eggs...'

The sun was bright in the room and, despite its large size, the Aga kept it reasonably warm.

Sylvia glanced across at Fred. He was eating with as much energy as the Rector. She wanted to touch him, feel his strength and kindness. Fred, kind? What an idea! Oh, Eddie if only you were here to see it, you whose absence has caused it.

Sylvia took a bite of bread and tried to stave off the pangs of terror that thinking of Eddie's absence always caused. Yesterday, she had asked Fred whether he still believed in God.

'Ah, there's a question.' He had looked at her closely. 'Ask me again when we're lying in bed together.'

So she had. The night was dark and cold but they were warm together under the blankets and eiderdown.

'You mean, because of Eddie?'

'Yes.'

'The Rector asked me that. I don't think he trusts my faith. I can't blame him.'

'No.' Sylvia waited.

'People with faith get comfort in times of trouble. Look at all the great poetry.'

'Some people can't understand why God allows so much unhappiness.'

'He asks you to put your faith in him. He sent his son to suffer with us.'

'Do you believe in that too?' Sylvia had seen her words appear in tiny puffs of white. The room was very cold. It was assumed Eddie had gone down over the sea. She thought of the cold of water, of its weight pressing down in steely fathoms. She didn't want to cry. She screwed her eyes tight shut in the dark. She had wanted Fred to answer.

'I prefer believing something to believing nothing.'

'I thought you'd be angry with God. People get very angry with God.'

'I don't know who all these people are you're talking about.' He'd turned over then to hold her with the length of his body. His breath was warm on her face. 'I'm bored of being angry. Where did it ever get me.'

She hadn't asked him anything more. Maybe he believed, maybe he didn't but while he held her lovingly, she tended to think he did and anyway it didn't matter.

'Sylvia, you've fallen asleep!' Lily, so endlessly tolerant, sounded cross. 'I was asking you when Eva arrives.'

Fred smiled. 'Don't you know, Sylvia never sleeps.' She's on guard, he thought, always waiting for Eddie. Waiting expectantly. She can't even cry.

'Sorry. Oh for a cup of real black coffee! This afternoon. Fred can meet her off the train.'

⚞

The train only stopped for a moment. Eva, case in hand, watched it steam off down the tracks. She remembered the summer's evening when she and Eddie had got off at the same halt. They had walked for a while in the soft, bird-filled dusk until Lily had picked them up in the trap.

'Sorry, I'm late!' Fred was calling from a very battered car on the lane.

'I'm late too.' Eva hurried down to him. The grass was still crisp under her feet and there were circles of ice around the car.

'Hop in. I can't stop the engine or it won't start again.'

'There's an awful lot of smoke coming out of the back,' Eva climbed in obediently.

'Duff petrol, probably. Journey all right?'

'There was no heating on the train.'

'We live in the kitchen.'

'That sounds good.'

Fred smiled. 'It is.' He was driving very slowly. 'We don't want to find ourselves pushing the car out of a ditch.'

Eva glanced at him curiously. He seemed different. Even his voice was different, perhaps less staccato, his Dorset roots more apparent. She hoped he wouldn't mention Eddie. She was good at not crying but in this intimate space she might lose control.

'It's very beautiful anyway,' she said. She gazed at the red sun, dipping majestically behind the horizon. Like a god, it spread a rich cloak over the countryside. Eddie was part of it.

'You brought your paints, I expect?'

'Oh, yes.'

'We'll have a few days of peace before the rest arrive.' Fred felt Eva's determination not to say anything about Eddie and respected it. She was stronger than she looked. Sylvia must have recognised a kindred spirit.

⋈

Eddie still had not been mentioned when later that day Sylvia told Eva she had invited Jack for Christmas.

Eva blushed but not with pleasure. Jack felt like a threat to her continued links with Eddie. When Eddie had been there, she could be with Jack safely; he was part of her painting life. But now it would feel like a disloyalty to talk or walk or eat with Jack in Eddie's home.

'When's he coming?' asked Eva. She failed to repress a shiver.

Sylvia rubbed her hands together. 'It is cool in here.' They were sitting in the small sitting-room. 'Perhaps we should go back to the kitchen.'

'It's OK.' Eva looked down at her own pale fingers with their paint-stained nails. 'You do look white. Are you sickening for something? My poor dear.' Sylvia's large grey eyes looked at Eva with such an intensity of sympathy that Eva could hardly bear it. It was Eddie between them, even if neither dared pronounce his name.

But as Eva looked back at Sylvia, thinking rather vaguely that, apart from Fred's cerulean blue eyes, Eddie looked like neither of his parents, something very strange happened. She put her hand to her face and gasped. It seemed suddenly obvious but it was only now she realised it, as if Sylvia's gaze had discovered the truth.

'What is it, Eva? Is something the matter?' Sylvia came over and crouched by her.

'I think...' began Eva, and then stopped.

'Is it something important?' Sylvia stood up but still gazed at Eva anxiously. 'Shall I go back to my chair and sit quietly? Would that be better than hovering over you?'

Ignoring this, Eva began again, 'I think...' and then stopped again.

'If it's a secret,' said Sylvia, 'you don't have to tell me.' She sat passively as if to prove her point.

'I'm pretty certain,' said Eva solemnly but with no more hesitations, 'that I'm going to have a baby.'

Sylvia sat absolutely still. Had she imagined the words? A baby? She stared at Eva's face, now flooded with colour and all kinds of thoughts flitted through her mind before she could respond with words. She thought this is a girl whose mother is in a camp in Germany or, more probably, dead. She thought this girl is too young to be a mother and then she thought of Gussie, pregnant at seventeen. She thought that Fred was too young to be a grandfather.

At length she allowed herself to think of Eddie and she said simply, 'I'm so glad.'

Eva stared at her with a shocked expression. 'I've only just realised it. When you looked at me.'

Sylvia knew she should hug her, indeed wanted to hug her, but she was struck by a darker thought: was this baby a swap for Eddie? Nothing should or could replace him. Ever. She suddenly felt she disliked the girl sitting there, so pretty, so alive. Perhaps she wasn't right. Perhaps she wasn't pregnant at all. Perhaps it was all in her imagination. A phantom pregnancy, conjured up from wishful thinking. After all, why would she just realise it now? How painful! How dreadful!

Eva watched Sylvia's face. What was happening? Why did she appear so tortured? 'I'm so sorry,' she said. 'Perhaps I'm wrong. I don't really know. It was only once…'

As her voice trailed off, Sylvia's emotions swung violently again. Of course Eva must be pregnant! It was joyous. Joyous! Now she took up Eva from her chair and into her arms. 'Don't be sorry. Whatever happens is good. But we must be calm. It's a shock. For both of us. We won't speak about it more just now. It's late. You need to sleep. Tomorrow we'll be clearer.'

Both women were tottering. They held on to each for safety.

It was in this state that Fred found them. He said kindly, 'Lily's offering hot chocolate in the kitchen, an Angela tin from the U.S. Not to be missed.'

Holding hands, the two women allowed themselves to be led out of the room.

※

In the night, Sylvia sat by her mother's bed. She could see her white, motionless face. She breathed regularly with no apparent effort. Perhaps she dreamt that the Colonel lay at her side.

Fred came up behind Sylvia and put his hand on her shoulder.

Without turning, Sylvia murmured, 'Why does your God arrange things so unnaturally?'

'Maybe he has a different agenda. It's a pretty meagre world we make for ourselves. There has to be something better.'

Still facing away from him, Sylvia said, 'Eva believes she's going to have a baby.'

'That child!' exclaimed Fred. His voice was loud enough to make Beatrice turn her head and her eyes opened for a second before they closed again and she slipped back.

Sylvia leant forward to touch her mother's forehead, then stood and took Fred's hand, 'I'm not swapping Eddie for anybody. Not even his own baby. And Eva's not a child.'

CHAPTER THIRTY-ONE
Christmas/New Year 1940-1941

A little boy was running as fast as he could along a grassy ridge. His arms were stretched wide to imitate an aeroplane. The low October sun gleamed on his yellow hair. To his left, the land dropped away steeply so that he felt as if he was more in the sky than on land.

'Brruhmm. Brruhmm.' He dipped his arms and felt the strong wind blowing from behind push him even faster. A cluster of black birds appeared over his head. We're all flying along together, thought the boy, but I'm bigger and faster because I'm an aeroplane.

To his right a flock of sheep grazed in a smooth green field and suddenly they too began to run, following each other in white puffy trails. Everything seemed to be going at top speed. If only I could get my legs off the ground, thought the boy, panting so hard he had no breath for engines noises.

The ungrazed grass at his feet was long and bumpy. Oh for lift-off! So nearly. So nearly. He only needed to run just a little bit faster. Face straining, legs pounding, he took several leaping strides before his toe caught a tussock. He landed on his face, arms still spread-eagled.

'Eddie! Eddie! Tea-time!' A woman's voice called thinly from down the hill.

The boy turned over and lay on his back. The sky whirled above him. He studied it with satisfaction. He really had been up there flying. He'd tell Aunt Lily so. He'd been keeping up with the birds until that mound had tripped him.

'Coming!'

Silver fluttered in the darkness. It disappeared and then returned again, like a star behind moving cloud. The silver was not fluttering, the silver was swinging. It was his eyelids that were fluttering, out of his control.

Eddie opened his eyes. The silver was very near, too near for his eyes to focus on it. He shut them again but the blackness was disappointing.

An intense voice whispered '*Ouvrez! Ouvrez! C'est Noël. Cette nuit le petit Jésus est né.*' The breath of the voice, a child's voice, warmed his skin.

'*Regardez l'ange. Je l'ai fait pour vous.*' A small hand nudged him and something touched his nose.

He opened his eyes again.

'*Bien, bien!*' The silver moved away a little and he saw the outlines of an angel with a spread of wings. It was dangling in front of his eyes, more like a bird than an angel. He thought of a buzzard. He thought of an aeroplane. He returned to the buzzard. Buzzards are not like other birds who use up energy flapping their wings. A buzzard sails majestically through the sky catching the wind currents, therms, dipping, circling, showing off to its mate with slow rolls. Afterwards it calls attention to its presence with mewing cries, like a kitten might make.

'*Maman! Maman!*' The child's voice was further away. '*Il est éveillé! Maman. Où êtes-vous?*'

The angel had gone too. It seemed likely he'd been in heaven for a moment or two: a child, an angel, another language which he seemed to understand.

Eddie shut his eyes but the buzzard stayed with him. A buzzard swooping on his prey a frightening sight: no warning, no sound, out of the blue. The poor little vole doesn't stand a chance, nor the baby rabbit nor the little birds or beetles, flitting or scrabbling.

He knew the buzzard meant more to him than that but his brain was leading him without his intention.

It was a relief to hear the child's voice again.

'*Voila!*' Once more near at hand. '*Ouvrez les yeux, Monsieur, s'il vous plait. Ma grand-mère vient. Je lui ai dit que vous serait eveillé pour Noël.*'

'*Tais-toi, Chérie!*' A new voice, slow and old took over. '*Il ne faut pas que le pauvre s'inquiète.*'

'*Mais, Titi, il aime beaucoup mon ange. Il a presque souri. Il ne peut pas dormir tout le temps*'. The child's voice, perhaps a girl's, was becoming a little petulant.

With some effort, Eddie opened his eyes.

'*Regardez! Regardez!*' Two black orbs which reminded Eddie of something, stared an inch from his face. A small finger was clearly planning to keep his eyelids open. He blinked in minor protest.

'*Fleur! Viens ici!*'

The orbs receded. The wrinkled face of an old lady took their place. '*Bonjour, Monsieur. Bienvenu dans le monde. Vous avez faim, peut-être?*'

Although the old woman spoke slowly with pauses to take wheezy breaths, Eddie found it hard to follow the words. He heard them but the meanings of which there seemed many, were too quick for him.

He managed, however, to associate the last sentence which stayed in his head longest, with another word, 'food'.

As if to help him, the little girl, Fleur – he had held on to that too, darted up and dangled a red crinkly apple near his mouth.

'*Non! Non, ma petite!*' The apple was removed. '*Je vais vous apporter de la soupe.*'

Eddie heard two sets of footsteps retreating, the slow and the quick, accompanied by a bright chattering until somewhere a heavy door closed.

He closed his eyes but now the darkness was filled with sounds. Whenever he moved, however slightly, sounds crackled round him, which eventually identified with the word, 'straw'. But directly under him there was something softer. No word came to him but he could feel his body lying on it, two legs, two arms, his trunk, his head. He remembered all of these and now he could hear his breath going in and out, quite regularly.

Further away, perhaps to the side or below there were heavier noises. He identified them with something big and moving but not, he decided, threatening. He listened for some time: there were movements he recognised and, eventually, the name 'animals' came to him. An image of a sturdy pony with a long tail immediately followed.

He was in a stable! The knowledge made him open his eyes and look around. There was nothing wrong with his sight or his hearing. Light came through two perpendicular slits and he could see that in fact he lay in a loft, partly filled with straw and hay bales. Something glinted at his side and, feeling with his fingers, he identified a glass bottle. He was even able to understand that it probably contained water.

Very slowly, his brain began to work: he was in a loft above a stable where there were animals or an animal, perhaps a horse or a cow. He thought of the brain, how clever it was to make all these links so it was hardly surprising he felt so tired.

He allowed himself to drift into the darkness for a while. But before long something was propelling him outwards. No little girl this time but a need to create more links. A curiosity. The word struck him as very important. Curiosity propelled the brain and turned him on, him, Eddie. Eddie. It was reassuring to have a name. But at the same time it seemed the doorway to a whole mass of information queuing to be allowed in. His brain pulsed and throbbed with the weight.

He felt himself drifting out, away from the stable and the shifting animals below. He wanted to let go but his curiosity clung to his brain, probing with sharp talons into the vulnerable softness. Memory, another word, was waiting for him, he knew, but he needed to rest. Prepare himself. '*Deux mois*', he remembered the old lady's voice but it linked to nothing. Later perhaps. '*Plus tard.*'

'*Je vous pousse, Titi. Ouph! Vous êtes plus grande que la vache.*'

The old woman's head with her tight grey bun and face as wrinkled as an old apple, appeared through the doorway to the loft. Despite her age, she was strong enough to climb up the wooden ladder nailed to the wall, with a bag over her shoulder. Nor was she big, as her granddaughter said, rather small and round and agile.

Fleur climbed like a monkey behind her and, reaching the top, ran across to Eddie.

'*Il dort encore!*' She cried disappointedly. Her grandmother unloaded the bag, with a jar of soup, water and a hunk of dark bread. '*Bien, ma petite. Maintenant nous devons nourrir les animaux.*'

'*Puis-je aller voir Maman?*'

'*Oui, oui.*' As the girl scrambled down the ladder, the woman bent over Eddie. '*Mangez, Monsieur. Il faut que vous repreniez des forces.*'

Eddie opened his eyes. Into his head came the words, '*Merci, Madame,*' but they were not yet ready to come out so he silently allowed the old lady to raise his head and feed him soup from a long spoon she took from her pocket. Her posture and his obedient swallowing seemed habitual, as if it had happened many times before. He would have liked to thank her. She smelled of strong soap, a smoky fire and the soup. She tore off a piece of bread and dipped it in before offering to him.

His hand reached up to hold it. His brain nudged and watched.

'*Bon, Monsieur.*' The woman nodded contentedly.

All these ministrations were performed as a ritual, calmly and firmly. After he had eaten and drank, she rolled him sideways and placed his penis neatly in a bottle. They both watched the dribble of dark liquid.

Again he reached out his hand, this time to steady the bottle. He was wearing a thick sweater, he saw, from which a long bony wrist protruded, ending in a hand, clad in a mitten. He wanted to ask, '*Il fait froid, Madame?*' It must be cold; she wore a black shawl, over her shoulders and crossed over her breasts, leaving her arms free. She too wore mittens, heavily darned. The darn was done in careful cross-stitch.

Before she left him, she sat down for a moment and it struck him she was praying, at least her lips moved soundlessly. Prayer was another idea that his brain seemed to enjoy. He watched her lips and after a while shut his eyes. This time he slept.

It was dark when he woke again, at least no light from the windows but something was approaching, a figure carrying a small covered lamp, perhaps containing a candle.

'*Bonsoir, Monsieur. On dit qu'aujourd'hui vous êtes revenu à la vie. Ma fille est très joyeuse. Elle dit qui vous avez choisi l'anniversaire du Christ! Comprenez-vous, Monsieur?*'

This woman's voice was light and bright and quick, not so easy to understand. The Christ, for example. What was that? The word, 'Christmas', hovered in his mind. But he wanted her to know he could understand, and he remembered now to raise his hand.

'*Ah! Très bien. Ma fille a raison. Ma mère espère toujours. Mais elle a la foi dans le Seigneur. Vous pouvez m'appeler Madame Sophie, qui n'est pas mon nom.*'

She withdrew with her light, leaving a sense of impatience. Madame Sophie, the child's mother.

⚎

The night was long now that Eddie was awake part of the time. He began to feel the cold more and wished he was down there with the animals, hugging their warm bodies.

At the first silvery slivers of light, he felt soft breath on his face. It smelled sweet and milky.

'*Alors, Monsieur. Je vais chanter pour vous — et le Christ,*' the little girl, Fleur, added reverently and she crossed herself. '*Ecoutez bien et ne parlez pas.*'

Eddie felt himself smiling at her confident bossiness, particularly as words still remained inside his head. She began singing in a pure treble.

Il est né le divin enfant,
Jouez hautbois, résonnez musettes!
Il est né le divin enfant,
Chantons tous son avènement!'

She broke off for a moment to shake Eddie's arm, *'C'est pour vous, ce vers.'*

Une étable est son logement
Un peu de paille est sa couchette,
Une étable est son logement
Pour un dieu quel abaissement.

Ah! Qu'il est beau, qu'il est charmant!
Ah! que ses grâces sont parfaites.
Ah! Qu'il est beau, qu'il est charmant!
Qu'il est doux ce divin enfant!'

As Fleur finished, she tipped herself backwards and lay panting on the straw beside Eddie.

Eddie felt his face wet with tears. He put up a hand to brush them away.

'*Vous pleurez, Monsieur,*' announced Fleur doubtfully; she had been studying him closely for a reaction to her singing. '*Vous n'aimez pas la chanson?*' Clearly, it was almost impossible that he would not like her carol but must be faced if true.

Eddie felt for her hand and squeezed it gently. Soon he would have to speak.

Fleur seemed to understand. She found a handkerchief in her pocket and wiped his face. Then she was off away, singing the carol as she went.

Memories began to pour into his mind against a background of sweet singing, even after Fleur had long disappeared. He tried to control the flood of names, places and faces and put them in some order. The singing, he decided, hung in the sky and it was there that he too stayed for a while. He explored its deep blues, trailing whites, puffed up grey and whites. He was flying, he realised, but not a bird, he was too big for that, too noisy, too fast. When he perceived the aeroplane, it was from the outside, although he was also inside, flying it. His heart lurched at the beauty of it, the power and the glory.

He contemplated it carefully, the smooth lines, the strong, graceful wings, the elegant nose. Inside he saw the narrow cockpit, the joystick, the instrument panel, the starter, the throttle. Everything came back to him with comfortable familiarity. But the name of this beautiful creature evaded him so he decided to leave the sky for the ground, land gently on green fields.

He became overcome at the amount to learn and, putting his hand to his forehead, found it burning hot, despite the icy cold of the air. He must rest '*Soyez calme*', had the old woman told him that? Stay calm. There seemed no hurry and the hours passed easily.

But now the hours had a purpose; it was no longer enough to accept being fed and washed, not enough to smile at Fleur's performances. He wanted to be involved and understand.

'*Ah, oui,*' commented the old woman, that afternoon or perhaps the afternoon after that, '*Vous avez retrouvé vos forces. Vous pouvez maintenant bouger votre jambe? Celle qui a été blessée.*'

His legs. Eddie had been too taken up with his mind to think of his legs. His arms had moved of their own accord. Apart from rolling over for the bottle, he had lain quite still. How could he have forgotten his legs. Now, with the Madame's strong little hands pushing at him, he slowly rolled one leg, then the other. They felt like logs.

'Tccht! Tccht!' grumbled the old lady.

But even this small amount of action seemed to stir new life and the next time she came in, he was sitting up, trying to flex his knees.

'*Mère de Dieu.*' He watched as she crossed herself and her face wrinkled even more with her smile.

It seemed that mind and body were working together because words joined every action. Sometimes in English, sometimes in French. He began to take pride in his progress.

Perhaps two mornings, later, the word 'Eva' came into his head. He felt it coming in with the light and savoured it for some time before a face came to join the name. Soon after, the aeroplane which he had admired so much called itself 'Spitfire'. After that, he began to remember everything that had happened. He wasn't always willing to remember, however, taking evading action, executing sharp turns and tight circles.

It was in this half-way stage of remembering and not remembering that he had a visitor from the outside world.

Eddie was sitting on a wooden stool, dragged up to the loft by Fleur, trying to make out a French newspaper. Every now and again, he stood up and down, marvelling at the weakness of his legs. The visitor was heralded by a disturbance among the animals below whose habits he knew intimately, although he had never seen them. They didn't stamp their feet when either Madame Sophie or the old Madame or Fleur appeared. But since he could hear Madame Sophie's voice, he knew there was nothing to fear. Fear was an unwelcome aspect of his returning strength or his *'retour de ses forces'*. His weakness, his presence in France, his knowledge of a Spitfire and the secrecy surrounding him, were all slowly coming together in his mind but still in a sketchy, unresolved, dream-like way.

A visitor, large and male, and speaking English as he came off the ladder and forced his shoulders into the loft, was an extraordinary shock.

'Good show, old chap. *Vive Britannia*! Or perhaps I should say '*Vive la France*' since they're the ones who saved you. Didn't know a thing about you until yesterday when the jolly old grapevine got buzzing like a swarm of bees, to mix my metaphors unforgivably. You are all right, are you?'

The man, wearing a scuffed leather coat, a black beret and an even blacker beard, stood over Eddie dubiously. 'Talk, can you? '*On dit*' you're a pilot with a uniform, or bits of it, spirited away. Thorough when they want to be, these continentals. Of course they never expected you to live. That's the other '*on dit*'. Know when you came down, do you, old chap?'

Eddie realised this was a test, that he had to speak to prove who he was. But did he know who he was?

'Must have been quite a while since you arrived with that growth on your chin. Or perhaps you're a navy fellow, not an air force chappie at all. Countries never too hot on each other's uniforms.' He paused again and looked questioningly and, as Eddie still said nothing, he asked in a slightly less jocular tone, 'You do speak English, do you?'

A word formed in Eddie's head, not quite the right word he knew but one embedded in his brain recently and not totally inapposite.

'*Oui.*' At least it came out as planned.

'*Oui*, is it? Well, better than '*non*', I suppose, but not exactly a word to bring confidence to a chap trying to establish the Englishness of another chap. Still, it shows you're not dumb.' The man looked round. 'Do you mind if I sit? Motorcycle broke down so I pinched a bike. Hate bikes.'

Eddie stood up, swaying slightly.

'Please.' He indicated the stool.

'Ha, ha! Further proof that you're a chip off the old bulldog. Jolly thin chip, I must say. You'd better sit down before you fall down. I'll squat on your bed.'

Just when Eddie was thinking that he'd never heard so many words in his life in any language, the man lay back and stared silently at the wooden rafters above his head.

Eddie looked at him and wondered if he was going to sleep. But his eyes remained open and, after five minutes, he began to talk again. 'You were brought here for dead, as I said. Plucked from the sea. Planned to stick you in the ground, nice they believe in burials, then your eyes opened. Head wound, they said, possibly bullet therein, and one of your legs shot up. All right, now?'

'Unsteady,' said Eddie, getting the hang of things. So he'd been a head case. That would explain a lot.

'I can see that. Need feeding up. Although Madame said you always drank her soup. You just lay here, she said. She seems to be the only one who thought you'd live. The doctor '*vous a donné pour mort*,' once he'd dealt with your wounds, so she told me clicking her tongue. You were lucky with her. You are a pilot, aren't you?'

'Yes,' said Eddie. 'I flew from Warmwell.' The word 'Warmwell' brought with it the image of a great curve of bright sea, and blue sky, dotted with clouds.

'Any idea when you hit the drink?' The man put his arms above his head and stared even more intensely at the rafters.

'No.'

'No. Well, *Madame* says you've been here since October and Christmas has been and gone. No hope you got your papers?'

Eddie made an effort to find an answer. 'I buttoned them into my jacket,' he said slowly, 'before I jumped.'

The man looked at him sympathetically. 'All coming back, is it?'

Eddie nodded.

'Not long ago I was put in touch with a rear gunner. Rest of them had been picked up. He'd lain in a drain for four days. Shocking state he was in. Got him out in the end. Through Spain. Long journey. And guess what, three days after he was back with his squadron, he was shot down over Germany and made a POW as quick as a gulp of a beer. Hardly worth my trouble. Still, it's all part of the war effort. Here's not to reason why. Now my principal occupation is dealing with things we don't talk about. Sometimes they come down from the sky. Not much at the moment, but growing. There're some brave Frenchies out there.' The man sat up and his words began to flow even faster. 'On my own a lot, though. Good to meet a fellow Brit. Speak French, do you?'

'A little.'

'Good. Spot on, in fact. You don't want more than a little if the *Boche* do get hold of you. Shoot you for a spy in a moment. Stick to swear words, that's my advice. The Germans know British servicemen only speak in swear words. Any that come to mind. Show a bit of guile and you've signed your death warrant. Want to cross back over the White Cliffs of Dover, do you? Don't fancy a cushy billet behind barbed wire?'

'No,' said Eddie.

'Thought as much. But can't get you out 'til you can walk more than a yard, or a metre, as they say here which is longer.'

'I'll work at it.'

'Then there's the whole question of your hosts. Can't take the risk with anyone nasty finding you were here. Not with that kind Madame and her pretty little grand-daughter. Need to find you an alternative. At a distance. As if you came down recently and looked after yourself. Chaps do. Like that chap in the drain. So you see, nothing will happen in a hurry.'

Eddie who had forgotten about being in a hurry looked across at the man wonderingly. 'No,' he agreed.

'It's not your problem, old boy. Think of yourself as a parcel, not a telegram, slow and sure.' The man leant forward a little, 'Talking of telegrams… Sorry and all that, but I'm not going to take a chance on a radio message to your loving folks back home. Let's face it, they think you're a gonner, so another few weeks won't matter. Never take unnecessary risks, that's what we're taught. Sorry, old boy. But no arguments.' The man held up his hand.

Eddie who had not been going to argue said carefully, 'Thank you. Thank you.'

'No names necessary. That's another thing. Never know when a name may pop into your head just when you don't want it. Yes. Yes. Well let's see how it goes. In one sense the sooner the better. The old Madame's daughter wants you out. Can't blame her. She blames the Virgin Mary for you being here at all. So let's say three weeks to get your walking boots on, then we'll make the first move.'

'Thank you,' repeated Eddie who was feeling so tired he thought he might topple off the stool.

'All in a day's work. Actually, you'll be the second one I've got out, if you do get out. All a bit hit and miss at the moment. Planning to get better. Route through Spain improved, that sort of thing.' The man stood over him and shook his hand. 'I bet you've smacked down a few Jerries in your time.'

'Yes,' agreed Eddie, remembering. 'But not on the day they got me. A second man on my tail.'

'Swings and roundabouts,' said the man cheerily as he headed for the opening to the ladder. 'Swings and roundabouts.' His legs disappeared. 'Now I'll see if I can scrounge for *moi* some of that soup you like so much. Cheerio! Or shall we say *Au revoir*'?'

CHAPTER THIRTY-TWO
January 1941

Fred decided to drive to Warmwell and collect Eddie's belongings. He had been putting off such a dismal trip but the New Year seemed to reproach him for being a coward.

He was pouring petrol into the car with a miserly hand when Eva came out to join him. At last the weather had relented from its sharp grip and the countryside presented itself in a mellow green. It was not so impressive as before, Eva decided, but somehow comforting. She stood a few yards away watching. Everybody else had left the day before and she could no longer lose herself in the crowd. Her father, in the end, had not been well enough to travel and she knew, guiltily, that she should go to him.

Fred looked up. 'I'm driving to Warmwell, if the car starts. Want to come?' He asked her because she looked expectant, although, in fact, she often did. The old term for pregnancy was 'expecting'. 'She's expecting', he could hear Lily's voice saying it happily about someone in the village. Odd when a woman expecting had far fewer expectations than a non-expecting woman. Perhaps she was not only expecting but also expecting him to say something congratulatory about the baby, if indeed there was a baby. It struck him that he had felt just as disbelieving when twenty years ago Sylvia had announced she was pregnant. Perhaps to believe you have to accept yourself in the role of a father or – as now – a grandfather. His own parents had died when he was a small child.

'I'm going to get Eddie's things,' Fred said, as Eva came closer, 'if they've still got them. I should have gone before.'

'Doesn't Sylvia want to come?'

'Not her.'

'What about Lily?'

'I haven't asked.' The two looked at each other. Fred noticed Eva's startling pallor against her black hair. 'It shouldn't take too long, if the car doesn't break down.'

Eva sneezed several times.

'I suppose you've caught a cold,' commented Fred not very sympathetically. Eva's nose now looked red in her white face.

'Not really.' Eva, who would have liked to pick up her pad and pencil from the house, got into the car firmly.

They drove down the driveway where pools of melted ice reflected the green all around.

'It's good to get out of the house,' said Fred after they reached the road. 'Too much emotion.'

'You mean George going back to fight,' said Eva.

'And Reggie being bombed out of the family home in London.' When asked by Sylvia where he now lived, he'd given an evasive answer incorporating the words 'old Buffy' and 'Islington'. Gussie, apparently convinced, had rolled her eyes and exclaimed, 'The war has made us all gypsies.'

Eva was quiet for a few minutes before saying softly, 'No-one mentioned Eddie at Christmas.'

'They all think he's dead.'

Eva gave a gasp.

'Sorry.' Fred *was* sorry. It had been unnecessary and cruel. 'Gussie apart, the English upper classes prefer to be silent about difficult subjects.'

'My father is silent about my mother, and he's not upper class. At least I don't think so.'

'He's an intellectual. Intellectuals pretend everything in life is theoretical. So they despise emotion.'

'But you haven't talked to me about Eddie either.' Here Eva looked down at her fingers entwined together in her lap. 'Nor have you mentioned our baby.' Eva blushed with a certain amount of defiance.

Fred felt a tremor of admiration for this brave girl beside him combined with fear at the idea of a new life at such a time. For this moment, the baby was real to him.

'Are you happy about it?' he asked.

'Of course I am!' Eva was obviously shocked at the question. 'The baby's part of Eddie. When he comes back, we'll marry.'

Now it was Fred's turn to be shocked. He had assumed only Sylvia, misled by a mother's love, seriously believed in Eddie's return. 'Yes,' he agreed weakly.

It was enough for Eva. She nodded. 'In the Tollorum church, I hope.'

Unable to endorse this with even pretended conviction, Fred concentrated on the road ahead, as if he might lose his way, as if he didn't know the way by heart, even though he'd only been there once.

Eva stared out of the window. Already there were a few snowdrops and quite soon there'd be primroses in the banks. She imagined that spring was approaching, and that Eddie was on his way back, winter past.

Fred knew that a quiet day like this was only a little break in the cold dark months. The sun was a lemony, half-hearted colour.

'I had been planning to visit Eddie at Warmwell,' said Eva.

'Last year,' said Fred.

The words were painful to Eva so she said nothing and looked out of the window once more. Ahead was a small grassy knoll with a group of beech trees on the top. Their leafless branches and trunks were almost black except where the dim sun turned them a ghostly grey-green. Because she thought of Eddie all the time, the sturdy trunks with their outstretched arms seemed to her like a group of men, struck by some wrathful hand, naked and immobile. Not, however, entirely lifeless.

'Trees never stop growing,' she said in a conversational tone. 'Even in winter.' She wondered whether the second part of her statement was true. She remembered that Fred had been brought up in the countryside. She added, 'I'm sure you know about things like that. Neither of my parents cared about nature.'

'I didn't care about it,' said Fred, 'I just lived in it and stole birds or animals when I could outwit the Tollorum gamekeeper. I was closest to nature in Gallipoli: heat that made your tongue swell, floods that flung men down ravines, cold that turned the blood to ice. There were some pretty sunsets, certainly, but the colours were no brighter than gunfire or blazing scrub. As soon as I could I gave up nature for ideas.'

Eva didn't follow Fred's imagination to Gallipoli. Instead she pictured Jack in his barn in the middle of a field. Very close to nature. Over Christmas, he had brought out some watercolour sketches. The colours were invariably pale, almost ethereal. 'Did you see Jack's paintings?' she asked.

'No. But I can imagine.'

'They're very beautiful.'

'I was never educated in art. Is beauty the aim? You're studying art. You must understand all about that?'

Eva decided it had been a mistake to mention art and couldn't now remember why she had.

Since she hadn't answered his question. Fred carried on, 'I suppose art is just another 'ism', like Communism and Fascism, a reason to get up in the morning and less harmful than either. Perhaps when I've mastered the message of Christianity, I'll move on to Art. Although I must say Christianity's keeping me interested. That's why we're going to Warmwell. Did I say?'

'You said we were collecting Eddie's belongings.'

'Yes, indeed. But I particularly wanted back the bible I lent him.' Fred found himself surprised at what he was telling Eva and paused for a moment. He hadn't even told Sylvia.

Eva watched him. She was no longer frightened by his abruptness and, now and again, she was reminded of Eddie.

'This bible belonged to Brigadier General Fitzpaine, Sylvia's father. He had it at Gallipoli. It survived the campaign, unlike its owner. I treasure survivors.'

'Perhaps Eddie took it with him?'

'No. He probably wouldn't be allowed.' Fred remembered that

Eddie had once taken up a dog and half-smiled. 'He wouldn't have taken up a bible.'

Eva returned to looking out of the window. They were passing through wide sweeps of green hills, with a great deal of silvery sky above.

'The sea's to our right now,' said Fred. 'We'll edge past Dorchester, take the Weymouth road and then go inland for a few miles. The airfield's very near a railway line but otherwise nothing to see or at least only a few little villages, Warmwell itself, Moreton, then Dorchester.'

Soon they were through Dorchester, turning off the bigger road and into woods and narrow lanes. 'I remember thinking that there'd be no room for a runway with all these trees,' said Fred. As he spoke three aeroplanes rose in front of them one after the other with a thunderous roar even though they were probably half a mile away.

Eva watched eagerly. When they'd gone far enough for Fred to hear her, she told him with shining eyes, 'Eddie took me up in a plane once. We flew from Oxford to Birmingham. It was called a Tiger Moth.'

'Did you feel safe?'

'Very safe. I loved every moment.'

Fred thought he'd never tried to make Sylvia safe. Except now when he held her and when it was too late. He swung the steering wheel sharply left and slammed on the brakes as two jeeps driven by young women in caps hurtled out across his path.

They had arrived. He turned into an entrance guarded by sentries.

Eva was amazed at the size of the place, at the movement of jeeps, cars, lorries, aeroplanes and bicycles all around. She could even see a tractor. There were huge buildings too, vast hangars, built of corrugated iron and painted green which did nothing to diminish their impact. There were rows of Nissen huts, a tower, square brick buildings and people everywhere, all in movement, all dressed in some sort of blue uniform or other. She supposed

Birmingham airfield must have been far bigger but there was something about coming across this place in the middle of such empty countryside that made it seem more extraordinary, more alien. She tugged her coat tight round herself and followed Fred out of the car.

Fred was already questioning an officer in his usual uncompromising tones. 'My son, Flight Lieutenant E. F. Chaffey, missing since October last year.' He named Eddie's Squadron.

Eva turned away. The engines of a row of aeroplanes, perhaps Spitfires, she thought, on the other side of the base, were starting up. Already the noise was terrific. How did anyone stand such noise! How had Eddie stood such noise?

'Ask me what you need.' There was a woman's voice close to her ear. 'Old Toby's never helped anybody in his life.' It was a WAAF officer, with plump cheeks and neat, rolled hair.

'We've come to collect my fiancé's things. He's been missing for a while.'

'Bad show. I know just the chap for you. If you're lucky, he'll make you a cup of tea too.'

As her new friend led them towards one of the brick buildings, Eva suddenly noticed how slight Fred was, scarcely taller than the WAAF and narrow as a boy.

The noise was only slightly less when they were shown into an office where a friendly officer with an absurd moustache opened files and inspected cupboards while explaining to Fred, 'These fighter boys are brave as lions but once they leave their cockpits they have no sense of order. Chuck their things anywhere or drop them on the floor. But don't you worry, Mr Chaffey, if there's nothing here and I know there was a little Bible unaccounted for – we don't have many Bible bashers in the RAF – I'll get in touch with his servant. Your son wasn't here long and never let on you lived so close.'

The droning voice, the moustache which seemed to move independently, the gigantic noise outside, combined to make Eva feel ill. 'I'll stand outside for a moment.'

She went quickly and leant against a wall. What if Eddie never did come back? It was the first time she'd allowed herself to consider the idea.

⋙

The following morning Eva took a train back to Oxford, or rather four trains and two buses. The rails were icy, the engines fed with the wrong coal, at least one station bombed, the engine driver bombed, a tunnel fallen in. The winter freeze had returned and it was wartime. What else could you expect?

The few civilian travellers were inclined to tell their life stories. Eva, wrapped in a thick paisley shawl pressed on her by Sylvia, didn't feel the cold. In fact she didn't feel anything very much. That question which had presented itself at Warmwell, 'What if Eddie never did come back?' played continuously in her head and all her emotional strength was needed to avoid an answer. Only tiny shivers of dread or an occasional heart-stopping intimation of disloyalty forced their way through her guard. In fact she could have wished the long bitter train journey to be even longer. It would be harder to avoid her feelings at home.

She walked slowly from Oxford station to her home. It was dark and the evening cold bit into her fingers. Her case was heavy with her painting equipment and clothes joined by a cheese, a pot of jam, a jar of honey and some pickled pears produced by Lily from the Tollorum larder. At last she was at her front door and into the silent house. She compared it unfavourably to Tollorum.

Ashamed, she called loudly, 'Papa! I'm back!'

When there was no answer, she went up to his bedroom which was empty, although the bed had been pulled back as if someone had slept there recently. She went to her studio and sat down, looking steadfastly at the first large oil portrait she'd painted of Eddie. It was nearly four months since she'd seen him. There had been a childhood portrait at Tollorum, showing a golden-haired angel with shining blue eyes. Hers was definitely better; the turbulent brush strokes where she'd over-painted it in dissatisfaction, gave it movement and life. The Ruskin term had already started. She would go the following day and make up for lost time.

She stood up to examine her brushes just as the telephone rang in the downstairs hall. She ran and jumped down the stairs, thinking defiantly as she landed at the bottom, I am young, I am young, young, young!

'Hello.'

It was Sylvia. She thought how childlike Eva sounded and felt sorry for her. 'Valtraud rang. She hoped to catch you before they left. Your father's been rushed to hospital. Valtraud's there too. I said I'd telephone you. I tried earlier.' She paused, 'You must have had an awful journey.'

Eva listened to Sylvia's voice and felt comforted, although she seemed to be a very long way away. 'Is he dying?' she asked. She thought it was possible to face her father's death. She sat on the bottom step. She felt exhausted all over again.

'I think you should go to the hospital.'

'I'm dreadfully tired. I only just got in.'

'I'm so sorry.' This girl is carrying my son's baby, thought Sylvia and she remembered how excited she'd been when she became pregnant; the war had ended, she had nearly completed her degree and Fred, to her surprise, had agreed to marry her. After the sorrows of her father's disappearance and death, she had felt full of new hope for the future. 'You must take care of yourself,' she added, 'of yourself and your baby.'

Eva stared at the telephone. Why hadn't she realised earlier that she had brought Eddie's baby to her home for the first time? Another burst of exhilaration made her jump to her feet. 'Yes! Yes! I feel much better already.'

Her voice made Sylvia smile. 'Go along then,' she said. 'I'll telephone you later.'

⟩≺

A nurse, old but robust, led Eva to her father's bedside. Laying her broad fingers on the neatly turned sheet by his face, she said,

'Even if it is too late, you can still say goodbye.'

Eva thought about this. So he was dead. He hardly looked different from when he sat at his desk at home.

'Your housekeeper went to look for you.'

'I came by bus.'

'So you missed each other. Never mind. His eyes were closed even before he arrived. Please touch him if you want. Perhaps you'd like to be left alone.'

Since there was no mention of her mother, Eva assumed Valtraud had explained her circumstances.

'He died peacefully,' said the nurse.

Eva glanced at her quickly and then bent to kiss her father. They had seldom kissed, but she didn't want to disappoint the nurse. The word 'orphan' came to mind.

'I expect you have other relatives?'

'Yes,' agreed Eva, 'although Cousin Phoebe lives in Scotland.' Was Cousin Phoebe her only relative? She really wasn't prepared to think about that. Both impatient and tired, she spotted a chair in the corner of the room and sat down on it. 'I'll stay here a moment.' As Sylvia said, she must look after her baby.

'I'll tell the doctor you've come.'

Left alone, Eva's thoughts drifted. Just when she'd decided that her father had never really got over the surprise of finding he had a daughter, which didn't mean he didn't love her, her head nodded and she fell asleep.

As she slept, the doctor and Valtraud returned together. 'He told me to bring the envelope from his desk. I have collected it.' Valtraud had been crying, her pretty face all puffed up.

The doctor who was young and tall and walked with a limp because he had been with the soldiers in France, saw the name of a local solicitors on the envelope and felt relieved. He knew that the sights he'd seen on the beaches of Calais had hardened his heart but he felt very moved by the sight of this young woman apparently alone in the world apart from a German refugee. A solicitor's letter was a start.

Eva sat drinking tea with Valtraud in the kitchen. It seemed there was nothing they could do till the morning. Both she and Valtraud were fairly certain there was nothing they knew how to do anyway.

Between drinking tea, Valtraud cried. She had loved the Professor and suffered with him the loss of his wife. Besides, what would happen to her now? She was still twenty but she could only see her life behind and nothing in the future. She wanted to scream out over and over again, 'What will happen to me now?' But she felt sorry for Eva so she drank tea which she had never liked, and cried.

Eva didn't cry. Her left hand was on her stomach and, although dimly aware of Valtraud's sufferings, her concentration was on a light fluttering under her fingers.

'Valtraud! Put your hand here!'

Valtraud heard the joy in her voice and, startled, put down her cup with a bang. She took out a handkerchief and dabbed her eyes.

Eva remembered she hadn't told Valtraud she was going to have a baby. But what was going on inside her body seemed far more important than who knew or who didn't.

'You have tummy ache?' asked Valtraud, deciding to discount the joyous note.

Eva laughed, this time thoroughly disturbing Valtraud. 'I'm going to have a baby,' she announced 'and I can feel it in there, moving around, tickling me. Isn't that amazing!'

Valtraud stared. Various possibilities, all tragic and including mania brought on by the noble Mrs Speke's disappearance and the poor Herr Professor's death, presented themselves.

'It's Eddie's.' said Eva, oblivious to the shocked speculation going on across the table. 'You remember Eddie, my pilot friend. You met him. Last time he came you asked him about the bombers flying over Oxford.'

Valtraud did remember. She had cried that night, not for the bomb in Birmingham but for her friends in Germany. Would she ever see them again? But here was this child in front of her talking about her baby. 'Ah, I see.' Was she to be a nurse for this baby? Was that a future?

Eva only thought in the present. 'Now I shall go to bed.' She stood up, kissed Valtraud gently on her still damp cheek, and left the room.

CHAPTER THIRTY-THREE
February 1941

In the weeks that passed following the visit from the Englishman, Eddie replayed much of his visitor's dialogue in his head. In place of a name he adopted the old *Madame*'s occasional reference to *Monsieur la Barbe*. His visit, like his beard, had been dramatic, or so it seemed to Eddie, a stage performance but also a guide to his past, present and future which was important to his returning self. Also, it had been carried out in English which gave him confidence. He began saying a few words to Madame in French while hearing the English in his head.

He reflected and he exercised, eating as much as he was brought. One afternoon, after Fleur came back from school, she guided him down to the stable. He stood behind the partly open door breathing in the first fresh air for months. Catching a glimpse of a wintry landscape, of flat fields with low crops, perhaps turnips or swedes, he was reminded of the afternoon in England when he'd parachuted into a turnip field. Everything reminded him of something, although there were areas where his memory remained vacant: his descent into *La Manche*, for example, and his rescue. But that he assumed, was due to whatever had been wrong with his head.

He was standing quietly, half-listening to Fleur's chatter as she fed hay to the cart-horse, when a bicycle was thrown down and Fleur's mother appeared like a whirlwind.

'*Je pouvais vous voir!*' she shouted. '*Je vous ai vu de dehors. Mon Dieu, Monsieur!*'

Smacking Fleur sharply, she sent her to the house, before turning back to Eddie.

'*Est-ce ainsi que vous remerciez pour notre gentillesse?* Now you go or we all are dead.'

'*Oh, Madame. Pardonnez-moi, je vous en prie.* I am so sorry.' In her anger she had revealed she knew some English. It was a shock to Eddie, who had assumed her an uneducated person like her mother. '*Je n'ai pas envisagé…* I should have realised.' There was nothing he could say and nothing she would listen to. She was right. His memory was no excuse. He understood his situation but he had ignored the risks. Anyone could have seen him. He had behaved like a child. Like Fleur, pretty, carefree Fleur.

'*Montrez-moi comment vous pouvez marcher. Walk!*'

The humiliation of walking in front of her, his thin, ungainly legs, his unbalanced stride, was a small punishment.

'*Une semaine de plus.* One week.' She clapped her hands together to end his pathetic parade. 'Enough. *Pratiquez la marche tout le temps. Dans le grenier.* In this place. Play with the rats. After you are strong *puis fichez le camp!*' Snapping her fingers in his face, she strode away, leaving behind the cold air tingling with the electricity of her rage.

Over the next six days, Eddie obeyed her instructions until he could walk briskly up and down a corridor between the hay and straw bales which stretched for forty feet, over half an hour without stopping. After that his bad leg which bore a double scar above the ankle would do no more. He hoped they were not expecting him to ride a bicycle.

Although the older Madame continued to bring him food, often garnished with a prayer or two, he needed her help with nothing else. Fleur, too, came seldom and fleetingly so that he suspected she had been forbidden to visit him. His solitary days gave him plenty of time to think and at last he allowed himself to remember the past year. He remembered making love with Eva under the table and smiled. He remembered Andy and Hank and their deaths in the context of all the other deaths as they took their planes up day after day. He remembered the weariness, the pride, the fizzing, thrilling, terrifying joy. He wondered if he would ever fly again. He wondered if he would ever make love again.

On the sixth day when the light was already dipping, Madame Sophie came up with a bowl of water, a knife and soap and shaved him. She performed it with tough efficiency so that he needed to grit his teeth.

She softened a little when his beard lay in thick golden curls on the floor.

'*Je ne savais pas que vous avez des brûlures, mais vous avez bien guéri.* You were burning, *alors*, when you go down.'

Eddie realised he had not seen his face since he left Warmwell for the op to Southampton.

Madame Sophie tipped the water on to the floor. '*Voilà.* Tomorrow you go.' She left unsmiling, satisfied with her task completed. For the first time Eddie wondered what had happened to her husband. She was a pretty woman, like her mother, small and dark but everything that was soft in the mother was hard in the daughter.

So he would leave tomorrow. The idea was scarcely real. Nevertheless, it led him to think more clearly about the world he'd once inhabited and to which he might now return. Now he heard again La Barbe's apologies for not feeding his name into the radio. 'Let's face it, they think you're a gonner so another few weeks won't matter.' Painfully, Eddie imagined Eva no longer believing in his existence, his mother, his father, Lily, his grandmother, cousin George, Les, his old friend the CO, Jenkins and Jones, the porter at his college, Oz, the medical student. In fact, everyone he'd ever known anywhere would assume him dead. 'Gone', as he'd dubbed all the pilots who did not come back, although dead was more accurate.

He began to stride up and down the loft faster than ever before. His previous passivity, which had lain on him like an eiderdown, had vanished as completely as his beard whose shreds were already interchangeable with the cornstalks on the floor. Now he was filled with restless impatience, buzzing with questions. What time would he leave? How would he leave? How would he get back to England? Would he get back to England?

He was so far away in his thoughts that he failed to notice a small reproachful face at the entrance to the loft.

'*S'il vous plait, Monsieur. Vous inquiétez les animaux. Vous marchez comme un soldat. Boum. Boum. Boum.*'

Eddie stared down at Fleur. Indeed he had been marching up and down like a soldier. '*Pardonnez-moi, ma petite Fleur. Voulez-vous parler avec moi?*' It struck him she had not appeared for the last week.

'*Non. C'est interdit.*' Blowing him a kiss, she disappeared downwards.

'*Au revoir!*' called Eddie after her, before thinking he should have said, '*Adieu*'.

But the next day, no one came to find him, except the faithful old Madame. Nor did anyone on the next two days and on the fourth day it began to snow. He could just see it flitting in white gasps past his narrow windows.

'*Ah, oui,*' agreed the old Madame, '*La neige est arrivée. Le voile blanc de la Vierge.*'

In Eddie's experience the Blessed Virgin wore a blue veil but, when he suggested this, Madame pursed her lips and told him that in the summer the Virgin wears a blue veil like the sky and in the winter a white veil like the snow. Then she left, more rapidly than usual.

But he suspected something was wrong.

Increasing strength made him feel like rushing out wildly, making his way to the sea, swimming the Channel. He realised that he had become twenty-one, an adult, towards the end of his blank two months. He remembered his last birthday in a snowy Scotland when he'd been training. It seemed like a century ago. It seemed a long time since Fleur had sung him '*Il est né le Divin Enfant.*'

He slept a little and walked more and more, stepping quietly to avoid disturbing the animals. He exercised, using the heavy wooden stool as a weight. Soon he could lift it above his head. When his whole body ached, he felt satisfied.

At the end of a week, Madame Sophie came to the loft. Without talking, she undid the heavy bar across the wooden doors in the wall and pulled them open.

Eddie took great breaths of cold air. The snow lay on the fields but not very deeply. Over the soft greyness came the sounds of church bells.

'Sunday,' he said.

Madame Sophie was rolling a large bale of hay towards the space. He helped and it dropped heavily down. They brought over another one, two of straw. She shut the doors again and sat down on the stool.

'Strong now. Yes?' She looked exhausted. *'Mais nous devons attendre que la neige fonde.* Too easy to see a man in the snow. Wait. Snow go.'

'*Vous êtes fatiguée*, Madame Sophie?'

'*Les cochons Boches*,' she stopped, glanced at Eddie. 'The dirty pigs Boches search.'

'Who are they looking for?'

'Not you… *Un autre. C'est la même chose. Ils cherchent.* They search.' She put her head in her hands.

'I will go now. It is dangerous for you. *Je vais partir.*' He wondered whether to put a hand on her shoulder. She seemed very small and alone.

'*Non! Non!* Tomorrow. *Demain la neige fondra, si Dieu le veut.*'

Eddie who had gathered Madame Sophie did not approve of the deity, supposed that this invocation, perhaps unconscious, expressed the depth of her anxiety.

'I owe your family my life,' he said in English because he had forgotten the French for 'owe'.

'*Oui.*' She got up and left.

A little later he could hear her with the chattering Fleur, rolling the bales into the stable.

Around noon, the following day, Madame brought him a bowl, soap and a knife. From her pocket she took a small broken piece of mirror.

'*Eh bien. La neige part et peut-être vous aussi.*'

'Tonight?'

She made the sign of the cross and left. He shaved slowly, noticing that indeed there were scars from burns around his chin and neck. Not very noticeable. That evening his plate held three slices of bread instead of the usual one or two. A few minutes later, Madame Sophie brought him his pilot's uniform, neatly folded. It was paler than he remembered, as if much washed.

'*Mettez–le sous vos vêtements.*' She seemed about to leave but paused. 'You understand? Uniform, clothes above.'

'I can never give you and your family enough thanks.'

'*On verra.*' Madame Sophie nodded and left.

Later, the old Madame came up and gave him a pair of hand-knitted gloves and a woollen hat. She kissed him on both cheeks and left.

Shivering, he took off his clothes and put on his uniform. He could see where it had been patched and the bottom half of one leg replaced with a piece of coarse blue cloth. He put all his clothes back on again, including the gloves and hat and his usual jacket and boots, and lay down again. It was totally black, not a sliver of light from moon or stars.

The rats, which he usually ignored, seemed closer and noisier and the animals moved restlessly below. It was time he left.

At what he estimated to be about midnight, he heard footsteps. He stood and went to peer down into the stable.

A voice said, '*Venez vite.*'

Legs shaking a little so that he recalled dogfights in the sky, he climbed down.

'*Vous pouvez marcher?*'

'*Oui.*' He felt rather than saw the presence of two men.

'You not see.' The man spoke English with a strong accent.

'*Non.*'

'*Ne parlez pas.* Not speak.'

Eddie said nothing. Blindfolded, he was put on the back of a motorcycle.

The roar of the engine was terrifying in the silent night. He sat squeezed between the two men. They smelled of sweat and onions. He felt two big panniers on either side of the bike. Then he realised they were bunches of onions. He thought onions didn't smell until they're cut or cooked. He wished he had seen the farm building from the outside just once.

They drove for two hours or more. Thirty or forty kilometres until he hoped to smell the sea. Sometimes they were on reasonable roads, often they bumped along tracks.

He was glad when they stopped. He was led, stumbling, across what he guessed was a field and into what seemed to be a stone shed. When he started to lift his blindfold, the man told him curtly,

'No! *Attendez que nous soyons partis.* Wait.'

Even when they'd gone and he lifted the blindfold, he could see nothing. Trying to loosen his stiff limbs, and expecting someone to come for him that night, he walked up and down the small space. But dawn, the sky streaked with pink and gold, came instead. He knew daylight was the most dangerous time when an unlucky chance could lead to his discovery. He felt his body begin to tremble and told himself it was the cold.

All he could do was wait. There was a bench in the corner where he sat down and ate the third piece of bread which he'd put in his pocket. He discovered an old wine bottle filled with water which he drank from. Quite fresh. He could smell that someone had been in the hut before him.

Later when he felt calmer he peered through the window and saw the field was grazing land but presently without animals. There was a water trough in one corner in which he longed to wash but guessed it would be frozen anyway.

Later again, he took in that the field was completely flat and closely grazed. A dazzling possibility hovered, too dazzling to be acknowledged.

The bright start of the day turned into a white mist which surrounded the hut as if to hide it from the rest of the world. Hunger became his main preoccupation. Desperately searching old cans, broken implements and rank-smelling sacks, he discovered a jar of black olives which he gobbled greedily. He became ashamed of his panic, lay down on the bench and told himself he'd waited for less than twenty-four hours. What was that, compared to the months he'd spent in the loft?

In a half doze, he thought that all pilots, men who were trained to be in charge and make their own decisions, hated waiting more than anything. Even with so much practice in the dispersal hut, they never got better at it.

Night came again and he drank the last of his water. He wondered how long he should stay there. Forever? Until he died of hunger and years later his bones were found and his identity discovered. He reproached himself for his childish hysteria and took slow, deep breaths.

He realised that he had never seen a single German, nor heard German spoken in all his time in France. For an hour on and off he heard German voices, even though he knew they were only in his head, and eventually they died away. He began to feel light-headed and when a spider abseiled from the ceiling on to his hand, he laughed uproariously. He told him he was the best friend he'd ever had even if he was a mad Englishman instead of Robert the Bruce.

On the second morning it was raining and he set the empty olive jar outside. It was consoling to hear the steady ping ping of the drips as it slowly filled.

He spent several hours thinking of all the people who would miss him if he never came back, before becoming ashamed of his self-pity. For the first time since he'd become conscious in France, he said 'Lord, protect thy servant.' Then he lay down and slept.

When he woke, the rain had cleared and there was a sunset even more beautiful than the pink and gold sunrise which had proved so short-lived. He had always loved a good sunset. He watched for an hour from the window as stripes of rich reds and yellows were darkened into orange, amber and purple. Gradually, the purple became deeper and wider, rising it seemed from the earth and forcing the brighter colours into the sky where they seeped away into blue and mauve. The blue and mauve met the purple and another night had come.

He sat on the bench and thought of Eva. But this time without self-pity. As a painter, she would know all about colours, the effect one had on another. For example, he had left out a luminous green from the sunset colours, made presumably by the mix of yellow against blue sky. Every child knows that yellow and blue make green.

He stood up and calmly began to do his exercises. He must stay strong. When he'd finished, he drank some olive-tasting water and lay on the bench. Some animal which hadn't been there the night before, scuttled about in a corner doing something or other. He understood now how prisoners made friends of rats. But he wasn't a prisoner. How long would he stay? How long should he stay? Perhaps the German voices had been real after all. His breath quickened. He pulled back these thoughts and his breath slowed.

He lay on the bench and drifted. Odd lines of poetry came into his head.

In the world's history lovers have a place
Just as Alexandra has or Caesar.

Shakespeare of course. He pictured Eva. He hadn't wanted to care for someone deeply. He'd tried so hard not to. He was a pilot, in love with his Spitfire, in love with the sky. In love with duty and his fellows. Prepared to die.

What was he doing, trapped in this hut?

Accustomed thoughts stretch to infinities,
And you alone can make the untrue true.

How do you tell time in a well of blackness? He opened his eyes. Just the same, of course, but something had disturbed him. Not the unknown animal who was quiet. He sat up and turned his head from left to right as if he could see.

A faint light seemed to come through one of the windows. Was it more than the moon? Could it be dawn already? He went to the door and opened it slightly. His sharp pilot's eyes saw four small flares spread across the field. A figure was briefly silhouetted against one. In another minute he appeared at his side. By the smell of onions, it was one of the men who'd brought him here.

'*Dépêche-toi*. Move!' He was gone before Eddie could say a word. He recognised the sound of a Lysander plane descending. He ran out and waited by a flare. He saw they would quickly burn out and leave no trace. One had already.

The aeroplane came in at a perfect line, landed without a bump and taxied almost to where he stood. The engines continued to turn over while a door opened.

A voice bellowed, 'Get a move on, old boy! My missus likes her breakfast and she's the impatient sort.'

Running the last few yards, Eddie reached the doorway and was heaved in by a strong arm.

He fell on the floor as the plane immediately began to taxi along the grass and in a few seconds was airborne.

He lay where he was and felt the rich surge of the engines, the hard vibration rush through his body, as life-giving to him as the blood in his veins. The plane was circling smoothly and there was no need to guess that they were heading west.

'Get in the back seat, you idiot!' Eddie crawled to the seat obediently.

The only light came from the instruments in front of the pilot. He half turned his head so Eddie could see a silhouette of a large nose, round rather than pointed. It looked very English to him.

'Well, you're the lucky one.' His voice was loud enough to carry above the engines. 'I was bidden to a hush-hush drop and told if that went okay and I happened to read our map and compass right and found that field in the middle of nowhere and you happened to come out unattended and we were unattended too and you hopped in within three seconds, then I'd take you off. Long odds, I'd say. Been waiting a while have you?'

Eddie found it impossible to respond. He was fighting back tears, and felt relieved when the pilot faced forward again. After a minute or two he managed to sit up straighter and do up his belt.

'Been over there long, have you?' This time the pilot spoke without turning round.

Again, Eddie felt unable to answer. He was shocked by what seemed his saviour's chatty assumption that all would go well. Lysander's were notoriously vulnerable to ground flak or enemy fire. How could he be anything but fearful and braced for the worst?

Slowly, he unbuttoned his heavy jacket and pulled it off, revealing his RAF uniform.

The pilot glanced backwards again. 'So that's who you are. Strike me down, thought I was picking up one of those agent chappies. Might have felt bad if you'd been left behind. 'Bomber pilot?'

'Fighter,' said Eddie and then had to shout louder, 'Fighter pilot! Out of Warmwell.' He was bellowing. Suddenly he felt stronger. 'Spitfires.' As long as he didn't burst into tears.

'Bloody hell.' The man whistled. 'I've picked up a buggering hero.'

Eddie saw he was joking about a bit but he didn't care. 'I didn't feel very heroic as I hit the sea.'

'Dipped your wick, did you. Never fancied that.'

'Didn't know much about it.' Things began to seem a little more real. Real brought hope.

There was no more talking as the pilot paid attention to his controls. Eddie's mind began to work faster. He guessed they would be flying at under 2000 feet, with any luck too low for enemy fighters and too high for ground fire. He revived enough to want to look out of a window. They must have passed the French coast and he wondered where they were heading. Not that it mattered. He found himself smiling idiotically. He was an idiot as the pilot had said.

At the same time, another part of his brain still informed him that no escape could be as easy as this. In a minute or two, there'd be the bright lines of tracer fire, the sharp rattle of bullets, the flicker of a first flame. He'd be thrown about on the floor as the pilot wrenched the stick, side to side, down up, circle, spin – Lysander's weren't any good at that either. He grasped the side of his seat and tried to stifle his gasps.

'Want a bun, do you?' The pilot threw a paper bag at him.

A bun? Eddie picked up the bag unbelieving. The fears disappeared. The bag smelled of England. How pathetic is that! The tears were near again. He'd almost forgotten he'd been starving for two days. He ate one in four big bites, choking with pleasure. This was more like it.

'Twenty minutes!' yelled the pilot.

'Where are we headed?' shouted Eddie.

'Hush. Hush!' yelled the pilot, laughing. He too would be relieved to be nearly back. 'Don't expect you've heard about rhubarbs and circuses. That's what you fighter lot are up to now,' he added with a kind of satisfaction.

'What's that?' asked Eddie because it was expected, although all his attention was on their flight and the possibility of arrival. He could not yet consider what awaited him, should they arrive.

'It's something they call targets of opportunity, railway lines and bridges or trying to lure up the enemy. Terribly risky business. Terrible losses.'

The pilot began to talk over the R/T. He had only just turned it on. Eddie picked up the word Manston. Not too far from his original posting. For the journey to have taken this long, he must have flown that doomed Spitfire a long way down the French coast.

The Lysander was dropping down very slowly. Eddie remembered its stalling speed was 650 mph. He couldn't remember when he'd last been in an aeroplane without flying it. In training probably. He remembered the person he'd been then with dispassionate curiosity. Such a child, when it came down to it. All that competitive excitement. Was he excited now? He should be dead. He had been lucky. His thoughts skittered about.

'Here we come! Prepare for landing!' shouted the pilot.

Eddie felt the roar in his body, the rush, the rumble and the light bumps as the Lysander's extra-large wheels hit the ground. They taxied fast, then slower, then stopped.

It reminded Eddie of so many other times when he'd come back from an op and sat unmoving for a moment as the adrenalin slowly settled and he took in that once again he'd survived and was home. Was he really about to enter that world again? It seemed impossible.

'Let's get going!' The pilot had the hood back and was preparing to climb out.

Almost reluctantly, Eddie undid his belt.

CHAPTER THIRTY-FOUR
February 1941

Eddie walked slowly along the apron at Manston airbase. The cold air gripped him viciously, making every step an effort. His saviour had disappeared as soon as they'd landed. His back was already to him when he shouted about refueling 'and not just the plane!' Any thanks were lost in the icy night. The usual dim flares at the edge of the runway seeped whispily upwards. He stood still and watched his own white breath puff into the air. It seemed the most energetic thing about him.

Two aircrew in blue dungarees, no coats, no hats, came briskly towards him, talking. 'Bloody cheek. At this time of the morning.'

Eddie watched them. Why did they seem familiar? They passed him, still talking, the cadences in their voices slightly unusual. Eddie turned to watch them go and, as he did so, one of the men swung around. He nudged the other who also turned.

Eddie swayed. His feet seemed insecure on the ground, which wavered, as did the swirling darkness, the glimmers of light, the puffs of white. A roaring started from somewhere or perhaps it was just in his head. Where was he? Had he died? Is this what happened after death? A dream peopled from the past. He put his hand to his head, hatless too, no need to salute.

'Sir?' The first man stepped towards him.

Eddie could not speak. Ghosts don't speak.

'It's him, all right.' The second man announced with certainty and took several steps forward.

'Sorry, sir. We didn't recognise you at first. You've lost that much weight.'

The two men, Jenkins and Jones, came level with each other,

stood to attention and saluted, despite the lack of a hat.

'Welcome back,' said Jones.

'Praise be the good Lord,' said Jenkins, who had never mentioned Him to Eddie before.

How strong they were! How kind! How comforting! How Welsh!

The ground steadied under Eddie's feet. He moved towards his two old friends and put a hand on each of their shoulders. 'You always were my guardian angels and for a moment there I thought you were welcoming me through the pearly gates.'

'No chance, sir. You just need feeding up and you'll be having Jerry for breakfast, if you catch my meaning.'

'Thank you, Jones.'

'We're off on a job sir, or we'd stay to hear the story.' Both men put their thumbs up and went sturdily on their way. It struck Eddie that they were probably looking after the plane that had brought him here.

He peered around and suddenly hail, like cold bullets, was falling round his head. Through it, he saw a tall officer in a heavy great coat striding purposefully towards him.

'Thought we'd lost you all over again.' He took Eddie's arm and led him forward. 'Come in before we both freeze to death. Bloody winter. Dark til lunch time. But doesn't even keep the planes on the ground these days. Not much to you, is there? Here we are. Take a pew. No ceremony. Not after what you've been through.'

Eddie found himself in a small office, hot and steaming with cigarette smoke.

'I'm the optimistically-named Intelligence Officer round here, Launcelot Smith-Garnier, known as Smithy. And now we can set about finding out who you are.' Smithy who wore thick-lensed glasses and had foregone the moustache usual for RAF officers over a certain age, lit himself a cigarette, acknowledged Eddie's shake of his head, and sat back in his chair.

Eddie supposed that his weeks of illness and silence followed by weeks which included little conversation, had made him particularly sensitive to all these words which men in this recovered world poured at him.

'I am Flight Lieutenant Eddie Chaffey,' he said carefully, 'from 609 squadron, flying out of Warmwell.'

'Good. Good. Well done. That's got us started. You know how it is. A war on and everyone under suspicion. Don't want to fatten you up, stick you in a Spitfire and find you're a Hun from the sun or even a Hun with a gun.'

Since Smithy paused, Eddie, wishing to co-operate, said, 'No, sir.'

'Yes. Quite. So, what more can you tell me? If I can clear things up, we won't have to bother anyone else. Though they may bother us. Can't entirely bank on them staying away. Nosey buggers.'

'Yes, sir,' agreed Eddie in another pause.

'So what else can you tell me?'

'Not very much, sir. I went down near the French coast. Got a bang on my head and a bullet in my leg.' He paused. 'But it might be the other way round.'

'When was that?'

'October, I think.'

'Bugger me!' exclaimed Smithy, and he exhaled smoke with such force that it turned into a prolonged coughing fit.

Eddie waited till he'd recovered and then added, 'A French family looked after me but I never knew who they were. I don't know how arrangements were made to pick me up either. I was kept in the dark.'

The sleuthing tendencies of the officer who was still coughing gently, seemed flattened by a combination of his failing lungs and his visitor's lack of knowledge. 'Good show anyway. I suppose getting you checked out by a medic is next on the agenda.'

As he leant forward to stub out his cigarette, the door behind Eddie was opened forcibly and a burly figure flung himself across the room. Seeing he was a Wing Commander, Eddie stood and saluted. He moved further aside as a beefy hand slapped the table.

'Guess what! The powers that shouldn't be want my lot up

to protect some damn convoy. In this weather! They won't see anything, least of all the airfield on their way back, if they don't end in the drink. It's a disgrace! It wasn't like this when Dowding was in charge!'

'Calm down, dear fellow,' coughed Smithy, 'You might think differently if you were a naval chappie in one of those old tubs.'

'If I believed it would do any bloody good. We lost two last week in the same sort of caper. And if it isn't convoys, it's bombers trundling across France. The Spitfire's a fighter plane not an escort. Even you understand that, Smithy.' The officer thumped down in the chair Eddie had just vacated.

'How many do they want?'

'They started with six and I've negotiated it down to three.' He took off his hat and banged it on his knee which sent raindrops flying. He swung back on the chair and surveyed the smoke-garlanded ceiling. 'Oh, well. Got to be done. Just letting off steam. Sorry old chap.' He straightened the chair and seemed to see Eddie for the first time. 'Hello, there. New are you. Not the best welcome. Sorry about that.' He peered a bit closer. 'You all right? Seem a bit off.' He stood up. 'Here, take a pew. See you later.'

He'd reached the door before Smithy got out, 'He's just been picked up from France.'

The officer did a double take. 'Thought you looked a bit knocked up. I'll just give the command they don't want to hear to my long-suffering pilots, then I'll treat you for a celebration in the jolly old Mess.'

Since the medic didn't turn up and Smithy became engaged in a wrangle on the telephone, Eddie found himself led over to the Mess by an obliging corporal.

'You'll be pleasurably surprised, sir. The Mess was bombed flat last summer so they moved into the old Station Commander's house before the war. This was a peace-time airfield too, sir.'

It was breakfast time in the Mess. The darkness and rain continued outside but inside there was a blazing log fire with deep armchairs grouped round it.

'Do you want to warm yourself or eat first, sir?'

Eddie glanced through the dining room where a lot of very young-looking pilots sat at a long table. He was still finding it hard to find a voice and the thought of answering all the eager questions that he was certain to be asked outweighed his hunger. It seemed his experiences in France had put a barrier between him and his fellows. Then he remembered hours slumped on his own in the Mess before he was moved to Warmwell.

'I'll stay here,' he said.

A few minutes later, the Wing Commander he'd met earlier appeared, throwing off his coat and calling for coffee. Eddie stood up but he waved him down.

'Good. Good. You found your way. More coffee?'

'Thank you.'

'Monty Crystal.'

'Eddie Chaffey.'

'Well, Eddie. I bumped into your old fitter and rigger on the way back from being a bloody executioner, so I know all about you now. Wouldn't mind getting you back here when you're up and running. Although it's a different sort of war, now. Seems you've been away a while.'

'I'm afraid I'm a bit of a Rip van Wrinkle.'

'No hurry. You've earned a rest. I bet your people weren't half chuffed hearing you're back. A kind of rebirth.'

Eddie stared at Monty's genial red face. He had not told anyone he was back. He had not even thought of them. It had been as if he'd been held in a dream, without will of his own. 'I haven't got through to them yet,' he said. 'I expect they think I'm dead.'

'Is that so.' Monty tried to disguise his surprise. 'Want a hand, do you?'

Eddie realised that was just what he needed. 'I believe I do.' He had nearly spoken in French.

'You tell me the number. I'll put you through and you can talk. Let's get this coffee under our belts first. Bit of a sensitive call, I'd say.'

There was a faint greyish light coming through the windows, struggling against the continuing rain, not enough to rival the room's lamps, when Monty took Eddie to a small room with a telephone and a single chair.

'You sit.'

Eddie sat and listened as Monty gave the Tollorum number. He wondered what time it was. He thought if he knew the time he might feel more connected. He needed a watch.

Monty was talking. He turned to Eddie, 'Mr. and Mrs. Chaffey are at a funeral. They'll be back later.' He put down the phone.

Too late Eddie realised that it was probably Lily who had given this information and that he could have spoken to her.

'What time is it?'

'Time for a second breakfast. Good news is it wasn't *your* funeral.'

Had Monty really said that? The dining-room was almost empty now and a clock on the wall told him it was eight-fifteen. Monty piled toast on his own plate and after he'd eaten it, went away saying, that if Eddie was waiting for the medic, there was no better place than this.

Eddie finished a small plate of porridge and a slice of toast before retiring gratefully to the chair by the fire. When he next looked up there was a small man in an M.O.'s uniform tapping his knee.

'What time is it?'

The medic looked at his watch. 'Nearly four. Sorry I've been so long. Had to take a chap to hospital.'

'I slept through lunch,' said Eddie.

'Good. Good. Now we'll find somewhere I can check you out.'

This checking out didn't take long because while expressing admiration for his scars, both in head and leg, without an X-ray he had no way of knowing what was going on. 'I could ask you to count from ten backwards, I suppose. But my advice is buzz off home before some idiot gets hold of you. Then, after a week or two, see how you feel. I can sign a chit right now if you like.'

Eddie agreed that sounded like an excellent plan and didn't tell the doctor that he still hadn't been in touch with his family.

He went back to the Mess to wait for the medic to arrange transport and was rather irritated when both chairs nearest the fire were occupied. The men sitting there were slumped backwards, each with a cigarette at the end of their fingers. Eddie remembered that position, after a difficult op, the angle of the slump ingrained forever in his body.

He knew he should go now and make the telephone call to Tollorum but instead he sat down and imagined how it would be if he just walked up the drive unannounced. How amazing that would be! He pictured Eva there, coming with her long stride towards him. But Eva might well be in Oxford; in fact she might be anywhere. Perhaps she had been sent up to Scotland to be with Cousin Phoebe. He was surprised to find himself remembering Cousin Phoebe.

Slowly, he got up and walked towards the room with the telephone. As he passed, one of the pilots looked up.

'Heard about you.' He pulled himself straighter. 'Jolly good show.'

The other pilot also sat up. 'Good to know a chap can get back from France. We're over it a lot these days. Taking the fight to the enemy. Flaps everywhere. You know.'

Eddie hesitated. He didn't know. The war could have been lost or won over the last few months for all he knew. 'I've got to make a call.'

'Buy you a pint when it suits,' offered the first pilot.

By the time Eddie reached the door both men had slumped back into position.

With some trepidation, he picked up the telephone receiver. He couldn't ring Eva because he didn't know her number by heart.

∞

The telephone rang in Tollorum's dark hallway. When it eventually stopped, the house breathed gently with no-one to command its creakings, scuttlings, squeaks, whispers and whistles.

Another hour passed before the sound of a car coming slowly up the driveway was followed by the front door opening and footsteps, stamping feet and voices. The voices were low, once the stamping stopped, the footsteps were slow.

'Straight to the kitchen,' said Lily. She switched on a light, showing the white faces of Sylvia and Eva. 'Food, drink, warmth, bed. It's a horrible night. Cold and wet. But at least your train wasn't too late. Let's hope Fred made it to London all right.' She would put a hot water bottle in each bed. At least the war couldn't stop her providing that bit of comfort. She put her arm round Eva's shoulders and led her forward.

'Thank you, dear Lily,' said Sylvia, lingering. It was terrible to return to the house and find Eddie still gone. And now there was no Beatrice it was even harder. It was the suddenness of death that was so particularly awful because it made everything seem so insubstantial. When Fred had come back from Gallipoli and they had studied Classics together with the Reverend Gisburne, all the most famous quotations had been about death. '*Thus have the gods spun the thread for wretched mortals: that they live in grief while they themselves are without cares.*'[2]

Beatrice had died in her sleep the week previously. Not that it was her funeral they'd just attended. That had been four days ago in the Tollorum village church. Sylvia had been glad her mother had not known she was dying or she might have relived her husband's disappearance.

Despite the extreme cold, Sylvia sat down on a small oak chair. It was good to be alone. Two funerals in a week and still Eddie missing. It was inconceivable. Neither death was caused by enemy action. The funeral they had just returned from was for Eva's father. They had travelled to Oxford to show support which turned out to be unnecessary as streams of elderly academics attended, including, of course, Arthur Lamb. Dear Arthur. Size apart, he never changed.

They had, however, borne off Eva and saved her from Cousin

---

2 *Iliad*, Book 24, l.525.

Phoebe. Cousin Phoebe was a bustling Scottish lady, used to the efficient management of seven children ranging in age from eight to eighteen. But what would she have made of the pregnant Eva? Perhaps she'd have taken it in her stride.

Sylvia stood up, stamped her feet once more to bring them back to life, and went to the kitchen.

Lily was making scrambled eggs on toast. 'A treat,' she said, glancing at Eva.

Sylvia and Lily both wanted to look after Eva. She was their closest link to Eddie, and Sylvia's visit to her cold and gloomy Oxford home had made her, in particular, understand Eva's unusual and solitary childhood. Sylvia told herself not to discount Eva's wish or even need to become a painter. Even so, she had abandoned the Ruskin to come with them, 'Just for a week,' she'd said, 'And I'll bring my painting things.'

Now she was being bullied into eating the eggs by Lily. Yes, it was good to have someone to look after.

※

Eddie thought he wouldn't mind being left alone to sit by the Mess fire forever. He was even irritated when a servant interrupted the peace by throwing on more wood; the resulting blaze, with sparks floating up the wide chimney, was far too dramatic. He thought he could do without drama for the rest of his life. Waking from a doze, he vividly pictured Fleur singing her carol and felt so much love and nostalgia that he half longed to be back in the loft.

But Smithy, the Intelligence Officer stood in front of him and then sat beside him. 'So the medic's arranged it all. By chance a chap's being taken to Salisbury Hospital. Don't ask me why. Miles away. But near your Middle Wallop base so has a semblance of good sense. You get properly checked, then their Wingco can take over.'

Eddie began to pay attention. 'I'm ready whenever you say, sir, although the medic did suggest I went home.'

'Did he now. Changed his mind, it seems.' Smithy began to cough.

As soon as he left, Eddie stood up. Now was the time to call Tollorum. It was seven-thirty. But as he hesitated, a group of officers came in and hurriedly, he took up his place again.

≫≪

Eva curled round the heavy china hot water bottle. She had safe-keeping of Eddie's baby. She slipped into sleep with his face before her.

≫≪

The ambulance had not yet turned up so Eddie had been put in a spare bed in the pilots' quarters. Vaguely he wondered in what kind of op the previous occupant had been lost. He woke up more fully as a man came into the room, smelling of beer, blundering but attempting to do it quietly.

'I don't mind if you put on the light,' said Eddie.

'Thanks.' The light went on immediately. 'I've never taken to night fighting.'

'Same here.'

'Bugger it.' The pilot, only half undressed, got into bed. 'They say you got out of France? After being shot down last year.'

'Yes,' agreed Eddie.

'We fly over France a lot now. Makes you realise the Hun didn't have it so easy coming this way. Sometimes I think I'd rather be posted abroad. All kinds of places to choose from: Italy, Africa, heard of Rommel, have you? I'd like something to remember if I'm still around after it's all over.'

Eddie thought, I must try and think about the war again. Find out what's going on. But the war sounded too big. Probably, he'd never thought about anything except the little bit where he was involved and now he was not involved at all.

'How are we doing?' he asked.

His companion seemed surprised by the question. Then he laughed, 'I'd need a few pints less to answer that one, if you mean, how's the war going. Let's say we haven't lost, but since you were away, Slovakia, Hungary and Romania have joined in on the wrong side. You probably know Italy invaded Greece. And of course, they're still bombing London. What else?'

The pilot was warming to his subject and Eddie heard him gulp, followed by the smell of whisky. He hadn't touched alcohol since his months in the loft and felt sickened.

'The bloody Yanks still aren't in, although Mr Churchill spends more time the other side of the Atlantic than here. The main point is the blessed RAF is needed all over the place, and nobody, except drama-seeking spinsters, talk of invasion anymore.'

Eddie listened as he talked on but closed his eyes and the intense words soon drifted away.

CHAPTER THIRTY-FIVE
February 1941

Fred, once communist, once pacifist, and now convinced of his only son's death, went along to the Chelsea section of the Home Guard. They were in the basement of a modern apartment, a building locally said to be bombproof. Piles of rubble on either side confirmed this reputation.

'Much safer than Churchill's bunker in Whitehall,' commented the uniformed man sitting behind a desk, 'Although if you believe the rumours, he never sleeps there, sensible chap.'

Bloody Churchill, thought Fred, but held to his purpose. 'As you can see, I'm veteran of the last war, but my body is able, my mind willing. There must be some way I can help the war effort.'

'The Home Guard is part of the Army,' said the man, noticing Fred's arm. 'The Army has regulations. I myself fought in the last war.. Survived Passchendaele. Perhaps you …'

'I have very good eyesight,' interrupted Fred, 'unlike that great one-armed hero, Admiral Nelson.' He tried to calm himself. 'I have no commitments and can work every night if necessary. Or cover for others at short notice. I am strong, not yet fifty.'

'I see,' the man was embarrassed, wanted to be on good terms with a fellow survivor of the Great War. But regulations were regulations and in another five minutes he'd be off duty and it would be someone else's problem.

'I'll do anything,' lied Fred. What he actually wanted was to put himself in danger. He wanted to confront death, look into his hot eyes. The air of continuing hopefulness at Tollorum, despite his determination to support Sylvia, had become more and more unbearable.

He had given up journalism altogether. His study of the Bible had made polemic of any sort seem ridiculous and that was the only writing he knew. He looked back now with despair at all the poses he had taken up for the *Daily Worker*. Poses, verging on gibberish, as he thought of them now. The spiritual side of religion had seemed to offer new hope but now he doubted even that. He began to believe that Eddie had been his future and Eddie was gone.

He could find women. Sonia, the pacifist, had never left the East End and still survived, helping the desperate. But now the thought of her made him picture Eddie, a handsome young boy sneaking off for sex with his father's lover. What did that say about him? What did it say about them both? Seeking out other women was even less possible when he considered Sylvia's tragic expectation of Eddie's return. Everything came back to Eddie.

He could drink. He did drink. But it was no longer deadening his feelings. Action was the only answer. So here he was begging this old soldier to take him into a section of the British Army, when he'd spent the last twenty years, based on first-hand experience, reviling everything it stood for, including the politicians who ran it. But then the last war had changed everything about him, so why wouldn't this one do the same?

'I'll tell you what,' said the man behind the desk, whose name was Alan Handyman, 'I'm off in a minute. Why don't we share a cuppa and talk it over?'

'We can do better than that,' said Fred. 'I'm only round the corner.'

So Handyman who only wanted to go to bed after his night shift, found himself being invited to a glass of whisky and told to push the books and papers off the sofa and on to the floor.

'With your help I'll be on to more useful things than pen-pushing now.'

The two men, apparently so unlike, hit it off. After two glasses of whisky, Fred recalled his fellow soldiers on Gallipoli: Ernie Wilkes, Parky, Joe Dingle, most of them dead or lost, some whose names he'd forgotten. Handyman answered with his own roll-call and the two knocked their glasses together and a warm glow lightened the burden of this war.

As Handyman left, he assured Fred that if he turned up at 10pm that night there would be something for him to do.

'Dangerous?'

'We can promise you that,' Handyman laughed.

⋙

Eva slept heavily and woke feeling lethargic. She got out of bed and pulled back the sprigged curtains. A hazy sun shone through drifting cloud over a sprinkling of snow. She thought that by the time her baby was born it would be summer, the fields and gardens golden and green. She went back to bed and slipped under the bed clothes. Normally, the pale wash of white would have challenged her to reproduce it in some form or other, watercolour, oil paint, perhaps pastel. But now she felt only the need for time. Time to grow strong, time to reflect calmly, Time to do nothing. Time to feel Eddie in every moment.

⋙

Sylvia turned off the wireless and Lily cleared away the breakfast.

'Let her sleep,' said Lily.

'I've got a meeting in Dorchester at ten-thirty,' said Sylvia. 'I'll pop down to the farm first. That new manager hasn't a clue how to handle the girls.'

'And why shouldn't there be a lady manager in the job!' Lily efficiently swung a heavy pan into its place above the range. Sylvia smiled. Lily was right. She'd been doing a man's job since 1914.

'We'll meet at lunch.'

⋙

In the afternoon, Eva had a telephone call from Cousin Phoebe. 'I have seen the solicitor, my dear, and we are agreed it will be best to sell the house. You'll not want something so big and the money will be useful for you. We can go into details later.'

'What about Valtraud?' asked Eva.

'She has decided to join Hildegard in Manchester.'

Everything is so simple, thought Eva, sitting quietly in the hall, if you just let things happen. One day she'd get back to the Ruskin.

'Thank you, Cousin Phoebe.'

≈

It had been dark for most of Eddie's journey from Manston to Salisbury but night lifted and the skies cleared to an overall whiteness as they reached the great open plain.

'I used to know all the roads round here,' said the driver of the ambulance chattily. 'But the Army have buggered it up with blocks here and there and everywhere.'

'I suppose they don't want to shoot us,' suggested Eddie, 'at least not by mistake.' He was sitting beside the driver while a male nurse travelled in the back with the patient. He was a pilot who'd lost both legs and was in danger of losing an arm.

This travelling first through darkness, now through hills, white with snow, like blank sheets of paper, seemed a continuation of his journey through France, of his flight in the Lysander, his long sojourns in the chair by the Mess fire at Manston. They had already been driving for nearly five hours, slowly and carefully. The bell had only been turned on once when a cow blocked their way.

Eddie thought that when they arrived at Salisbury, he should be ready to telephone Tollorum. Stumbling stiffly out of the ambulance, he automatically looked up at the sky but the only planes were too far away to identify.

Doctors, shocked by his scars in head and leg, insisted on X-rays, but there were queues and then a stray bomb was dropped on a village near the town. It was hard enough to find a sandwich, let alone a telephone.

Instead he found an empty chair with a neatly folded copy of *The Times* on it and sat down. He read: 'Hitler's marching orders for a spring offensive.'

By the time the X-rays were done it was dark again and there were no doctors or beds available so he was told to come back for the results in the morning. Eddie knew the sensible thing would be to ring the Wing Commander at Middle Wallop but why should he do that before ringing Tollorum?

He tried leaving the hospital but the cold made him shake, so he came back inside and found another chair in a warm corridor. It was a relief that no one troubled him. Only an elderly cleaner asked him to raise his legs while she swabbed the lino underneath. By then light was coming through the windows.

He walked back to the waiting room where the same newspaper lay on the same chair. The receptionist said brightly, 'Good morning, sir. Can I help you?' as if he had just arrived in the hospital, so he told her who he was and why he had come.

She consulted a list, nervously patting her hair where the grips predominated, as if her experiences with the list were less than positive. Eventually she announced with a triumphant smile, 'Here we are: Flight Lieutenant E. F. Chaffey. No appointment time, so just stay close.'

Eddie resumed his seat, noticing that *The Times* had been removed by his neighbour, a large man with a dressing over one eye. Like Eddie, he didn't seem to be making much headway with the paper, finally stuffing it under his chair.

Winking his one eye, he said, 'Bad enough living through it. What's wrong with you, then? Got all your bits have you? Looks like it. Picked up a Jerry pilot out of our field last year. Head one place, legs the other. Never found the hands. I expect you've seen some sights?' He waited expectantly.

Not keen on this sort of gruesome bartering, Eddie opened his mouth, pointed to it with his finger and shook his head sorrowfully.

'Oh, dearie dearie me. I bet they never told you boys war would be like this. No voice. Well I never.'

Eddie looked down modestly. In the next several hours, he moved only once, to collect a roll and tea from a trolley. At last his name was called by the receptionist.

The doctor receiving him, was peering closely at the X-ray of his head with a baffled expression.

'Is it all right, sir?' asked Eddie.

'That's the point.' The doctor was very small, with a big face. 'Your leg has healed of course. You're a young chap and if it's not dead straight, you won't know about that for decades.'

'But what about my head?' Eddie was suddenly alarmed. He had been behaving oddly since he arrived in England. Perhaps he had a screw loose. The description of madness came to him with a nasty lurch of his heart.

'That's the point as I'm trying to tell you,' the doctor was suddenly irascible. 'Your head, despite that deep scar, seems perfectly fine. I suppose there was a bleeding on the brain which the Frog medic fixed. But I was informed that you were out for weeks or even months.'

Eddie thought about this. 'So you can't find much wrong?'

'*Nothing* wrong! It doesn't make sense if your story's true. Most confusing.' The doctor who'd been standing, staring at the screen with the X-ray pinned to it, suddenly sat down. Frankly, I was expecting to see a bullet lodged in your brain which I'd have to extricate or you'd face dangers of swelling and meningitis. It's the problem of the failed suicide.' He looked up at Eddie. 'How do you explain it?'

Eddie waited but the doctor seemed to be expecting an answer. 'I suppose I could be a German spy and have made up the whole story.'

'Quite.' The doctor took up his pen. 'I'll diagnose traumatic wounds and exhaustion and suggest a month's rest. That do?'

'Yes, sir. Thank you, sir.'

Outside the hospital the sun had come out, shining in a hard, cold way. Eddie buttoned up the jacket that had come all the way from France with him. He was free. Or at least another layer of freedom.

A taxi, lights dimmed, drove carefully up to the hospital. The passenger had trouble opening the door. Eddie went to help her.

A woman, a fur stole ending in a fox's head round her shoulders, got out. 'Thank you. So kind.'

The driver joined Eddie and they both watched as the woman, a striking figure in her fur, jaunty hat and very high heels walked through the hospital doors.

'Husband in there,' commented the driver, 'Expected to come out in a bag.'

'I'll tell you what,' said Eddie, 'Are you up for a bit of a drive?'

'It all depends on the petrol, doesn't it. What do you mean, bit of a drive?'

As he was speaking somewhat suspiciously, Eddie saw a jeep draw up and a man wearing an RAF overcoat got out. Instinctively, Eddie turned slightly aside but not before he'd recognised his mother's admirer, the Wing Commander. He edged closer to the taxi.

'We can fill up when we arrive if you can get us there.' He suggested to the driver. 'With any luck, we'll make it in daylight.'

'Hop in, then, sir. No time like the present.'

Eddie climbed carefully into the back of the car. Even as he sat there, heart beating jerkily, his mother's admirer passed by.

'Where to?' asked the driver.

The moment they were on their way, Eddie closed his eyes. He thought that the Wing Commander would never have known who he was anyway, in his French jacket and at his new weight.

<hr />

Eva sat at one end of the large kitchen. As always, it was the only warm room, but she had begun to love the long, scrubbed wooden table, the brass pots and pans, and the old range which in theory heated itself, the water and the whole house, except that there was never enough coal to feed it. She could imagine the days, not so long past, when the room would have been filled with servants, preparing with the maximum of effort, huge meals, while they, with butler and man-servants, ate and lived in other rooms, now shut up, along the corridor. The kitchen was a relic, presided over by Lily. Eva sat there and felt comforted by friendly ghosts from the past.

Sylvia, preparing for one of her many meetings of the WVS, watched her. Since Beatrice's death, she had begun to think about the future of the house. The war had given the garden a purpose as it turned into a market garden with acres of potatoes, turnips, leeks, cabbage. The home farm just about paid the expenses of the house but what was its purpose? Resolutely refusing to accept the probability of Eddie's death, and now watching over the coming of his child, she nevertheless decided that she must turn Tollorum Manor over to the government if it could find a use for it.

Outside, the gardens were quiet and the sun only showed in a rim over the hills. Silently, a frost descended and the grass began to curl and crisp as damp patches and the occasional puddle tightened and hardened against the ground.

Eva stood up. 'I think I'll get a breath of air before the light goes completely.'

Sylvia understood how much Eva dreaded the moment when they put up the black-out and shut themselves away from the world. From Eddie. She felt the same herself. 'You've probably got another ten minutes. Once the sun's gone, it gets dark so quickly. Wrap up warm.'

Eva put on an old coat of Beatrice's because hers wouldn't button up and went out through a side door. She stood for a moment breathing deeply, before bending down to a pot by the door and picking a sprig of rosemary. She held it close to her nose as she walked, enjoying the slightly bitter smell. She loved Tollorum more and more, the garden with its old stone walls, the fields that rose in graceful folds to the sky. Every day now, she did sketches, usually from windows inside but sometimes finding a sheltered corner away from any wind where she could sit for an hour and draw a tree or a slice of a view.

Looking up, she saw the sun had quite disappeared and the night was sweeping towards her.

She walked more quickly, planning to pass by the front of the house to the walled garden beyond. It would be darker still there.

339

Dim lights, as golden as a cat's eyes, wide and blank, turned off the road and down the driveway. The leafless trees hung like skeletons overhead.

'I won't deny I'll be glad of a cup of tea.' The driver, who had been keeping awake by talking to himself, gave a brave chuckle. The Manor house appeared ahead.

Eddie, who had woken from a long sleep in time to direct him through the narrow lanes, looked out of the window and tried to make out the shapes of his childhood.

How could it be that he was returning? It felt as if he was dreaming. He reassured himself by touching the doctor's note in his pocket. He tried to concentrate on what lay ahead but suddenly it all felt too quick. He should speak to the driver.

'We'll get you petrol, money, a cup of tea and a sandwich, at least a sandwich.'

'Thanks for that, sir.' He should have guessed his passenger came from a posh family. An odd bloke, not a talker anyway, but who knows what he'd been through. Just for a moment the driver allowed himself to think of his son fighting on some front, against the Ities maybe. The driveway forked and he slowed down.

'Front door, sir?'

'Turn left here. We'll park in the stable yard.'

'Okey dokey.' An odd one, no joke. You'd think he'd want a grand home-coming.

Followed by the driver, Eddie walked slowly up to the house which was in complete darkness. For a flash he imagined that he was coming to an empty house, until he remembered the black-out.

'What time is it?'

'Four thirty. It's lucky my missus doesn't worry where I am. I tell her driving a taxi is like being in the Army. Never know where you'll find yourself.

'So dark,' said Eddie. He was glad to be going in by the side door. 'So quiet.'

'Could be midnight,' agreed the driver.

As Eddie neared the door, he felt a growing sense of foreboding. Why was he coming back here? What could be bring but suffering? It was too much. The separation was too great to cross. Without his driver behind him, he'd have turned and run, hid like a wild animal in the undergrowth. He turned away from the door, mumbled to the driver, 'I just need a moment.' He started walking back the way they'd come.

The driver stood aside, watching.

Everywhere was black below now, even the dimmest glow dropped behind the hills but high up in the sky the evening star appeared with bright glimmering.

><=

Eva recognized Eddie and walked towards him with her arms open wide. She felt as if she could see him every detail, as if that single star was lighting him up for her.

Eddie, who had been walking with bowed head, looked up.

They came together quickly, silently, holding on to each other, faces close, breathing the same cold air.

The driver watched approvingly. He thought how he would describe it to his wife and how she would sigh sentimentally and feel happy there were some good endings in the war.

'You're shaking,' Eva held Eddie tightly. 'It's freezing. We must go inside.'

They walked with arms still around each other. Eddie felt that he might fall down if he let go. Eva felt that he might disappear back into her dreams.

'Come inside,' she nodded to the driver, without altering her grasp round Eddie.

Even the dim lights of the corridor seemed harsh. Ahead were the even brighter lights of the kitchen.

Eva and Eddie stood at the doorway. They had been so quiet that nobody inside had heard them coming.

Eddie stared at the tranquil scene in front of him.

Sylvia sat at the table reading *The Times* and Lily was lifting the black kettle onto the Aga. 'This kettle gets heavier every day,' she was saying.

Sylvia smiled, 'Do you ever think it might be you that's getting weaker?'

'Not for a moment!'

Eva took her arms away from Eddie and started to speak. At once the two women turned.

Sylvia stood, then seemed unable to move any further. 'It is you! Is it you? Can it be true? Is it true? It is true!'

The joyful, loving sounds, wordless in Eddie's head, reminded him of Fleur. They were drawing him out of the night.

Behind him, the driver stayed at a respectful distance.

Eva took Eddie's hand and looked into his face. 'It is Eddie. Of course it is.'

Lily who had not come to greet Eddie, slid the kettle further onto the stove. She took off the padded gloves she was wearing and stuffed them in her apron pocket. The driver came in a little further and stopped. Suddenly there was stillness.

It seemed that the room and everybody in it held their breath, like a stage before the curtain goes up. Eddie was there in front of them. But was he really there?

'You're back,' Sylvia said tenderly. 'We knew you would be.' She moved towards him.

This affirmation reached Eddie. 'Yes. Hello Eva. Hello Mother. Hello Aunt Lily.' He paused over the driver, before remembering. 'Thank you for bringing me here. Please, sit down. I'm going to.'

Sylvia and Eva took chairs on either side of Eddie. They did not even think of rejoicing excitedly or asking questions. He was back from the dead and just now accepting a cup of tea from Lily, then pleased at the idea of a cheese sandwich. His extreme thinness and slow, quiet movements, so unlike the Eddie they knew, warned them to be careful.

He was not yet as he was, *not yet,* they all three thought. How patiently they would tend him back to good health! The expression as he looked at them, shocked them by its vulnerability and sweetness. Their love was so great that they could hardly bear it.

Eventually it was too much for Eva who began to sob. 'I haven't even told him we're going to have a baby.'

'Not taking in the meaning of what she had said, but recognizing the appeal, Eddie put down his sandwich. 'I'm sorry.' He looked seriously at Eva. 'It was my fault I went into the sea. A stupid trick. Two of them when I thought there was one. But I was lucky. Picked up and looked after by a French family. Odds very long. But now I'm back. Here I am. Don't cry, Eva. It makes me sad.'

So Eva stopped crying and accepted a cup of tea and after a bit, when the driver said he'd better push on, she and Sylvia led Eddie up to his bedroom.

She helped him as he took off his uniform and didn't look away as his terrible thinness was revealed. Lily piled hot water bottles round him.

Sylvia went to the door. 'Would you like the light left on, darling?'

'I'm not afraid of the dark.'

Eva found Eddie's hand and kissed it.

"I've had a long day.' Eddie touched Eva's cheek. 'I'll be brighter in the morning.' He paused, then tried again, 'I'm looking forward to it.'

The three women left him reluctantly. 'I want to sleep on the floor beside him,' whispered Eva to Sylvia.

'I know. But I think he wants to be alone.'

Eddie, cradled in the warmth of the hot water bottles, heard their whispers and felt the beginnings of a smile. He had forgotten the sensation and was surprised. Perhaps he really was looking forward to the morning. He half wanted to call back Eva but he was too comfortable, too tired and, his mother was right, he did want to be alone.

CHAPTER THIRTY-SIX
Spring 1941

The banks and verges were a thick mass of primroses as the wedding party walked down the drive to Tollorum Church. They could have gone through the garden but it had been raining earlier and the women wore pale satin slippers that Angela had brought from America. Eva's were white, Sylvia's eggshell blue, Gussie's lemon and Lily's lilac. Valtraud had a silvery pink pair which she had to be persuaded to wear after Lily pronounced that grass stains would do none of the shoes any good.

'A wartime wedding should still be beautiful,' said Sylvia firmly.

Since Eddie's return, an air of rejoicing, which had gradually emerged as Eddie grew stronger, coloured each day with an artificial glow.

They began to believe that he was there to stay. Still thin, frail, but already with them for a full month. His arrival that extraordinary evening, projected amongst them with no forewarning, had produced a similar sense of shocked disbelief as his disappearance. Even Sylvia, who had never lost faith, continued to touch him often as if to confirm his presence.

Eva, prohibited by tradition from sharing his bed and also by his obvious need for complete rest, clung to him in the day.

Amongst all this loving concern, Eddie walked obediently, saying little and telling them no more about how he had spent the last few months than he had on that first evening. It was as if the motor that had driven him to so much action as a pilot had slowed down to an old man's plodding or perhaps, as Eva wondered, placed him in another dimension, so that he was not fully with them. He never complained, never laughed, although smiled a little, drank no alcohol and seemed happiest outside, walking slowly round the fields or the long stretches of vegetables.

His eyes were usually downcast where before they had been most often turned upwards, searching the sky.

It was not that he seemed unhappy, just different. When Eva, on the first of their pottering walks told him once more about their baby, he said with a kind of sweetness that had brought tears to her eyes, 'I'm so glad.' He paused, before murmuring 'A little girl called...', but when she'd questioned him, he'd added nothing further but held her hand on his cheek. Later in their walk as they'd stood together near a chestnut tree whose buds were already swelling and sticky, he took her hand again, 'I love you. We love each other. Now we should marry. Now.' His firm repetition of the words seemed significant but Eva was happy so she didn't dwell on it. Probably it was just concern over the length of his leave. But then, after a return visit to hospital, it was extended from one to three months. He did not explain why. He did not know why.

The date of the wedding was fixed for the beginning of April and two days earlier Angela had arrived with her case of satin slippers. Eddie had put his hand on her shoulder. 'You shall be my Best Man.' He didn't need to explain.

So the wedding party, all of them, not just the women but Fred and Eddie walked to the church where the Reverend Gisburne would officiate. Also waiting was the Wing Commander who had refused to be disinvited when Eddie had declined his offer of a guard of airmen. 'I am on sick leave,' he said, without further explanation.

Gussie was still bewailing this lack of a guard as they walked down the driveway. 'And no bridesmaids. Jemima,' this was her youngest daughter, 'is *so* disappointed. And Artemis too.'

'Artemis would hate being a Maid of Honour,' said Sylvia, as usual exasperated by her sister. 'And Jemima's at boarding school.'

Eva looked at Eddie who was walking ahead with his father and then at the trees on either side of the road. They were old chestnuts – they had stood under one of them when he asked her to marry him. Their branches spread across, almost reaching the trees opposite, and now the buds had unfolded into bright green fans.

'The trees stand guard over Eddie and me,' she said and, in order to avoid Gussie's chattering, half ran to join Fred and Eddie.

Both men turned and stared. Two nearly identical sets of blue eyes took in the apparition smiling at them. Eva was now over five months pregnant which only made her more beautiful; her skin as smooth and white as Beatrice's satin wedding dress that she was wearing, her black hair coiled up on the top of her head like a crown and circled by waxy camellias. Around her shoulders she clutched a shawl patterned with red roses which had belonged to her own mother. It was nearly two years since Eva had last seen her mother. With her father dead, it seemed that both he and her mother had inhabited another world now lost forever. Even the Ruskin, which had been so important to her, no longer mattered. Her whole being centred on Eddie and their baby.

Eddie turned to Fred and said, 'I'm so lucky.'

Fred glanced at him but said nothing. Despite Eddie's return, Fred still spent most of his week in London. Even more than Sylvia, Eva and Lily, he found it hard to believe that Eddie was truly with them and not a ghost as likely to depart as precipitately as he'd returned. On the other hand, the work Fred did on the streets gave him a strong sense of reality. He had become a fixer, known to all the different services. When a wall was in danger of falling, Fred would locate engineers and bring them in. When a fire threatened to overwhelm the local service, he would find a team from another station. If a fire-watcher failed to turn up, Fred was there. He wore a fire-watcher's helmet, picked up when a man ran for his life and lost it anyway.

He squeezed Eddie's arm and smiled. There's no such thing as luck, he wanted to say to Eddie but perhaps that wasn't true anyway. Sometimes he thought he stayed in London because he couldn't bear to witness Sylvia's pain when Eddie recovered, as was inevitable, and was called back to the RAF.

'You mean you're lucky to have Eva as your bride?'

'Yes,' said Eddie.

'Well, that's true enough,' agreed Fred, smiling again. Why did he have to take such a grim view of the world!

Behind them, Gussie was reminiscing about her own wedding, also at Tollorum Church, although she didn't mention that she, too, had been pregnant, and the marriage a quick, hushed-up affair. 'Oh, how Reggie would love to be here!'

Sylvia who knew this to be untrue, moved away, soon followed by Lily and Angela, leaving only Valtraud to listen with polite attention to Gussie's chatter, not gossip because she never talked about anyone but herself.

The Fitzpaines had been soldiers for generations. Their coats of arms and regimental flags shone red and blue and yellow in the stained glass windows. The names of the dead were carved in stone memorials on the walls. Eva, standing at the altar, felt their shadow, so many of them, like Eddie's grandfather, dying in war. But then the aged Rector began the service with a loud cough, followed by a series of sneezes, which so exhausted him that he staggered into the choir stalls and plonked himself down, and Eva failed to repress a laugh.

Such happiness! Eddie at her side, the baby kicking inside her tummy, the Rector honking and snorting, it all seemed wonderfully funny. She put her arm through Eddie's and leant her weight on him. She believed he was here for good, her husband. The Rector put away a huge white handkerchief, dragged himself to his feet and got to work joining them together.

'I love you,' Eva whispered to Eddie.

⸎

Reverentially, Eva took off Beatrice's wedding dress. Despite Lily putting in a gusset, it had been tight across her stomach so she was glad to get out of it. She hung it in a cupboard that still held layers of Eddie's life, school cricket whites, a black-tie suit, even an oar stuffed in the back.

Now he has me, thought Eva with immodest delight. She

couldn't help being glad that there was nothing of the Air Force visible. When she turned round to face Eddie, she was aware of her round stomach pressing on the slip she had borrowed from Sylvia.

'I couldn't fit under a table now,' she said, smiling.

'Another time,' Eddie murmured.

He sat on a wooden chair that had been in bedroom since childhood. He watched her and wondered whether the peacefulness he felt in Eva's company had outflanked passion.

She came closer to him. 'Do you want to take it off.' She held up her arms like a child.

The beauty of those raised arms astounded him. He stood up and lifted off the slip. He smoothed his hands all over her body, the long slim arms, the soft full breasts with dark nipples that hardened as he touched them, the swelling stomach perfectly poised above her strong fine legs.

Eva stayed quite still. She could wait under his hands forever.

Eddie sighed and held her closer.

'Can we make love? With ...'

'The baby, you mean. The doctor said I can do anything, anything I enjoy. He's a very nice doctor.'

They began to kiss. Eddie remembered how his body had been in the past. Not a maimed, sad thing, in hiding, lost. This same body had been powerful and confident.

'Come to bed.' Eva felt like a siren, a mother, a little girl. Had ever any woman been filled with such love! She lay down on the bed, expectant for him.

Eddie took off his wedding suit. He had thought it too black for anything but a funeral and he was glad to get rid of it.

'You're still thin.' Now Eva watched him as he came towards her and lay beside her on the bed. She crouched over him and ran her fingers over his shoulders. 'That other time, it was so quick.'

Eddie shut his eyes and felt her fingers firm and warm on his skin. He felt the generosity and determination of her love.

'I love you Eva.' Tears slid out of his eyes and, unashamed, he allowed her to wipe them away.

They lay in each other's' arms and after a while their faces met and they began to kiss again and in that time everything else was shut out except their desire for each other.

⋙

Downstairs in the small sitting room, Angela and Fred sat up drinking. Fred had just opened another bottle of champagne.

'It's not every day one's son gets married.'

'It's not every day a girl gets to be Best Man,' said Angela who sat on the sofa with her legs curled under her. 'I'll feel ill tomorrow if I carry on drinking like this.'

'You're a brave woman.' Tomorrow night, Fred would be back on the London streets. Sometimes putting himself in danger felt like a protection for Eddie. He began to talk. 'The bombing is worse again. Last night I pulled out the oddest woman. Wouldn't come. She kept wailing, 'Me woo! Me woo!' I said, we'll get you out first, dear. I thought it was her husband or dog or something. 'Woo! You mug!' she was shrieking so hard I thought she'd bring the house down on both of us. Then I saw she was holding knitting needles. 'Your *wool*,' I said. There she was on the floor with the ceiling under her and half the walls and only a small space to squeeze her out through and she was going on about her bloody wool. 'Now, my old dear,' I began more firmly. 'Don't you old dear me, I'll have you know you're talking to the proud possessor of a knitter's medal.' She couldn't draw herself to her full height or she'd have clonked herself on the cornice, but her beady eyes fixed on mine, 'I have knitted 220 pairs of socks and 21 pullovers.' I finally clocked that one hundred per cent homage was the only way to get her out, homage and a promise of wool. 'Congratulations, Madam. You're an important part of the war effort. And when we're out, I'll lead you personally to a wool bank I happen to know.' That was a lie, of course, but it got her out and another life saved.'

During this recital, Angela had shut her eyes but when Fred stopped speaking, she opened them again. She swung down her legs and stared into her glass, 'Do you think Eddie will fly again?'

'I suppose so. He's been given another two months' sick leave. He is getting better.'

'Seeing Eddie makes me think of Hank again. He was always Henry to me but I think he enjoyed being Hank. He loved being the squadron, being accepted as part of a team.'

'It was an extraordinary time to be part of the RAF. Do you miss him?' added Fred with a dutiful expression.

'Sure I miss him. But now it's been so many months, I've begun to wonder whether we would have made such a great team. I'm very conventional, you know.'

'What? Flying over here in the middle of a war and making a role for yourself!'

Angela laughed. 'War encourages wild behaviour. Later, I would have reverted to type.'

Unnoticed, Sylvia stood at the door. She was dressed in a sky-blue robe, patterned with silver clouds and, on the back, a golden dragon. She had been to bed before returning downstairs to collect Fred. She didn't like Fred drinking too much. Or perhaps she was jealous of Angela.

Fred looked at her. He stared admiringly at the clouds. 'I've never seen that gown before.'

'It was my mother's. Eva and I found it when we were looking for her wedding dress.' She held out her hand.

'You look like a guardian angel,' said Angela. 'Lucky Fred.'

'But you're called angel.'

'I couldn't guard Hank, could I?' She stood up and shook out her hair. 'Sorry. It's the champagne talking. Time I went to bed.'

After she had gone, Sylvia and Fred sat side by side on the sofa. Sylvia said, 'They're such children.'

Fred remembered that he had said that to her and she'd reproved him. Now it was his turn. 'Eddie's fought for his country and will again. Eva's going to be a mother. They're married. How much more grown up can you be?'

'They've had no time to grow up. Not really grow up. The war has made everything happen too fast. That's what war does.' She looked up at Fred and repeated, 'They're still children.'

Fred took her hand and said nothing.

※

As Fred predicted, Eddie grew stronger, but more quickly than he or anyone else had expected. It was as if Eva breathed life into him. They were together all the time, walking round the fields and woods for hours as the weather softened and warmed. They discovered hidden banks of primroses, skirted round the stretches of bluebells, some already showing colour, discovered a copse entirely under-grown with wild garlic.

They went further afield still, taking picnics. One day they followed a stream overhung by catkins growing from budding hazel trees, until they reached its source high in the hills. There gorse grew, its yellow flowers making the air around smell of honey.

Eva wanted to say, 'Do you really have to fight again? Surely you've done enough? Suffered enough?' But she dreaded the blank face that he would surely turn towards her, and said nothing.

They heard woodpeckers in the woods and eventually saw the flash of a brilliant red belly. They heard the first cuckoos in the hills, the harsh croak of pheasants and watched larks rise from the field in a flurry of trills. They saw a row of baby owls in the dim interior of an old barn and, if, just then, Eva thought of Jack, she said nothing. Jack, although so close, was also part of another world.

They held their breath when a doe appeared from the hillside scrub with her fawn behind and watched as the deer took off, bounding so high with the little fawn close at her side that when they reached the crest of the hill, it looked as if they were flying across the sky.

Leaves appeared, pale green flags on bushes and trees. As the sun shone more warmly, they lay down on the grass, face-to-face, wondering at the new life curled between them.

There were interruptions to this idyll. Aircraft went overhead, flying north to Bristol or south to Southampton, Yeovil or Portland, Eddie's old beat. He watched them go over and disappear but made no comment, no excited listing of their names as Eva remembered from the past. She tried not to think of them as rival sirens calling to him. She feared he might want to visit Warmwell, perhaps he still had friends there, although nearly six months had passed since his disappearance. She learnt to live in the present, grateful for every day with Eddie. It was Sylvia who reminded her to let the Ruskin know that she was unable to attend at the moment.

The nights were best of all, when she had Eddie totally captive. When they made love, they were scarcely separate at all. And all the time she felt him getting healthier and she knew when the bluebells died and the scent of the wild garlic faded, his sick leave would be up and he would go to London for his medical.

About ten days before that time, they were passing by some workers weeding and trimming a field of kale when Eddie stopped and said he would give them a hand. He joined them immediately; an old man, a young boy and two land girls.

Eva watched him. He worked well, far quicker than the others but he also looked purposeful. It was as if he was in training. *In training.* The words stuck with her. She began to walk slowly away.

'I'll be back for supper.' Eddie waved cheerfully.

That evening Fred arrived from London and began his usual stories – of dogs on chimney pots, sacks of flour swept into the Thames, a fire whose flames danced like a row of high-kicking girls in scarlet tutus on the empty boards of a building without walls.

Sylvia listened tolerantly. Eddie listened and asked questions, 'How many bombers went out? 'What sort of bombs did they drop?' What causes most harm? Incendiaries? Am I right in guessing that?' He'd never shown so much interest in the war since his return.

On the same evening Eva watched him read *The Times*. It was the first time he'd picked up the paper. Since the warm weather, they'd sat in the small sitting-room and he looked comfortable in an armchair methodically turning the pages. He was well, Eva could see that.

The next supper time, while Fred was still present, she pushed aside her plate of potato pancakes and said, failing to hide a nervous blush, 'If you're passed fit in your medical what will happen next?'

Eddie turned to her seriously. 'It's not up to me. It's up to the RAF.'

'It's a fair question,' said Fred. 'After such a gap, perhaps they'll put you back in training.'

'I'd have to get back to operational standards again, that's true enough.'

'They always need instructors,' said Sylvia. 'The Wing Commander told me.'

Eva looked at her hopefully.

'Don't tell me that old bore's been hanging around,' said Fred.

'When the cat's away, the mice do play,' Lily smiled at her brother.

'I don't invite him,' protested Sylvia. 'But he might be useful to Eddie. He knows the whole story. He knows how he suffered. An outsider might not get it, seeing him now.'

They all looked at Eddie who said nothing for a moment and then smiled, 'I was talking to a couple of our land girls today and they seem to have appalling digs. How many do we have? On the whole estate, I mean? What about moving at least some in here?'

Sylvia remembered her plan to hand over Tollorum to the government. 'I can't imagine why I didn't think of that myself.'

⨯

Eddie took the train up to London. He wore a new Royal Air Force uniform on which his Distinguished Flying Cross had been sewn by Lily. It had arrived in his absence and, at some point in the not too distant future, he had been assured by a letter from his former CO, that King George VI would be pleased to welcome him and a member of his family at the Palace. It was clear by the wording that, initially, this had been assumed to be a posthumous award. Eddie was resilient enough now to find the idea amusing. He was expecting to be passed fit for flying.

It was a perfect early summer's morning. The long train – there were fewer trains now, but longer – moved slowly through the countryside, the same countryside that Eva and Eddie had walked through so joyfully. The hawthorn flowers were still like a galaxy of white stars, the gorse flowers as yellow. He even saw a group of deer dashing along as if racing the train. But it was not just a glass window that made them seem another world. Eddie was conscious of leaving behind one way of life, with all the natural beauty he and Eva had shared and entering a future which was also his past. He recognised how quickly he would be absorbed back into days filled with dangerous exhilaration and the ever-present possibility of death.

'Looks like we're diverting,' an Army major, who'd been smoking his pipe contentedly up 'til now, leant close to the window and tapped one foot impatiently.

'Going north,' agreed Eddie. 'There's probably a raid further south.'

'Yes, that will be it.' The major puffed furiously.

The other passengers who had become more interested at the word 'raid' began to discuss their new route, 'It'll be through Salisbury,' advised one old farmer with First World War-style whiskers.

'At least we won't get bombed there,' added a nervous spinsterish lady wearing a thick felt hat as if it was a helmet. 'Those Jerry pilots set their fix on the cathedral spire, that's what I've heard. You don't bomb your guide, do you now.'

Then began a lively discussion about camouflage and its limitations which lasted until they did indeed enter Salisbury station and there was the great spire, reaching far into the bright blue sky. To Eddie this Salisbury seemed another place to the town whose hospital he had arrived at not so many months earlier. Just as he seemed another man. Already he began to think of his time with Eva nostalgically.

Even though the train diverted for a second time and arrived three hours late into Paddington station, Eddie still had time to cross London in a leisurely way for his appointment with the Medical Board at 5pm. He had planned to take the bus and was immediately surprised to find that the red London bus had diversified into all kinds of surprising colours, one labelled 'The Corporation of Manchester' with destinations to match: Deansgate, Salford Quays and Castlefield.

He decided to walk anyway and found himself as surprised by the buildings that had survived as by those which had gone.

In the slanting afternoon sun, some of the bomb sites had already gathered a sense of timelessness like much more ancient ruins. There were even wildflowers poking up through the rubble, a dash of mauve or white. Those buildings that stood seemed more substantial than ever, presumably only a trick of the imagination which one night's close attention from the Luftwaffe would quickly disperse. He was staying overnight with Fred in Chelsea so perhaps he would experience their attentions for himself. He found the prospect undaunting. It surprised him a little how ready he was for war.

Eddie walked more quickly. His appointment was in Astradel House where he'd had his original board in 1939. Then he'd thought of nothing but how to get into the RAF. It was where he'd met Andy. He could feel little link with the confident, even arrogant nineteen-year-old boy he'd been then. His life seemed to fall into separate compartments with no obvious doors between them.

≍

'Flight Lieutenant Chaffey? Please come this way. The doctor will see you first.'

How different it all was to that first time! No waiting, a sense of deference. Well, he deserved, it didn't he?

The doctor, an elderly man in uniform, stood up from behind his desk. 'Sit down. Which isn't to suggest you aren't fit enough to stand. I've had your notes and X-rays. In fact, you're a bit of a talking point in our profession. You were semi-conscious or even unconscious for a couple of months, is that right?'

'Yes, sir. I can't remember anything from my leaving the plane in October until Christmas Eve.'

'But you must have been operated on?' The doctor had fierce grey eyebrows above kindly blue eyes.

'Yes, sir. But I never saw the doctor. An Englishman who arranged my departure told me I was expected to die by the people who picked me up. Sounds unlikely, sitting here right as rain.'

'Must have been a bit of a genius, your doctor. French, I assume. So you feel recovered now?'

'Yes, sir.'

'Enough to fly a plane.'

'I just got married.'

The doctor smiled and waited.

'When I was still in France, my speech was slow coming back. I was very weak. Even back in England I had lost something. Everything seemed distanced and too fast. I couldn't quite make sense of things. But gradually I returned to normal. Now I can walk all day, talk ...'

'And get married.' The doctor smiled again. 'So how is your brain, your reflexes, your understanding, your head turning when there's a Me 109 at front and back?'

'I'm back to normal, sir,' Eddie said it stolidly. He did not feel like pleading. It seemed that he'd been wrong; the decision did, to some extent at least, depend on him.

'You are a decorated fighter pilot. One of the men who kept the wolf from the door. The men who inspired Churchill's famous phrase, 'Never were so many saved by so few.'

Eddie wondered if the man was being ironic. He had never liked that phrase.

'I cannot see into your mind, Flight Lieutenant,' continued the doctor, 'which is why I ask for your help.'

'Are you *that* sort of doctor?' asked Eddie.

'My job is to see if you are fit in every way to be put in charge of a machine that flies through the air at nearly 400 mph, climbs to 35,000 feet in a matter of minutes and costs many thousands of pounds to build. And that's leaving out the eight Browning machine guns.'

Eddie thought of the pilots he'd known who hadn't been fit to ride a bicycle, let alone fly an aeroplane. There weren't many and most of them had been spotted before they'd killed anyone. There was a story of pilots who shot down their own squadron-leader because he'd become such a danger to them. Had he become like that?

'I believe, sir, that I am a hundred per cent fit.' As he spoke, he felt an enormous sense of relief. It seemed that he needed to pass himself fit for service and he had.

'Well done, Chaffey. It's not for me to do more than make a recommendation but you have that. You're a fine young man and I'm proud of you.' Standing, he came to Eddie and shook his hand.

'Thank you, sir.'

'I'm afraid your wife may not share our view but unfortunately, just at the moment, there's nothing we can do about that.'

Eddie left the building with his sense of relief intact. He had not acknowledged consciously how much he wanted to pass fit. The beautiful day had turned into a cool evening and the streets were almost as crowded as in previous times or perhaps, more people were forced to walk. He didn't notice those who stared at the tall pilot with the buoyant stride who looked as if he knew just where he was going.

The doctor's mention of his wife had not affected Eddie. Flying was what he did. What he was.

CHAPTER THIRTY-SEVEN
July 1941

Eddie was in Manchester operating as a flight instructor when he was handed a message after returning from a flight with a man who continually failed to hear, ignored or misunderstood his instructions. It was difficult to believe that he'd ever been so casual. It would be an irony of fate if, having survived the Germans, he was killed by the ineptitude of a patriotic Englishman. Recently one trainee had overshot the runway by so much, they'd come to a stop among a herd of milking cows. He put away the note in his pocket – notes were never interesting – and continued to the Mess.

It was only when he reached his quarters later and took off his jacket, checking the pocket as he always did, that he found the note and read it. It was a transcribed from a telephone call. *You are a father. Healthy baby boy born at 3am today.*

Eddie sat down on the bed. Then lay back, smiling. A baby boy! He was a father. What sort of father would he be? He thought of Fred. He could do better than that. When he got the chance. If he got the chance.

He knew he must pull himself up and try to find an available telephone. But just now he was comfortable where he was. A baby. Eva's baby. His baby. It took a bit getting used to.

≈

Eva knelt up in bed, studying the baby who was lying there fast asleep. She had picked him out of his cot against the protective order of Lily and Sylvia so she could get to know him better. Both of them were out of the house, this light summer morning, Sylvia gone to London and Lily down to the village.

Carefully, so as not to wake the sleeping baby, she untied and removed the knitted cardigan, the long cotton nightdress, then the vest and finally undid the nappy pin and, since the nappy seemed dry enough , laid it open.

There he was, a perfect little boy, naked as the day he was born, just ten days ago on another lovely July day. Soon she would have him outside on the lawn, kicking his legs on the lawn, waving his hands at the trees. She felt so well, so very pleased with herself for creating such a delicious creature. Fleetingly, it crossed her mind that she had never made anything half so successful on canvas.

'What would you like to be called, my little wonder? Fred? Charlie? Augustus? Cornelius?' She made a face, and noticed that the sound of her voice had made the baby's eyelids flutter. 'Sam is what I'd like. No reason, in case you ask, I just like the name.' She sat back a little. 'On the other hand, we must take into consideration your papa's views.'

This thought made her frown. Stuck up in the North, Eddie still hadn't seen his son. 'We must take action, Sam.' Leaning sideways, she reached for a pad and pencil. She would make him a sketch, label it *Sam, your son* and put in the post.

Sitting cross-legged now, Eva began to draw, noting the high forehead, the wide-spaced eyes (still closed as Sam was a very contented baby) the wispy fair curls and the narrow red mouth. Lily had told her that his eyes were too dark to stay blue. How handsome he would be with her brown eyes and Eddie's yellow hair!

Sylvia was in London. She hadn't left Tollorum for months but now that Eva's baby was safely born, she felt she could spend a day or two away. Her exhilaration was tempered by a guilty sense that it was inappropriate when visiting a city lambasted by bombing raids. But Angela, once more in London, had begged her to come to a dinner party. 'It's about Eddie,' she'd said. 'I've had an idea.'

The dinner was to be held in the Savoy. But first of all, Angela had arranged a trip to the infamous 'Tilbury' shelters in Stepney where East Enders had taken up habitation. When Sylvia had protested, 'I don't want to be a tourist of squalor and misery,' Angela had explained, 'My paper wants me to bear witness to the terrors of being a Londoner and with you and Fred along, I will seem less like a nosey Yank.'

Their guide for the jaunt was a cheerful, bird-like woman called Marigold who worked for the Citizens Advice Bureau in Whitechapel. She hopped into the seat beside the driver of Angela's Daimler and immediately turned round to put them in the picture. 'About four thousand of the younger folk have been induced to leave Tilbury but,' she added with a kind smile for Angela, 'they've plenty left to make good copy.'

From the west to the east end of London was a long, slow journey. As they came nearer to their destination the slowly falling light failed to disguise the narrow, smashed streets.

'Nearly six thousand Londoners were killed last September,' said Marigold chattily, 'most of them from this part of the world. But there's been nothing huge since the middle of May. Incendiaries cause most problems.'

Angela got out her notebook and scribbled for a few minutes. She seemed to feel no need to look out of the window.

As the car progressed like a closed capsule in the direction of the river and Marigold and Fred began to talk facts and figures, Sylvia, disturbed at the level of destruction, worse than she'd expected, stared out of the window. She supposed she had become soft in her green countryside with all her fears circling round Eddie and then little Sam. She focused again to hear Fred explaining that his son was a pilot.

'Based where?' asked Marigold.

'He's up North at the moment. As an instructor. He was injured.'

'Where now, Madam?' asked the driver. They had arrived at the docks, at a vast expanse of black buildings beside the Thames, some of them curiously clawed apart, a few standing and some apparently sinking into the ground.

'We'll go to the loading bays. They're worst.'

Soon, they were among people. Fred wound down his window. Immediately, a girl jammed her head in. She was heavily made up and very cheerful. 'Quickie, for ten bob, luv?' She seemed to be joking before seeing his missing arm and yelling to a friend, 'Don't you love the one-armed sort! Millie, over here fast or you'll miss your chance.'

As Fred laughed and the car inched forward between the growing crowds, Angela addressed Marigold, 'I suppose we'll have to get out of the car.' She seemed to be losing her nerve.

One of several large men in shirt-sleeves, arm in arm with a group of seamen of all nationalities shouted. 'Who can spot a Yank?' He mimed a kiss at Angela. 'I can't go further, Madam,' the driver announced.

'Five or six women, nearly as large as the men, two pushing wheelbarrows, thrust their faces against Sylvia's window, 'Come to see how the other half live, have you?'

'You can't blame them wanting a bit of fun,' said Marigold in a motherly voice. 'Most of them have useful jobs in the day.'

As the car stopped, the crowd swelled round it and continued on, they were headed down into the rotted darkness of one of the buildings. Or many of the buildings. It was not clear how many there where or whether they were linked or whether the arches, visible just about, were corridors, entrances or part of the whole. Whatever was ahead, the people were pouring towards it, in a confident, unstoppable flow.

Fred quoted, '*Whoever is generous to the poor lends to the Lord and he will repay you.*' Proverbs 19:17.

'They're not really supposed to be here,' commented Marigold. 'But the older folk knew it from the last war. Safety is in the eyes of the beholder, even though there're not many bombs now. You never know, though, and an awfully lot of their homes have been flattened. Shall we descend? I told my dear warden eight-thirty and it's just about that now.'

The highlight of their tour was a to be a visit to the woman's latrines. Jean, the warden, a young woman with bright red hair which made it easy to follow in the dim light and crowds, explained, 'I've tried endlessly to persuade the children to use them.' Her trilling laugh was less convincing than Marigold's.

'However do you stick it?' asked Angela, hand to nose. Already all the bunks, squeezed between rolls of newspaper and giant pots of defiled margarine, were taken. 'Those are not the latrines,' commented Jean, with her laugh, 'although you might think so.'

'Waste of good marge,' said Marigold robustly. 'I shall have a go to get them moved in the morning. I can make myself a horrible nuisance in a good cause.'

Angela who had been scribbling, head down for most of their tour, whispered to Sylvia, 'What is the vile smell made up of?'

'How about urine, faeces, fish, rancid margarine, unwashed clothes, animals, beer, rotting meat, tea,' Sylvia began to warm to her theme, 'chips, cheese, sour milk, smelly feet, armpits, body odours all over actually.' She stopped, noticing Angela's disgusted face. 'Sorry.'

'I think you missed vomit off your list,' volunteered Marigold. 'Have you got enough copy, Miss Hope?'

'I've seen quite enough, thank you, Marigold,' said Angela hastily.

After Tilbury, there was dinner at the Savoy where Reggie joined them. As they entered the dining room, Fred looked across at Sylvia, and saw how beautiful she was in her mother's silver-grey gown. In the past this effortless beauty had the power to make him angry. It had seemed the product of class and money, inherited without justice. But on this evening he also noticed the lines deepening on her face, her eyes wary as if the fear that had taken hold when Eddie was missing had never quite gone away.

Reggie, resplendent in his Lieutenant-Colonel's uniform and determined not to hear about Tilbury horrors, took over the table, ordering champagne and hors d'oevres.

'A toast,' said Angela, when their glasses were filled, 'To gallant men and women!'

'To Hank!' said Sylvia. She drank and thought of Eddie. Every day she waited to hear that he had been summoned back into a fighter squadron.

Reggie ordered a feast of salmon and steak and ice-cream gateau and when the steak became *poulet*, the salmon an unnamed grey fish, no-one complained.

Angela began to speak seriously, 'My idea involves Eddie but, it's also a memorial to Hank and most of all a bit of added pressure to bring my country into the war. You remember Moira Lipscombe, Sylvia, the actress who came to Tolorum. We'll go together to America where Moira is famous and her film about this war in England is screening – a love story, of course, but with an heroic pilot – and tour the big cities. I'll describe my experiences of London bravery under bombing, like tonight's trip, while Eddie will talk modestly about being one of 'the few' and tell Hank's story. We'll tour the big cities, New York, Washington, L.A., Chicago.'

Sylvia was dazed. She could hardly understand. Eddie out of the war? Safe in America?

'But would the Air Force ever let him go?' said Fred

'He fought for ages,' said Angela, 'even if he's not at the frontline now. That might make it easier to get him out.'

Sylvia thought that Eddie had only fought for months but that it had felt like endless ages.

'The RAF invest a lot in their pilots,' Fred said, 'although there are more than there were.'

Sylvia frowned at her husband. Surely he wanted Eddie far away from the war?

Angela looked at Reggie who was swirling his champagne in his glass. 'What do you think, Reggie? You're the only one with powerful connections.'

Reggie was flattered. 'Oh, very minor powerful connections.' Attempting modesty, he became pompous. 'I do have a passing acquaintance with the Minister of Propaganda who gave his backing to Moira's film. I could put in a word.'

'Please Reggie!' breathed Sylvia.

It was nearly midnight before they left. Like everyone else in the room, they'd ignored the wail of the sirens and, if there had been bombs, they didn't hear them.

They came out on to the dark streets and Angela lent Fred and Sylvia her car.

In its cosy interior, Sylvia appealed to Fred, 'It would be Eddie's patriotic duty. It would not be running away.'

'The most important thing is to pull the Americans in,' agreed Fred, trying not to wonder whether Eddie himself would play along with Angela's plan. The whole idea seemed unrealistic and almost irrelevant. The Americans would come in soon without a little bit of half-baked propaganda.

Sylvia caught hold of Fred's hand. 'Wouldn't it be wonderful. Wonderful!'

In the flat, they quickly got into bed, lying naked in each other's arms, 'Don't let me dream of Tilbury,' said Sylvia, smiling. 'I'll picture Eva and Sam instead.' The lines had gone from her face.

CHAPTER THIRTY-EIGHT
December 1941 – June 1942

Eddie was still in the North when he heard the news of the Japanese bombing of Pearl Harbour and the American entry into the war.

Angela rang him to exult, 'I know I didn't do it all on my own but I'm giving no credit to the Japs.' She had found a boyfriend among the U.S. Press Corps and neither of them mentioned Hank, although Eddie at least, thought of him.

Fred also rang, 'You won't be needing those puny boys you're training. Prepare yourself for brave hunks of New World manhood.'

A day or two later, Angela rang Sylvia who was standing in the hall at Tollorum watching while Eva piled more blankets on Sam's pram. 'I guess my plan to take Eddie on a tour of the US isn't a starter any more. Now we're in!' Angela wanted Sylvia to celebrate with her.

'That was months ago.' Sylvia didn't want to remember how excited she'd been at the thought of Eddie safe in America. 'I gave up hoping once poor Moira met such a horrible end.'

'Poor Moira,' agreed Angela automatically. She made an effort. 'Being drowned like that with a whole crowd of other people didn't suit her personality. I suppose she crossed the Atlantic once too often.'

'I blame the torpedoes,' said Sylvia, anxious to tuck in a corner of the blanket that Eva had missed. 'At least Eddie is still out of the fighting. Training is very important, of course.'

'Certainly is, particularly with all these new American flyers.'

Sylvia waved Eva out of the door and thought she and Angela had nothing left to say to each other. Since she had been to London over five months ago, her focus had narrowed further. She relied on Fred's visits for any news outside of Dorset.

※

Eddie was given a whole week's holiday over Christmas. As he made the long journey south, he remembered how he'd spent his last Christmas and recalled the little Fleur, prising open his eyelids and singing about the birth of Christ. In many ways, it remained a dream which he was reluctant to examine too closely. Only briefly, as he stared out at the black towns and grey fields, did he wonder about the French family.

Once he was back at Tollorum, everything was planned for his pleasure. Watching his son rolling round on the old carpet, whose patterns he knew from childhood, Eddie had the sense of a future which had seemed impossible only a few months earlier. It was partly to do with the entry of the US into the war but also by the exuberant confidence of Sam.

He told Eva as they lay in bed clasped together for warmth, 'I never thought I'd have a son.'

'She half-smiled into the darkness. 'We were far too young.' Sometimes Eddie's apparent happiness frightened her, as if she sensed it was not quite real.

'Are we still too young?' He moved away enough so he could stroke her shoulders and breasts. She was still feeding Sam and he loved to feel the tautness of the skin.

'We're the perfect age. Kiss me now.'

※

Eddie's optimistic mood continued as he returned to Manchester and the days gradually grew longer, lighter.

Then in May 1942, he was posted back to a Spitfire fighting squadron. He had been expecting it, hoping for it, but it was still a shock. He told himself it was just because he knew what it would mean for Eva and Sylvia.

The flying was hard, death still out there waiting. But Spitfires

366

whose main job was as bomber escort, didn't have the fuel t
follow the bombers into Germany so the most hazardous part of
the journey was avoided. When Eddie turned his aeroplane round
and saw the steady, onward course of the massive bombers, mostly
British but gradually being joined by Americans, he knew his own
life was easy. It seemed to him that luck was more important to
a bomber pilot than anything their brave gunners could do. The
ground fire was often so intense that it seemed impossible any
planes or men should return.

After only a few weeks his new role, he was summoned to a
medical board in London and given a 24-hour leave, not enough
time to get to Tollorum and back.

Instead, he met Fred in a pub where, as a legacy of the Blitz, all
the windows were boarded up. Outside the sun shone.

'Why do they want to see you?' Fred looked reasonably
concerned. 'You're flying, aren't you? Fighting for your country.'

'Annual head check,' Eddie pushed away his drink. 'Routine.
I've never felt better.'

'I won't tell Sylvia.'

'No point. I don't even get headaches.'

'Never?' Fred drank his beer thirstily.

Eddie smiled, 'You look well.'

'Night life suits me.'

'Is that why you like this cave?'

Fred peered round. 'It is strangely dark. I hadn't noticed. I
should have been a sapper. Terrifying lot they were. Burrowing
along with enough explosions strapped to them to blow up a
mountain.'

'I've always been a sky man.'

For the first time, respectful of each other and comfortable
together, they didn't feel the need to say anything important. The
war defined their days but they didn't have much to say about it.

Eddie's check-up was as slow and unimportant as he'd expected.
It was early evening when he came out on to the street again.
He had made no plans and began to wander aimlessly through

afalgar Square where, since the lessening in the bombing, the
igeons had returned in numbers, and on towards Pall Mall and
St James's.

He reached Club-land, all the buildings apparently untouched
by war, the impressive colonnades of the Athenaeum first. With
Fred as his father, there was no leather armchair waiting for Eddie
in any of these emporiums of the establishment. Yet if he'd gone
inside some of them, White's, perhaps, the Travellers' Club, even
Boodle's, he'd have been fairly certain to recognise some of his
fellow Etonians, even if he had been thrown out. Why had he
been so rebellious? Without the war would he have gone on
fighting *against*, never *for*? Not a very good reason for a war. Those
lounging Etonians he was imagining, how many of those had died
or were fighting in some bloody awful place or sitting behind
barbed wire watching their life go by? He'd been lucky, that was
the thing, lucky to survive being shot, dipped in the channel and
dumped half-dead in a country occupied by the enemy.

Eddie seldom thought about the French family who'd saved
him, although they sometimes entered his dreams, but now he
found himself picturing the old Madame tenderly caring for him
and Fleur's bright chatter, both in their own way, determined to
bring him back into the world.

At the same time as he saw these images, he was half-consciously
watching a man striding towards the steps of White's. He was
noticeable because of his thick black beard.

Words came into his head just as the pictures had: '*Monsieur La
Barbe.*'

'Do I know you, old chap?' The man stopped beside him.

'Sorry, sir. I was staring.' Eddie hesitated. Instinctively, he wanted
to deny all knowledge.

'You do faintly ring a bell. Just the tiniest tinkle. But that's war,
isn't it. You meet people in the oddest places and then haven't a
clue when you're back on dry land, if you know what I mean.'

'Yes. You did me a good turn once.'

'That's good. I shan't expect a knife in my back. Tell you what,

I'm half an hour ahead of my guest. One of those American generals who think you're late if you're ten minutes early. Why don't I do you another good turn and buy you a drink.'

Eddie looked below the beard and saw the uniform of an army colonel. Very few army colonels have beards. Probably none. 'Thank you, Colonel.' Had the Colonel recognised him? Healthy and four stone heavier, it seemed unlikely. Just a friendly fellow. War made quick friends.

The two men sat in adjoining chairs, each holding a glass of whisky.

'Never liked drinking alone,' said the Colonel. 'And some of these Yanks think we can win the war on orange juice.' He swivelled to face Eddie. 'France, wasn't it? Not far into '41. Near the start of things over there. You've changed a bit.'

'It didn't take too long once I was back.'

'Wonderful thing, the human body. Still bloody dangerous out there. Can't talk about it, of course.'

'Of course not, sir. I just wanted to say I was grateful.'

'Yes. Well. Pilots are worth a lot. Not so bad now we've got the big boys in.' He paused, seemed to be reflecting on something.

Eddie sipped his whisky and enjoyed the warm glow. He'd only started drinking again recently and preferred a single shot to pints of beer. 'Nice whisky, sir.'

'Laphroiag. Single malt. I tell them to keep it under wraps.' The Colonel looked up at Eddie and then down again. 'Bloody terrible business yours, I remember more of it now. Can't even blame the Gestapo. They hadn't arrived back then. Savages!' His voice was suddenly charged with so much bitter anger that Eddie, despite taking another sip, wanted to drop the glass and run.

'Machine-gunned the lot of them, mother, daughter and little girl. Wasn't there a little girl? No reason. Just spite because you got away. No idea how they traced you back. I hope we're cleverer now. That was early days. Barbarians!' The Colonel drank the remainder of his whisky and banged the glass on the table.

'I'm sorry.' Eddie stood. 'I'm afraid I've got to go to…'

He managed to get to the lavatory a few seconds before he was violently sick. He stood over the bowl, shaking. When he could walk again, he left the building, carefully by-passing the bar. All the same, as he neared the door an American General was being shown through and, turning, Eddie saw the Colonel greeting him with a warm smile.

The light was fading in the streets. Head down, half running, he made his way back to Fred's flat. Everything that had happened in France and that he had encouraged to disappear, reawakened and whirled about in images and words. He was aware that tears were streaming down his face but he had no way of stopping them. As he neared the flat, Fleur's voice accompanied him with all the words that he could remember of the Christmas Carol she had sung:

'Il est ne, le divin Enfant, Jouez hautbois, resonnez, musettes ... Une étable est son lodgement, Un peu de paille est sa couchette ... ah, qu'i lest beau, qu'il est charmant ...'

The flat was empty, no longer a wild muddle of papers and books as it had been in Fred's days as a journalist. Even the large table was clear of anything but sheets of information and a couple of boxes holding paper-clips and pens. On the wall hung two helmets and two gas masks and several waterproof capes.

Noticing nothing of this and too tortured by his imagination to keep still, Eddie walked up and down, up and down. But even that reminded him of Fleur's imitation of his long strides in the loft, '*Boum, boum, boum.*'

While he had been growing stronger and happier, marrying, becoming a father, the three people who had helped him most in his life, who had saved his life, were dead. 'Murdered!' Eddie shrieked the word and, slumping on the sofa, put his head in his hands. This felt like play-acting. There must be something he can do. 'What can I do!' Once again, Eddie shouted the words.

The door to Fred's bedroom opened and he came out, looking as if he'd wakened from sleep.

'What is it?' He rubbed his hand over his face.

'Oh, my God!' Eddie began to pace again.

Fred sat down on the sofa and watched him. 'Tell me.'

Eddie only heard when he repeated the words. 'What can I tell you?' He stared like a madman.

Eva? Sam? Sylvia? thought Fred, suddenly wide awake. Sometimes German bombers got so off course that the most unlikely places received a hit. Fred sat up straighter. It was approaching the time he usually set out for the streets. 'What can be so terrible? Tell me.'

Only the unbearable pain in Eddie's head made him even consider telling his father the story. 'My head's splitting,' he muttered. 'I want to bang it on the wall.'

'Don't do that,' said Fred patiently.

'It's the family who looked after me in France. Three generations. Grandmother. Mother. Daughter. I just heard.'

'Yes?'

'They were murdered, machine-gunned in revenge after I left. Even the little girl, Fleur.' Tears began to roll down Eddie's cheeks once more. 'Because of me,' he managed before unable to say anything more.

'You never told us what happened.' Fred stood up and tried to put his arm round his son's trembling shoulders but Eddie shook him off.

'Don't you understand? I killed them! Three innocent people, a girl not more than six or seven. Wiped out because I was selfish, because I wanted to live!'

'I'll get you a glass of water.' Fred went to the kitchen. When he came back, Eddie was sitting on the sofa. He had stopped crying and his face wore a grim, determined look. Fred sat down beside him.

'Tell me the whole story.'

'If you want. It doesn't matter anymore. I know what I must do now.' Eddie told the story carefully through his parachute drop, his regaining consciousness in France, the months there, his eventual escape. He told it simply, without tears or any emotion. He was surprised by how much he could remember.

Fred listened without interruption until the end. Then he got up, drew the black-out which covered the few gaps in the boarding, and put on a small light. He looked at Eddie, head in his hands, and sat down again. 'So you blame yourself?'

'Who else was responsible? My presence there was the sole reason for their death. Do you want to know the worst thing? One day Fleur, the little girl, led me outside. Her mother was furious in case someone had seen me. Maybe someone *had* seen me!'

'How long were you outside?'

'A few minutes. A minute or two. Less. I don't know.'

'You must know you weren't seen.'

'Yes. Yes, I suppose so. But I'm still guilty. Don't you understand!'

'I understand you want to punish yourself?'

Eddie avoided his father's gaze. 'That seems fair.'

Fred sat back in the sofa. He thought of all the arguments he could put forward to Eddie. Then he thought of everything he'd seen in Gallipoli, the horrors that he would never describe to anyone. He had hated the politicians most, but hated the Generals too, even the officers who had obeyed them and most of all he'd hated himself for being part of it. Filled with rage, and minus an arm entirely due to his own idiocy, he'd come home and tried to drink himself to death. The young think suicide is the easy option.

'The young think suicide is an easy option, although they kid themselves it's brave, even heroic. That is, if they're in their right mind. Are you in your right mind?'

Eddie kept his face turned away. 'I didn't say I was going to commit suicide. I thought you'd understand.'

'I do understand. If you mean, do I understand self-hatred. Tell me, why is this so different from the death of Hank, Andy, all the others?'

'Oh, Dad, you know the difference! These aren't pilots or soldiers. We've signed up for the war, for whatever comes. The old Madame, Madame Sophie, Fleur, they were *murdered*.'

'Did the two women know the risks?'

'That's not the point. Madame Sophie only got involved

because her mother wanted to offer it up to God. The old woman saw looking after me as her Christian duty. And what about Fleur?'

Fred noticed that Eddie's calm determination had broken and he relaxed a little. 'They chose to look after you. They didn't expect to be shot but people in London or Liverpool or Coventry didn't expect to be bombed.'

'If I hadn't been there, they'd still be alive.'

'You've decided to thank them for saving your life by throwing it away. Do you think that's the sort of thanks they want?' Fred stared at his son attentively.

'But how can I *live?* Why should I live when they're dead!"

Fred waited a moment, then stood up again. If Eddie did not feel a wife and son enough reason to live then he was not going to be able to persuade him. 'I'm hungry. I'll make some sandwiches.' How selfish is grief! Fred hacked out some stale bread and topped it lavishly with Tollorum jam. He knew he couldn't take away Eddie's suffering however much he wanted to. Eddie's grief was well-founded. The story was a tragic one. Eddie's description of the loving little Fleur had touched even his tough old heart, but would it have been better if she had survived with her mother and grandmother bleeding to death beside her?

Fred pictured the scene in all its vile cruelty, only too easily. But he would say nothing more to Eddie, beyond suggesting he told Eva at least something of what had happened. With any luck, once he was back at the airfield, he would take comfort in his role fighting the Nazi.

'Grub's up!' said Fred, bringing through two great wedges of bread and jam.

CHAPTER THIRTY-NINE
June 1942

In the morning neither man mentioned the conversation of the night before. It was easily avoided because Fred was out working all night and only returned to see Eddie off to the train.

'I'll have proper leave soon,' Eddie said. 'We can meet at Tollorum.'

Fred was reassured, as Eddie meant him to be, but all the same, he got drunk and picked up a prostitute who had been eyeing him up for weeks. After a few minutes he let her go, returned to the flat and rang Sylvia.

When Sylvia heard the story she said, 'I won't tell Eva just yet,' and a note of dread was in her voice.

'He'll be alright,' said Fred unconvincingly.

Eddie, who had not slept all night, dozed on the train. Images of Fleur continued as half dreams and the weight of guilt lay over him in a thick mass. He remembered times when he had flown into such darkness, terrified and nearly panicking that there was no way out. The cloud that never lifted. But always he had found a path into brightness until he was surrounded once more by clear blue and filled with the intense exhilaration of escape.

As the journey progressed, filled with stops and starts and the fetid heat of overcrowding, none of which Eddie noticed, his images of Fleur began to change and she became a much younger child.

Eddie whose head had been nodding, sat up with a jerk and said out loud, 'Sam.' He mustn't desert Sam.

Nobody in the carriage, mostly asleep, or staring vacantly, reacted.

Eddie then remained awake until he reached his station. He was met by a corporal who began talking at once as he led the way to the car.

'Been away a long time, sir?'

'No. Twenty-four hours.' But so very long. He sat in the back of the car and shut his eyes.

'Night on the town, dare I suggest.'

'Yes,' agreed Eddie. It seemed he must continue forwards as if nothing had happened. He wondered if talking to Eva would help but how could he spell out such love and such tragedy over a Mess telephone? Perhaps he would write.

That afternoon there was a big operation. Eddie liked his squadron, one or two survivors of the Battle of Britain, but many more, new to fighter ops, no older than Eddie but looking up to him.

Rafi who was lounging beside Eddie in the dispersal hut, had become a particular friend. His full name was Augustus Rafaelo Georgione Penworthy. His father was an art critic and had only moved from his home in Florence just before being interned. Rafi had been studying at the Courtauld Institute in London and told Eddie that he preferred German music, writing and especially art to anything Italian and certainly English. 'I'm one of the few men who will admit to admiring Neville Chamberlain.'

It was Rafi who insisted on decorating the dispersal hut. Whereas most of them were drab slovenly places, smelling of tired men and smoke, this one had a large vase of flowers on a round table, two Turkish rugs, maps and photographs on the walls, and curtains of a yellow and green geometric pattern at the windows. 'I cannot sit for hours surrounded by crap,' Rafi had explained to Eddie.

On this afternoon, their five-minute standby was lengthened to half an hour, so at the sound of an incoming flight, they wandered outside. Eddie felt a little stronger outside. He found himself thinking that the sky was his friend, for better or worse.

A Spitfire was coming in, landing gracefully and stopping exactly where directed. The two men watched, the hood was open already and a figure jumped, without accepting an arm from the ground staff. The leather helmet was swept off, revealing shoulder-length dark hair. The girl, seeing Eddie and Rafi watching, waved cheerfully before striding off to the CO's office.

'Sometimes I find myself wishing I fancied the female sex,' commented Rafi. Eddie stared vaguely before noticing Rafi's questioning look. He tried to smile. 'As a married man, I can't comment.'

'So you are. Don't you find women horribly squishy?'

Eddie didn't bother to answer this one. Rafi knew all about Eva but liked to pretend forgetfulness. He also knew that she was a painter, although Eddie floundered when trying to describe her style. Rafi had helped him by tolerantly suggesting she might like work by Vanessa Bell. 'Quite a nice painter until she got into the hands of the Omega workshop and started overdosing on hexagons. She designed the dispersal hut curtains, as it happens.'

As they stood in the sun waiting, Rafi's sharp chatter was particularly welcome, as if he might tie him into the world, however venial. Now he was talking about the war.

'Of course the war's moved on from England. You especially, who were fighting when it really mattered, must feel like a bit of flotsam after the tide's gone out.'

'We're kept busy enough.' Eddie was watching the pilot from the Air Transport Auxiliary who'd already come out of the CO's office. She was called Joy and when he met her in the Mess a few weeks' ago after delivering another Spitfire, she'd reminded him of Eva. For a few moments he'd flirted with her. How seldom he saw Eva now!

Rafi was talking about Malta. 'If I had your experience that's where I'd want to be. Flying from that poor smashed island over the Med to Africa or Italy. Sicily, too. I wouldn't mind dropping a few bombs on those hideous Roman mosaics.'

Before he could elaborate on what was wrong with these

famous jewels of Roman art, the telephone rang in the dispersal hut behind them and both men turned.

'Nothing special boys. Someone's spotted what might be a couple of raiders advancing on a convoy. Eddie, why don't you take three bright chaps up with you and have a deco.'

The Squadron Leader's instincts turned out to be right. They flew out, rising only to five thousand feet so they could see the line of ships below them, a tanker escorted by two destroyers, but the sky was clear above them apart from a few billowing clouds sailing rather more majestically from west to east than the ships below them.

They romped about for an hour or so and Eddie didn't bother to stop Rafi and a Sergeant Pilot, Doug, playing a game of I Spy, over the R/T:

'I spy with my little eye something beginning with SP,' said Rafi.

'Sergeant Pilot?'

'No. Seagull pissing.'

'I spy with my little eye something beginning with HFTS.'

'Hun from the sun.'

'No. Home faster than shit.'

'If you can't do better than that, shut up,' said Eddie eventually.

On the way back, even the clouds which had grouped into an ungainly heap, failed to impress, but Eddie wasn't unhappy. The tragedy had not followed him into the sky. As they crossed the coast and flew over the light green fields and darker trees billowing like the clouds, he felt something of the freedom that had been with him during the early months of the summer of 1940. Why this brightness should come back to him now when only a few hours ago his life seemed a place of torture and darkness, he had no idea. Perhaps someone was praying for him somewhere. Whoever or whatever, he was immensely grateful. For the first time since his return from France, he said to himself, 'O Lord, protect thy servant.'

While he was in the sky, Madame Sophie, the old Madame,

even Fleur seemed alive again. That was it, they were up there with him, loving him and looking after him. If he could, he'd have flown on for hours.

It didn't seem strange or morbid when he heard Fleur's voice singing into his headphones.

CHAPTER FORTY
August 1942

Eva ran round and round the chestnut tree. Her black hair bounced and twisted and her white blouse reflected green under the leaves. She was followed by Sam, his fat little legs racing to keep up with her.

'I didn't mean you have to run!' Jack called out, a long, dark figure standing near two wooden easels. 'I just said check it out from all angles, even if your canvas is one-dimensional.'

Eva wasn't listening, any more than she listened to Sam's cries of delight. She liked that Jack came once a week to give her painting lessons, instituted by Sylvia, saying, 'A woman needs something to care for apart from men and babies.' Eva had remembered then that Sylvia had published novels and asked about them. But Sylvia had shaken her head, 'For another time.' Eva was glad that Jack took her painting seriously but sometimes his intensity inspired her with the spirit of rebellion. So now she ran round the tree.

Every now and again, she stopped to stare upwards and admire the thick leaves which entirely obscured the sky. On these occasions Sam caught up with her and clasped her legs; she kissed him for a moment before carrying on.

'Enough!' shouted Jack.

'Nuff!' imitated Sam. 'Nuff. Nuff. Nuff.'

Eva laughed before relenting and coming back to stand panting by Jack. She didn't want to make him too angry.

'So what did you learn?'

'A tree blots out the sky.' At the word sky, spoken out loud into the bright, clear air, Eva felt her expression changing. Sky meant Eddie and she didn't want to introduce him into the afternoon.

She added hastily, as if more words might dilute his presence, 'In the summer a tree is bigger than the sky.' But that only made it worse. Where was Eddie? Would he come back soon? He must be due for leave.

'Perspective,' said Jack, placing a paint-stained finger on Eva's canvas. 'Everything in the world is about perspective.' His love for her had never wavered, even when she married and gave birth to Sam in quick succession. He knew she loved Eddie with all her heart, it was only too obvious that he was the sort of man a girl would fall for, handsome, heroic, but he also believed that he, Jack, artist, had something to offer her. He was part of her private life, her independent dreams of becoming a good painter, her feelings of the importance of her existence outside her husband and baby and the Fitzpaine grandeur.

Sometimes he flattered himself that he was an alternative choice to Eddie and that, should something happen to Eddie – it was not wrong to imagine something so imminently possible – then, he, Jack, living in his barn, like a peasant, like an artist, might stand a chance. So when Sylvia invited him to come over once a week to teach Eva, Jack agreed at once and believed that Sylvia understood the other side of Eva just as he did.

He came out gladly and tried not to mind if Eva was rude. Perhaps, consciously or unconsciously, she felt the contradictions in the two sides of her life and it made her difficult. Nothing would stop him loving her.

Eva began to mix colours on her palette and Sam sat and then lay on the grass. He was a beautiful little boy, just as Eva had imagined, with her own dark eyes and Eddie's golden hair. Confident in the devotion of three women, his mother, Sylvia and Lily, he believed himself the king of all around him and, with nothing to thwart him, had a sunny, relaxed disposition.

As the shadows lengthened and a chill rose from the grass, more of Sam's admirers appeared from beyond the garden. These were the Land Girls, heading back to the house where they stayed, but deviating to find Sam.

'Six-thirty already,' said Eva, reluctantly putting down her brush. She had at last found a relationship between the canopy of leaves and the trunk.

Jack also put down his brush. The Land Girls, particularly the three who were advancing singing cheerfully, 'Land of muck and slurry' were a challenge to his celibacy. 'I hope you've managed to visualise the roots. Even if you don't paint them, you have to visualise them or your tree won't stand up. Most people think shadows will do it but they really won't, you know.'

Eva was interested. It struck her as one of Jack's really imaginative suggestions but Sam had jumped up and was running towards the girls. The girl in the lead, picked him up and swung him in the air.

'Sam loves Daisy,' Eva watched, pleased with the sight. Perhaps she could paint them one day.

'She's so happy all the time,' commented Jack noting how Daisy's full breasts lifted as she raised her arms.

'It's because she's escaped the munition factory.'

'Just wait for the winter.'

'I think she's escaped her mother too.' Eva heard herself pronounce the word 'mother' without a tremor. She was the mother now. Sylvia was a mother.

But the girls were upon them, thickly clad in regulation dungarees and Wellington boots.

'Phew, you're smelly.' Eva grimaced and held her nose.

'Why do you think we were singing 'Land of muck and slurry?' asked Daisy, tall and broad and fair like a warrior. The other two girls, from further away were small and dark, sisters, not twins, but almost identical.

'We'll take Sam up for his bath if you like,' said Joan, one of the sisters.

'Would you really,' Eva glanced at her painting, 'it's going to be light for ages yet and I've hardly started.'

Maurie, the younger sister, peered curiously. 'It's just like a tree,' she said, as if surprised.

Eva laughed. 'Do you hear that, Jack?'

Daisy settled Sam onto her shoulders. 'I love muck spreading. Ooh, the shocking filth and stink! My mum would have a fit.'

'I thought you were a country girl?'

'My mother married out of Hackney, although I'm Yeovil born and bred. None of us allowed out of the house on market day and never near a field, particularly the hill called Babylon.'

Off Daisy strode, followed by Joan and Maurie who were pulling on Sam's legs. Both Eva and Jack followed their progress admiringly.

'Is it wrong to be having so much fun when Eddie is facing death every day?' By mistake Eva spoke out loud.

'Fighter pilots think *they're* having fun and you should know by now that painting isn't fun at all.'

Eva glanced at Jack warily; he hadn't seemed in a bad mood earlier. She wondered whether she had offended him more than just being unavailable. Dismissing the idea, she went back to her painting. She had always been unavailable and he kept on coming and, where painting was concerned, she was glad he did.

'The sun, of course, is making everything quite different,' said Jack after fifteen silent minutes, save for the cooing of the homeward pigeons. 'Quite soon it will drop below the tree's canopy and then we might as well stop.'

'It could light up my roots.' She wasn't trying to be funny. Inspired by Jack's advice, she'd gone further and made the roots visible, snaking and humping above the grass so that they took up the same amount of space below the trunk as the leaves above. She was pleased with the effect but their colour, a root-like greyish brown seemed dull. It struck her, as she stood back and critically surveyed her canvas, that, since she had already broken free from reality, she could paint them any colour she liked: pink (briefly she remembered Salome) yellow, purple. Perhaps purple. She grabbed her palette excitedly.

But Jack was already clearing up his things, screwing on tops, stacking them neatly, stowing them into a canvas bag.

'Am I invited to supper?' he asked.

'Naturally,' answered Eva smiling nicely.

Tollorum kitchen suppers had changed with five or more Land Girls to feed and one Land Boy, a conscientious objector who had found his way to the farm. He was the only quiet one. For Eddie's next leave, thought Eva, I shall find a country pub where we can stay at peace together. She joined Jack who was staring at her painting.

'I like the roots,' he said, 'a daring move, saved by the soft underground colour you've chosen for them.' He turned to her and, although as always semi-blinded by her beauty, he couldn't ignore the willfulness in her expression. 'What?' he asked.

'Nothing,' said Eva. After all, purple was an underground colour too. Safe. As far away from the sky as possible. 'I must go in and read to Sam.'

CHAPTER FORTY-ONE
August 1942

'You're off, old boy.'

Eddie stared at the CO. The man had only arrived at the base three days ago and had the worst characteristics of a desk–job pilot who'd been an ace in the last war and still thought he knew all the answers, despite never having flown anything that wasn't a box made of canvas. Or so Eddie thought rebelliously. Rafi agreed and had immediately christened him Sir Box Wallah.

'What do you mean, *off,* sir?'

'I can't tell you more because I don't know more.'

'I've got leave due next week.'

'You did have leave due next week.' Sir Box waved a piece of paper. 'Orders. You and Penworthy. London train to Scotland. From there darkness falls. Top secret. There's a war on, they tell me. Get your train tickets from Dibs and don't bother with too much luggage.'

'Thank you, sir.' Eddie stood up.

'My pleasure.'

Fat slob, thought Eddie viciously. Outside the door Rafi lounged smoking a cigarette. He raised an eyebrow.

'You'll know soon enough,' said Eddie.

By the time they'd boarded the train for London, Rafi had worked out their destination. 'It's obvious. They're shipping us off to Malta. All this cloak and dagger stuff is nonsense to amuse themselves. Everyone knows that since Park's taken over in Malta they're flying Spitfires over there as quickly as they can get the pilots. Wasn't I going on about it to you just the other day?'

'I see you arranged it all, Rafi. But I wish you'd asked me if I wanted to come along.'

On the sleeper to Glasgow, Rafi worked out his first moves on arriving in Valletta. 'There's an amazing painting by that sublime murderer Caravaggio in the Cathedral. He fled to Malta after the Pope went for him. A chap in the act of hacking off St John the Baptist's head. Perfectly revolting, I'm assured. Even shocked my fish-eyed father. I'll be along there in a flash. Then there's …'

'Malta's been bombed to pieces, you bloody idiot,' protested Eddie. They were now trying to force their way along a crowded corridor to the buffet car and he didn't feel like a lecture on art. 'If we are going to where you say we are, you shouldn't be shouting about it and if we do get there, we'll have a job to do and we won't have time to go on one of your bloody Baedeker tours.' Eddie was beginning to think Rafi wasn't such a great companion. He was fearless, that was it, fearless, filled with curiosity and utterly insensitive to everything except the content of his own head. Although they were much the same age, he made Eddie feel old, careful and anxious. It had not felt good being unable to tell Eva or his parents where he was going. Perhaps he should have ignored the CO and told them Malta. If it was Malta.

At Glasgow they were not the only pilots getting out of the train. Eddie counted at least a dozen. Since it was six-thirty on a grey cold morning – Eddie had forgotten just how cold summer in Scotland could be – nobody bothered much with greetings. Even Rafi, pale from a night at the bar, was silent. Eddie had chosen a bunk where he'd rested, if not slept.

They were transported by Nessie Coaches Ltd, painted with Loch Ness and its monster, rising with jaws open, direct to Abbotsinch Air Base Mess where they joined a further thirty or so pilots who competed with devouring porridge and powdered scrambled eggs on toast. Most agreed there was no difference between the two.

'I suppose we are going to Malta?' Eddie tried question-ing an Australian Flight Lieutenant at his table. In his experience Aussies were keen and knowledgeable and certainly more reliable than Rafi.

'Can't think where else, old mate, unless it's somewhere like Burma and, I'll tell you what, I'll jump into the Clyde rather than face their rainy season.'

After a day of sitting around doing nothing, it was a relief when service police arrived and more respectable buses transported them to Greenock Harbour.

'So what have you been doing all day?' asked Eddie as Rafi sat beside him.

'Smoking. I hear Malta's totally run out of ciggies.' Rafi lit a cigarette as he spoke. 'This is my 55th. I'm aiming for a record'

'I think you'd need hundreds to win that.' In the afternoon Eddie had roused himself to write a letter to Eva. He had handed it to an intelligence officer, commenting 'Maybe when we're gone you can tell my wife where we've gone. Just scribble on the envelope, "Malta, Tally Ho" or wherever it may be.'

'Jolly funny, sir.' The man had taken the letter without smiling. But then Eddie hadn't been smiling either.

It was raining hard when they were turned out on the quayside but even so the sight of such an array of ships was impressive.

'Well, there's always the Navy,' said Rafi.

Out of the gathering gloom, a naval trawler came to pick them up.

'I've got a brother in the Navy up here somewhere. Thinks they stopped the invasion.' This was Eddie's flight lieutenant breakfast companion.

'Were you in Fighter Command during the summer of '40?' asked Eddie mildly.

'Got my wings last year.'

'Tell him to stuff it anyway.' The puff of anger Eddie felt passed quickly. It was enjoyable to be handed down to the trawler and to set off through the ranks of ships. They were heading for a flight carrier. Whatever their destination they'd be leaving England, in future flying from foreign soil, over foreign water. It made him feel slightly lightheaded, whether with trepidation or anticipation, he couldn't tell. Even in the hardest days of that summer of '40, when they'd been operational for five times a day, they were always at home, or at least in England by nightfall. Either that or they were at the bottom of the sea or burnt to ashes. They'd been flying over the country they were defending. It had helped. Or had it made things harder?

He was trying to keep the memories of France buried. Even in this latest letter he had not written to Eva about it.

The aircraft carrier was immense, built into tiers with room for thirty-eight Spitfires. They were shown into the wardroom which, with its mahogany fittings, gilt-edged mirrors and leather armchairs, was more like a London club than a military meeting room. There would be a briefing at 1800 hours for the four flight lieutenants who would be leading the planes.

Since it had stopped raining, Eddie with Stu and Rafi, went in search of their Spitfires. They found them in a gigantic hanger.

'How small they look!' Eddie went closer to smooth the flank of the nearest. All the planes were painted with desert camouflage which made it certain they were heading south. Next door some RAF armourers seemed to be taking the ammunition out of the boxes.

'Come over here,' he called. Stu and Rafi wandered over. 'Am I dreaming or did I just see the ammunition being removed?'

The armourer looked up and smiled. 'You wait till you see what's going in, sir.'

The three pilots waited. Soon men came up carrying boxes of cigarettes which they began to load, one singing cheerfully, 'All the nice girls love a sailor.'

The other who'd spoken before said, 'I know what you're thinking but don't ask us, we just obey orders.'

'We're fighter pilots, not travelling salesmen,' said Eddie.

'Well, if they're going to Malta with us,' said Rafi, 'I needn't have nearly choked to death on seventy-eight gaspers in twelve hours.'

'We don't know where we're bloody going,' said Stu.

'My only advice, sir,' said the talkative armourer who didn't know his place – he was a big man with a boxer's broken nose – 'is once you've gone, stay gone, wherever you're going. You're the third lot of planes we've seen off this floating platform and they all think the same, getting off may be difficult but flying back on would be suicide.'

The three pilots walked away.

'Bloody cheek,' said Stu.

'Probably explains the removal of the ammunition,' said Eddie. 'Weighs a lot and that runway looked horribly short.'

They all began to think that the briefing couldn't come soon enough. This limbo of unknowing surrounded by sheets of blank grey water got on your nerves. Perhaps it would be better when they were moving.

The briefing was postponed with the news that it would take place when they were at sea. The wardroom began to look less welcoming and everybody, except Rafi who took to his bunk with a book, spent more time with the Spitfires which seemed to get smaller compared to the grey horizon but larger compared to the flight deck.

'What the hell is the point of that ruddy great ramp in the middle of the deck?' asked Stu of no one in particular.

As it happened, Group Captain Tim Holder who they'd seen earlier in the boardroom was prepared to give them the answer. 'Set up for the old biplanes. Threw up into the air.'

'That won't work for Spitfires, sir.' Eddie tried to sound calm. 'Won't have enough speed, not with the propellers fitted on those planes in the hangers.'

'You've hit the nail on the head, Chaffey. That's why we're waiting. Don't mind if you put the word around, as a matter-of-fact. Hydromatic airscrews on the way, put us well over the 3000 revs we need. Progress, boys, progress.'

Later, in the bar, the boys agreed that someone should have foreseen this little difficulty. 'So that armourer was a hundred per cent wrong,' pointed out Stu. 'It's just as hard to get off this bloody ship as to get back on.'

The only answer to this was to order another round of drinks. Another two days of waiting passed.

Eddie wrote a second letter to Eva. Although it was not particularly long, it filled up most of the day. He still did not talk about his time in France and the tragedy that followed. Instead he described the ship, the food, the routine, his companions.

In the afternoon he felt the ship moving and going on deck saw they were well out into the Clyde.

After the others had gone — the bar opened early on board ship — Eddie stayed to watch the carrier which had been into the wind steaming along at a good thirty knots, slow down and make a wide circle back to Greenock Harbour. Out at sea, a naval rating pointed out two ships which he identified as destroyers. 'They'll be escorting us, no doubt.' He put his finger against his nose. 'Been to Malta before, have you?' The man scurried away without waiting for an answer, although he turned round twice to check the effect of his words.

This was definitely somebody else's world. Eddie went down once more to the giant hangar where the Spitfires were kept. He saw that a dozen men were working on them. Clearly the famous hydromatic airscrews had arrived and were being fitted in a hurry. He had little experience of them and looked forward to the boost of power. Surely now, they'd get their briefing.

It came at 9 pm that night about an hour after the carrier had begun to move out of the harbour. The Group Captain called in Eddie, Stu and two other flight lieutenants.

'So now it's official. We're flying these Spitfires to Malta. We are also part of a sizeable naval convoy going in the same direction. So don't be surprised when you see more ships than you've ever seen before. Malta has been essentially in a state of siege, little food, drink, oil, cigarettes.'

'Ah,' said Eddie.

'You've seen the packets of cigarettes?' The Group Captain frowned. He was a fussy little man who held a notepad like a shield.

'What if we meet a 109, sir?'

'You're not expected to engage the enemy.'

'But if the enemy engage us?'

'You run. Look, with the extra fuel you need to carry, you'll be already heavier than I'd like. As I was saying, we're one part of a plan to relieve Malta. Operation Pedestal. She's put up a damned fine show being bombed worse than London, but now she needs some help. Think of the grateful Forces when you unload your cigarettes.'

Eddie decided not to say he was thinking of the faces of German pilots coming in for the kill. There was no point. Orders are always orders.

'The important thing is to choose a route where you won't meet any 109s.' The Group Captain unfolded a map. 'Best to keep well south and up at 20,000 feet. You'll fly off south-west of the Balearic Islands and I suggest you drop down to Algeria, heading for Bizerta and Tunis, before cutting through the Gulf of Tunis and heading north to Malta, using Linosa Island as a marker. That's 650 miles, about six hours flying time. Any questions so far?'

Nobody had any questions. Assuming the extra fuel tank kicked in and no 109s materialised, it seemed doable.

'Good. You'll each lead either eight or nine Spitfires and you can choose your number twos. You'll keep R/T contact to the minimum and once you're in range of Malta, you'll follow their orders. You'll be flying into Luqa airport.'

After the meeting was over, the four pilots swapped reactions. Without radio contact, they'd be flying with their eyes and a map, a compass and a watch.

'Like the good old days,' said Eddie, but nobody smiled. Perhaps they thought he could actually remember some good old days. Perhaps he could.

'We can't avoid spotting the coast of bloody Africa,' said Stu.

Eddie went to find Rafi. He was propped against the bar, one hand held a whitish drink, the other an open book.

'Want to hear the news?' Eddie waved at the immaculate barman. 'We're going to Malta,' Rafi lifted his book so Eddie could see the title: *Ancient Maltese − at the Crossroads of History.* 'The captain lent it me. A very educated man. Did you know we're part of Operation Pedestal? Getting on for forty ships involved. I'm hoping we'll join up with them before we fly off. Should be a magnificent sight. The captain wasn't too clear on timing.'

'I suppose he also told you you're my number two?' said Eddie ironically. 'Or was that top secret?'

'Ha. Ha. Glad I'm not tail-end Charlie, though.'

'There haven't been any tail-end Charlies since the last one was shot down in 1940, cursing the RAF and crying for his mother.'

Eddie sipped his whisky. There *had* been good old days at the RAF, Fighter Squadron days when he'd drunk too much beer with his friends, Hank, Andy, others, another age. Rafi, although quite unlike any of them, gave him the same feeling of comradely piss-taking. 'What's that filthy brew you're drinking?'

'Pernod, Monsieur. Not quite the Maltese brew. We won't be off for days so no point in holding back.'

Eddie didn't question Rafi's information but couldn't resist a jibe. 'Are you sure it's the captain you've been talking to? I'd thought the naval ratings would be more your level.'

'You may have a point there, although I've never met a ship's boy, to use the colloquial terminology, who was interested in ancient Malta.'

'Stolen from the ship's library?' Around him, Eddie was aware of other pilots drinking and laughing. 'So do you want me to tell you more details of our mission?'

'Later, later. Don't you find the pulse of the ship's engine thrilling?'

Eddie laughed. 'I preferred the throb of a Rolls-Royce Merlin engine and, incidentally, they've been fitting hydromatic airscrews since teatime.'

CHAPTER FORTY-TWO
August 1942

The ship became familiar to Eddie and the rest of the pilots. Each man was allocated his own Spitfire with identifying letters and numbers. Eddie's was NB440. The pilots appeared to ignore the mission ahead; they sat about in the wardroom, played dominoes and draughts and very occasionally threw a ball around on the deck. The carrier was pounding through the waves at 35 knots and on the whole it was more entertaining to lean over the railings and estimate the green depths of the water or admire the clean lines of the escorting cruiser whose sharp hull threw up thick rolls of white spray, or the two small destroyers on either side of them. All the pilots, watching the scrubbing, the sluicing, the polishing, waited on by servants in spotless white, agreed they could get used to the life at sea. They gave up staring at the sky to see how the winds moved the clouds and how fast and from what direction and particularly avoided remarking on the ramp in the middle of the flight deck, although it stuck out like a nose in a face.

In the evening, Eddie picked up a book from a table and began reading when he saw it was a history of eighteenth-century balloonists. After a few pages he found a paragraph which someone had marked, '*I felt we were flying away from Earth and all its troubles and persecutions forever. It was not mere delight. It was a sort of physical rapture ... I explained to my companion, 'I'm finished with the earth. From now on our place is in the sky'*.

Was the sky a seductress? Eddie copied out the passage in a letter he had began to Eva. He told her that he pictured her on the lawn with Sam. That the sky was just another element. Then he started a letter to his father.

You have always made my life difficult but now I see that as a good thing. Life is difficult and you prepared me for it. War has made us what we are. When I told you about the unhappy fate of the French family, it came as no surprise to you and I knew the story was safe with you. This is beginning to sound like a farewell letter but it's not supposed to be. Soon I shall write to Eva and tell her what happened. I assume you already told mother. This is a thank you letter, a letter from a loving son who has grown up a bit lately . . .

※

The following morning, as predicted by Rafi, they found themselves joining a huge convoy of ships. Suddenly their virtually empty sea was filled with vessels of every size and shape, from a vast tanker that rode in the centre to two dozen destroyers and in between, more cruisers, two battleships, several aircraft carriers and more than a dozen merchant ships. It was like going from a walk in the country to Piccadilly Circus.

The pilots, used to operating individually within the structure of squadrons, could hardly believe these moving islands, filled with hundreds of men.

'Bloody hell,' exclaimed Stu. 'Let's hope their guns aren't loaded with cigarettes.'

'Ever heard the expression 'sitting ducks'?', added Rafi.

'It's an amazing show of strength,' protested Eddie. He was exhilarated by the beauty and power of all this great naval display, moving round the world. It made him think how isolated he'd been up to now moving from one airbase to another, operational for an hour or so, fighting his own battles.

He mostly preferred to be alone and that evening, he continued his letter to Eva. He told her that the sea and the sky were joined into one around the ships. Pilots had already been informed they could only take one small bag so he planned to entrust the delivery of his letters to the Admiralty.

Early the next morning, just as a rating was bringing him his tea, there was a colossal noise which literally made him jump out of bed.

'Don't worry, sir.' The rating deftly held the cup and saucer out of Eddie's way, 'It isn't Armageddon yet. It's just them show-off sailors testing their guns. Quite a rattle if you're not used to it,' he added with satisfaction. 'Next stop Gibraltar now. I expect you've been to old Gib often, sir?'

'No,' Eddie accepted the tea and sat drinking it in his bed.

'Never fancied living on a rock, myself, although from what I've heard, they're mostly inside it now, cave-dwellers, like. Not that we will be there long enough to check, I dare say.'

The vast shock of massive guns firing in unison had passed away, leaving the steady pulse of the engine and the sounds of wind and waves outside Eddie's porthole.

'So when do you think we'll be off?' Rafi had taught him the omniscience of naval ratings.

'Well, sir. Gib tomorrow, a day or less there, then out to Mallorca, keeping it north. Then we'll get you off as quick as a cargo of fleas.'

'I suppose our presence makes this ship a prime target?'

'Of course, sir. Nothing personal, it's our job. But bearing in mind the Luftwaffe and the Ities above, and those subs, like nasty old sharks, we'll sing Hallelujah when you're all off and we can head for home. In short, the Med's not the healthiest place to fly the Red Ensign.'

That night Eddie found himself caught up in a discussion about fear with a group of very young and very drunk pilots. Most of them agreed that they never felt an ounce of fear on the job. Waiting to be called out was bad, they admitted, but the worst time of all was when they went home and felt their father's fear, heavily disguised by inappropriate jollity and their mother's thinly disguised by unnecessary provisioning. 'I had to dump three boxes of tea,' laughed one pilot. 'It's true. It's other people's fear that gets you,' said another. 'You can't tell them to brace up. Last leave I made an excuse and went to London.'

Eddie wondered whether his fear of Eva's fear had held them

apart. It had only been while he was recuperating and there had been no chance of his flying, no danger, that they had become close. Those days, the long walks in the beautiful countryside with Eva's swelling stomach, seemed dreamlike now. Now fear of her fear was back, if that was a true analysis, there could be no way that calm happiness could be repeated until the war was over. Yet Eva's was an independent spirit. He never imagined her waiting at home for him sorrowfully. She had her painting as well as Sam. That evening Eddie wrote a fourth letter to Eva.

At last he described to her what had happened in France, explaining the tenderness with which the old Madame had cared for him, the joyous determination of Fleur to make him well and Madame Sophie's indomitable courage in saving him. Their deaths took only a sentence but he had no doubt Eva would understand everything he felt. He pictured her finding comfort in the green folds of Tollorum's hills. He pictured Sam flinging his arms round her neck.

He felt happier as he sealed the letter. Now there was nothing between them.

Gibraltar was reached just before sunrise. The pilots went on deck and watched its black flank being painted white by the brilliant light. It seemed they wouldn't stay long. The carriers wanted to get off their aeroplanes as soon as possible and the escorting destroyers and battleships wanted to get the tanker and merchant ships to Malta as quickly as possible.

Still, there was another night to be got through. The pilots began to bond with their designated planes. Many, like Eddie, hung his parachute ready on the wing. It was another op., this stated clearly, just another op.

It had been very hot for the last few days and all of them had noticed a haze that collected over the sea as the morning progressed. Eddie's planes were going last which gave time for a build-up. After a while no one could think of anything more to say, so Eddie, suddenly needing company, strolled over to the bar where he found Rafi with a bottle of champagne.

'I hear there's a shortage on Malta,' he smiled at Eddie's raised eyebrows. 'All set for a happy flight?'

'All set,' responded Eddie seriously. 'We'll fly in a loose formation. More relaxed than bunching up with such a relatively long flight. Have you checked the switchover on your overload tank?'

'We all have. More than once. Want a glass?'

≈

Early the next morning everybody turned out to watch the first Spitfires fly off. Despite the additional revs, it took a steady nerve and there was general relief when the first nine got off without a problem. On the other end of the deck, the Marine band, sun glinting on its instruments, played *We'll Meet Again* and *Wish me Luck as I Wave you Goodbye*, but nobody took much notice. All eyes were fixed on the planes as they circled round before taking off east.

Nobody even took much notice of the convoy spread on the glittering waters around them. They were on the job now, nothing else mattered.

The second squadron came out, throttled up to full speed, mounted the ramp and, like birds release from a cage, soared up into the sky.

'Not terrifying at all,' said Eddie to Rafi.

'A thing of beauty is a joy forever,' agreed Rafi.

The two men stood watching admiringly as each Spitfire took wing with perfect grace. Soon the third squadron, led by Stu, set off one by one. There was no fear now, it looked almost easy. Eddie was just turning to go to his Spitfire when something caught his eye.

'Oh lordy Lord!' A sailor who had helped the last pilot into his plane was staring, frozen-faced out to sea. '*Eagle* is it?' He shouted at another sailor.

Eddie peered in the same direction. He didn't know the names of all the ships but now he could see a battleship listing badly.

'It's been torpedoed,' he heard someone say. The fact that he'd heard and seen nothing of the attack made the sight not only shocking, but surreal, difficult to believe.

'What the hell are you lot up to?' It was the fussy Group Commander, now showing impressive and justified rage. 'Get into your planes and get them off this deck now!'

Eddie and Rafi ran. Everybody ran. It was a relief not to see what was going on, instead to concentrate on the Spit, the throttle and the revs and the undercarriage and the stick.

Someone was under attack, that was for sure but it was not them yet, nor even their flight carrier. Their job was to get off into the sky before those cigarette packs had to line up against guns.

Eddie, circling right, counted all his flight off the carrier, then, dipping his wings to Rafi, turned east and pulled back the stick. 20,000 feet was what the CO suggested and 20,000 feet it would be.

Tally Ho! Malta.

CHAPTER FORTY-THREE
August 1942

Rafi was enjoying himself. He had a leader he trusted, a good kite, the weather was perfect, even if there was a little bit of haze where the land should be, and he was on a heroic mission to save an historic island. He began to sing, inappropriately, with any luck, but it came into his head:

> *Fear no more the lightning flash,*
> *Nor the all-dreaded thunder stone...*

Ahead of him he could see Eddie's plane and spread around him, in very loose formation as Eddie had wanted, were the seven other Spitfires. They had quickly left behind the scenes of the attack on the convoy and in Rafi's case, it was out of sight, out of mind. The only pity was he couldn't slide open the cockpit roof and breathe in the dulcet Mediterranean air. But at 20,000 feet it would be cold, not dulcet, and in fact it was time to step on the oxygen and keep his mind sharp. Even if Eddie was the leader, as number two he needed to double-check their position.

The truth was that, despite his good spirits, he was suffering from an excess of champagne, head thick, eyes sticky, hands not with their wonted grip. He turned up the oxygen further and immediately felt a great deal better. For every problem there is a remedy.

Shakespeare certainly knew how to get death across. Rafi began to sing again:

> *Thou hast finished joy and moan:*
> *All lovers young, all lovers must*
> *Consign to thee and come to dust.*

One of the advantages of not being on R/T was that he could sing to his heart's content and no one would tell him to shut up and not block the airways. Also, the loose formation meant he really couldn't do very much about the other Spitfires. He kept Eddie in view and the rest of them kept him in sight. There was none of that 'Where are you, blast you, Rafi? Don't you yet know about wing formation?' There wasn't even much point in searching for the enemy since in a clear blue sky and cigarettes for ammunition, there was little he could do anyway.

So Rafi sailed along, occasionally looking up and occasionally looking down, where he noted that the haze was so thick that it might have been one of those bands of clouds that can give a pilot a bit of a challenge. Not that he felt challenged; Eddie was going steady enough, using his compass to follow the line of the North African coast, even if he couldn't see it.

Nevertheless, he wasn't surprised when Eddie started to drop height, first to 15,000 feet, then to 10,000 feet. No need for oxygen now but he still took a precautionary whiff. Didn't want to doze at the controls.

He looked at his watch. They'd been going nearly two hours. Extraordinary how quickly time passes when you're happy. Another couple of hours and he'd be admiring Valetta's Cathedral. Meanwhile it was time to switch over to his overload tank. Wouldn't do to forget that. He glanced down but the haze was as thick as ever. Warm pea soup. The Spitfire had warmed up too so that he felt a bit dozy again. Maybe being dry in Malta wouldn't be such a bad idea.

Soon it would be time to keep a serious look-out for Bizerta and, there that's definitely the Tunisian coast, fairly definitely anyway. Eddie had dropped lower still. So he was in and out of the haze and not so easy to see. Not that he was essential. Bizerta was the only city on this bit of the coast. Then it was 160° to Hammamet. Scarcely higher mathematics. Hammamet, Linosa, remembering to avoid falling down into the volcanoes. Malta. Bingo!

Rafi lowered his speed to 200 mph and peered with sudden concentration. Might show Eddie the way. Couldn't see Eddie just now but all the other planes were tucked in behind him so that was all right.

Aha! Spot on. A town just where it should be. Rafi checked his compass and prepared to turn. And that looked like Eddie ahead doing the same. Pleased, Rafi screwed round to watch the planes behind him make the turn too. Follow my leader. Although he seemed to have lost Eddie again. Now for Hammamet.

Maybe after the war he'd travel these parts, learn something about Arab culture. Englishmen were supposed to have a special feeling for nomadic Arabs, think Lawrence of Arabia. Was there much desert below him? It was shocking how little he understood about the war being fought out here, or the politics of the region before the war if it came to that.

Rafi mused on and he'd passed Hammamet without taking much notice and now it was Linosa. That was important. He straightened up, pushed his goggles which were darkened, and looked about him. Jolted into awareness by the sudden glare, he screwed up his eyes and peered ahead. This time there really was no reason not to see Eddie. But he still wasn't there. Nervously, Rafi checked his compass and watch, but he was just where he should be. He'd never had a problem with that sort of thing. Never. Not ever. Eddie had to be somewhere close.

He swivelled in his seat and for a dreadful moment, didn't see the other planes. Just a second or two of feeling all alone. Then he saw them higher than him, but not by much. He waggled his wings to draw their attention and make sure they took the course over the sea to Linosa.

But where was Eddie? It wasn't as if he could stop and look for him. In fact now he had to keep checking the map. Best to come down another few thousand feet. With any luck there wouldn't be any Germans nor Italians here, and the island was small enough to miss.

Perhaps Eddie had flown high and fast. Strange, but no time to worry. Must concentrate. Soon after Linosa, they'd be in Maltese radio space and he could get the story.

The haze that had been so impenetrable earlier had now thinned to white shreds, like the white trails of vapour left behind by planes. But they were quite low on the water and below them the sea shone a rich ultramarine blue, occasionally decorated by curling ripples, forming a zigzag pattern or a series of wriggling stripes. And there amidst it all, a black blob in just the right place, was Linosa Island.

Twisting round for a moment to make sure the other Spitfires were following, Rafi flew directly over it. What a splendid display the islanders were getting! Or perhaps it was uninhabited. Their briefing hadn't run to that detail. He turned on his R/T.

For a second he imagined hearing Eddie's voice, 'What the hell do you think you're doing? Put another way, where the bloody do you think you are, blast you!'

Instead, after a few minutes the voice of the air controller from Luqa airport came over remarkably clearly, 'Calling Red Section.' The amount of relief Rafi felt showed just how anxious he'd been. Now it was a matter of concentrating on instructions and not buggering things up at the end.

⚍

'What do you mean, "He disappeared"?' The Intelligence Officer was a don-like chap with glasses and a stoop. He also had an accent Rafi couldn't quite place.

It had been a heroes' welcome for the pilots. Men lined up and cheered, women in black scarves crossed themselves, thanked God for their safe arrival. They were like angels from heaven, indicated one old lady with appropriate gestures. At first, the assumption had been that Rafi was Eddie Chaffey, despite his repeated assertions that he was Rafaelo Penworthy. Rejoicing that all four Spitfire sections had safely arrived, despite reports of a costly battle at sea, overrode any minor discrepancy.

But after several hours when the light was turning golden

over the golden ruins of Valetta, Rafi found himself in front of an intelligence officer. Then he tried to explain.

'Are you telling me Flight Officer Chaffey dematerialised somewhere between your leaving the flight carrier and Bizerta when you noticed he was missing? That you took over the section and led them into Luqa?'

'Yes, sir,' said Rafi. An immense sorrow and weariness came over him.

'So, what did you do about it? Did you look for him? Did you try and make contact over the R/T?'

'No,' said Rafi. 'We were told to avoid contact.' But he had not even thought of trying.

'I see,' the officer made a note.

'Let's try and pinpoint when you last saw Chaffey.'

'I thought he might have gone down into the haze, searching for Bizerta.' But he hadn't thought that. He hadn't known what to think. 'The heat haze was very, very thick. He might have got lost. Sometimes in very thick cloud, you don't know which way you're going. Are you a pilot, sir?'

'No. If you want to know I'm a historian.'

Rafi put his head in hands and shut his eyes. 'I've got a thumping headache.'

'Did you have a headache when you were flying?'

'No, sir.'

The officer made a note. 'I ask because you'll be operational again tomorrow. Every pilot is needed here. You know what I mean?'

'Yes, sir.' Rafi made an effort and raised his head.

'Let's try and do our best.' The officer lifted his glasses as if about to take them off, then dropped them down again and sighed.

The action drew Rafi's attention to his skin which was a pale purplish colour, as if infused with an ink wash. On the other hand, maybe he wasn't seeing too well. 'Where will we be going, sir?'

'That's for tomorrow. So, let's see, was Chaffey behaving normally when you left the carrier?'

'Quite normal.' Rafi thought. 'Of course, we'd had a shock. A battleship had been torpedoed in front of our eyes. Not used to ships being blown up like that. Used to aeroplanes.'

'A shock? Do you know something, Penworthy, I don't think anything we've said has much relevance to Flight Lieutenant Chaffey's disappearance.'

'No, sir.' The Intelligent Officer's eyes were flashing behind his glasses and his skin had gone a deep purple. 'Pilots go missing all the time. I expect we could do the numbers from the RAF if we tried. Enemy action only the half of it, mechanical faults, pilot error, unexpected weather, mental problems, all sorts of reasons pilots and planes go unaccounted for.' He seemed to be on a roll. Then he paused and said more soberly, 'Most often, they're missing in action, one has to admit that. But I've no doubt that we both know that planes disappear in unknown circumstances right across the world. Was Chaffey a friend of yours?'

'Yes, sir.'

'Shall we just write "missing". He leant forward. 'Absolutely no chance you saw a 109?'

'I don't know, sir.' Rafi took a breath. 'I can't help imagining him in the desert, sir, walking in the heat, no water, no compass.' He hesitated. 'Probably Eddie would have his compass.'

'Desert? Ha! Shot down?'

'Or the extra fuel tank developed a fault and he glided down, landed OK – Eddie's a very experienced pilot – landed safely, as I said, and even now is walking under a sun of a hundred or more degrees.' Rafi realised he'd had this image in the back of his mind all the time. Why hadn't he tried to look for him?

'It is a possibility,' the Intelligence Officer conceded, 'but I served in North Africa before I came here, I can tell you the desert is not half as empty as we are led to believe. Not so deserted you might say. Tribes all over the place, mostly on our side.' He sat back in his chair and this time did take off his glasses. 'It's the African sun that turned me this peculiar colour. I was what's laughably called white before. But that's a diversion.' He replaced his glasses and leant over his pad. 'I should say we have reached a conclusion.'

'Sir?'

The Intelligence Officer scribbled: *Flight Lieutenant Eddie Chaffey missing on August 15th, 1942*. 'I'll write to his parents. Anything more you want to add?'

'He has, had, has, a wife, sir, and a son.'

'Good fellow.' The officer scribbled again before standing up. 'So you'll be on standby 0600 hours tomorrow morning. Destination Sicily, I might as well tell you. No secrets on Malta.'

Sicily. Rafi remembered his joke to Eddie about smashing up the Roman mosaics at Piazza Armerina. The Intelligence Officer had put on his cap and was saluting. It was time to leave.

CHAPTER FORTY-FOUR
September 1942

Lily saw the bicycle coming up the drive and turn left to the kitchen door. She took Sam by the hand who, because the day was hot, wore only a nappy, and went out of the kitchen to meet the boy who rode the bike. She had been stewing apples and the sweet smell clung about her.

'It's a package!' shouted the boy before they reached him. He was too small for the large, heavy bike and his face was scarlet with his sweaty hair clinging to his forehead.

'Ike!' cried Sam, holding out his arms hopefully.

The boy somehow got off the saddle and let the bike crash to the ground thankfully. 'It came from the Navy so old Bidder sent me off in a hurry. Phew it's hot!'

'Come into the kitchen, and I'll find you a drink,' said Lily, automatically. The sight of Jimmy from the post office had been a fearful one but, if the package was from the Admiralty not the RAF, it could be anything. 'Who's it for?' she asked as Jimmy tucked the package importantly under his arm.

'It's for Mrs Chaffey and that's who I'm handing it to,' he said. 'Mrs. Edward Chaffey.'

'Well, we'll see if we can find her once you've had your drink. I expect you wouldn't mind a biscuit neither.'

Jimmy sat at the table drinking cold apple juice and eating two home-made biscuits.

He made no protest when Lily picked up the package. 'I'll take it to Mrs Chaffey while you cool down.'

Eva had made a studio for herself in one of the empty stables. Daisy, the Land Girl, who was handy with a mallet, had enlarged a window to give more light. Sometimes, the pony Rosie joined her in the next-door stable and hung her head over the partition.

Lately, Eva's paintings had become more abstract. She was on her own that morning painting the top segment of her large canvas with a heavy white. She stared up at Lily blankly. Lily never interrupted her; Sylvia sometimes did, but Lily never.

'It's a package for you.'

'Can't it wait?'

'It's from the Admiralty.'

Eva put down her brush and came to the door. In her long blue smock, and with her still unfocused expression, she had the look of a priestess interrupted at the altar.

'It's lovely and cool in here,' commented Lily approvingly.

'I'm painting a hot white. I'm *trying* to paint a hot white.'

Sam who had been collecting stones outside heard his mother's voice and came running in.

'I can never quite solve things,' Eva frowned to herself. 'I like to pretend it's a lack of time but it may be a lack in my brain.' She took the package and sat on a straw bale. Immediately, Sam climbed on to her lap. 'Oh, Sam, you're so delicious!' She squeezed him and kissed his cheek. Then she opened the package over his head.

'Me,' suggested Sam, reaching upwards.

Deftly, Eva avoided him. She pulled out an envelope. 'It's a letter from Eddie.' She looked further. 'Four of them.'

'Well, now. Shall I take the baby away?'

'Yes, please, dearest Lily.'

Eva carried the package to the walled garden and sat on the bench where long ago Eddie had fallen asleep and she had drawn him. She both longed to read the letters and wanted to slow the process. They might be all she'd have of Eddie for weeks. But she did want to know where he was so eventually she opened the envelope with the earliest date. Even then, she hesitated.

Ahead of her stretched the decorative ranks of carrot tops, a second crop. Although the plot had been ruthlessly ploughed for two years now a few plants from the past survived, including a tall artichoke bearing several heads which were just spouting bright blue hair. Eva noted them and wondered how their weirdness could be achieved on canvas.

My darling Eva. I am onboard ship! A flight carrier with all the Spitfires stowed below. As much a surprise to me as you, although by the time you read this, I'll have flown off it long ago. Not sure about naval censorship so I won't tell you much more just now. Main excitement, once you discount the water all around instead of the usual green grass, is the food and comfort. No wonder naval chaps consider themselves the senior service. Hot buttered scones with strawberry jam for tea, bacon, eggs and sausages for breakfast, three courses for lunch.

The lengthy descriptions of food surprised Eva.

There was a new friend: Rafi. Eva approved of this, although having little experience of friendship herself; perhaps Betty had been one, perhaps Jack was now. But she knew how important Andy and Hank had been to Eddie. That Rafi was a student at the Courtauld Institute and his father an art critic was interesting. Eddie's attitude to her painting, which had once seemed ambivalent, in the last year had been far more positive – as if he wanted her to have a life outside himself.

Putting aside the first letter, Eva took up the second. She was suddenly struck with fear. Why had they all come together? Where was he now? This moment. They were undated but it could have taken to weeks for them to reach her. They seemed to have been written very quickly one after the other. What was the meaning of that? Often, Eddie let weeks go without writing at all.

Eva put the four letters on the bench and tried to calm herself. She knew she could manage with a lack of knowledge. From her childhood onwards she had understood so little – of her father, of her mother, of what it means to be alive – she had become practiced in not knowing; it was a state she expected and could deal with. It had surely helped with her faith in Eddie's eventual return over that winter of 1940/41. Only very recently, painting had given her a language to explain to herself what she was feeling.

Eva gathered the envelopes into her lap, played with them as if they were cards. 'I love you, Eddie,' she said out loud. But she didn't open more of them.

Eventually, she tucked the envelopes into the large pocket on the front of her smock and wandered out of the walled garden and back to the stable. Her painting waited for her. She stared critically at the band of white. Even though it had been mixed with many other colours, it had a flat deadness which had not been her intention.

She took out the letters and placed them out of sight behind a horse brush and a curry comb on a high shelf. Then she went back to the doorway and sat on the straw bale. The sky stretched out above the trees and the green lines of garden and fields. The sun had not appeared all day, although the air was very warm. She supposed the thick whiteness had got into her head. But the real sky wasn't like that at all. It seemed filled with secrets. Not only rain and wind and that summer sun pressing hotly behind it. Eva's mind veered away and she shut her eyes.

'Eddie, I love you,' she said again.

≫≪

Sylvia found her later. 'Supper time, my darling.'

Eva who was still sitting on the bale, looked up, 'Did Lily tell you some letters came from Eddie?'

'Yes. From the Navy, she told me.'

'I've only read the first. I hid them in the stable. We waited so long sometimes for even one.'

'What do you mean?' Sylvia sat down beside Eva and put her arm round her shoulders. 'It's a good thing he's written. Where is he?'

'I don't know. He couldn't tell me. Or maybe.' Eva jumped up and ran into the stable. She returned clutching the letters. 'I just lost my nerve a little. Silly.'

'You want me to open one?'

'Yes. Please.' Eva handed over the letters and clasped her hands together. 'I sat here too long and began imagining things. I suppose I've missed Sam's bedtime. What a fool I am! You read the third, dearest Sylvia while I read the second. I don't know why I got in such a state.'

Sylvia opened the envelope and tried not to show that her heart was beating too fast. Fear is catching.

Eddie's handwriting was reassuringly even and readable. He wrote about the Spitfires, about some sort of special adjustment to the propellers which was needed so that they could get off the short deck of the flight carrier. They were now heading for Gibraltar, he said, strange, that had got past the censor. It was very hot but sometimes the heat threw up a haze, almost like a fog. He wrote about the coast of Africa which was only eight miles away. In the last paragraph, he gave a summary of Malta's wartime history. Even though he didn't explicitly say so, it was quite obvious that was where he was going.

Sylvia put down the letter and took a breath. She started to speak but her voice cracked. She tried again, 'It's all right, Eva. He was part of the convoy that went to relieve Malta. I read about it. It was on the news too. They broke the siege. There was no mention of any planes being lost. Malta is so important. It's wonderful he was part of saving it.'

'Oh. Oh.' Eva put down the letter she was reading and put her arms round Sylvia, pressing her cheek against hers. 'I was so frightened. I don't know why.' She began to laugh and cry at the same time. 'What would I do without you? Now I can pull myself together and will go and have jolly fun with Daisy and the others.'

Sylvia stroked Eva's hair back from her face. The sky was so dark now, a heavy indigo as if the sun would never rise again. Again, she told herself that she mustn't be affected by Eva fears. That afternoon she'd read in *The Times* about the siege of Malta. Her head was filled with too many horrors. Hardly any of the ships had got through.

'Come on now. We should go in. You can get a chill even on an August evening.'

When supper was eaten and cleared away, Sylvia, still disturbed, went back to the stable. Lily had mentioned four letters but Eva had only produced three. Torch in hand, she found the letter behind the horse brush and comb. It had already been opened. She took it out and read the sad story of the French family which Fred had already described to her.

She wondered why Eva had not talked about it. The letter was not tragic in itself. The French story was told calmly and Eddie ended with warm love for Eva and Sam. It was no surprise that he hadn't mentioned coming back or the future. Why had Eva hidden it here as if she didn't want it near her? What did she understand from it that Sylvia could not. She paused, holding the letter. Or would not.

∞

Fred woke early and reached out to his bedside table. In his orderly flat he found what he wanted at once: his bible. Inside it was the letter from Eddie which had arrived the day before. Unusually, he had not been out overnight and he felt fully awake. He sat up, put aside the letter and a marker of plaited straw made by Eva, and began to read.

For this is the blood of the new Testament, which is shared for many for the remission of sins. Matthew 26:28.

The Old Testament had taken him more than a year to finish, determined as he was not to overlook a word. But he was now well into the New Testament, beginning with the four Gospels. It was not altogether what he'd expected. The moral teaching was clear enough, love, forgiveness and generosity of spirit – virtues he had never managed. This he expected. It was the emphasis on suffering and death that took him aback. Whereas in the Old Testament he had entered the dark world, occasionally charged

410

with purple passages or garishly lit beauty, he had expected the New Testament to be literally enlightened, impregnated with the spirit of the Lord, illuminated with hope. He supposed it was there in the resurrection, but how much agony was described on the road there!

Fred was confused. Where did that put his own sufferings? He stared now at his naked stump, the ugly scar at the end like the twist sealing a lump of pink sausage meat. He remembered, although it was always in his head, what he had seen on Gallipoli. And now, all around him, another world war, with ever more monstrous news, of atrocities, in Europe against the Jews, in Russia against whoever was losing, in Korea, Burma, Japan. But these New Testament gospellers wanted him to accept and forgive. Was there no limit set?

Even here, in the free western rim of the globe, his nightly work led him to people tortured, lives destroyed. Two nights ago there'd been Millie, a fat ugly drunk prostitute, four children buried under their house, husband out somewhere or other to clean an officer's boots. Must he offer Millie and everyone else to God? Was it not more honourable to shout with fury and hatred?

Eddie had written to thank him for showing him the difficulties of life. He had sent him love. Where was he? What new burdens of sorrow there be? They had become close over the tragedy of the French family who had saved him. Is that what war does to you? Extracts love out of horror? Was that Christian teaching?

Restlessly, Fred got out of his bed and went naked to the kitchen. Banging down his stump on the counter, he thought, I am just a simple country boy, my only education through war. How can I expect to understand? Honourable? How stupid is that! I'll be talking about patriotism next! How laughable! A one-armed naked old man stamping his feet in a frenzy. How ridiculous! He banged down his stump again and gave a howl.

The telephone rang.

'Fred. Are you there?'

Fred stood holding the receiver. He pictured Sylvia,

unconsciously recreating the slender, tentative creature he'd known twenty years ago. He sat down. 'Yes. I'm here.'

'I needed to hear your voice.'

'Perhaps I should come to you.' He heard her sigh. Fred once more pictured the younger Sylvia.

'I want you here so much. Eddie's in Malta. Eva had some letters from a flight carrier taking him there or, I suppose, part of the way there.'

'I had one too. I love you, Sylvia.'

She sighed again. 'I know. I need you, Fred. But can you leave all those people you help?'

Fred leant back in the chair and took a breath. 'You are more important than all those people.'

'Darling. Oh, darling.'

Fred dressed calmly and made himself breakfast. It would be a long journey. It was always a long journey. There was no hurry.

><=

Eva was painting her sky again. Unsatisfied with yesterday's attempt, she had picked up her palette knife and was making small slashes of white mixed with indigo and a tinge of cadmium yellow. Perhaps they were clouds. She didn't know. Through the open door of the stable, she could see the sky and that there were clouds gathering in all sorts of forms, none of them like her slashes. A wind was blowing, that was the thing, so that the patterns changed every second, sharp lines, billowing flounces, puffy trills, all dashing across the sky.

Eva put down her brush and stepped out of the stable in time to see an old man on a bicycle, approaching the kitchen door. She stood quite still.

It came to her with absolute certainty that yesterday's fears had been a dress rehearsal and today was the real thing.

She waited for Sylvia to come out and hand over the telegram.

EPILOGUE
15 August 1942

Eddie spread his wings.

It seemed that however hard he tried, he was not destined to return from his crash into the English Channel. He'd just been on loan to the world, with time to do a bit more growing up.

The French family had tried so hard to bring him back, with all their care, love and prayers. He had even been given Fleur to lure him into life.

Eva had tried, showing him what was most beautiful about the world, winding him into herself so that he should be safe forever. She had taught him how to love and he had loved her. She had given him Sam.

He had been given so much but it hadn't lasted. Now the end was coming to him fast. Even within the thick blinding haze all around, he could sense the red earth of Tunisia rising up to meet him. It was the blistering hot red earth of the desert, scorching, panting flames.

There wouldn't be much of him left to find. Perhaps he would be missing forever. If he was found, he would be just part of the Spitfire, the Spitfire, number NB440, that had failed. Mechanical failure – what an epitaph! Dear Spit, I don't blame you; you were rushed on to that flight carrier. Even if it had been your fault, I would forgive you anyway. I forgive the whole world.

What about, *He met his destiny over the Mediterranean Sea and the African Desert?*

Enough.

Although the skin of Eddie's face was drawn rigidly backwards with the force of the plane's dive, and his eyes were shut, he tried to smile.

He knew about death, he had seen it so close, so often. He had cried out 'O Lord protect thy servant', although he knew it wasn't really possible.

But now death had arrived, he felt a calm that overrode his bursting head, that took over his spirit and told him to spread his wings.

Eddie spread his wings and flew onwards.

END

He is born the Divine Child

He is born, the divine child,
Sound the oboes, ring out the bagpipes!
He is born, the divine child,
Let us all serenade his coming!

A stable is his place of rest,
A bed of straw to make his cradle.
A stable is his place of rest,
Our God in all humility!

Ah! But he is handsome, and so charming!
What perfection in his graces!
Ah! But he is handsome, and so charming!
This divine child, so tender there.

ACKNOWLEDGEMENTS

Many thanks to Ian Strathcarron, my outstanding publisher, to Lucie Skilton, the perfect editor, to Ryan Gearing, Dawn Monks, Lauren Tanner and all my brilliant new friends at Unicorn Publishing.

My family, as always, have been endlessly encouraging, particularly Rose Gaete and Chloe Billington and my sister, Antonia Fraser. Thanks also to Elisabeth Salina Amorini, Belinda Wingfield Digby, and Victoria Gray who have supported me in important ways. My husband, Kevin Billington, has shown unflagging enthusiasm for all aspects of my research, including trips to airfields, some still used, others only recognisable by an ancient hangar losing the battle against rampant nature, or a runway like a disintegrating road going nowhere.

I have read widely about the role of the fighter pilot in the course of writing this book. Patrick Bishop is the master of the subject and endlessly useful. But the books that have inspired me most (with thanks to the London Library) are memoirs written by the pilots themselves. They include Richard Hillary, Brian Kingcome, Geoffrey Wellum and Peter Townsend, to name only a few. With the exception of Hillary, these were survivors who lived to tell with all modesty their extraordinary stories of courage an endurance.

The women in *Clouds of Love and War* would never have made history books. Yet they are of my mother's and grandmothers' generation whose stories were part of my childhood. So I remember them here also and thank them.

Finally, anyone who would like to know more about the older characters in this novel, may be interested in reading my last novel, *Glory – A Story of Gallipoli*.